ORIGIN

MANIFOLD 3

Stephen Baxter

ORIGIN

MANIFOLD 3

HARPER
Voyager

Harper*Voyager*
An imprint of HarperCollins*Publishers*
1 London Bridge Street
London SE1 9GF

www.harpervoyagerbooks.co.uk

This paperback edition 2015
1

First published in Great Britain by
Harper*Voyager* 2001

Stephen Baxter asserts the moral right to
be identified as the author of this work

A catalogue record for this book is
available from the British Library

ISBN: 978-0-00-813449-5

Printed and bound in Great Britain

MIX
Paper from
responsible sources
FSC **FSC™ C007454**

FSC™ is a non-profit international organisation established to promote
the responsible management of the world's forests. Products carrying the
FSC label are independently certified to assure consumers that they come
from forests that are managed to meet the social, economic and
ecological needs of present and future generations,
and other controlled sources.

Find out more about HarperCollins and the environment at
www.harpercollins.co.uk/green

DEDICATION

To my nephew, William Baxter.

Emma Stoney:

Do you know me? Do you know where you are? Oh, Malenfant . . .

I know *you*. And you're just what you always were, an incorrigible space cadet. That's how we both finished up stranded here, isn't it? I remember how I loved to hear you talk, when we were kids. When everybody else was snuggling at the drive-in, you used to lecture me on how space is a high frontier, a sky to be mined, a resource for humanity.

But is that all there is? Is the sky really nothing more than an empty stage for mankind to strut and squabble?

And what if we blew ourselves up before we ever got to the stars? Would the universe just evolve on, a huge piece of clockwork slowly running down, utterly devoid of life and mind?

How – desolating.

Surely it couldn't be like that. All those suns and worlds spinning through the void, the grand complexity of creation unwinding all the way out of the Big Bang itself . . . You always said you just couldn't believe that there was nobody out *there* looking back at you down *here*.

But if so, where is everybody?

This is the Fermi Paradox – right, Malenfant? *If the aliens existed, they would be here.* I heard you lecture on that so often I could recite it in my sleep.

But I agree with you. It's powerful strange. I'm sure Fermi is telling us something very profound about the nature of the universe we live in. It is as if we are all embedded in a vast graph of possibilities, a graph with an axis marked *time*, for our own future destiny, and an axis marked *space*, for the possibilities of the universe.

Much of your life has been shaped by thinking about that cosmic graph. Your life and, as a consequence, mine.

Well, on every graph there is a unique point, the place where the axes cross. It's called the origin. Which is where we've finished up, isn't it, Malenfant? And now we *know* why we were alone . . .

But, you know, one thing you never considered was the subtext. Alone or not alone – why do we *care* so much?

I always knew why. We care because we are lonely.

I understood that because *I* was lonely. I was lonely before you stranded me here, in this terrible place, this Red Moon. I lost you to the sky long ago. Now you found me here – but you're leaving me again, aren't you, Malenfant?

. . . Malenfant? Can you hear me? Do you know me? Do you know who you are? – oh.

Watch the Earth, Malenfant. Watch the Earth . . .

Manekatopokanemahedo:

This is how it is, how it was, how it came to be.

It began in the afterglow of the Big Bang, that brief age when stars still burned.

Humans arose on an Earth. Emma, perhaps it was your Earth. Soon they were alone.

Humans spread over their world. They spread in waves across the universe, sprawling and brawling and breeding and dying and evolving. There were wars, there was love, there was life and death. Minds flowed together in great rivers of consciousness, or shattered in sparkling droplets. There was immortality to be had, of a sort, a continuity of identity through copying and confluence across billions upon billions of years.

Everywhere humans found life: crude replicators, of carbon or silicon or metal, churning meaninglessly in the dark.

Nowhere did they find mind – save what they brought with them or created – no *other* against which human advancement could be tested.

They came to understand that they would forever be alone.

With time, the stars died like candles. But humans fed on bloated gravitational fat, and achieved a power undreamed of in earlier ages. It is impossible to understand what minds of that age were like, minds of time's far downstream. They did not seek to acquire, not to breed, not even to learn. They needed nothing. They had nothing in common with their ancestors of the afterglow.

Nothing but the will to survive. And even that was to be denied them by time.

The universe aged: indifferent, harsh, hostile and ultimately lethal. There was despair and loneliness.

There was an age of war, an obliteration of trillion-year memories, a bonfire of identity. There was an age of suicide, as even the finest chose self-destruction against further purposeless time and struggle.

The great rivers of mind guttered and dried.

But some persisted: just a tributary, the stubborn, still unwilling to yield to the darkness, to accept the increasing confines of a universe growing inexorably old.

And, at last, they realized that something was wrong. *It wasn't supposed to have been like this.*

Burning the last of the universe's resources, the final down-streamers – lonely, dogged, all but insane – reached to the deepest past . . .

I

WHEEL

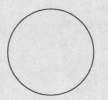

Reid Malenfant:

'. . . Watch the Moon, Malenfant. Watch the Moon!'

So here was Reid Malenfant, his life down the toilet, chasing joky UFO reports around a desolate African sky. Emma's voice snapped him to full alertness, for just about for the first time, he admitted to himself, since takeoff.

'What about the Moon?'

'Just look at it!'

Malenfant twisted his head this way and that, the helmet making his skull heavy, seeking the Moon. He was in the T-38's forward blister. Emma was in the bubble behind him, her head craned back. The jet trainer was little more than a brilliant shell around them, white as an angel's wing, suspended in a powder-blue sky. Where was the Moon – the west? He couldn't see a damn thing.

Frustrated, he threw the T-38 into a savage snap roll. A flat brown horizon twisted around the cockpit in less than a second.

'Jesus, Malenfant,' Emma groaned.

He pulled out into a shallow climb towards the west, so that the low morning sun was behind him.

. . . And then he saw it: a Moon, nearly full, baleful and big – *too* big, bigger than it had any right to be. Its colours were masked by the washed-out blue of the air of Earth, but still, it had *colours*, yes, not the Moon's rightful palette of greys, but smatterings of a deep blue-black, a murky brown that even had tinges of green, for God's sake – but it was predominantly red, a strong scorched red like the dead heart of Australia seen from the flight deck of a Shuttle orbiter . . .

It was a Moon, but not *the* Moon. A new Moon. A Red Moon.

He just stared, still pulling the T-38 through its climb. He sensed Emma, behind him, silent. What was there to say about this, the replacement of a Moon?

That was when he lost control.

Fire:

The people walk across the grass.

The sky is blue. The grass is sparse, yellow. The ground is red under the grass. Fire's toes are red with the dust. The people are slim black forms scattered on red-green.

They are called the Running-folk.

The people call to each other.

'Fire? Dig! Fire?'

'Dig, Dig, here! Loud, Loud?'

Loud's voice, from far away. 'Fire, Fire! Dig! Loud!'

The sun is high. There are only people on the grass. The cats sleep when the sun is high. The hyenas sleep. The Nutcracker-men and the Elf-men sleep in their trees. Everybody sleeps except the Running-folk. Fire knows this without thinking.

As his legs walk Fire holds his hands clamped together. Smoke curls up from between his thumbs. There is moss inside his hands. The fire is in the moss. He blows on the moss. More smoke comes. The fire hurts his palms and fingers. But his hands are hard.

His legs walk easily. Walking is for legs. Fire is not there in his legs. Fire is in his hands and his eyes. He makes his hands tend the fire, while his legs walk.

Fire is carrying the fire. That is his name. That is what he does.

It is darker. The people are quiet.

Fire looks up. A fat cloud hangs over him. The sun is behind the cloud. The edge of the cloud glows golden. His nose can smell rain. His bare skin prickles, cold. Immersed in this new moment, he has forgotten he is hungry.

The clouds part. There is a blue light, low in the sky. Fire looks at the blue light. It is not the sun. The blue light is new.

Fire fears anything new.

The fire wriggles in his hands.

He looks down, forgetting the blue light. There is no smoke. The moss has turned to ash. The fire is shrinking.

Fire crouches down. He shelters the moss under his belly. He feels its warmth on his bare skin. He hoots. 'Fire, Fire! Fire, Fire!'

Stone is small-far. He turns. He shouts. He is angry. He begins to come back towards Fire.

Loud comes to Fire. Loud hoots. His voice is loud. Loud is his name. Loud kneels. He looks for bits of moss and dry grass. He pushes them into the bit of fire.

Dig comes to Fire. Her hand holds arrowhead roots. She squats beside Fire. Her taut dugs brush his arm. His member stiffens. He rocks. She grins. Her hands push a root into his mouth. He tastes her fingers, her salty sweat.

Loud hoots. His member is stiff too, sticking out under his belly. He crams bits of grass into Fire's hands.

Fire snaps his teeth. 'Loud, Loud away!'

Loud hoots again. He grabs Dig's arm. She laughs. Her legs take her skipping away from both of them.

Others come to Fire. Here are women, Grass and Shoot and Cold and Wood. Here are their babies with no names. Here are children with no names. The children jabber. Their eyes are round and bright.

Here is Stone. Stone is dragging branches over the ground. Blue is helping Stone drag the branches. Sing is lying on the branches. Sing is white-haired. She is still. She is asleep.

Stone sees the dying fire. He sees Fire's stiff member. He roars. Stone's hands drop the branches.

Stone has forgotten Sing, on the branches. Sing tips to the ground. She groans.

Stone's axe clouts Fire on the back of the head. There is a hard sound. Stone shouts in Fire's face. 'Fire, Fire! Hungry, feed!' His face is split by a scar. The scar is livid red.

'Fire, Fire,' says Fire quietly. His arms drop and his head bows. He keeps hold of the fire.

Sing moans. Her eyes are closed. Her dugs are slack. The men pick her up by shoulders and legs and lift her back on the branches.

Stone and Blue grab the branches. Their legs walk them back the way they had come.

Fire tells his legs to stand him up. They can't. His hands are still clasped around the fire. Lights fill his head, more garish than that blue stripe in the sky. He nearly falls over backwards.

Loud's hand grabs his armpit. Loud lifts him until his legs are straight.

Loud laughs. Loud walks away, fast, after Dig.

Fire's head hurts. Fire's hands hurt. Fire's member wants Dig.

He starts walking. He wants to stop thinking.

He thinks of the blue light.

Emma Stoney:

Emma had accompanied Malenfant, her husband, on a goodwill tour of schools and educational establishments in Johannesburg, South Africa. It had been a remarkably dismal project, a throwback to NASA PR malpractices of old, a trek through mostly prosperous, middle-class-and-up neighbourhoods, with Malenfant running Barco shows from his two missions to the Space Station before rows of polite and largely uncaring teenagers.

In darkened classrooms Emma had watched the brilliance of the students' smiles, and the ruby-red winking of their earpiece phones like fireflies in the night. Between these children growing up in the fractured, complex, transformed world of 2015, and Reid Malenfant, struggling worker astronaut, all of fifty-five years old and still pursuing Apollo dreams from a boyhood long lost, there was a chasm as wide as the Rift Valley, she thought, and there always would be.

Still, for Emma, it had been a holiday in the African sun – the reason she had prised herself away from her work as financial controller of OnlineArt – and she and Malenfant had gotten along reasonably well, for them, even given Malenfant's usual Earthbound restless moodiness.

But that had been before the word had come through from the Johnson Space Center, headquarters of NASA's manned spaceflight programme, that Malenfant had been washed out of his next mission, STS-194.

Well, that was the end of it. With a couple of phone calls Malenfant had cut short their stay in Joburg, and begun to can the rest of the tour. He had been able to get out of all of it except for a reception at the US ambassador's residence in Nairobi, Kenya.

To her further dismay, Malenfant had leaned on Bill London – an old classmate from Annapolis, now a good buddy in the South African Navy – to let him fly them both up to Nairobi from out of a Joburg military airfield in a T-38, a sleek veteran supersonic jet trainer, a mode of transport favoured by the astronauts since the 1960s.

It wasn't the first time Emma had been taken for a ride in one of those toy planes, and with Malenfant in this mood she knew she could expect to be thrown around the sky. And she shuddered at the thought of how Malenfant in this wounded state was going to behave when he got to Nairobi.

But she had gone along anyhow. Somehow she always did.

So that was how Emma Stoney, forty-five-year-old accountant, had found herself in a gear room getting dressed in a blue flight suit, oxygen mask, oversized boots, helmet, going through the procedures for using her parachute and survival kit and emergency oxygen, struggling to remember the purpose of the dozens of straps, lanyards and D-rings.

Malenfant was ready before she was, of course. He stomped out into the bright morning sunlight towards the waiting T-38. He carried his helmet and his flight plan, and his bald head gleamed in the sun, bronzed and smooth as a piece of machinery itself. But his every motion was redolent with anger and frustration.

Emma had to run to keep up with him, laden down with all her absurd right-stuff gear. By the time she reached the plane she was hot already. She had to be hoisted into her seat by two friendly South African female techs, like an old lady being lifted into the bath. Malenfant was in his cockpit, angrily going through a pre-takeoff checkout.

The T-38 was sleek and brilliant white. Its wings were stubby, and it had two bubble cockpits, one behind the other. The plane was disturbingly small; it seemed barely wide enough to squeeze in a whole person. Emma studied an array of controls and dials and softscreen readouts at whose purpose she could only guess. The venerable T-38 had been upgraded over the years – those shimmering softscreen readouts, for instance – but every surface was scuffed and worn with use, the metal polished smooth where pilots' gloved hands had rubbed against it, the leather of her seat extensively patched.

The last few minutes of the prep wore away quickly, as one of the ground crew took her through her final instructions: how she should close her canopy bubble, where to fasten a hook to a ring on a parachute, how to change the timing of her parachute opening. She watched the back of Malenfant's head, his jerky tension as he prepared his plane.

Malenfant taxied the jet to the end of the runway. Emma watched the stick move before her, slaved to Malenfant's movements. Her oxygen mask smelled of hot rubber, and the roar of the jets was too loud for her to make out anything of Malenfant's conversation with the ground.

Do you *ever* think of me, Malenfant?

There was a mighty shove at her back.

Fire:

Stone drops the branches. Sing rolls to the ground. Stone has forgotten her again.

The sun is low. They are close to a thick stand of trees. Fire can smell water.

Fire is tired. His stomach is empty. His hands are sore. 'Hungry Fire hungry,' he moans.

Sing, on the ground, looks up at him. She smiles. 'Hungry Fire,' she says. He thinks of her feeding him. But she is small and withered. She does not get up to feed him.

Stone walks over the branches he hauled across the savannah, the branches that transported Sing. He kicks them aside. He has forgotten he hauled them here. He bends. His hands seek out a piece of dung on the ground. His tongue tastes it. It is Nutcracker-man dung. The dung is old. The dung crumbles.

Fire is not fearful. There are no Nutcracker-men near here.

Stone's feet kick aside more branches and twigs. He uncovers a round patch of black ground. Fire's nose smells ash. Stone hoots. 'Hah! Fire Fire.'

Fire crouches over the ash. The fire is warm in his hands.

Loud and Dig and others huddle near him. Their hands scrape dry stuff from the floor, dead leaves and dry moss and grass and bits of bark. Their hands pick up rocks, and rub the tinder against the rocks. Their fingers turn the tinder, making it fine and light.

Wood's legs walk to the forest. She comes back with a bundle of sticks, of wood. That is what she does. That is her name. She piles the sticks on the ground.

The hands of the others push the tinder into the middle of the pile of wood.

Working closely, the people jostle each other. They are hot from the walk. Their bare skin is slick with sweat. They grunt and yap, expressing tiredness, hunger, irritation. But they do not speak of the work. They are not thinking as their hands gather the fire materials. Their hands have done this all their lives. Their ancestors' hands have done this for hundreds of thousands of years.

Fire waits while they work.

He sees himself.

He is a child with no name. Another cups fire in his hands. He cannot see this other's face. The adults' huge hands make tinder. Fire is fascinated. They push him out of the way.

A woman picks him up. It is Sing. Her arms are strong. Her mouth smiles. She swings him in the air. The leaves are green and big.

. . . The leaves are small. The leaves are yellow. Sing is lying on the ground.

Fire's hands push into the tinder. He makes his hands put his precious bit of fire inside the tinder. His mouth blows on the fire. His hands want to come out of the prickling heat. He makes them stay in the tinder. Flame flickers. The wood smokes and pops, scorches and burns.

People laugh and hoot at the fire.

Fire pulls out his hands. His hands are sore.

Emma Stoney:

The plane shot almost vertically into the air, and its white nose plunged through a layer of fine, gauzy cloud. The ground imploded below her, the rectilinear patterns of the airfield shrinking into insignificance as the glittering carcass of Joburg itself shouldered over the horizon, agricultural land beyond showing as patches of greyish green and brown. On the eastern horizon the sun was unimaginably bright, sending shafts of light spearing through the cockpit glass, and to the west she spotted the Moon, almost full, its small grey face peering back at the sun's harsh glare.

Already the sky above was turning a deeper blue, shading to purple.

Emma felt her stomach lurch, but she knew it would pass. One of the many ironies of their relationship was that Emma was more resistant to motion sickness than her astronaut husband, who had spent around ten per cent of the time on his two spaceflights throwing up.

Malenfant banked to the north, and the horizon settled down, sun to right, Moon to left. As they headed towards the interior of the continent, the land turned brown, parched, flat.

'What a shithole,' Malenfant said, his voice a whisper over the jet's roar. 'Africa. Cradle of mankind my ass.'

'Malenfant –'

He hurled the T-38 forward with a powerful afterburner surge.

Within seconds they had reached 45,000 feet and had gone through a bone-shaking Mach 1. The vibrations damped away and the noise of the jets dwindled – for, of course, they were outstripping most of the sound they made – and the plane seemed to hang in shining stillness.

Emma, as she had before, felt a surge of exhilaration. It was at such paradoxical moments of stillness and speed that she felt closest to Malenfant.

But Malenfant was consumed by his gripes.

'Two years. I can't fucking believe it. Two years of training, two years of meetings and planning sessions, and paddling around in hydro labs and spinning around in centrifuges. All of it for nothing.'

'Come on, Malenfant. It's not the end of the world. It's not as if Station work was ever such a prize anyhow. *Looking at stars, pissing in jars.* That's what you used to say –'

'Nobody was flying to fucking Mars. Station was all that was available, so I took it. Two flights, two lousy flights. I never even got to command a mission, for Christ's sake.'

'You got washed out this time. That doesn't mean you won't fly again. A lot of crew are flying past your age.' That was true, of course, partly because NASA was having such difficulty finding willing applicants from younger generations.

But Malenfant growled, 'It's that asshole Bridges. He even called me into the JSC director's office to *explain* the shafting. That fucking horse holder has always had it in for me. This will be the excuse he needs to send me to purgatory.'

Emma knew whom he meant. Joe Bridges was the director of flight operations – in effect, in NASA's Byzantine, smothering internal bureaucracy, in charge of astronaut selection for missions.

Malenfant was still muttering. 'You know what Bridges offered me? ASP.'

Emma riffled through her mental file of NASA acronyms. ASP: Astronaut Support Personnel, a non-flying astronaut assigned to support the crew of a mission.

'I'd have been point man on STS-194,' Malenfant spat. 'The Caped Crusader. Checking the soap dispensers in the orbiter john. Strapping some other asshole into *my* seat on the flight deck.'

'I gather you didn't take the job,' Emma said dryly.

'I took it okay,' he snapped. 'I took it and shoved it sideways up that pencil-pusher's fat ass.'

'Oh, Malenfant,' she sighed.

She tried to imagine the meeting in that rather grand office, before a floor-to-ceiling office window with its view of the park-like JSC campus, complete with the giant Saturn V Moon rocket lying there on its side as if it had crashlanded beside the driveway. Even in these days of decline, there were too few seats for too many eager crew-persons, so – in what seemed to Emma his own very small world – Bridges wielded a great deal of power indeed.

She had never met this man, this Bridges. He might be an efficient bureaucrat, the kind of functionary the aviator types would sneer at, but who held together any major organization like NASA. Or perhaps this Bridges transcended his role; perhaps he was the type who had leveraged his position to accrete power beyond his rank. With the gifts at his disposal, she thought, he might have built up a network of debtors in the Astronaut Office and beyond, in all the places in NASA's sprawling empire ex-astronauts might reach.

Well, so what? Emma had encountered any number of such people in her own long, complex and moderately successful career in the financial departments of high-tech corporations. No organization was a rational place. Organizations were bear pits where people fought for their own projects, which might or might not have something to do with the organization's supposed mission. The wise person accepted that, and found a way to get what she wanted in spite of it all.

But to Malenfant – Malenfant the astronaut, an odd idealist about human behaviour, always a loner, always impatient with the most minimal bureaucracy, barely engaged with the complexities of the world – to Malenfant, Joe Bridges, controlling the most important thing in his entire life (more important than me, she thought) could be nothing but a monster.

She stared out the window at the baked African plain. It was huge and ancient, she thought, a place that would endure all but unchanged long after the little white moth that buzzed over it today was corroded to dust, long after the participants in this tiny domestic drama were mouldering bones.

Now she heard a whisper from the ground-to-air radio. It sounded like Bill London, good old bullshitter Bill from Annapolis, with some garbled report about UFOs over central Africa.

The plane veered to the right, and the rising sun wheeled around the cockpit, sparking from scuffs in the Plexiglas around her.

'Let's go UFO-hunting,' Malenfant snapped. 'We got nothing better to do today, right?'

She wasn't about to argue; as so often in her relationship with Malenfant she was, literally, powerless.

Fire:

Stone and Blue put branches into the fire. Leaves and twigs burn. Stone and Blue pull out the burning branches. Their legs carry them into the wood. Small animals squeal and run before the fire. Stone and Blue pursue, their eyes darting, their hands hurling rocks and bits of wood.

Fire's hands are very red and raw.

Dig comes to him. Water is in her mouth. The water spills on his hands. The water is cool. Dig has leaves. Her hands rub them on his burns.

Fire has no name. Sing is huge and smiling. Sing's hands rub his palms with leaves.

Fire has his name again. It is Dig who tends his burned hands, smiling.

'Blue light!' he shouts, suddenly.

Dig looks at him. Her eyes narrow. She tends his hands.

Fire's hand reaches out. It cups one conical breast. The breast is hot in his hand.

The fire is hot in his hand. A captured bat is hot in his hand.

His member does not rise. Dig tends his hands.

Blue and Stone return. Their hands carry rabbits. The rabbits are skinned. There is blood on the mouths of the men. The rabbits fall to the ground.

The children with no names fall on the rabbits. They jabber, snapping at each other. The children's small faces are bloody. The adults push the children aside, and growl and jostle over the rabbits. All the people work at the meat, stealing it from each other.

Grass and Cold throw some pieces of meat on the fire. The meat sizzles. Their hands pick out the meat. Their mouths chew the burned meat, swallowing some. Fire sees that their mouths want to swallow all the meat. But their fingers take meat from their

16

mouths. They put the meat in the mouths of their babies with no names.

Sing groans. She is on the ground near the branches. Her nose can smell the food. Her hands can't reach it.

Fire is eating a twisted-off rabbit leg. His hands pluck meat off it, and put the meat in Sing's mouth.

Her head turns. Her mouth chews. Her eyes are closed. She chokes. Her mouth spits out meat.

Fire's hands pop the chewed meat in his mouth.

Sing is shivering.

Fire thinks of a bower.

There are branches here, on the ground. He has forgotten that they were used to transport Sing. He keeps thinking of the bower.

He makes his hands lay the branches on the ground. He thinks of twigs and grass and leaves. He gathers them, thinking of the bower. He makes his hands pile everything up on the branches.

He makes his arms pick up Sing.

It is sunny. He has no name. Sing is carrying Fire. Sing is large, Fire small.

It is dark. His name is Fire. Fire is carrying Sing. Fire is large, Sing shrunken.

He lays her on the crude bower. She sinks into the soft leaves and grass. The branches roll away. The grass scatters. Sing falls into the dirt, with a gasp.

Fire hoots and howls, kicking at the branches.

One of the branches is lodged against a rock. It did not roll away.

Fire makes his hands gather the branches again. He puts the branches down alongside the rock he found. His hands pile up more grass. At last he lowers Sing on the bower. The branches are trapped by the rocks. They do not roll away.

Sing sighs.

Every day he makes a bower for Sing. Every day he forgets how he did it before. Every day he has to invent a way to fix it, from scratch. Some days he doesn't manage it at all, and Sing has to sleep on the dirt, where insects bite her.

She sings. Her voice is soft and broken. Fire listens. He has forgotten the rocks and the branches.

She stops singing. She sleeps.

People are sleeping. People are huddled around the children. People are coupling. People are making water. People are making dung. People are chattering, for comfort, through rivalry.

Beyond the glow of the flames, the sky is dark. The land is gone. Something howls. It is far away.

Dig is sleeping near the fire.

Fire's legs walk to her. His hand touches her shoulder. She rolls on her back. She opens her eyes and looks at him.

His member is stiff.

'Hoo! Fire!'

It is Loud. He is on the ground. Fire's eyes had not seen him. Fire's eyes had seen only Dig.

Loud's hands throw red dirt into Fire's eyes. Fire blinks and sneezes and hoots.

Loud has crawled to Dig. His hands paw at her. His tongue is out, his member hard. Her hands are pushing him away. She is laughing.

Fire's hands grab Loud's shoulders. Loud falls off Dig and lands on his back. He pulls Fire to the ground and they roll. Fire feels hot gritty dirt cling to his back.

Stone roars. His scar shines in the fire light. His filth-grimed foot separates them with a shove. His axe clouts Loud on the head. Loud howls and scuttles away.

Stone's axe swings for Fire. Fire ducks and scrambles back.

Stone grunts. He moves to Dig. Stone's big hand reaches down to her, and flips her onto her belly.

Dig gasps. She pulls her legs beneath her. Fire hears the scrape of her skin on red dust.

Stone kneels. His hands push her legs apart. She cries out. He reaches forward. His hands cup her breasts. His member enters her. His hands clutch her shoulders, and his flabby hips thrust and thrust.

He gives a strangled cry. His back straightens. He shudders.

He pulls back and stands up. His member is bruised purple and moist. He turns. He kicks Fire in the thigh. Fire yells and doubles over.

Dig is on the ground, her hands tucked between her legs. She is curled up.

Loud is gone.

Fire's legs walk.

Fire stops.

Dig is far. The fire is far. He is in a mouth of darkness.

Eyes watch him.

He makes his legs walk him back to the fire.

Sing is lying on a bower. He has forgotten he made the bower. Her eyes watch him. Her arm lifts.

He kneels. His face rests on her chest. The bower rustles. Sing gasps.

Her hand runs over his belly. Her hand finds his member. It is painfully swollen. Her hand closes around it. He shudders.

She sings.

He sleeps.

Emma Stoney:

If this really was the close of Malenfant's career at NASA, Emma thought, it could be a good thing.

She wasn't the type of foolish ground-bound spouse who palpitated every moment Malenfant was on orbit (although she hadn't been able to calm her stomach during those searing moments of launch, as the Shuttle passed through one of NASA's 'non-survivable windows' after another . . .). No, the sacrifices she had made went broader and deeper than that.

It had started as far back as the moment when, as a new arrival at the Naval Academy, he had broken his hometown girl's seventeen-year-old heart with a letter saying that he thought they should break off their relationship. Now he was at Annapolis, he had written, he wanted to devote himself 'like a monk' to his studies. Well, that had lasted all of six months before he had started to pursue her again, with letters and calls, trying to win her back.

That letter had, in retrospect, set the course of their lives for three decades. But maybe that course was now coming to an end.

'You know,' she said dreamily, 'maybe if it is ending, it's fitting it should be like this. In the air, I mean. Do you remember that flight to San Francisco? You had just got accepted by the Astronaut Office . . .'

It had been Malenfant's third time of trying to join the astronaut corps, after he had applied to the recruitment rounds of 1988 – when he wasn't even granted an interview – and 1990. Finally in 1992, aged thirty-two, he had gotten an interview at the Johnson Space Center in Houston, and had gone back to his base in San Diego.

At last the Astronaut Office had called him. But he was sworn to secrecy until the official announcement, to be made the next day. Naturally he had kept the secret strictly, even from Emma.

So the next day they had boarded a plane for San Francisco, where they were going to spend a long weekend with friends of Emma's (Malenfant tended not to have the type of friends you could spend weekends with, not if you wanted to come home with your liver). Malenfant had given the pilot the NASA press release. Just after they got to cruise altitude, the pilot called Emma's name: *Would Emma Malenfant please identify herself? Would you please stand up?*

It had taken Emma a moment to realize she was being called, for she used her maiden name, Stoney, in business and her personal life, everywhere except the closed world of the Navy. Baffled – and wary of Malenfant's expressionless stillness – she had unbuckled her seat belt and stood up.

I hope you like barbecue, Ms Malenfant, said the pilot, *because I have a press release here that says you are going to Houston, Texas. Commander Reid Malenfant, US Navy, has been selected to be a part of the 1992 NASA astronaut class.*

'. . . And everybody on the plane started whooping, just as if you were John Glenn himself, and the stewards brought us those dumb little plastic bottles of champagne. Do you remember, Malenfant?' She laughed. 'But you couldn't drink because you were doubled over with air sickness.'

Malenfant grunted sourly. 'It starts in the air, so it finishes in the air. Is that what you think?'

'It does have a certain symmetry . . . Maybe this isn't the end, but the beginning of something new. Right? We could be at the start of a great new adventure together. Who knows?'

She could see how the set of his shoulders was unchanged.

She sighed. Give it time, Emma. 'All right, Malenfant. What UFOs?'

'Tanzania. Some kind of sighting over the Olduvai Gorge, according to Bill.'

'Olduvai? Where the human fossils come from?'

'I don't know. What does that matter? It sounds more authentic than most. The local air forces are scrambling spotter planes: Tanzania, Zambia, Kenya, Mozambique.'

None of those names was too reassuring to Emma. 'Malenfant, are you sure we should get caught up in that? We don't want some trigger-happy Tanzanian flyboy to mistake us for Eetie.'

He barked laughter. 'Come on, Emma. You're showing your prejudice. We trained half those guys and sold the planes to the other half. And they're only spotters. Bill is informing them we're coming. There's no threat. And, who knows? Maybe we'll get to be involved in first contact.'

Under his veneer of cynicism she sensed an edge of genuine excitement. From out of the blue, here was another adventure for Reid Malenfant, hero astronaut. Another adventure that had nothing to do with her.

I was wrong, she thought. I'm never going to get him back, no matter what happens at NASA. But then I never had him anyhow.

Losing sympathy for him, she snapped, 'You really told Joe Bridges to shove his job?'

'Sweetest moment of my life.'

'Oh, Malenfant. Don't you know how it works yet? If you took your punishment, if you sweated out your time, you'd be back in rotation for the next assignment, or the one after that.'

'Bullshit.'

'It's the way of the world. I've had to go through it, in my own way. Everybody has. Everybody who wants to get on in the real world, with real people, anyhow. Everybody but you, the great hero.'

'You sound like you're writing my appraisal,' he said, a little ruefully. 'Anyhow, ass-kissing wouldn't have helped. It was the Russians, that fucking Grand Medical Commission of theirs.'

'The *Russians* scrubbed you?'

'It was when I was in Star City.'

Star City, the Russian military base thirty miles outside Moscow that served as the cosmonauts' training centre.

'Malenfant, you got back from there a month ago. You never thought to tell me about it?'

Through two layers of Plexiglas, she could see him shrug. 'I was appealing the decision. I didn't see the point of troubling you. Hell, Emma, I thought I would win. I *knew* I would. I thought they couldn't scrub me.'

Far off, to left and right, she saw contrails and glittering darts. Fighter planes, perhaps, converging on the strange anomaly sighted over Olduvai, whatever it was, if it existed at all.

She felt an odd frisson of anticipation.

'It took them a morning,' Malenfant said. 'They brung in a dozen Russian doctors to probe at my every damn orifice. A bunch of snowy-haired old farts with pubic hair growing out of their noses, with *no* experience of space medicine. They ought to have no jurisdiction over the way we run our programme.'

'It's their programme too,' she said quietly. 'What did they say?'

'One of them pulled me up over my shoulder.' Malenfant suffered from a nerve palsy behind his right shoulder, the relic of an ancient football injury, a condition NASA had long ago signed off on. 'Well, our guys gave them shit. But the fossil stood his ground.

'Then they took me into the Commission itself. I was sat on a stage with the guy who was going to be my judge, in front of an auditorium full of white-haired Russian doctors, and two NASA guys who were as mad as hell, like me. But the old asshole from the surgical group got up and said my shoulder was a "disqualifying condition" that needed further tests, and our guys said I wasn't going to do that, and so the Russians said I was disqualified anyhow . . .'

Emma frowned, trying to puzzle it out. It sounded like a pretext to her; Malenfant had after all flown twice to the Station before, and the Russians must have known all about his shoulder, like everything else about him. Why should it suddenly become a mission-threatening disability now?

Malenfant put the little jet through a gut-wrenching turn so tight she thought she heard the hull creak. 'I knew we'd appeal,' he said. 'Those two NASA surgeons were livid, I'm telling you. They said they'd pass it all the way up the line, I should just get on with my training as if I was planning to fly, they'd clear me through. Hell, I believed them. But it didn't happen. When it got to Bridges –'

'Was your shoulder the only thing the Russians objected to?'

He hesitated.

'Malenfant?'

'No,' he said reluctantly. 'They smuggled shrinks' remarks into their final report to NASA. They should have presented them at the Commission . . . Hey, can you see something? Look, right on the horizon.'

She peered into the north. The horizon was a band of dusty, mist-laden air, grey between brown earth and blue sky, precisely curving. Was something there? – a spark of powder-blue, a hint of a circle, like a lens flare?

But the day was bright, dazzling now the sun was climbing higher, and her eyes filled with water.

She sat back in her seat, and her various harnesses and buckles rustled and clinked around her, loud in the tiny cockpit. 'What did it say, Malenfant? The Russian psych report.'

He growled, ' "Peculiarities".'

'What kind of peculiarities?'

'In my relations with the rest of the crew. They gave an example about how I was in the middle of a task and some Russkie came over nagging about how we were scheduled to do something else. Well, I nodded politely, and carried right on with what I was doing, until I was finished . . .'

Now she started to understand. The Russians, who rightly believed they were still far ahead of the West in the psychology of the peculiarly cramped conditions of space travel, placed great collectivist emphasis on teamwork and sacrifice. They would not warm to a driven, somewhat obsessive loner-perfectionist like Malenfant.

'I should have socialized with the assholes,' he said now. 'I should have gone to the cosmonauts' coldwater apartments, and drunk their crummy vodka, and pressed the flesh with the guys on the gate.'

She laughed, gently. 'Malenfant, you don't even socialize at NASA.'

'My nature got me where I am now.'

Yeah, washed out, she thought brutally. 'But maybe it's not the nature you need for long-duration space missions. I guess not everybody forgives you the way I do.'

'What is that supposed to mean?'

She ignored the question. 'So the psych report is the real reason they grounded you. The shoulder was just an excuse.'

'The Russians must have known the psych report would never stand up to scrutiny. If Joe Bridges had got his thumb out of his ass –'

'Oh, Malenfant, don't you see? They were giving you cover. If you're going to be grounded, do you want it to be because of your shoulder, or your personality? Think about it. They were trying to help you. They all were.'

'That kind of help I can live without.' Again he wrenched the plane through a savage snap roll.

Her helmet clattered against the Plexiglas, as varying acceleration tore at her stomach, and the brown African plain strobed around her. She was cocooned in the physical expression of his anger.

She glared at the back of Malenfant's helmeted head, which cast dazzling highlights from the African sun, with a mixture of fondness and exasperation. Well, that was Malenfant for you.

And because she was staring so hard at Malenfant she missed seeing the artefact until it was almost upon them.

Malenfant peeled away suddenly. Once again she glimpsed pale blue-white sky, dusty brown ground, shafts of glowering sunlight – and an arc, a fragment of a perfect circle, like a rainbow, but glowing a clear cerulean blue. Then it fell out of her vision.

'Malenfant – what was that?'

'Damned if I know.' His voice was flat. Suddenly he was concentrating on his flying. The slaved controls in front of her jerked this way and that; she felt remote buffeting, some kind of turbulence perhaps, smoothed out by Malenfant's skilful handling.

He pulled the jet through another smooth curve, and sky and ground swam around her once more.

And he said, 'Holy shit.'

There was a circle in the sky.

It was facing them full on. It was a wheel of powder-blue, like a hoop of the finest ribbon. It looked the size of a dinner plate held before her face – but of course it must be much larger and more remote than that.

Emma saw this beyond Malenfant's head and shoulders and the slim white fuselage. The jet's needle nose pointed straight at the centre of the ring, so that the wheel framed her field of view with perfect symmetry, like some unlikely optical flare. Its very perfection and symmetry made it seem unreal. She had no idea of its scale – it would seem so close it must be hanging off the plane's nose, then something in her head would flip the other way and it would appear vast and distant, like a rainbow. She found it physically difficult to study it, as if it was an optical illusion, deliberately baffling; her eyes kept sliding away from it, evading it.

It's beyond my comprehension, she thought. Literally. Evolution has not prepared me for giant wheels suspended in the air.

Fire:

Water runs down his face.

He is lying on his back. The sky is flat and grey.

Rain falls. His ears hear it tapping on the ground. His eyes see the drops fall towards his face. They are fat and slow. Some of them fall on his face.

Water runs in his eyes. It stings. He sits up.

Fire is sitting on the ground. He is wet. His eyes hurt. His burned hands hurt.

He stands up. His legs walk him towards the trees.

People walk, run, stumble over muddy ground, adults and children. They move in silence, in isolation. Nobody is calling, nobody helping. They are cold and they hurt. They have each forgotten the other people, all save the mothers with their babies with no names. The mothers' arms carry the infants, sheltering them.

Fire reaches the trees.

The wind changes. His nose smells ash.

He remembers the fire. His legs run back.

The fire is out, drowned by the rain. The back of Fire's head hurts in anticipation of Stone's punishing axe.

Sing is calling. She is lying on a bower. The bower is falling apart, the leaves damp and shrivelled.

Loud is walking back to Sing.

Sing screams. Fire spins and crouches.

There is a Mouth. It is bright blue. The Mouth is skimming over the shining grass. The Mouth is approaching Fire, gaping wide.

Cats have mouths. A cat's mouth will take a person's head. This Mouth would take a whole person, standing straight. It is coming towards him, this Mouth with no body, this huge Mouth, widening.

It makes no noise. The rain hisses on the grass.

Fire screams. Fire's legs carry him off into the forest.

Still the Mouth comes. It towers into the sky.

Sing is at its base. Her arms push at the bower. Her legs can't stand up. She screams again.

Loud runs. His hands are throwing dirt at the Mouth.

The Mouth scoops him up.

There is a flash of light. Fire can see nothing but blue.
Loud screams.

Emma Stoney:

'Malenfant – you see it too, right?'

He laughed. 'It ain't no scratch in your contacts, Emma.' He
seemed to be testing the controls. Experimentally he veered away
to the right. The ride got a lot more rocky.

The blue circle stayed right where it was, hanging in the African
sky. No optical effect, then. This was *real*, as real as this plane. But
it hung in the air without any apparent means of support. And still
she had no real sense of its scale.

But now she saw a contrail scraped across the air before the wheel,
a tiny silver moth flying across its diameter. The moth was a plane,
as least as big as their own.

'Damn thing must be a half-mile across,' Malenfant growled. 'A
half-mile across, and hovering in the air eight miles high –'

'How appropriate.'

'My God, it's the real thing,' Malenfant said. 'The UFO-nauts
must be going crazy.' She heard the grin in his voice. 'Everything
will be different now.'

Now she made out more planes drawn up from the dusty ground
below, passing before the artefact – if artefact it was. One of them
looked like a fragile private jet, a Lear maybe, surely climbing well
beyond its approved altitude.

Malenfant continued his turn. The artefact slid out of sight.

Dusty land wheeled beneath her. She was high above a gorge, cut
deeply into a baked plain, perhaps thirty or forty miles long. Perhaps
it was Olduvai itself, the miraculous gorge that cut through million-
year strata of human history, the gorge that had yielded the relics
of one ancient hominid form after another to the archaeologists'
patient inspection.

How strange, she thought. Why here? If this wheel in the sky
really is what it appears to be, an extraordinary alien artefact, if
this is a first contact of a bewilderingly unexpected type (and what
else could it be?) then *why here*, high above the cradle of mankind
itself? Why should this gouge into humanity's deepest past collide
with this most unimaginable of futures?

The plane dropped abruptly. For a heartbeat Emma was weightless. Then the plane slammed into the bottom of an air pocket and she was shoved hard into her seat.

'Sorry,' Malenfant muttered. 'The turbulence is getting worse.' The slaved controls worked before her. The plane soared and banked.

She suddenly wished she was on the ground, perhaps holed up in her well-equipped hotel room back in Joburg. The world must be going crazy over this. She would have every softscreen in the room turned to the coverage, filling her ears and eyes with a babble of instant commentary. Here, in this bubble of Plexiglas, she felt cut off.

But this is the real experience, she thought. I am here by the sheerest chance, at the moment when this vision appeared in the sky like the Virgin Mary over Lourdes, and yet I pine for my online womb. Well, I'm a woman of my time.

The artefact settled into place before Emma once more, vast, enigmatic, slowly approaching. Planes criss-crossed before it, puny. Emma spotted that small private jet, lumbering through the air so much more slowly than the military vehicles around it. She wondered if anybody had tried to make contact with the wheel yet – or if it had been fired on.

'Holy shit,' said Malenfant. 'Do you see that?'

'What?'

He lifted his arm and pointed; she could see the gesture through the Plexiglas blisters that encased them. 'There. Near the bottom of the ring.'

It looked like a very fine dark rain falling out of the ring, like a hail of iron filings.

Malenfant lifted small binoculars. 'People,' he said bluntly. He lowered the binoculars. 'Tall, skinny, naked people.'

She couldn't integrate the information. *People* – thrust naked into the air eight miles high, to fall, presumably, all the way to the welcoming gorge of bones . . . Why? Where were they from?

'Can they be saved?'

Malenfant just laughed.

The plane buffeted again. As they approached the wheel the turbulence was growing stronger. It seemed to Emma that the air at the centre of the ring was significantly disturbed; she made out concentric streaks of mist and dust there, almost like a sideways-on storm, neatly framed by the wheel's electric blue frame.

And now that lumbering business-type jet reached dead centre of the artefact. It twisted once, twice, then crumpled like a paper cup in an angry fist. Glittering fragments began to hail into the ring.

It was over in seconds. There hadn't even been an explosion.

Fire:

Wind gusts. Lightning flashes.

There is no Loud.

People come spewing out of the Mouth. They fall to the grass.

The rain falls steadily on the grass, hissing.

Emma Stoney:

'Like it got sucked in,' Malenfant said with grim fascination. 'Maybe the wheel is a teleporter, drawing out our atmosphere.' The plane juddered again, and she could see him wrestling with the stick. 'Whatever it is it's making a mess of the air flow.'

She could see the other planes, presumably military jets, pulling back to more cautious orbits. But the T-38 kept right on, battering its way into increasingly disturbed air. Malenfant's shoulders jerked as they hauled at the recalcitrant controls.

'Malenfant, what are you doing?'

'We can handle this. We can get a lot closer yet. Those African guys are half-trained sissies –'

The plane hit another pocket. They fell fifty or a hundred feet before slamming into a floor that felt hard as concrete.

Emma could taste blood in her mouth. 'Malenfant!'

'Did you bring your Kodak? Come on, Emma. What's life for? This is history.'

No, she thought. This is your wash-out. *That's* why you are risking your life, and mine, so recklessly.

The artefact loomed larger in the roiling sky ahead of her, so large now that she couldn't see its full circle for the body of the plane. Those iron-filing people continued to rain from the base of the disc, some of them twisting as they fell.

'Makes you think,' Malenfant said. 'I spend my life struggling to get into space. And on the very day I get washed out of the programme, *the very same day*, space comes to me. Wherever the hell this thing comes from, whatever mother ship orbiting fucking Neptune, you can bet there's going to be a clamour to get out there. Those NASA assholes must be jumping up and down; it's their best day since Neil and Buzz. At last we've got someplace to go – but whoever they send it isn't going to be *me*. Makes you laugh, doesn't it? If Mohammed can't get to the mountain . . .'

She closed her hand on the stick before her, letting it pull her passively to and fro. What if she grabbed the stick hard, yanked it to left or right? Could she take over the plane? And then what? 'Malenfant, I'm scared.'

'Of the UFO?'

'No. Of you.'

'Just a little closer,' he said, his voice a thin crackle over the intercom. 'I won't let you come to any harm, Emma.'

Suddenly she screamed. '. . . Watch the Moon, Malenfant. Watch the Moon!'

Reid Malenfant:

It was a Moon, but not *the* Moon. A new Moon. A Red Moon.

It was a day of strange lights in the sky. But it was a sky that was forever barred to him.

The plane was flung sideways.

It was like a barrel roll. Suddenly his head was jammed into his shoulders and his vision tunnelled, worse than any eyeballs-back launch he had ever endured – and harder, much harder, than he would have wanted to put Emma through.

His systems went dead: softscreens, the clunky old dials, even the hiss of the comms, everything. He wrestled with the stick, but got no response; the plane was just falling through an angry sky, helpless as an autumn leaf.

The rate of roll increased, and the Gs just piled on. He knew he was already close to blacking out; perhaps Emma had succumbed already, and soon after that the damn plane was going to break up.

With difficulty he readied the ejection controls. 'Emma! Remember the drill!' But she couldn't hear, of course.

. . . Just for a second, the panels flickered back to life. He felt the stick jerk, the controls bite.

It was a chance to regain control.

He didn't take it.

Then the moment was gone, and he was committed.

He felt exuberant, almost exhilarated, like the feeling when the solid boosters cut in during a Shuttle launch, like he was on a roller-coaster ride he couldn't get off.

But the plane plummeted on towards the sky wheel, rolling, creaking. The transient mood passed, and fear clamped down on his guts once more.

He bent his head, found the ejection handle, pulled it. The plane shuddered as Emma's canopy was blown away, then gave another kick as her seat hurled her clear.

And now his own canopy disappeared. The wind slammed at him, Earth and sky wheeling around, and all of it was suddenly, horribly real.

He felt a punch in the back. He was hurled upwards like a toy and sent tumbling in the bright air, just like one of the strange iron-filing people, shocked by the sudden silence.

Pain bit savagely at his right arm. He saw that his flight-suit sleeve and a great swathe of skin had been sheared away, leaving bloody flesh. Must have snagged it on the rim of the cockpit on the way out.

Something was flopping in the air before him. It was his seat. He still had hold of the ejection handle, connected to the seat by a cable.

He knew he had to let go of the handle, or else it might foul his 'chute. Yet he couldn't. The seat was an island in this huge sky; without it he would be alone. It made no sense, but there it was.

At last, apparently without his volition, his hand loosened. The handle was jerked out of his grip, painfully hard.

Something huge grabbed his back, knocking all the air out of him again. Then he was dangling. He looked up and saw his 'chute open reassuringly above him, a distant roof of fully blossomed orange and white silk.

But the thin air buffeted him, and he was swaying alarmingly, a human pendulum, and at the bottom of each swing G forces hauled on his entrails. He was having trouble breathing; his chest laboured. He pulled a green toggle to release his emergency oxygen.

The artefact hung above him, receding as he fell.

He had been flung west of it, he saw now, and it was closing up to a perfect oval, like a schoolroom demonstration of a planetary orbit. There was no sign of the other planes. Even the T-38 seemed to have vanished completely, save for a few drifting bits of light wreckage, a glimmer that must have been a shard of a Plexiglas canopy.

And he saw another 'chute. Half open. Hanging before the closing maw of the artefact like a speck of food before the mouth of some vast fish.

Emma, of course: she had ejected a half-second before Malenfant, so that she had found herself that much closer to the artefact than he had been.

And now she was being drawn in by the buffeting air currents.

He screamed, 'Emma!' He twisted and wriggled, but there was nothing he could do.

Her 'chute fell into the portal. There was a flash of electric-blue light. And she was gone.

'Emma! *Emma!*'

. . . Something fell past him, not ten yards away. It was a man: tall and lithe like a basketball player, stark naked. He was black, and under tight curls, his skull was as flat as a board. His mouth was working, gasping like a fish's. His gaze locked with Malenfant's, just for a heartbeat. Malenfant read astonishment beyond shock.

Then the man was gone, on his way to his own destiny in the ancient lands beneath.

A new barrage of turbulent air slammed into Malenfant. He rocked viciously. Nursing his damaged arm he fought the 'chute, fought to keep it stable – fought for his life, fought for the chance to live through this day, to find Emma.

As he spun, he glimpsed that new Red Moon, a baleful eye gazing down on his tiny struggles.

Fire:

The Mouth is gone.

The new people are nearby. The smallest is a child. They are all yelling. Their skin is bright, yellow-brown and blue. They are trying to stand up, but they stumble backwards.

31

Fire's legs walk forward. He walks over the soaked fireplace. The ashes are still hot. He yelps and his feet lift up, off the ashes.

Sing is nearby, on her branches, weeping.

Fire's eyes see Dig. They can't see Loud. Fire calls out. 'Loud, Loud, Fire!' But Loud is gone.

Shrugging, the rain running down his back, he turns away. Fire will never think of his brother again.

A new person is coming towards him. This stranger has blue and brown skin on his body. Fire can't see his member. It is a woman. But he can't see breasts. It is a man.

The new person holds out empty hands. '*Please, can you help us? Do you know what happened to us? What place is this?*'

Fire hears: '*Help. What. Us. What.*' The voice is deep. It is a man.

Stone is standing beside Fire. 'Nutcracker-man,' he says softly.

'No,' says Fire.

'Elf-man.'

'No.'

'*Please.*' The new person steps forward. '*I have a wife and child. Do you speak English? My wife is hurt. We need shelter. Is there a road near here, a phone we could use –*'

Stone's axe slams into the top of the new person's head. The head cracks open. Grey and red stuff splashes out.

The new person's eyes look at Fire. He shudders. He falls backwards.

Stone grunts. 'Nutcracker-man.' Stone slices off the new person's cheek and crams it into his mouth.

Fire hoots at the kill. Nutcracker-folk fight hard. This kill was easy.

Other people's legs bring them running from the trees to join Stone at his feast. They have forgotten the rain. They get wet again. But they are all drawn by the scent of the fresh meat.

The new person's skin yields easily to Stone's axe. It comes off in a sheet. Fire's finger touches the sloughed skin. It is blue and brown, thick and dense. Fire is confused. It is skin. It is not skin.

The flesh under the strange skin is white. Stone's axe cuts into it easily. The axe butchers the body rapidly and expertly, an unthinking skill honed across a million years.

The other new people are screaming.

Fire had forgotten them. He straightens up. He has a chunk of flesh in his mouth. His teeth gnaw at it, while his hands pull on it.

The new people's legs are trying to run away. But the new people fall easily, as if they are weak or sick.

Grass and Cold catch the new people. They push them to Stone. One of the new people is bleeding from her head and staggering. Its arms are clutching the small one. When it screams its voice is high. It is a woman.

The other new person has no small one. It has blue skin all over its body. '*We don't mean you any harm. Please. My name is Emma Stoney.*' Its voice is high. It is a woman.

Shoot's hand grabs the hair of this one, pulls her head back.

The new woman's elbow rams into Shoot's belly. '*Get your hands off of me!*' Shoot doubles over, gasping.

The men laugh at the women fighting.

The woman with the child speaks to Stone. '*Please. We're American citizens. My name is Sally Mayer. I – my husband . . . I know you can speak English. We heard you. Look, we can pay. American dollars.*' She holds out something green. Handfuls of leaves. Not leaves. Her arm is bleeding, he sees.

I. You. That is what Fire hears.

The woman has fallen silent. Her eyes are staring at the top of Stone's head. Her mouth is open.

The top of the woman's head is swollen.

Fire makes his hand run over his own brow. He feels thick eye ridges. He feels a sloping brow. He feels the small flat crown behind his brow. His fingers find a fly trapped in his greasy hair. He pulls it out. He pops it into his mouth.

Stone studies the new woman. Stone's fingers squeeze the woman's dug. It is large and soft, under its skin of green and brown. The woman yelps and backs away. The child, eyes wide, cringes from Stone's bloody hand.

Fire laughs. Stone will mount the woman. Stone will eat the woman.

'*No.*'

The other new woman steps forward. Her hands pull the other woman behind her. '*We are like you. Look! We are people. We are not meat.*' She points to the child.

The child has no hair on his face. The child has wide round eyes. The child has a nose.

Nutcracker-folk have hair on their faces. Nutcracker-folk have no noses. Nutcracker-folk have nostrils flat against their faces.

33

Running-folk have no hair on their faces. They have round eyes. They have noses.

Stone's axe rises.

Fire takes a step forward. He is afraid of Stone and his axe. But he makes his hand grab Stone's arm.

'People,' Fire says.

'*Yes.*' The new woman nods. '*Yes, that's right. We're people.*'

Slowly, Stone's arm lowers.

The smell of meat is strong. One by one the people drift away from the new people, and cluster around the corpse.

Fire is left alone, watching the new people.

The fat new person is shaking, as if cold. Now she falls to the ground. The other puts the child down, and cradles the fat one's head on her lap.

The other's face lifts up to Fire. '*My name is Emma. Em-ma. Do you understand?*'

Fire carries the fire. That is his name. That is what he does.

Emma is her name. Emma is what she does. He doesn't know what *Em-ma* is.

He says, 'Em-ma.'

'*Emma. Yes. Good. Please – will you help us? We need water. Do you have any water?*'

His eye spots something. Something moves on a branch on the ground nearby. He has forgotten that he used these branches to make a bower.

His hand whips out and grabs. His hand opens, revealing a caterpillar, fat and juicy. He did not have to think about catching it. It is just here. He pops it in his mouth.

'*Please.*'

He looks down at the new people. Again he had forgotten they were there. 'Em-ma.' The caterpillar wriggles on his tongue. His hand pulls it out of his mouth. He remembers how he caught it, a sharp shard of recent memory.

He makes his hand hold out the caterpillar.

Emma's eyes stare at it. It is wet from his spit. Her hand reaches out and takes it.

The caterpillar is in her mouth. She chews. He hears it crunch. She swallows, hard. '*Good. Thank you.*'

Fire's nose can smell meat more strongly now. Stone's axe has cracked the rib cage. Whatever is in the new person's belly may be good to eat.

The other new woman wakes up. Her eyes look at the corpse, at what the people are doing there. She screams. Emma's hand clamps over her mouth. The woman struggles.

The people crowd close around the corpse. Fire joins them.

He has forgotten the new people.

2

RED MOON

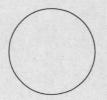

Emma Stoney:

Her chest hurt. Every time she took a breath she was gasping and dragging, as if she had been running too far, or as if she was high on a mountainside.

That was the first thing Emma noticed.

The second thing was the dreaminess of moving here.

When she walked – even on the slippery grass, encumbered by her clumsy flight suit – she felt light, buoyant. But she kept tripping up. It was easy to walk slowly, but every time she tried to move at what seemed a normal pace she stumbled, as if about to take off. Eventually she evolved a kind of half-jog, somewhere between walking and running.

Also she was strong here. When she struggled to drag the woman – Sally? – out of the rain and into the comparative shelter of the trees, with the crying kid at her heels, she felt powerful, able to lift well above her usual limit.

The forest was dense, gloomy. The trees seemed to be conifers – impossibly tall, towering high above her, making a roof of green – but here and there she saw ferns, huge ancient broad-leafed plants. The forest canopy gave them some shelter, but still great fat droplets of water came shimmering down on them. When the droplets hit her flesh they clung – and they *stung*. She noticed how shrivelled and etiolated many of the trees' leaves looked. Acid rain? . . .

The forest seemed strangely quiet. No birdsong, she thought. Come to think of it she hadn't seen a bird in the time she'd been here.

The flat-head people – hominids, whatever – did not follow her into the forest, and as their hooting calls receded she felt vaguely reassured. But that was outweighed by a growing unease, for it was very dark, here in the woods. The kid seemed to feel that too, for he went very quiet, his eyes round.

But then, she thought resentfully, she was disoriented, spooked, utterly bewildered anyhow – she had just been through a plane wreck, for God's sake, and then hurled through time and space to wherever the hell – and being scared in a forest was scarcely much different from being scared on the open plain.

. . . *What* forest? What plain? What is this place? *Where am I?*

Too much strangeness: panic brushed her mind.

But the blood continued to pulse from that crude gash on Sally's arm, an injury she had evidently suffered on the way here, from wherever. And the kid sat down on the forest floor and cried right along with his mother, great bubbles of snot blowing out of his nose.

First things first, Emma.

The kid gazed up at her with huge empty eyes. He looked no older than three.

Emma got down on her knees. The kid shrank back from her, and she made an effort to smile. She searched the pockets of her flight suit, seeking a handkerchief, and finding everything but. At last she dug into a waist pocket of Sally's jacket – she was wearing what looked like designer safari gear, a khaki jacket and pants – and found a paper tissue.

'Blow,' she commanded.

With his nose wiped, the boy seemed a bit calmer.

'What's your name?'

'Maxie.' His tiny voice was scale-model Bostonian.

'Okay, Maxie. My name's Emma. I need you to be brave now. We have to help your mom. Okay?'

He nodded.

She dug through her suit pockets. She found a flat plastic box. It turned out to contain a rudimentary first aid kit: scissors, plasters, safety pins, dressings, bandages, medical tape, salves and creams.

With the awkward little scissors she cut back Sally's sleeve, exposing the wound. It didn't look so bad: just a gash, fairly clean-edged, a few inches long. She wiped away the blood with a gauze pad. She could see no foreign objects in there, and the bleeding seemed mostly to have stopped. She used antiseptic salve to clean up, then pressed a fresh gauze pad over the wound. She wrapped the lower arm in a bandage, and taped it together.

. . . Was that right? How was she supposed to know? Think, damn it. She summoned up her scratchy medical knowledge, derived from what she had picked up at second-hand from Malenfant's training

– not that he'd ever told her much – and books and TV shows and movies ... She pressed Sally's fingernail hard enough to turn it white. When she released it, the nail quickly regained its colour. Good; that must mean the bandage wasn't too tight.

Now she propped the injured arm up in the air. With her free hand she packed up what was left of her first aid kit. She had already used one of only two bandages, half-emptied her only bottle of salve ... If they were going to survive here, she would have to ration this stuff.

Or else, she thought grimly, learn to live like those nude hominids out there.

She turned to the kid. She wished she had some way to make this experience easier on him. But she couldn't think of a damn thing. 'Maxie. I'm going to find something to keep the rain off. I need you to stay right here, with your mom. You understand? And if she wakes up you tell her I'll be right back.'

He nodded, eyes fixed on her face.

She ruffled his hair, shaking out some of the water. Then she set off back towards the plain.

She paused at the fringe of the forest.

Most of the hominids were hunched over on themselves, as if catatonic with misery in the rain. One, apparently an old woman, lay flat out on the floor, her mouth open to the rain.

The rest seemed to be working together, loosely. They were upending branches and stacking them against each other, making a rough conical shape. Perhaps they were trying to build a shelter, like a tepee. But the whole project was chaotic, with branches sliding off the pile this way and that, and every so often one of them seemed to forget what she was doing and would simply wander off, letting whatever she was supporting collapse.

At last, to a great hoot of dismay from the workers, the whole erection just fell apart and the branches came clattering down.

The people scratched their flat scalps over the debris. Some of them made half-hearted attempts to lift the branches again, one or two drifted away, others came to see what was going on. At last they started to work together again, lifting the branches and ramming them into the ground.

It wasn't like watching adults work on a project, however unskilled. It was more like watching a bunch of eight-year-olds trying to build a bonfire for the very first time, figuring it out as they went along, with only the dimmest conception of the final goal.

But these hominids, these *people*, weren't eight-year-olds. They were all adults, all naked, hairless, black. And they had the most beautiful bodies Emma had ever seen, frankly, this side of a movie screen anyhow. They were tall and lean – as tall as basketball players, probably – but much stronger-looking, with an all-round grace that reminded her of decathletes, or maybe Aussie Rules footballers (a baffling, sexy sport she'd tried to follow as a student, long ago).

With broad prominent noses and somewhat rounded chins, they had human-looking faces – human below the eye line, anyhow. Above the eyes was a powerful ridge of bone that gave each of them, even the smallest child, a glowering, hostile look. And above that came a flat forehead and a skull that looked oddly shrunken, as if the top of their heads had somehow been shaved clean off. Their hair was curly, but it was slicked down by the rain, showing the shape of their disturbingly small skulls too clearly.

The bodies of humans, the heads of apes. They spoke in hoots and fragmentary English words. And not one of them looked as if he or she had ever worn a stitch of clothing.

She had never heard of creatures like this. What *were* these people? Some kind of chimp, or gorilla? – but with bodies like that? And what chimps used English?

What part of Africa had she landed in, exactly?

The rain came down harder still, reminding her she had a job to do.

She made her way out into the open, working across increasingly boggy ground, until she reached her parachute. She had been worried that the hominids might have taken it away, but it lay where it had fallen when she had come tumbling from out of the sky.

She took an armful of cloth and pulled it away from the ground. It came loose of the mud only with difficulty, and it was soaked through. She'd had vague plans of hauling the whole thing into the forest, but that was obviously impractical. She hunted through her pockets until she found a Swiss Army knife, kindly provided by the South African air force. She quickly discovered she had at her disposal a variety of screwdrivers, a can and bottle opener, a wood saw, scissors, a magnifying glass, even a nail file. At last she found a fat, sturdy blade. She decided she would cut loose a piece of cloth perhaps twenty feet square, which would suffice for a temporary shelter. Later, when the rain let up, she would come back and scavenge the rest of the silk.

She began to hack her way through the 'chute material. But it was slow work.

For the first time since that dreadful moment of mid-air disintegration, she had time to think.

It was all so fast, so blurred. She remembered Malenfant's final scream over the intercom, her sudden ejection – without warning, she had been thrust into the cold bright air, howling from the pain as the seat's rockets slammed into the small of her back – and then, even as her 'chute had begun to open, she saw the wheel opening like a mouth all around her – and she had realized that for better or worse she was going to fall *through* it . . .

Blue light had bathed her face. There had been a single instant of pain, unbearable, agonizing.

And then, *this*.

She had found herself lying on scrubby grass, in a cloud of red dust, all the breath knocked out of her. *Lying on the ground*, an instant after being forty thousand feet high. From the air to the ground: that was the first shock.

She was aware of the others, the strangers, the couple and the kid, who had appeared beside her, out of nowhere. And she glimpsed that blue portal, foreshortened, towering above her. But it had disappeared, just like that, stranding her here.

Yes, but where was *here*?

She had cut the 'chute section free. She sat back on her haunches, flexing arms that were not conditioned for manual work. She closed up the knife.

Then, on an impulse, she lifted up the knife and dropped it. It seemed to fall with swimming slowness.

Low gravity. As if she was on the Moon.

That was ridiculous. But if not the Moon, *where*?

Get a grip, Emma. Where you are surely matters a lot less than what you are going to do about it – specifically, how you plan to stay alive, long enough for Malenfant to alert the authorities and come find you.

. . . *Malenfant*.

Had she been shying away from thinking about him? He certainly wasn't anywhere near here; he would be making enough noise if he was. Where, then? On the other side of the great blue portal?

But he'd been through the crash too. Was he alive at all?

She shut her eyes, and found herself rocking gently, back and forth, on her haunches. She remembered how he had been in those last instants before the destruction of the plane, the reckless way he had hurled them both at the unknown.

Malenfant, Malenfant, what have you done?

A scream tore from the forest.

Emma bundled up her parachute cloth and ran back the way she had come.

On her bed of dead leaves, Sally was sitting up. With her good arm she held her kid to her chest. Maxie was crying again, but Sally's face was empty, her eyes dry.

Uneasy, Emma dumped the parachute cloth. In the seeping rain, she got to her knees and embraced them both. 'It's all right.'

The kid seemed to calm, sandwiched between the two women.

But Sally pushed her away. 'How can you say that? Nothing's *right*.' Her voice was eerily level.

Emma said carefully, 'I don't think they mean us any harm . . . Not any more.'

'Who?'

'The hominids.'

'*I saw them*,' Sally insisted.

'Who?'

'Ape-men. They were *here*. I just opened my eyes and there was this face over me. It was squat, hairy. Like a chimp.'

Then not like the hominids out on the plain, Emma thought, wondering. Was there more than one kind of human-ape, running around this strange, dreamy forest?

'It was going through my pockets,' Sally said. 'I just opened my eyes and looked right in its face. I yelled. It stood up and ran away.'

'It *stood up*? Chimps don't stand upright. Not habitually . . . Do they?'

'What do I know about chimps?'

'Look, the – creatures – out there on the plain don't sound like that description.'

'They are ape-men.'

'But they aren't squat and hairy.' Emma said hesitantly, 'We've been through a lot. You're entitled to a nightmare or two.'

Doubt and hostility crossed Sally's face. 'I know what I saw.'

The kid was calm now; he was making piles of leaves and knocking them down again. Emma saw Sally take deep breaths.

At least Emma was married to an astronaut; at least she had

had her head stuffed full of outré concepts, of other worlds and different gravities; at least she was used to the concept that there might be other places, other worlds, that Earth wasn't a flat, infinite, unchanging stage . . . To this woman and her kid, though, none of that applied; they had no grounding in weirdness, and all of this must seem unutterably bewildering.

And then there was the small matter of Sally's husband.

Emma was no psychologist. She did not kid herself that she understood Sally's reaction here. But she sensed this was the calm before the storm that must surely break.

She got to her feet. Be practical, Emma. She unwrapped her parachute silk and started draping it over the trees, above Sally. Soon the secondary forest-canopy raindrops pattered heavily on the canvas, and the light was made more diffuse, if a little gloomier.

As she worked she said hesitantly, 'My name is Emma. Emma Stoney. And you –'

'I'm Sally Mayer. My husband is Greg.' (*Is?*) 'I guess you've met Maxie. We're from Boston.'

'Maxie sounds like a miniature JFK.'

'Yes . . .' Sally sat on the ground, rubbing her injured arm. Emma supposed she was in her early thirties. Her brunette hair was cut short and neat, and she wasn't as overweight as she looked in her unflattering safari suit. 'We were only having a joy ride. Over the Rift Valley. Greg works in software research. Formal methodologies. He had a poster paper to present at a conference in Joburg . . . Where are we, do you think?'

'I don't know any more than you do. I'm sorry.'

Sally's smile was cold, as if Emma had said something foolish. 'Well, it sure isn't *your* fault. What do you think we ought to do?'

Stay alive. 'Keep warm. Keep out of trouble.'

'Do you think they know we are missing yet?'

What 'they'? 'That wheel in the sky was pretty big news. Whatever happened to us probably made every news site on the planet.'

Here came Maxie, kicking at leaves moodily, absorbed in his own agenda, like every kid who wasn't scared out of his wits. 'I'm hungry.'

Emma squeezed his shoulder. 'Me too.' She started to rummage through the roomy pockets of her flight suit, seeing what else the South African air force had thought to provide.

She found a packet of dried foods, sealed in a foil tray. She laid out the colourful little envelopes on the ground. There was coffee and dried milk, dried meal, flour, suet, sugar, and high-calorie stuff like chocolate powder, even dehydrated ice cream.

Sally and Emma munched on trail mix, muesli and dried fruits. Sally insisted Maxie eat a couple of digestive biscuits before he gobbled up the handful of boiled sweets he had spotted immediately.

Emma kept back one of the sweets for herself, however. She sucked the cherry-flavour sweet until the last sliver of it dissolved on her tongue. Anything to get rid of the lingering taste of that damn caterpillar.

Caterpillar, for God's sake. Her resentful anger flared. She felt like throwing away the petty scraps of supplies, rampaging out to the hominids, demanding attention. Wherever the hell she was, she wasn't supposed to be here. She didn't want anything to do with this. She didn't want any responsibility for this damaged woman and her wretched kid – and she didn't want her head cluttered up with the memories of what had become of the woman's husband.

But nobody was asking what she wanted. And now the food was finished, and the others were staring at her, as if they expected her to supply them.

If not you, Emma, who else?

Emma took the foil box and went looking for water.

She found a stream a few minutes' deeper into the forest. She clambered down into a shallow gully and scooped up muddy water. She sniffed at it doubtfully. It was from a stream of running water, so not stagnant. But it was covered with scummy algae, and plenty of green things grew in it. Was that good or bad?

She carried back as much water as she could to their improvised campsite, where Sally and Maxie were waiting. She set the water down and started going through her pockets again.

Soon she found what she wanted. It was a small tin, about the size of the tobacco tins her grandfather used to give her to save her coins and stamps. Inside a lot of gear was crammed tight; Maxie watched wonderingly as she pulled it all out. There were safety pins, wire, fish hooks and line, matches, a sewing kit, tablets, a wire saw, even a teeny-tiny button compass. And there was a little canister of dark crystals that turned out to be potassium permanganate.

Following the instructions on the can – to her shame she had to use her knife's lens to read them – she dropped crystals into the water until it turned a pale red.

Maxie turned up his nose, until his mother convinced him the funny red water was a kind of cola.

Habits from ancient camping trips came back to Emma now. For instance, you weren't supposed to *lose* anything. So she carefully packed all her gear back into its tobacco tin, and put it in an inside pocket she was able to zip up. She took a bit of parachute cord and tied her Swiss Army knife around her neck, and tucked it inside her flight suit, and zipped that up too.

And while she was fiddling with her toys, Sally began shuddering.

'Greg. My husband. Oh my God. *They killed him.* They just crushed his skull. The ape-men. Just like that. I saw them do it. It's true, isn't it?'

Emma put down her bits of kit with reluctance.

'Isn't it strange?' Sally murmured. 'Greg isn't here. But I never thought to ask *why* he isn't here. And all the time, in the back of my mind, I *knew* . . . Do you think there's something wrong with me?'

'No,' Emma said, as soothing as she could manage. 'Of course not. It's very hard, a very hard thing to take –'

And then Sally just fell apart, as Emma had known, inevitably, she must. The three of them huddled together, in the rain, as Sally wept.

It was dark before Sally was cried out. Maxie was already asleep, his little warm form huddled between their two bodies.

The rain had stopped. Emma pulled down her rough canopy, and wrapped it around them.

Now Sally wanted to talk, whispering in the dark.

She talked of her holiday-of-a-lifetime in Africa, and how Maxie was doing at nursery school, another child, a daughter, at home, and her career and Greg's, and how they had been considering a third child or perhaps opting for a frozen-embryo deferred pregnancy, pending a time when they might be less busy.

And Emma told her about her life, her career, about Malenfant. She tried to find the gentlest, most undemanding stories she could think of.

Like the one about their engagement, at the end of Malenfant's junior year as a midshipman at the Naval Academy. He had received his class ring, and at the strange and formal Ring Dance she had worn his ring around her neck, while he carried her miniature version in his pocket. And then at the climax of the evening the couples took their turns to go to the centre of the dance floor and climb up under a giant replica of the class ring. Filled with youth and love and hope, they dipped their rings in a bowl of water from the seven seas, and exchanged the rings, and made their vows to each other . . .

Oh, Malenfant, where are you now?

Eventually they slept: the three of them, brought together by chance, lost in this strange quasi-Africa, now huddled together on the floor of a nameless forest. But Emma came to full wakefulness every time she heard a leaf rustle or a twig snap, and every time a predator howled, in the huge lands beyond this sheltering forest.

Tomorrow we have to make a proper shelter, she thought. We can't sleep on the damn ground.

Shadow:

She woke early.

She turned on her back, stretching her long arms lazily. Her nest of woven branches was soft and warmed by her body heat, but where her skin was exposed to the cold, her hair prickled, standing upright. She found moist dew on her black fur, and she scooped it off with a finger and licked it.

Scattered through the trees she could see the nests of the Elf-folk, fat masses of woven branches with sleek bodies embedded, still slumbering.

She had no name. She had no need of names, nor capacity to invent them.

Call her Shadow.

The sky was growing light. She could see a stripe of dense pink, smeared along one horizon. Above her head there was a lid of cloud. In a crack in the cloud an earth swam, bright, fat, blue.

Shadow stared at the earth. It hadn't been there last time she woke up.

Loose associations ran through her small skull: not thoughts, not memories, just shards, but rich and intense. And they were all blue. Blue like the sky after a storm. Blue like the waters of the river when it ran fat and high. Blue, blue, blue, clean and pure, compared to the rich dark green of night thoughts.

Blue like the light in the sky, yesterday.

Shadow's memories were blurred and unstructured, a corridor of green and red in which a few fragments shone, like bits of a shattered sculpture: her mother's face, the lightness of her own body as a child, the sharp, mysterious pain of her first bleeding. But nowhere in that dim green hall was there a flare of blue light like that. It was strange, and therefore it was frightening.

But memories were pallid. There was only the now, clear and bright: what came before and what would come after did not matter.

As the light gathered, the world began to emerge out of the dark green. Noise was growing with the light, the humming of insects and the whirring flight of bats.

Here, in this clump of trees high on an escarpment, she was at the summit of her world. The ground fell away to the sliding black mass of the river. The trees were scattered here, the ground bare and grey, but patches of green-black gathered on the lower slopes, gradually becoming darker and thicker, merging as they tumbled down the gullies and ravines that led to the river valley itself.

She knew every scrap of this terrain. She had no idea what lay beyond – no real conception that *anything* lay beyond the ground she knew.

The others were stirring now. Her infant sister, Tumble, sat up on the belly of their mother, Termite. Termite stretched, and one shapely foot raised, silhouetted against the sky.

Shadow slid out of her nest. The pliant branches rustled back to their natural positions. This was a fig tree, with vines festooned everywhere. Shadow found a dense cluster of ripe fruit, and began to feed.

Soon there was a soft rain all around her, as discarded skins and seeds fell from the lips of the folk, towards the ground.

Above her there was a sharp, sudden crack. She flinched, looking up. It was Big Boss. His teeth bared, without so much as a stretch, he leapt out of his nest and went leaping wildly through the trees, swaying the branches and swinging on the vines.

Everywhere people abandoned their nests, scrambling to get out of the way of Big Boss. The last peace of the night was broken by grunts and screams.

But one man wasn't fast enough. It was Claw, Shadow's brother, hindered by his need to favour his useless hand, left withered by a childhood bout of polio.

Big Boss crashed directly into the nest of the younger male, smashing it immediately. Claw, screeching, fell crashing through the branches and down to the ground.

Big Boss scrambled after him, down to the ground. He strutted back and forth, waving his fists. He shook the vegetation and threw rocks and bits of dead wood. Then he sat, black hair bristling thick over his hunched shoulders.

One by one, Big Boss's acolytes approached him, weaker men he dominated with his fists and teeth and shows of anger. Big Boss welcomed them with embraces and brief moments of grooming.

Claw was one of the last, loping clumsily, his withered hand clutched to his belly. Shadow saw how his back was scratched and bleeding, a marker of his rude awakening. He bent and kissed Big Boss's thigh. But Claw's obeisance was rewarded only by a cuff on the side of his head, hard enough to send him sprawling.

The other men joined in, following their leader's example, kicking and punching at the howling Claw – but each of them retreated quickly after delivering his blow.

Big Boss spread his lips in a wide grin, showing his long canines.

Now Termite strode into the little clearing, calm and assured, her infant clinging to the thick black hair on her back. Claw ran to her and huddled at his mother's side, whimpering as if he was an infant himself.

One of the men pursued Claw, yelling. Like most of the men he was a head taller than Termite, and easily outweighed her. But Termite cuffed him casually, and he backed away.

Now Big Boss himself approached Termite. He slapped her, hard enough to make her stagger.

Termite stood her ground, watching Big Boss calmly.

With a last growl Big Boss turned away. He bent over and defecated explosively. Then he reached for leaves to wipe his backside, while his acolytes jostled to groom his long black fur.

Termite walked away, followed by Claw and her infant, seeking food.

The incident was over, power wielded and measured by all concerned.

Another day had begun in the forest of the Elf-folk.

Shadow, her long arms working easily, swung down to the ground to join her family.

The people lingered by the trees where they had slept. They sat with legs folded and groomed each other, picking carefully through the long black hairs, seeking dirt, ticks and other insects.

Shadow sat her little sister on her lap. Tumble squirmed and wriggled – but with an edge of irritation, for she had picked up blood-sucking ticks some days before. Shadow found some of the tiny, purplish creatures in the child's scalp now. She plucked them away between delicate fingernails and popped them in her mouth, relishing the sharp tang of blood when they burst beneath her teeth.

All around her people walked, groomed, fed, locked into an intricate geometry of lust, loyalty, envy, power. The people were the most vivid thing in Shadow's world; everything else was a blur, barely more noticed than the steady swell of her own breathing.

At eleven years old, Shadow was three feet tall. She had long legs under narrow hips, long, graceful arms, a slim torso, a narrow neck and shoulders. She walked upright. But her legs were a little splayed, her gait clumsy, and her long, strong arms were capable of carrying her high in the trees. Her rib cage was high and conical, and her skull was small, her mouth with its red lips prominent. And over pink-black skin, her body was covered with long black fur.

Her eyes were clear, light brown, curious.

A few days before, Shadow had begun the bleeding, for the first time in her life. Several of the men and boys, smelling this, had begun to pursue her. Even now a cluster of the boys pressed close to her, dragging clumsy fingers through her hair, their eyes bright. But Shadow desired none of them, and when they got too persistent she approached her mother, who growled deeply.

Termite herself was surrounded by a group of attentive men and adolescent boys, some of them displaying spindly erections. Termite submitted to the gentle probing of their fingers. Though she was growing old now, and some of her fur was shot through with silver, Termite was the most popular woman in the group, as far as the men were concerned. On some patches of her head and shoulders her fur had been worn away by the constant grooming; her small skull was all but hairless, her black ears prominent.

That allure, of course, made her one of the most powerful women. Just as the weaker men would compete for the friendship of Big Boss, so the women were ambitious to be part of Termite's loose circle. Shadow – and Tumble, and even Claw – had special privileges, as Termite's children, arising from that power.

And it was real power, the only power, even if the women had to endure the blows and bites of the powerful men. Everybody knew her mother and her siblings, and that was where loyalty lay; for nobody knew her father. No man, not even Big Boss, would have achieved his status without the backing of a powerful mother and aunts.

At last it was time to move on. Little Boss – the brother of Big Boss, his closest lieutenant – led off, working his way down the hillside towards the river. He paused frequently, watching nervously to be sure that Big Boss followed.

The people gave up their grooming and wandered after them.

The Elf-folk entered thicker swathes of forest. The day grew hot, the air oppressive in the greenery. The people walked easily, save where the vines and brambles grew too dense, and then they would use their powerful arms to climb into the trees. They moved slowly, stopping to feed wherever the opportunity arose.

Even at its most dense the forest was sparse. Many of the trees' leaves were yellow, shrivelled and sickly, and some of the trees themselves were dead, no more than gaunt stumps with broken-off branches at their roots. There was much space between the big trees, and the gaps in the forest canopy allowed the sunlight to reach the ground, where shoots and bushes grew thickly.

Shadow, like the others, kept away from the more open clearings. Though her long slim legs carried her easily over the clear ground, the denser green of the forest pulled at her, while the blue-white open sky and green-brown undergrowth repelled her.

They came to a knot of low shrubs.

Termite lowered Tumble to the ground. This was a bush Termite knew well, and her experienced eyes had spotted that some of the leaves had been rolled into tubes, held together by sticky threads. When Shadow opened up such a tube she was rewarded by a wriggling caterpillar, which she popped into her mouth.

The three of them rested on the ground, relishing the treat.

Little Tumble snuggled up to her mother, seeking her nipples. Gently Termite pushed the child away. At first Tumble whimpered, but soon her pleading turned to a tantrum, and the little ball of fur ran in circles and thumped the ground. Her mother held her close, subduing her struggles, until she was calm. Tumble took some of the caterpillars her mother unpacked for her. But later, Tumble made a pretence of having eaten her fill, and began to groom her mother with clumsy attentiveness. Termite submitted to this as she fed – and pretended not to notice as Tumble worked her way ever closer to her nipple, at last stealing a quick suck.

Shadow stretched out on the grass, legs comfortably crossed. She plucked caterpillar leaves from the bushes with one hand, holding the other crooked behind her head.

The sky was a washed-out blue, but clouds were tumbling across it. She had a dim sense of the future: soon it would be dark, and it would rain, and she would get wet and cold. But she saw little further than that, little further than the bright sunny warmth of the sun and the softness of this patch of grass, and she relaxed, her thoughts warm and yellow.

She raised her free hand before her eyes. She stretched her fingers, making slats through which the sun peeked. She moved her hand back and forth, rapidly, making the sun flicker and dance.

Now, with a single graceful movement, she turned over and got to her knees. She gazed at the sharp shadow the sun cast on the leaf-strewn ground before her. She raised her hands, making the shadow do the same, and then she spread her fingers, making light shine through the hands of her shadow.

She got to her feet and began to whirl and dance, and the shadow, this other self, capered in response, its movements distorted and comical. Her dance was eerily beautiful.

The wind shifted, bringing a scent of smoke. Smoke, and meat.

Big Boss stood tall and peered into the green. His nostrils flared.

He rooted around on the ground until he found a cobble the size of his fist. He hurled the cobble against a large rock embedded in the ground, smashing it. Then, with some care, he fingered the debris, searching for flakes of the right size and sharpness.

He stood tall, hands full of sharp flakes, a small trickle of blood oozing from one finger. He issued his summoning cry – 'Ai, ee!' – and, without looking back, he began to stalk off to the west, the way the smoke had come from. His brother Little Boss and another senior man, Hurler, scurried to follow him, keeping a submissive few paces back.

Claw had been crouching in the grass. He stood up now, and took a few steps after the men, uncertainly.

Little Boss slapped him so hard in the back that Claw was sent sprawling on his chest.

But Hurler helped him get back to his feet with a fast, savage yank. Hurler, a big man with powerful hands and a deadly accuracy with thrown rocks, was Termite's brother – Claw's uncle – and so favoured him, more than the other men anyhow. The two of them trotted after Big and Little Boss.

As the men receded, Termite shrugged her slim shoulders and returned to her inspection of the shrubs.

Emma Stoney:

Emma clung to sleep as long as possible. When she could sleep no longer, she rolled on her back, stiff and cold. There was sky above her, an ugly lid of cloud.

Still here, she thought. Shit. And there was an unwelcome ache in her lower bowels.

Nothing for it.

She went behind a couple of trees – close enough that she could still see her parachute canopy tent – and stripped to her underwear. She took a dump, her Swiss Army knife dangling absurdly around her neck. The problem after that was finding a suitable wipe; the dried leaves she tried to use just crumbled in her hands.

Where am I? Answer came there none.

Maybe some kind of adrenaline rush had gotten her through yesterday. Today was going to be even worse, she thought. This morning she felt cold, stiff, dirty, lost, miserable – and with a fear that had sunk deep into her gut.

She got dressed and kicked leaves over the, umm, deposit she'd left. We have *got* to build a latrine today.

Sally and Maxie, waking slowly, showed no desire to leave the forest. But Emma decided she ought to go say hello to the neighbours.

She stepped out of the forest.

It had stopped raining, but the sky was grey and solid and the grassy plain before her was bleak, uninviting. If she had not known otherwise she would have guessed it was uninhabited; the heapings of branches and stones seemed scarcely more than random.

And yet hominids – *people* – sat and walked, jabbered and argued, from a distance just as human as she was, every one of them as naked as a newborn. And they were talking English. The utter strangeness of that struck her anew.

I don't want to be here, facing this bizarreness, she thought. I want to be at home, with the net, and coffee and newspapers, and clean clothes and a warm bathroom.

But it might not be long before she was begging at these hominids' metaphorical table. She had no doubt that those tall, powerful qua-people had a much better ability to survive in this wilderness than she did; she sensed that might become very important, unless they were rescued out of here in the next few days. So she forced herself forward.

Some of the women were tending to nursing infants. Older children were wrestling clumsily – and wordlessly, save for an occasional hoot or screech. The children seemed to her to have the least humanity; without the tall, striking, very human bodies of the adults, their low brows and flat skulls seemed more prominent, and they reminded her more of chimps.

Listening to the hominids yesterday, she had picked up a few of their functional names. The boy who had given her the caterpillar was called Fire. Right now Fire was tending the old woman on the ground, who was called Sing. He seemed to be feeding her, or giving her water. Evidence of kinship bonds, of care for the old and weak? It somewhat surprised Emma. But it was also reassuring, she thought, considering her own situation.

The largest man – Stone, the dominant type who had groped Sally – was sitting on the ground close to the smoking remains of the fire. He was picking through a pile of rocks. He was the leader, she figured – the leader of the men anyhow.

She plucked up her courage and sat opposite him.

He glowered at her. His brown eyes, under a heavy lid of brow, were pits of hostility and suspicion. He actually raised his right fist at her, a mighty paw bearing a blunt rock.

But she sat still, her hands empty. Perhaps he remembered her. Or perhaps he was figuring out all over again that she was no threat. Anyhow, his hand lowered.

Seeming to forget her, he started working at the rocks again. He picked out a big lump of what looked like black glass; it must be obsidian, a volcanic glass. He turned it this way and that, inspecting it. His movements were very rapid, his gaze flickering over the rock surface.

His muscles were hard, his skin taut. His hair was tightly curled, but it was peppered with grey. His face would have passed in any city street – so long as he wore a hat, anyhow, to conceal that shrivelled skull. But an *Aladdin Sane* zigzag crimson scar cut right across his face.

She thought he looked around fifty. Hard to tell in the circumstances.

He picked out another rock from his pile, a round pebble. He began to hammer at the obsidian, hard and confident. Shards flew everywhere, and for the first time Emma noticed that he had a patch of foliage over his lap, protecting his genitals from flying rock chips. He worked fast, confident, his eyes flickering – faster than a human would have, she thought, faster and more instinctively. It was less like watching the patient practising of a human craft than a fast-reaction sport, like tennis or soccer, where the body takes over.

He may not have a wide repertoire of skills, she thought. Maybe this is the one type of tool he can make. But there was nothing limited in what she saw, nothing incomplete; it was as efficient a process as eating or breathing. The contrast with the way the people had struggled to build their heaped-up tepees couldn't have been more striking. How was it possible to be so smart about one thing, yet so dumb about another?

She felt her ideas adjust, her preconceptions dissolve. These people are not like me, she thought.

After a time, Stone abruptly stood up. He dropped his hammerstone, his lap cover, even the tool he had been making, and wandered away.

Emma stayed put.

Stone hunted around the grass, digging into the red dust beneath, picking out bits of rock or perhaps bone, discarding them where he found them. At last he seemed to have found what he wanted.

But then he was distracted by an argument between two of the younger men. He dropped the bone fragment and waded into what was fast becoming a wrestling match. Pretty soon all three of them were battling hard.

Others were gathering around, hooting and hollering. At last Stone floored one of the young men and drove off the other.

Breathing hard, sweating heavily enough to give him a pungent stink, he came back to the pile of rocks, where Emma waited patiently. When he got there he looked around for his bit of bone – but of course it had never made it this far. He bellowed, apparently frustrated, and got up again and resumed his search.

A human craftsman would have got all his tools together before he started, Emma supposed.

Stone came back with a fresh bit of bone. It was red, and bits of meat clung to it; Emma shuddered as she speculated where it might have come from. He used it to chip at the edge of his obsidian axe.

When he was done he dropped the improvised bone tool at his

feet without another thought. He turned the axe over and over in his hands; it was a disc of shaped rock four inches across, just about right to fit into his powerful hand.

Then he hefted it and began to scrape at his neck with it.

My God, she thought. He's shaving.

He saw her looking. 'Stone Stone!' he yelled. He turned away deliberately, suddenly as self-conscious as a teenager.

She got up and moved away.

Shadow:

The people were moving again, working deeper into the forest, seeking food. She spotted Termite and Tumble, walking hand-in-hand, and she followed them.

There had been a shower here. The vegetation was soaking, and droplets sprayed her as she pushed past bushes and low branches. But the droplets sparkled in the sun, and the wet leaves were a bright vivid green. The people's black hair was shot with flashes of rust brown, smelling rich and damp.

Termite came to an ants' nest, a mound punctured by small holes. She reached out and broke a long thin branch from a nearby bush. She removed the side branches and nibbled off the bark, leaving a long, straight stick half as long as her arm. She pushed one hand into the ants' nest and scooped out dirt.

Soon the ants began to swarm out of the nest. Termite plunged her stick into the nest, waited a few heartbeats, and then withdrew it. It was covered with squirming ants. She slid the tool through her free hand so that she was left with a palm filled with crushed and wriggling ants, which she scooped into her mouth, crunching quickly. There was a strong acid smell. Then she returned her stick to the mound and waited for a fresh helping.

Shadow and the other women and children joined in the feast with sticks of their own. Occasionally they had to slap at their feet and thighs as the ants swarmed to repel the invaders; these were big, strong ants that could bite savagely. But Shadow's stick was too spindly and it bent and finally snapped as she shoved it into the loose earth.

More people crowded around. The ants' nest became a mass of jostling and poked elbows and slaps and screeching.

Shadow quickly tired of the commotion. She straightened up, brushed dirt from her legs, and slipped further into the forest.

She came to a tall palm. She thought she could see clusters of red fruit, high above the ground. Briskly she began to climb, her strong arms and gripping legs propelling her fast above the ground.

She found a cluster of fruit. She picked one, then another, stripping off the rich outer flesh, and letting the kernels fall with a whisper to the distant ground. This was one of the tallest trees in the forest. The sky seemed close here, the ground a distant place.

There were eyes, watching her.

She yelped and recoiled, gripping the palm's trunk with her arms.

She saw a face. But it was not like her own. The head was about the size of Shadow's, but there was a thick bony crest over the top of the skull, and immense cheekbones to which powerful muscles were fixed. The body, covered in pale brown fur, was squat, the belly distended. Two pink nipples protruded from the fur, and an infant clung there, peering back at Shadow with huge pale eyes. The infant might have been a twin of Tumble, but already that bony skull had started to evolve its strange, characteristic superstructure.

Mother and child were Nutcracker-folk.

Emma Stoney:

All the tepee shelters had fallen down.

One younger man was struggling, alone, to hoist branches upright. It was Fire, the teenager-type who had gifted her the caterpillar. But nobody was helping him, so his branches had nothing to lean on, and they just fell over. Still he kept trying. At one point he even ran around his construction, trying to beat gravity, hoisting more branches before the others fell. Of course he failed. It was as if he knew what he wanted to build, but couldn't figure out how to achieve it.

Cautiously, Emma stepped forward.

Fire was startled. He stumbled backwards. His branches fell with a crash.

She held her hands open and smiled. 'Fire,' she said. She pointed to herself. 'Emma. Remember?'

At length he jabbered, 'Fire Fire. Fire Emma.'

'Emma, yes. Remember? You gave me the caterpillar.' She pointed to her mouth.

His eyes widened. He ran away at startling speed, and came back with a scrap of what looked like potato. With impatient speed, he shoved it into her mouth. His fingers were strong, almost forcing her jaws open.

She chewed, feeling bruised, tasting the dirt on his fingers. The root was heavy and starchy. 'Thank you.'

He grinned and capered, like a huge child. She noticed that in his excitement he had sprouted an erection. She took care not to look at it; some complications could wait for another day.

'I'll help you,' she said. She walked around his pile of branches. She picked up a light-looking sapling and hoisted it over her shoulder until it was upright. Though her strength still seemed boosted, she struggled to hold the sapling in place.

Mercifully Fire quickly got the idea. 'Fire, Emma, Fire!' He ran around picking up more branches – some of them thick trunks, which he lifted as if they were made of polystyrene – and rammed them into place against hers.

The three or four branches propped each other up, a bit precariously, and the beginning of their makeshift tepee was in place. But, hooting with enthusiasm, Fire hurled more branches onto the tall conical frame. Soon the whole thing collapsed.

Fire shouted his disappointment. He did a kind of dance, kicking viciously at the branches. Then, with a kind of forgetful doggedness, he began to pick up the scattered branches once more.

Emma said, 'I've a better idea.' Raising her hands to make him wait, she jogged over to the muddy remnant of her parachute. She cut free a length of cord – taking care not to show her Swiss Army knife to any of the hominids – and hurried back.

Fire had, predictably, wandered away.

Emma squatted down on the ground to wait, as Fire dug more tubers from the ground, and spent some time throwing bits of stone, with startling accuracy, at a tree trunk, and went running after a girl – 'Dig! Dig, Fire, Dig!' Then he happened to glance Emma's way, appeared to remember her and their project, and came running across as fast as a 100-metre record holder. Straightaway he began to pick up the branches again.

She motioned him to wait. 'No. Look.' She took one of the branches, and pulled another alongside, and then another. Soon he got the idea, and he helped her pile the branches close together.

Now she wrapped her cord around them, maybe three feet below their upper extent, and tied a knot.

. . . Emma Stoney, frontier woman. What the hell are you doing? What if the knot slips or the cord breaks or your sad tepee just falls apart?

Well, then, she thought, I'll just think of something else, and try again. And again and again.

All the time the bigger issues were there in her mind, sliding under the surface like a shark: the questions of where she was, how she had got here, how long it was going to be before she got home again. How she felt about Malenfant, who had stranded her here. How come these ape-folk existed at all, and how come they spoke English . . . But this was *real*, the red dust under her feet, the odd musk stink of the ape-boy before her, the hunger already gnawing at her belly. Right now there was nobody to take care of her, nobody but herself, and her first priority was survival. She sensed she had to find a way of working with these people. So far, in all this strange place, the only creature who had showed her any helpfulness or kindness at all was this lanky boy, and she was determined to build on that.

Find strength, Emma. You can fall apart later, when you're safely back in your apartment, and all this seems like a bad dream.

She laboured to tie her knot tight and secure. When she was done, she backed away. 'Up, up! Lift it up, Fire!'

With terrifying effortlessness he hoisted the three branches vertical. When he let go, they immediately crashed to the ground, of course, but she encouraged him to try again. This time she closed her hands around his, making him hold the branches in place, while she ran around pulling out the bases of the branches, making a pyramidal frame.

At last they finished up with a firmly secured frame, tied off at the top – and it was a frame that held as Fire, with exhilaration and unnerving vigour, hurled more branches over it.

Now all I have to do, Emma thought, is make sure he remembers this favour.

'. . . Emma! *Emma!*'

Emma turned. Sally came running out of the forest, with Maxie bundled in her arms.

Creatures pursued her.

They looked like humans – no, not human, like chimps, with long, powerful arms, short legs, covered in fine black-brown hair – but *they walked upright*, running, almost emulating a human gait. There were four, five, six of them.

Emma thought, dismayed, What now? What new horror is this?

One of the creatures, despite the relative clumsiness of his gait, was fast closing on Sally and the child.

Stone stepped forward. The old male stood stock still, reached back, and whipped his arm forward. His axe, spinning, flew like a Frisbee.

The axe sliced into the ape-thing's face. He, it, was knocked flat, dead immediately. The hominids hooted their triumph and ran to the fallen creature.

The other ape-things ran back to the forest's edge. They screeched their protest, but they weren't about to come out of the forest to launch a counter-attack.

Sally kept running until she had reached Emma. They clutched each other.

'Now we know why our friends keep out of the forest,' Emma said.

Fire was standing beside them. 'Elf-folk,' Fire said, pointing at the ape-things. 'Elf-folk.'

'That's what I saw yesterday,' Sally murmured. 'My God, Emma, they could have come on us while we slept. We're lucky to be alive –'

'They took the ice cream,' Maxie said solemnly.

Sally patted his head. 'It's true. They took all your food, Emma. I'm sorry. And the damn canopy.'

Maxie said, 'What are we going to eat now?'

It appeared the hominids had their own answer to this. From the spot where the ape-like 'Elf' had fallen came the unmistakable sounds of butchering.

Shadow:

For long moments Nutcracker-woman and Shadow gazed at each other, fearful, curious.

Then the Nutcracker-woman took a red fruit, stripped off the flesh, and popped the kernel into her mouth. She pressed up on her lower jaw with her free hand. Caught between her powerful molars, the shell neatly cracked in two. She extracted the nut's flesh and pushed it into her infant's greedy mouth.

Shadow's fear evaporated. She took a fruit herself and stripped it of flesh. But when she tried to copy the Nutcracker-woman's smooth destruction of the nut, she only hurt her jaw.

She spat out the shell and, cautiously, passed it to the Nutcracker-woman.

Just as hesitantly, the Nutcracker-woman took it. Her hand was just like Shadow's, the back coated with fine black hairs, the palm pink.

Shadow had grown used to meeting Nutcracker-folk.

The Elf-folk favoured the fringes of the forest, for they could exploit the open land beyond, where meat could often be scavenged. The Nutcracker-folk preferred the dense green heart of the forest, where the vegetation grew richer. But as the forest shrank, the Elf-folk were forced to push deeper into the remaining pockets of green.

Sometimes there was conflict. The Nutcracker-folk were powerful and limber, more powerful than most Elf-folk, and they made formidable opponents.

All things considered, it was better to try to get along.

But now, as Shadow and the Nutcracker-woman amiably swapped fruit back and forth, there was a screech and crash at the base of the tree. The Nutcracker-woman peered down nervously, her child clinging to her shoulders.

It was the hunting party – or rather, what was left of them. She saw the two powerful brothers, Big Boss and Little Boss, and there was her own brother, Claw, trailing behind. They were empty-handed, and there was no blood around their mouths, or on their pelts. Big Boss seemed enraged. His hair bristled, making him a pillar of spiky blackness. As he stalked along he lashed out at the trees, at his brother – and especially at Claw, who was forced to flee, whimpering. But he needed to stay with the men, for he was in more danger from the predators of the forest than from their fists.

And there was no sign of Hurler, her uncle.

It was Hurler who had been killed by Stone's obsidian axe.

Images of him rattled through Shadow's memory. By tomorrow, though she would be aware of a loss, she would barely remember Hurler had existed.

The men abruptly stopped below Shadow's tree. They peered upwards, silent, watchful.

The Nutcracker-woman had clamped her big hand over her baby's mouth, and it struggled helplessly. But now a nut-shell slipped from the baby's paw, falling with a gentle clatter to the ground.

Big Boss grinned, his hair bristling. Little Boss and Claw spread out around the base of the tree.

Shadow slithered down the tree trunk. The men ignored her.

The three of them clambered into nearby trees. Soon there was an Elf-man in each of the trees to which the Nutcracker-woman could flee.

She began to call out, a piercing cry of fear. '*Oo-hah!*' Nutcracker-people were fierce and strong, and would come rushing to the aid of their own.

But if any Nutcrackers were near, they did not respond.

Suddenly Big Boss made a leap, from his tree to the Nutcracker-woman's. The Nutcracker-woman screeched. She leapt to Claw's tree, her big belly wobbling.

But Claw, small as he was, was ready for her. As the Nutcracker-woman scrambled to get hold of a branch, Claw grabbed her infant from her.

He bit into its skull, and it died immediately.

The Nutcracker-woman screamed, and hurled herself towards Claw. But already, with his kill over his shoulder, Claw was scurrying down the tree trunk to the ground. Blood smeared around his mouth, he held up his limp prize, crying out with triumph.

But Big Boss and Little Boss converged on him. With a casual punch, Little Boss knocked Claw to the dirt, and Big Boss grabbed the infant. The two of them huddled over the carcass. With firm strong motions, they began to dismember it, twisting off the infant's limbs one by one as easily as plucking leaves from a branch. When Claw came close, trying to get a share of the meat, he was met by a punch or a kick. He retreated, screeching his anger.

In the tree above, the Nutcracker-woman could only watch, howling: '*Hah! Oo-hah!*'

Claw came up to the men time and again, pulling at their shoulders and beating their backs.

A powerful blow from Big Boss now sent Claw sprawling. Clutching his chest, he groaned and lay flat.

Shadow approached her brother. She held out a hand, fingers splayed, to groom him, calm him.

He turned on her.

There was blood on his mouth, and his hair bristled around him, and his eyes were crusted with tears. He punched her temple.

She found herself on the ground. The colours of the world swam, yellow leaching into the green.

Now Claw stood over her, breathing hard. He had an erection. She reached for him.

He grabbed her hand and squeezed it, hard, so that her fingers were bent back. She cried out as bones bent and snapped.

Then he walked around her, legs splayed, erection sticking out of his fur. He grabbed at the trees and waved branches at her.

She understood the signs he was making. She knew what he wanted, in his frustration, in his rage. But he was her brother. The thought of him lying on her filled her head with blackness, her throat with bile.

She turned over and tried to stand. But when she put her injured hand on the ground, pain flared, and she fell forward.

He stamped hard on her back. She was driven flat into the undergrowth. She felt his hands on her ankles. He dragged her back towards him and pulled her legs apart. He was stronger than she was; sprawled face-down on the ground, she could not fight him.

His shadow fell over her, looming.

In another bloody heartbeat he was inside her. He screamed, in pain or pleasure. Shadow called for her mother, but she was far away.

Emma Stoney:

The days here lasted about thirty hours. Emma timed them with her wristwatch and a stick stuck in the ground to track shadows.

Thirty hours. No possibility of a mistake.

Not Earth, she thought reluctantly. But that thought was unreal. Absurd.

She knocked over her stick and took her watch off her wrist and stowed it in a pocket, so she wouldn't have to look at it.

After the Elf attack, the three of them stayed on the open plain.

But every morning it was strange, disorienting, to wake among

64

the hominids. Whichever of them woke first would take one look at the strangers and hoot and holler in alarm. Soon they would all be awake, all of them yelling and brandishing their fists, and Emma and the others would have to cower away, waiting for the storm to pass. At last, somebody would recognize them – Fire, or Stone, or one of the younger women. 'Em-ma. Sal-ly.' After that the others would gradually calm down.

But Emma would have sworn that some of them *never* regained their memories of the day before, that every day they woke up not recognizing Emma and the others. It seemed they came awake with the barest memory of the detail of their lives before, as if every day was like a new birth.

Emma wasn't sure if she pitied them for that, or envied them.

The days developed a certain routine. Emma and Sally worked to keep themselves clean, and Maxie; they would rinse out their underwear – they had only one set each, the clothes they had arrived in – and scrub the worst of the dirt off the rest of their clothes and gear.

The women had precisely two tampons between them. When they were gone, they laboured to improvise towels from bits of cloth.

As evening drew in Emma and little Maxie would help build the hominids' haphazard fire by throwing twigs and branches onto it. Paying dues, Emma thought; making sure we earn our place in the warmth.

In the dark the hominids gathered close to the fire, she supposed for safety and warmth. But they didn't form into anything resembling a circle, as humans would. There were little knots of them, men testing their strength against each other, women with their children, pairs coupling with noisy (and embarrassing) enthusiasm. But there was no story-telling, no singing, no dancing. They even ate separately, each hunched over her morsel, as if fearful of having it stolen.

The group did not have the physical grammar of a group bound by language, Emma thought. This was not a true hearth. Their bits of words, their proto-language, were surely a lot closer to the screeches of chimps, or even the songs of birds, than the vocalizations of humans. Though the Runners huddled together for security, they lived their lives as individuals, pursuing solitary projects, each locked forever inside her own head.

They aren't human, Emma realized afresh, however much they might look like it. And this wasn't a community. It was more like a herd.

As night fell, Emma and the others would creep into the shelter she had made with Fire. A few of the hominids followed them, mothers with nursing infants. Maxie cried and complained at the pungent stink of their never-washed flesh. But Emma and Sally calmed him, and themselves, assuring each other that they were surely safer here than in the open, or in the forest.

One child, looking no more than five or six years old in human terms, fell ill. Her eyelids, cheeks, nose and lips were encrusted with sores. The child was skinny, and was evidently in distress; her gestures were faint, her movements listless.

'I think it's yaws,' Sally said. 'I've seen it upriver, in Africa . . . It's related to syphilis. But it's transmitted by flies, who carry it from wound to wound. That's where the first signs show: little bumps in the corners of your eyes, or your nostrils, where the flies go to suck your moisture.'

'What's the cure?'

'A shot of Extencilline. Safeguards you for life. But we don't have any.'

Emma rummaged through her medical pocket. 'What about Floxapen?'

'Maybe. But you're crazy to use it up on *them*. We're going to need it ourselves. We'll get ulcers. We need it.'

Emma struggled to read the directions on the little bottle. She found a scrap of meat, embedded a pill in it, and fed it to the child. It was hard to hold her hand near that swollen, grotesque face.

The next morning, she did the same. She kept it up until the Floxapen was gone. It seemed to her the child was getting gradually better.

Maybe it helped the Runners accept them. She wasn't sure if they understood what she was doing, if they saw the cause-and-effect relationship between her treatment and any change in the girl's condition.

Sally didn't try to stop her. But Emma could see she was silently resentful at what she regarded as a waste of their scarce resources. It didn't help relations between them.

Five or six days after their arrival, she woke to find shards of deep blue sky showing through the loosely stacked branches above her. She threw off her parachute-silk blanket and crawled out of the shelter's rough opening.

It was the first time the sky had been clear since she had got here. The sun was low, but it was strong, its warmth welcome on her face. The sky was a rich beautiful blue, and it was scattered with clouds, and it was *deep*. She saw low cumulus clouds, fat and grey and slow, and higher cirrus-like clouds that scudded across the sky, and wispy traces even above that: layers of cloud that gave her an impression of tallness that she had rarely, if ever, seen on Earth.

She tried to orient herself. If the sun was *that* way, at this hour, she was looking east. And when she looked to the west – oh, my Lord – there was a Moon: more than half-full, a big fat beautiful bright Moon.

. . . *Too* big, too fat, too bright. It had to be at least twice the diameter of the pale grey Moon she was used to. And it was no mottled grey disc, like Luna. This was a vibrant dish of colour. Much of it was covered with a shining steel-blue surface that glimmered in the light of the sun. Elsewhere she saw patches of brown and green. At either extreme of the disc – at the poles, perhaps – she saw strips of blinding white. And over the whole thing clouds swirled, flat white streaks and stripes and patches, gathered in one place into a deep whirlwind knot.

Ocean: that was what that shining steel surface must be, just as the brown-green was land. That wasn't poor dead Luna: it was a planet, with seas and ice caps and continents and air.

And she quickly made out a characteristic continent shape on that brightly lit quadrant, almost bare of cloud, baked brown, familiar from schoolbook studies and CNN reports and Malenfant's schoolkid slideshows. It was Africa, quite unmistakably, the place she had come from.

That was no 'Moon'. That was *Earth*.

And if she was looking at Earth, up in the sky, her relentlessly logical mind told her, then she couldn't be *on* Earth any more. 'Stands to reason,' she murmured.

It made sense, of course: the different air, the lightness of walking, these alien not-quite humans running around everywhere. She had known it the whole time, on some level, but she hadn't wanted to face it.

But, if not on Earth, *where was she*? How had she got here? How was she ever going to get home again? All the time she had been here, she realized, she had got not one whit closer to answering these most basic questions.

Now a shadow passed over them, and Emma felt immediately cold. A new cloud was driving overhead, flat, thick, dark.

Sally was standing beside her. 'They talk English.'

'What?'

'The flat-heads. They talk English. Just a handful of words, but it is *English*. Remember that. They surely didn't evolve it for themselves.'

'Somebody must have taught it to them.'

'Yes.' She turned to Emma, her eyes hard. 'Wherever we are, we aren't the first to get here. We aren't alone here, with these apes.'

She's right, Emma realized. It wasn't much, but it was a hope to cling to, a shred of evidence that there was more to this bizarre experience than the plains and the forests and the hominids.

Emma peered into the sky, where Earth was starting to set.

Malenfant, where are you?

Reid Malenfant:

Malenfant parked at the Beachhouse car park. Close to the Kennedy Space Center, this was an ancient astronaut party house that NASA had converted into a conference centre.

Malenfant, in his disreputable track suit, found the path behind the house. He came to a couple of wooden steps and trotted down to the beach itself. The beach, facing the Atlantic to the east, was empty, as far as he could see. This was a private reserve, a six-mile stretch of untouched coastline NASA held back for use by astronauts and their families and other agency personnel.

It wasn't yet dawn.

He stripped off his shoes and socks and felt the cool, moist sand between his toes. Tiny crabs scuttled across the sand at his feet, dimly visible. He wondered whether they had been disturbed by the new Moonlight, like so many of the world's animals. He stretched his hams, leaning forward on one leg, then the other. Too old to skip your stretching, Malenfant, no matter what else is on your mind.

The Red Moon was almost full – the first full Moon since its appearance, and Emma's departure. A month already. The light cast by the Red Moon was much brighter than the light of vanished silvery Luna, bright enough to wash out all but the brightest stars, bright enough to turn the sky a rich deep blue – but it was an eerie glow, neither day nor night. It was like being in a movie set, Malenfant thought, some corny old 1940s musical with a Moon painted on a canvas sky.

Malenfant hated it all: the light, the big bowl of mystery up there in the sky. To him the Red Moon was like a glowing symbol of his loss, of Emma.

Breathing deep of the salty ocean air, he jogged through gentle dunes, brushing past thickets of palmetto. It wasn't as comfortable a jog as it used to be: the beach had been heavily eroded by the Tide, and it was littered with swathes of sea-bottom mud, respectably large rocks, seaweed and other washed-up marine creatures – not to mention a large amount of oil smears and garbage, some of it probably emanating from the many Atlantic wrecks. But to Malenfant the solitude here was worth the effort of finding a path through the detritus.

It had been another sleepless night. He was consumed with his desire to reach the Red Moon.

Frustrated by the reception his proposals were receiving at NASA Headquarters in Washington, he had decided to take his schemes, his blueprints and models and Barco shows, around the NASA centres, to Ames and Marshall and Kennedy and Johnson, trying to drum up grass-roots support, and put pressure on the senior brass.

We can do this. We've been to the Moon before – a Moon, anyhow – and this new mother is a lot more forgiving than old Luna. Now we have an atmosphere to exploit. No need to stand on your rockets all the way from orbit; you can glide to the ground . . . We can throw together a heavy-lift booster from Shuttle components in months. That one the challenge for Marshall, where von Braun had built his Moon rockets. For Kennedy and Johnson, where the astronauts worked: *We have whole cadres of trained, experienced and willing pilots, specialists and mission controllers itching to take up the challenge of a new Moon. Hell, I'll go myself if you'll let me . . .* He had appealed to the scientists, too: the geologists and meteorologists and even the biologists who suddenly had a whole new world to study: *It will be a whole new challenge in human spaceflight, a world with oceans and an atmosphere – an oxygen atmosphere, by God – just three days away. It's the kind of world we were hoping we might find when we sent our first fragile ships out on the ocean of space half a century ago. And who knows what we'll discover there . . .*

And then there were the groups he had come to think of as the xeno-ologists: the biologists and philosophers and astronomers and others who, long before the sudden irruption of the Red Moon, had considered the deeper mysteries of existence: Are we alone? Even if not, why does it *seem* that we are alone? If we were to meet others – what would they be like?

Come on, people. Our Moon disappeared, and was replaced by another. How the hell? Can this possibly be some natural phenomenon? If not, who's responsible? Not us, that's for sure. The greatest mystery of this or any other age is hanging up there like some huge Chinese lantern. Shouldn't we go take a look?

But, to his dismay and surprise, he had gotten no significant support from anybody – save the wacko UFO-hunting fringe types, who did him more harm than good. NASA, through the Jet Propulsion Laboratory, was working on a couple of unmanned orbital probes and a lander to go visit the Red Moon. But that was it. The notion of sending humans to Earth's new companion was definitively out of the question.

So he had been told, gently but firmly, by Joe Bridges.

'In these road shows of yours you underestimate the magnitude of the task, Malenfant. Whether you're doing that deliberately or not isn't for me to say. We know diddley about the structure of the Red Moon's atmosphere, which is somewhat essential data before you even begin to develop your gliding lander. And then what about the cost and schedule implications of putting together your "Big Dumb Booster" – a brand-new man-rated heavy-lift launcher, for God's sake? Our analysis predicts a schedule of years and a cost of maybe a hundred billion bucks. We just don't have that kind of money, Malenfant. And NASA can't go asking for it right now. Get your head out of your ass and take a look around. *The Tide.* The human race has other priorities . . .'

The first sunlight began to seep into the Atlantic horizon, smears of orange and pink banishing the Red Moon's unnatural light. Malenfant's calves were beginning to tingle, and he could feel his breathing deepening, his heart starting to pound.

Too long since I did this.

He had gotten hooked on running in the dawn light during the preparation for his first spaceflight. Emma had complained that he was spending even less time with her, but as long as he crept out of bed without waking her she had seemed to forgive him. But then there always had been a lot she had had to forgive him for. *Is that why I want to reach her – just so I can say I'm sorry? Well,* is that so bad? Or is it selfish – do I just want to get to her so I can project even more of my own shit onto her? . . .

Emma!

He pounded on, the moist sand cold under every footstep. As his blood pumped he felt the structure of his thoughts dissolve, his obsessive night-time round of planning and worrying and agonizing over I-should-have-said and I-should-have-done, all of it washing away. The main reason to exercise, he thought: it stops your brain working, lets your body remind you you're still an animal.

It was the only respite he got from being himself.

He'd meant to run a couple of miles before doubling back. But when he reached his turn-back point he spotted something on the beach, maybe a mile further south: blocky, silhouetted, very large, returning crumpled orange highlights to the approaching sun. A beached whale? The Tide had played hell with migration patterns. No, too angular for that. A wreck, then?

On impulse he continued on down the beach.

The washed-up object was the size of a small house, twenty-five or thirty feet high. It was heavily eroded, its walls sculpted by wind and water into pits and pillars. When Malenfant stood at its foot the sea breeze that washed over it was distinctly colder.

He ran his hand over its surface. Under stringy seaweed he found a grey, pitted surface, cold and slick under his palm. Ice, of course. The dawn light was still dim, but he could make out the cold clean blue-white shine of the harder ice beneath. He wondered how long the berg would sit here before it melted into the sand.

It was here because of the Tide.

The first few days had been the worst, when Earth's oceans, subject to a sudden discontinuous shock, had sloshed like water in a bathtub. Millions of square miles of coastal lowland had been scoured. In some places, pushed by currents or channelled by sea bottoms, the oceans had spawned waves several hundred feet high, walls of water that had crushed everything in their paths.

After that, with twenty times the mass of Luna, the Red Moon raised daily tides twenty times as high as before – roughly anyhow; the new Moon's spin complicated the complex gravitational dance of the worlds.

The coastlines of the world had been drastically reshaped. The English Channel was being widened as the soft white chalk of the lands that bordered it, including Dover's white cliffs, was worn away. Even rocky coastlines like Maine were being eroded. The lowest tides on the planet used to be in the Gulf of Mexico, the Mediterranean, and elsewhere: now those tides of two feet or less had become forty feet, and around the shores of the Mediterranean many communities, with roots dating back to the dawn of civilization, had been smashed and worn away in a matter of weeks. Meanwhile the tides had forced their way into the mouths of many of the world's rivers, making powerful bores a hundred feet high, and vast floodplains filled and drained with each ebb and flow, drowning some of the planet's most fertile land in salt water.

People had fled inland, a secondary tide of misery, away from the devastated coasts. Already there had been too many deaths even to count, from flooding and tsunamis and 'quakes – and there were surely many more to come, as the displaced populations succumbed to disease, and flooded-out farmers failed to return a crop, and as the wars broke out over remaining stocks.

Meanwhile, as the polar seas flexed, titanic rafts of ice broke away from the shelves of Antarctica and the glaciers of Alaska and Greenland. The larger bergs broke up in the tempestuous seas, but many of them survived to the Equator, filling the oceans, already all but impassable, with an additional hazard. And so bergs like this one were now common sights at all latitudes on the seaboards of the Atlantic and Pacific. In some places they were actually being mined to make up for the disrupted local supplies of clean fresh water. Always a silver lining, Malenfant thought sourly.

He stripped off his sweaty track suit and ran naked into the surf. Deeply mixed by the Tide with the waters of the deep ocean, the sea was icy cold and very salty, stinging when it splashed his eyes and the scar tissue on his healing arm. He took care not to go far out of his depth; he could feel a strong undercurrent as the sea drew back.

He swam a few strokes and then lay on his back, studying the sky, buoyant in the salty water.

The Red Moon was fat and swollen in the sky above him. Though it had (somehow) inserted itself into the same orbit as the old, vanished Moon, it was more than twice Luna's diameter, as large in area as five old Moons put together – and a lot more than five times as bright, because of its reflective cloud and water.

And this morning, the Red Moon was blue. The hemisphere facing him showed a vast, island-strewn ocean, blue-black and cloud-littered, with the shining white of ice caps at the northern and southern extremes. The Red Moon's north pole was tilted towards Earth by ten degrees or so, and Malenfant could see a huge high-pressure system sitting over the pole, a creamy swirl of cloud. But dark bands streaked around the equator, clouds of soot and smoke.

Malenfant, for all his personal animosity, admitted that the new Moon was hauntingly lovely. It even *looked* like a world: obviously three-dimensional, with that shading of atmosphere at the sunlit limb, and sun casting a big fat highlight on its wrinkled ocean skin, as if it were some immense bowling ball. Poor Luna had been so dust-choked that its scattered light had made it look no more spherical than a painted dinner plate.

Malenfant, understandably obsessive, had kept up with the evolving science of the Red Moon.

The new Moon turned on its axis relative to Earth – unlike departed, lamented Luna – with a 'day' of about thirty hours, so that Earthbound watchers were treated to views of both sides. The other hemisphere was dominated by the worldlet's main landmass: a supercontinent, some called it, a roughly circular island-continent with a centre red as baked clay, and fringed by grey-green smears that might be forests. The Red Moon was hemispherically asymmetric, then: like Mars and Luna, unlike Earth and Venus.

That great continent was pitted by huge, heavily eroded impact craters: to Malenfant they were an oddly pleasing reminder of true, vanished Luna. And the centre of the supercontinent was marked by a single vast volcano that thrust much of the way out of the atmosphere. Its immense, shallow flanks, as seen in the telescope, were marked at successively higher altitudes by (apparent) rings of vegetation types, what appeared to be glaciers, and then by bare rock, giving it to terrestrial observers something of the look of a shooting target. (And so the commentators had called it Bullseye.)

The Red Moon's mightiest river rose on the flanks of the Bullseye. Perhaps that great magma upwelling had lifted and broken ancient aquifers. Or perhaps air uplifted by the great mountain was squeezed dry of its water by altitude. Anyhow the river snaked languidly across a thousand miles to the eastern coast, where it cut through a mountain chain there to reach the sea at a broad delta.

There were mountains on both east and west coasts of the supercontinent. They were presumably volcanoes. Those on the east coast appeared to be dormant; they were heavily eroded, and they seemed to cast a rain shadow over the desiccated interior of the continent. There was, however, a comparatively lush belt of vegetation between the mountains and the coast. The commentators had called it the Beltway. The greenery pushed its way into the interior of the continent in a narrow strip along the valley of that great river, which was a Nile for this small world.

But the mountains on the west coast were definitely not dormant. Presumably prompted by rock tides induced by Earth's gravity field, they had been observed to begin erupting a few days after the Red Moon's arrival in orbit around Earth.

They must have been spectacular eruptions. Thick, dense rock near the surface appeared to have blocked the magma flows, bottling up increasing pressure before yielding explosively like a champagne cork flying out of a bottle. On Earth, such stratovolcanoes – like Mount Fuji, Mount Rainier – could eject debris miles into the air. On the Moon the volcanoes had blown debris clear of the planet altogether. Meanwhile vast quantities of dust and gases had been pumped into the atmosphere, to spread in thick bands around much of the Moon's middle latitudes.

There was a great deal you could tell about the Red Moon, even from a quarter-million miles, with telescopes and spectrometers and radar, as the two hemispheres conveniently turned themselves up for inspection. For instance, those oceans really were water. The temperature range was right – as you'd expect since the Moon shared Earth's orbit around the sun – and examination of the visible and infra-red spectra showed that the clouds' caps were made of water vapour, just the right amount to have evaporated off the oceans.

The Red Moon's surface gravity was some two-thirds Earth's – a lot more than Luna's, and, crucially, enough for this miniature planet to have retained all the essential ingredients of an Earthlike atmosphere: oxygen, nitrogen, carbon, water vapour, carbon dioxide – unlike poor barren Luna. So the Red Moon had water oceans and a nitrogen-oxygen atmosphere.

Already the study of the Red Moon had revolutionized the young science of planetology. With a quarter of Earth's mass – but four times the mass of Mars, some twenty times the mass of Luna – the Red Moon was a planet in its own right, intermediate in size between the Solar System's small and large denizens, and so a good test-bed for various theories of planetary formation and evolution.

It differed in key ways from Earth. Because it was so much smaller, it must have started its formation (wherever *that* had occurred) with a much smaller supply of heat energy than Earth.

And that inner heat had been rapidly dissipated through its surface.

Like a shrivelled orange, the Red Moon's rind was thick. Probably aeons ago, the tectonic plates fused, and continents no longer slid over its face. There was no continental drift, no tectonic cycling, no oceanic ridges. Unlike Earth, the Moon's uncycled surface was very ancient; and that was why the interior of the continent bore those huge eroded craters, the scars left by immense impacts long ago.

And that was why the Bullseye was so vast. The huge shield mountain had probably formed over a fountain of magma erupting through a flaw in the crust layers. The crust beneath it must have been held in place over the flaw for hundreds of millions of years – so it more resembled Mars's Olympus Mons than, say, Earth's Hawaiian islands.

But there was more than geology up there. On the Red Moon, it appeared, there was life.

The air was Earthlike, containing around a sixth oxygen – a smaller proportion than Earth's atmosphere, but difficult to explain away by non-living processes. It hadn't taken long to establish that the green-grey pigment that stained the fringes of the supercontinent and its wider river valleys, as well as the shallower sections of the world ocean, was chlorophyll, the green of plants. There were other fingerprints of a living world: an excess of methane in the air, for example, put there perhaps by bacteria in bogs, or burning vegetation, or even the farts of Moon-calves. Though some scientists remained sceptical – and though nobody could say for sure if the Red Moon harboured anything like bogs or bacteria or cows – most people seemed to concur that there was indeed life on the Red Moon, life of some sort.

But was there intelligence?

Nobody had detected any structured radio signals. There had been no response to various efforts to signal to the Red Moon using radio and TV and laser, not to mention a few wacko methods, like the cutting of a huge right-angled triangle of ditches into the Saharan desert filled with burning oil.

But what were the mysterious lights that flickered over the night lands? Most observers claimed they were forest fires caused by lightning or drought. Perhaps, perhaps not. Could the streaming 'wakes' sometimes visible on the great oceans be the wakes of ships, or were they simply peculiar meteorological features? And what about the geometrical traces – circles, rectangles, straight lines – that some observers claimed to have made out in clearings along the coasts and river valleys of the Red Moon's single huge continent? What were they but evidence of intelligence?

And if any of these signs were artificial, what kind of being might live up there to make them?

Malenfant was willing to admit that one manned expedition could do little to probe the mysteries of a world with fully half the surface area of Earth. But there were mysteries that no amount of remote viewing could unravel. The fact was, the most powerful telescope could not resolve an individual human being up there.

Malenfant was never going to find Emma by staring up from Earth.

But at this time of crisis, nobody wanted to see Malenfant's drawings of rocket boosters and gliding spaceships.

Of course there was the question of resources, of priorities. But Malenfant suspected that people were shying away from dealing with the most fundamental issue here: the existence of the Red Moon itself. It was just too big, too huge, impossible to rationalize or grasp or extrapolate. The Wheel was different. A blue circle in the air, a magic doorway? Yes, we can imagine ways we might do that, even if we can't think why we should. Peculiar-looking human beings falling out of the air? Yes, we know about the plasticity of the genome; we can even imagine time travel, the retrieval of our flat-browed ancestors. But *what kind of power hangs a new Moon in our sky?*

He didn't last long in the water; it was too cold. He took a few brisk strokes until the water was shallow enough for him to walk. He splashed out of the surf, shivering, briskly dried himself on his shirt, and began to pull on his pants.

There was somebody standing beside the beached berg fragment, just a slim shadow in the grey dawn light, watching him.

Fire:

Maxie is running around Fire's feet. 'Hide and seek. Hide and seek, Fire. Hide and seek.'

Fire stares at Maxie. To him the boy is a blur of movement and noise, unpredictable, incomprehensible, fascinating.

Maxie has leaves on his head. They flutter away as he runs.

Sally puts them back on. 'No, *Maxie,*' she says. '*Be careful of the sun.*'

'*Hide and seek, hide and seek.*' He stands still. His hands cover his eyes. '*Hands, Fire, eyes, Fire.*' His hands cover his eyes.

Fire puts his hands over his eyes. It is dark. The night is dark. He starts to feel sleepy.

Maxie calls, '*Eight nine ten ready! Fire Fire Fire!*'

Fire lowers his hands. It is not night. The sunlight is bright. The world is red and green and blue. He blinks.

Maxie has gone away.

Fire sees Sing on her bower of leaves. He walks towards her. He has forgotten Maxie.

Maxie is at his feet. '*Here I am, here I am!*' Maxie stamps his foot. Red dust rises and sticks to Maxie's white flesh. '*You have to try, you silly. You have to play it right. Try again, try again. Eyes, Fire, hands, Fire.*' He covers his eyes.

As the sun climbs into the sky, the game goes on. Every time Maxie disappears Fire forgets about him. Every time he comes back Fire is surprised to see him.

Fire grows hungry. Fire thinks of himself in the forest, eating nuts and berries and leaves. Fire lopes towards the forest.

'*Come back, come back, you nasty!*' Maxie falls to the dirt and howls.

Emma comes running to Fire. 'Fire, are you going to the forest? Can I come with you?'

Fire. Forest. That is what Fire hears.

'Em-ma,' he says.

Emma has blue hair. Fire frowns. He thinks of Emma with brown hair. Fire's hand touches Emma's hair. The blue hair is smooth like skin. It has bits of white vine stuck to it.

Emma says, '*It's just a hat, Fire. Just parachute silk.*' She puts the blue hair back on her head and pulls the vines under her chin. '*Can I come to the forest?*'

There is something on Emma's chest. It is bright red. Berries are bright red. Fire touches the berry. It is hard. It is stuck to a vine. The vine is around Emma's neck. His teeth bite the berry-thing. It is hard, like a nut. His teeth cannot break the shell.

Emma pulls it back from him. '*It's my knife, Fire. I showed you yesterday. And the day before. And the day before that. Look.*' Emma touches her knife. When she shows him again, there is a red part, and a part like a raindrop. There is a spot of light behind the raindrop, on Emma's hand. Emma is smiling. '*See, Fire? The lens? Remember this?*'

Fire sees the raindrop and the light. He hoots.

Emma steps away. '*Emma hungry. Emma forest. Fire forest. Emma Fire forest.*'

Fire thinks of Emma and Fire in the forest, gathering berries, eating berries. He smiles. 'Emma Fire forest. Berries trees nuts.'

Emma smiles. '*Good. Let's go.*' She takes his hand.

The forest is a huge mouth. It is dark and green and cool.

He waits at the edge of the forest. His ears listen, his eyes see. The forest is still.

His legs walk into the wood. His feet explore the ground, finding soft bare earth. His arms and his torso and his head duck around branches. He is not thinking of how his body is moving.

His eyes learn to see the dark. His nose smells, his ears listen. He is not aware of time passing, of the sun climbing in the sky, of the dappled bits of light at his feet sliding over the forest-floor detritus.

He sees a pitcher plant. It is a big purple sac, high above his head. His hands pull it down. There is water in the pitcher plant. There are insects in the water. His hand scoops out water and insects. He drinks the water. It tastes sweet. His teeth crunch the insects.

Emma is here. He has forgotten she was here. He gives her the pitcher plant.

Her hand lifts water and bugs to her mouth. She coughs. She spits out insects.

His eyes see a cloudberry plant. It has white flowers and pink fruit. His hands pull the fruit from the plant, avoiding the spiky brambles. His mouth chews the berries.

Here is Emma. Her hands explore the blue skin on her legs. Now she has a soft shining thing in her hands. Her hands open a mouth in the shining thing. She feeds the mouth with berries. He can see them in the stomach of the shining thing.

She holds up the shining thing. '*This is a bag, Fire. These berries are for Sally and Maxie. I can carry more in the bag than I can with my hands. You see? . . .*'

He thinks of Sally eating berries. He thinks of Maxie eating berries.

He thinks of Sing, on her bower. He thinks of Sing eating berries.

His hands pluck berries. His mouth wants to eat the berries, but he thinks of Sing eating them. He keeps the berries in his hands.

His legs move him on. Soon he forgets about Sing, and his mouth eats the berries.

He finds a chestnut tree. It has leaves the size of his hands and sticky buds and nuts. Beneath the chestnut something white is growing. His hands and eyes explore it. It is a morel, a mushroom. His hands pull great chunks of it free, and lift them to his mouth.

Emma is here. Her hands are taking nuts from the chestnut. The nuts want to hurt Emma. He slaps her hands so they stop taking the nuts.

His ears hear a grunt, a soft rustle.

He stops thinking. He stops moving. His ears listen, his nose smells, his eyes flicker, searching.

His eyes see a dark form, squat. It has arms that move slowly. He sees eyes glinting in the green gloom. He sees ears that listen. He sees orange-brown hair, a fat heavy gut, a head with huge cheeks, a giant jaw.

It is a Nutcracker-man.

The Nutcracker-man grunts. He lifts pistachio nuts to his huge mouth. Fire can see his broad, worn teeth, glinting in the dappled light. The Nutcracker-man grinds the nuts between his giant teeth.

Fire's mouth fills with water, to tell him it wants the nuts.

Fire stands up suddenly. He rattles branches and throws twigs. 'Nutcracker-man. Ho!'

The Nutcracker-man screeches, startled. His arms lift him into a tree and swing him away, crashing through foliage, bits of nut falling from his mouth.

Fire pushes through the brush. His hands cram the nuts into his grateful mouth.

Emma is here. Her hands are taking nuts and putting them into the mouth of the shining thing.

His nose can still smell the dung of the Nutcracker-man. He thinks of many Nutcracker-folk, out in the shadows of the forest.

His legs take him away from the place with the pistachio nuts, back towards the open daylight.

Emma follows him. But he has forgotten Emma. He remembers the nuts and the fungus and the Nutcracker-man.

Reid Malenfant:

He kept right on pulling on his pants. When he was done, his breath misting slightly, he walked up the slope of the eroded beach.

His silent observer was a woman: little more than a girl, really, slim, composed, dark. She was wearing a nondescript jumpsuit. She was very obviously Japanese.

'I know you,' he said.

'We have not met.' Her voice was deep, composed. 'But, yes, I know you too, Reid Malenfant.'

'Just Malenfant,' he said absently, trying to place her. Then he snapped his fingers. 'You were on Station when –'

'– when the Moon changed. Yes. My name is Nemoto.' She bowed. 'I am pleased to meet you.'

He bowed back. He felt awkward. He couldn't care less if she had glimpsed his wrinkly ass. But he wished, oddly, that he had his shoes on.

He looked up and down the beach. He saw no sign of transportation, not so much as a bicycle. 'How did you get here?'

'I walked. I have a car, parked at the Beachhouse.'

'As I have.'

'Yes.'

'Will you walk back that way with me?'

'Yes.'

Side by side, in the gathering pink-grey light, they walked north along the beach.

Malenfant glanced sideways at Nemoto. Her face was broad, pale, her eyes black; her hair was elaborately shaved, showing the shape of her skull. She could have been no more than half Malenfant's age, perhaps twenty-five.

'The Red Moon is very bright,' she said.

'Yes.'

'It is a great spectacle. But it will be bad for the astronomers.'

'You were an astronomer . . .'

'I am an astronomer.'

'Yeah. Sorry.'

Nemoto was a Japanese citizen trained as an astronaut at NASA. Her speciality had been space-based astronomy. She had been the brilliant kid who had made it all the way into space at the incredibly young age of twenty-four. He remembered Nemoto as being bright, excitable, even bubbly. Well, she wasn't bright and bubbly now. It was as if she had gone into eclipse.

'I have been looking for you,' she said now. 'I have missed you several times in your tour of the NASA centres. Malenfant, when you are not at your scheduled meetings, you are something of a recluse.'

'Yeah,' he said ruefully. 'Nowadays more than I'd like to be.'

'You miss your wife,' she said bluntly.

'Yes. Yes, I miss my wife.'

'I almost found you at your church.'

'The chapel at Ellington Air Force Base?'

'I had not realized you are Catholic.'

'I guess you should call me lapsed. I converted when I married Emma, back in '82. Emma, my wife. It was for the sake of her family. When I joined NASA we looked around for a chapel. Ellington was near Johnson, and a lot of my colleagues and their families went there, and we liked the priest . . .'

'Are you religious now?'

'No.' He had tried, for the sake of the priest, Monica Chaum, as much as anybody else. But, unlike some who came back from space charged with religious zeal, Malenfant had lost it all when he made his first flight into orbit. Space was just too *immense*. Humans were like ants on a log, adrift in some vast river. How could any Earth-based ritual come close to the truth of the God who had made such a universe?

'So I gave up the chapel. It caused some problems with Emma's family. But she supported me. She always did.'

'But now you have returned to the faith?'

'No. I do find the chapel kind of restful. But I get a lot more comfort from going out on a toot with Monica Chaum over at the Outpost. She has quite a capacity for a woman Catholic priest. I make no excuses; I'd been through a lot.' He eyed her. 'As have you.'

'Yes.' Her face, never beautiful, was empty of expression. 'As is well known.'

Nemoto had been aboard the International Space Station, in low Earth orbit, when the Red Moon had made its dramatic entrance. Nemoto had been forced to watch from orbit as the first great tides battered at Japan.

'I returned to Earth as soon as I could. I and my colleague used our Japanese Hope shuttle. You may know that our landing facility was at Karitimati Island in the South Pacific –'

'Where? Oh, yeah, Christmas Island.'

'There is little left of Karitimati. We were forced to come down here, at KSC.'

He said carefully, 'Where was your home?'

'I have no home now,' was all she would reply.

He nodded. 'Nor do I.' It was true. He had an empty house in Clear Lake, but the hell with that. His home was with Emma – wherever she was.

Nemoto paused and looked into the sky. Although the first liquid glimmer of sun was resting on the horizon, the Red Moon still shone bright in the sky. 'If you have abandoned your attempts to acquire faith, you do not believe that God is responsible for *that*?'

He grinned, rubbing his hand over his bare scalp, feeling a rime of salt there. 'Not God, no. But I think *somebody* is.'

'And you would like to find out who.'

'Wouldn't you?'

'Do you believe that the bodies which fell through the African portal were human?'

He frowned, taken aback by the question. 'Nobody can make much of the mashed-up remains that they scraped out of the savannah.'

'But they appear to be human, or a human variant. You *saw* them, Malenfant. I've read your testimony. They share our DNA – much of it, though the recovered sequences show a large diversity from our own genome. There is speculation that they are more like one of our ancestors, a primitive hominid species.'

'Yeah. So there are ape-men running all over our new Moon up there, right? I read the tabloids too.'

'Malenfant, what do *you* believe?'

He said fiercely, 'I believe that the Wheel was some kind of portal. I believe it linked Earth to its new Moon. And I believe it transported those poor unevolved saps, here from there. What I don't know is what the hell it all means.'

'And you believe your wife made the return journey. That she is still alive up there on the Red Moon, breathing its air, drinking its water, perhaps eating its vegetation.'

'Where else could she be? . . . I'm sorry. It's what I want to believe, I guess. It's what I have to believe.'

'Yes.' She smiled. 'Everybody knows this, Malenfant. Your longing to reach her is tangible. I can see it, now, in your eyes, the set of your body.'

'You think I'm an asshole,' he said brutally. 'You think I should let go.'

'No. I think you are fully human. This is to be admired.'

He felt awkward again. He'd only just met this girl, yet somehow she'd already seen him naked every which way a person could be naked.

They reached the Beachhouse. They sat on its porch, facing the ocean. Malenfant sipped water from a plastic bottle. 'So how come you've been pursuing me around NASA? What do you want, Nemoto?'

'I believe we can help each other. You want to set up a mission to reach the Red Moon. So do I. I believe we should. I believe we must. *I can get you there.*'

Suddenly his heart was pumping. 'How?'

Rapidly, with the aid of a pocket softscreen, she sketched out a cut-down mission profile, using a simplified version of Malenfant's Shuttle-based Big Dumb Booster design, topped by a Space Station evacuation lander, adapted for the Moon's conditions. 'It will not be safe,' she said. 'But it will work. And it could be done, we believe, in a couple of months, at a cost of a few billion dollars.'

It was fast and dirty, even by the standards of the proposals he had been touting himself. But it could work . . . 'If we could get anybody to fund it.'

'There are many refugee Japanese who would support this,' Nemoto said gravely. 'Of all the major nations it is perhaps the Japanese who have suffered most in this present disaster. Among the refugees, there is a strong desire at least to *know*, to understand what has caused the deaths of so many. Thus there are significant resources to call on. But we would need to work with NASA, who have the necessary facilities for ground support.'

'Which is where I come in.' He drank his water. 'Nemoto, maybe you're speaking to the wrong guy. I've already tried, remember. And I got nowhere. I come up against brick walls like Joe Bridges the whole time.'

'We must learn to work with Mr Bridges, not against him.'

'How?'

She touched his hand. Her skin was cold. He was shocked by the sudden, unexpected contact. 'By telling the truth, Malenfant.

You care nothing for geology or planetology or the mystery of the Red Moon, or even the Tide, do you? You want to find Emma.' She withdrew her hand. 'It is a motive that will awaken people's hearts.'

'Ah. I get it. You want me to be a fundraiser. To blub on live TV.'

'You will provide a focus for the project – a *human* reason to pursue it. At a time when the waters are lapping over the grain fields, nobody cares about science. But they always care about family. We need a story, Malenfant. A hero.'

'Even if that hero is a Quixote.'

She looked puzzled. 'Quixote's was a good story. And so will yours be.'

She didn't seem in much doubt that he'd ultimately fall into line. And, looking into his heart, neither did he.

Irritated by her effortless command, he snapped, 'So why are *you* so keen to go exploring the new Moon, Nemoto? Just to figure why Japan got trashed? . . . I'm sorry.'

She shrugged. 'There is more. I have read of your speeches on the Fermi Paradox.'

'I wouldn't call them speeches. Bullshit for goodwill tours . . .'

'As a child, your eyes were raised to the stars. You wondered who was looking back. You wondered why you couldn't see them. Just as I did, half a world away.'

He gestured at the Moon. 'Is that what you think this is? We were listening for a whisper of radio signals from the stars. You couldn't get much less subtle a first contact than *this*.'

'I think this huge event is more than that – even more significant. Malenfant, *people rained out of the sky*. They may or may not belong to a species we recognize, but they were people. It is clear to me that the meaning of the Red Moon is intimately bound up with *us*: what it is to be human – and why we are alone in the cosmos.'

'Or *were*.'

'Yes,' she said. 'And, consider this. This Red Moon simply appeared in our sky . . . It is not as if a fleet of huge starships towed it into position. We don't know how it got there. *And we don't know how long it will stay*, conveniently poised next to the Earth. The Wheel disappeared just hours after it arrived. If we don't act now –'

'Yes, you're right. We must act urgently.' The sun was a shimmering globe suspended on the edge of the ocean, and Malenfant began to feel its heat draw at the skin of his face. 'We've a lot to talk about.'

'Yes.'

They walked up the path to their cars.

Fire:

The sun is above his head. The air is hot and still. The red ground shines brightly through brittle grass. People move to and fro on the red dust.

Fire thinks of Dig. He thinks of himself touching Dig's hair, her dugs, the small of her back. His member stiffens. His eyes and ears seek Dig. They don't find her.

He sees Sing.

Sing is lying flat on her bower, in the sun. Her head does not rise. Her hand does not lift from where it is sprawled in the red dirt. Her legs are splayed. Flies nibble at her belly and eyes and mouth.

Fire squats. His hands flap at the flies, chasing them away. He shakes Sing's shoulder. 'Sing Sing Fire Sing!'

She does not move. He puts his finger in her mouth. It is dry.

Fire picks up Sing's hand. It is limp, but her arm is stiff. He drops the hand. The arm falls back with a soft thump. Dust rises, falls back.

Emma is beside him.

'*Fire. Maxie is ill. Perhaps you can help. Umm, Maxie sore Maxie. Fire Maxie . . . Fire, is something wrong?*'

Her eyes look at Sing. Her hands press at Sing's neck. Emma's head drops over Sing's mouth, and her ear listens.

Fire thinks of Sing laughing. She is huge and looms over him. Her face blocks out the sun.

He looks at the slack eyes, the open mouth, the dried drool. This is not Sing.

His legs stand him up. He bends down and lifts the body over his shoulders. It is stiff. It is cold.

Emma stands. '*Fire? Are you all right?*'

Fire's legs jog downwind. They jog until his eyes see the people are far away. Then his arms dump the body on the ground. It sprawls. He hears bones snap. Gas escapes from its backside.

Bad meat.

He jogs away, back to the people.

He goes to Sing's bower. But the bower is empty. People are here, and then they are gone, leaving no memorials, no trace but their children, as transient as lions or deer or worms or clouds. Sing is gone from the world, as if she never existed. Soon he will forget her.

He scatters the branches with his foot.

Emma is watching him.

Sally is here, holding Maxie. Maxie is weeping. Emma says, '*Fire, I'm sorry. Can you help us? I don't know what to do . . .*'

Fire grins. He reaches for Maxie.

Maxie cringes. Sally pulls him back.

Emma says, '*No, Fire. He doesn't want to play. Fire Maxie ill sick sore.*'

Fire frowns. He touches Maxie's forehead. It is hot and wet. He touches his belly. It is hard.

He thinks of a shrub with broad, coarse-textured leaves. He does not know why he thinks of the shrub. He doesn't even formulate the question. The knowledge is just there.

He lopes to the forest. His ears listen and his eyes peer into the dark greenery. There are no Nutcracker-folk. There are no Elf-folk.

He sees the shrub. He reaches out and plucks leaves.

His legs take him out of the forest.

Maxie stares at the leaves. Water runs down his face.

Fire pokes a leaf into his small, hot mouth. Maxie's mouth tries to spit it out. Fire pushes it back. Maxie's mouth chews the leaf. Fire holds his jaw so the mouth can't chew.

Maxie swallows the leaf, and wails.

Fire makes him swallow another. And another.

Somebody is shouting. 'Meat! Meat!'

Fire's head snaps around. The voice is coming from upwind. Now his nose can smell blood.

Something big has died.

His legs jog that way.

He finds Stone and Blue and Dig and Grass and others. They are squatting in the dirt. They hold axes in their hands.

The meat is an antelope. It is lying on the ground.

Killing birds are tearing at the carcass.

The killing birds tower over the people. They have long gnarled legs, and stubby useless wings, and heads the size of Fire's thigh.

The heads of the birds dig into the belly and joints of the antelope, pushing right inside the carcass.

The people wait, watching the birds.

A pack of hyenas circles, warily watching the birds and the people. And there are Elf-folk. They sit at the edge of the forest, picking at their black-brown hair. The bands of scavengers are set out in a broad circle around the carcass, well away from the birds, held in place by a geometry of hunger and wariness. The Running-folk are scavengers among the others – not the weakest, not the strongest, not especially feared. The people wait their turn with the others, waiting for the birds to finish, knowing their place.

One by one the birds strut away. Their heads jerk this way and that, dipping. Their eyes are yellow. They are looking for more antelopes to kill.

The hyenas are first to get to the corpse. Their faces lunge into its ripped-open rib cage. The hyenas start to fight with one another, forgetting the killing birds, forgetting the people.

Blue and Stone and Fire hurl bits of rock.

The dogs back away. Their muzzles are bloody red, their eyes glaring. Their mouths want the meat. But their bodies fear the stones and sticks of the people.

The people fall on the carcass.

Stone's axe, held between thumb and forefinger, slices through the antelope's thick hide. The axe rolls to bring more of its edge into play. It slices meat neatly from the bones. The birds have beaks to rip meat. The hyenas and cats have teeth. The people have axes. The people work without speaking, not truly cooperating.

Fire's hands cram bits of meat into his mouth, hot and raw. Fire thinks of the other people by the fire, the women and their infants and children with no name. He tells his mouth it must not eat all the meat. He holds great slabs of it in his hands, slippery and bloody.

Fire's ears hear a hollering. His head snaps around.

More Elf-folk are boiling out of the forest fringe, hooting, hungry. They have rocks and stones and axes in their hands. They run on their legs like people. But their legs are shorter than a person's, and they have big strong arms, longer and stronger than a person's.

Stone growls. His mouth bloody, he raises his axe at the Elf-folk.

The Elf-folk show their teeth. They hoot and screech.

A bat swoops from the sky. It is a hunter. Its wings are broad and flap slowly. The people scatter, fearing talons and beak.

The bat falls on the Elf-folk. It caws. It rises into the air. It has its talons dug into the scalp of an Elf-woman. She wriggles and cries, dugs swinging.

One Elf-man throws a rock at the bat. It misses. The others just watch. She is gone, in an instant, her life over.

Suddenly Stone charges forward at the Elf-folk. Blue follows. Dig follows.

The Elf-folk scamper away, into the safety of their forest.

Stone hoots his triumph.

The people return to the antelope. The hyenas have approached again, and bats have flown down, digging into the entrails of the antelope. The people hurl stones and shout. The people's hands take meat and bones from the carcass, until their hands are full. The people's mouths dig into the carcass and bite away final chunks of meat.

Other scavengers move in. Soon there will be nothing left of the antelope but scattered, crushed, chewed bones, over which insects will crawl.

The children fall on the meat. Their mouths snap and their hands punch and scratch as they fight over the meat.

Fire approaches Dig. He holds out meat. Her hands grab it. She throws it away. A child with no name falls on the discarded scrap.

Dig laughs. She turns her back on Fire.

Emma comes to Fire. She smiles, seeing the meat. His belly wants to keep all the meat, but he makes his hands give her some.

Emma takes it to the fire. There are rocks in the fire. Emma beats the meat flat and puts it on the hot rocks. She peels it off the rocks and carries it to Sally and Maxie.

Fire squats on the ground. His hands tear meat. His teeth crush it.

Emma stands before him. She is smiling. She pulls his hand.

His legs follow her.

She stops by a patch of dung. The dung is pale and watery and smelly. There is a leaf in the dung. There is a worm on the leaf, dead.

Emma says, '*I think you did it, Doctor Fire. You got the damn worm out of him.*'

Fire does not remember the leaf, or Maxie. Emma's mouth is still moving, but he does not think about the noises she makes.

Reid Malenfant:

A flock of pigeons flew at the big Marine helicopter. Such was their closing speed that the birds seemed to explode out of the air all around them, a panicky blur of grey and white. The pilot lifted his craft immediately, and the pigeons fell away.

Nemoto's hands were over her mouth.

Malenfant grinned. 'Just to make it interesting.'

'I think the times are interesting enough, Malenfant.'

'Yeah.'

Now the chopper rolled, and the capital rotated beneath him. They flew over the Lincoln, Jefferson and Washington monuments, set out like toys on a green carpet, and to the right the dome of the Capitol gleamed bright in the sunlight, showing no sign of the hasty restoration it had required after last month's food riots.

The helicopter levelled and began a gentle descent towards the White House, directly ahead. The old sandstone building looked as cute, or as twee, as it had always done, depending on your taste. But now it was surrounded by a deep layer of defences, even including a moat around the perimeter fence. And, save for a helipad, the lawn had been turned to a patchwork of green and brown, littered with small out-buildings. In a very visible (though hardly practical) piece of example-setting, the lawn had been given over to the raising of vegetables and chickens and even a small herd of pigs, and every morning the President could be seen by webcast feeding his flock. It was not a convincing portrait, Malenfant always thought, even if the Prez was a farmer's son. But for human beings, it seemed, symbolism was everything.

The helicopter came down to a flawless landing on the pad. Nemoto climbed out gracefully, carrying a rolled-up softscreen. Malenfant followed more stiffly, feeling awkward to have been riding in a military machine in his civilian suit – but he was a civilian today, at the insistence of the NASA brass.

An aide greeted them and escorted them into the building itself. They had to pass through a metal-and-plastics detector in the doorway, and then spent a tough five minutes in a small security office just inside the building being frisked, photographed, scanned and probed by heavily-armed Marine sergeants. Nemoto even had to give up her softscreen after downloading its contents into a military-issue copy.

Nemoto seemed to withdraw deeper into herself as they endured all this.

'Take it easy,' Malenfant told her. 'The goons are just doing their job. It's the times we live in.'

'It is not that,' Nemoto murmured. 'It is this place, this moment. From orbit, I watched the oceans batter Japan. I felt I was in the palm of a monster immeasurably more powerful than me – a monster who would decide the fate of myself, and my family, and all I possessed and cared for, with an arbitrary carelessness I could do nothing to influence. And so, I feel, it is now. But I must endure.'

'You really want to go on this trip, don't you?'

She glanced at him. 'As you do.'

'You always deflect my questions about yourself, Nemoto. You are a *koan*. An enigma.'

She smiled at that fragment of Japanese.

At last they were done, and the aide, accompanied by a couple of the armed Marines, took them through corridors to the Oval Office, on the West Wing's first floor, which the Vice-President was using today. Her official residence, a rambling brick house on the corner of 34th Street and Massachusetts Avenue, was no longer considered sufficiently secure.

Nemoto said as they walked, 'You say you know Vice-President Della.'

'Used to know her. She's had an interest in space all her career. As a senator she served on a couple of NASA oversight committees.' Now the President had asked Della to take responsibility for Malenfant's project, in her capacity as chair of the Space Council.

Nemoto said, 'If she is a friend of yours –'

'Hardly that. More an old sparring partner. Mutual, grudging respect. I haven't seen her for a long time – certainly not since she got *here*.'

'Do you think she will support us?'

'She's from Iowa. She's a canny politician. She is – practical. But she has always seen a little further than most of the Beltway crowd. She believes space efforts have value. But she's a utilitarian. I've heard her argue for weather satellites, Earth resources programmes. She even supports blue-sky stuff about asteroid mining and power stations in orbit. Moving the heavy industries off the planet might provide a future for this dirty old world . . . But robots can do all that. I don't think she sees much purpose in Man in Space. She never supported the Station, for instance.'

'Then we must hope that she sees some utility in our venture to the Red Moon.'

He grimaced. 'Either that or we manage to twist her arm hard enough.'

As they entered the Oval Office, Vice-President Maura Della was working through documents on softscreens embedded in a walnut desk. The desk was positioned at one of the big office's narrow ends – the place really was oval-shaped, Malenfant observed, gawking like a tourist.

Della glanced up, stood, and came out from behind the desk to greet them. Dressed in a trim trouser-suit, she was dark, slim, in her sixties. She shook them both briskly by the hand, waved them to green wing-back chairs before the desk, then settled back into her rocking-chair.

The only other people in the room were an aide and an armed Marine at the door. Malenfant had been expecting Joe Bridges, and other NASA brass.

Without preamble Della said, 'You're trying to get me over a barrel, aren't you, Malenfant?'

Malenfant was taken aback. This was, after all, the Vice-President. But he could see from the glint in Della's eye that if he wanted to win the play this was a time for straight talking. 'Not you personally. But – yes, ma'am, that's the plan.'

Della tapped her desk. Malenfant glimpsed his own image scrolling before her, accompanied by text and video clips and the subdued insect murmur of audio.

Maura Della always had been known for a straightforward political style. To Malenfant she looked a little lost in the cool grandeur of the Oval Office, even after three years in the job, out of place in the crispness of the powder-blue carpet and cream paintwork, and the many alcoves crammed with books, certificates and ornaments, all precisely placed, like funerary offerings. This was clearly not a room you could feel you lived in.

There was a stone sitting on the polished desk surface, a sharp-edged fragment about the size of Malenfant's thumb, the colour of lava pebbles. No, not stone, Malenfant realized, studying the fragment. *Bone.* A bit of skull, maybe.

Della said, 'Your campaign has lasted two weeks already, in every media outlet known to man. Reid Malenfant the stricken hero, tilting at the new Moon to save his dead wife.' She eyed him brutally.

'It has the virtue of being true, ma'am,' Malenfant said frankly. 'And she may not be dead. That's the whole point.'

Nemoto leaned forward. 'If I may –'

Della nodded.

'The response of the American public to Malenfant's campaign has been striking. The latest polls show –'

'Overwhelming support for what you're trying to do,' Della murmured. She tapped her desk and shut down the images. 'Of course they do. But let me tell you something about polls. The President's own approval ratings have been bouncing along the floor since the day the tides began to hit. You know why? Because people need somebody to blame.

'The appearance of a whole damn Moon in the sky is beyond comprehension. If as a consequence your house is smashed, your crops destroyed, family members injured or dead, you can't blame the Moon, you can't rage at the Tide. In another age you might have blamed God. But now you blame whoever you think ought to be helping you climb out of your hole, which generally means all branches of the federal government, and specifically this office.' She shook her head. 'So polls don't drive me one way or the other. Because whatever I decide, your stunt isn't going to help *me*.'

'Perhaps not,' said Nemoto. 'But it might help the people beyond this office. The people of the world. And that is what we are talking about, isn't it?'

Malenfant covered her hand. *Take it easy.*

Della glared. 'Don't presume to tell me my job, young woman.' Then she softened. 'Even if you're right.' She turned to a window. 'God knows we need some good news ... You know about the 'quakes.'

'Yes, ma'am,' Malenfant said grimly.

This was the latest manifestation of the Red Moon's baleful influence. Luna had raised tides in Earth's rock, just as in its water. Luna's rock tides had amounted to no more than a few inches.

But the Red Moon raised great waves several feet high.

Massive earthquakes had occurred in Turkey, Chile and elsewhere, many of them battering communities already devastated by the effects of the Tide. In fault zones like the San Andreas in California, the land above the faults was being eroded away much more rapidly than before, thus exposing the unstable rocks beneath, and exacerbating the tidal flexing of the rocks themselves.

Della said, 'The geologists tell me that if the Red Moon stays in orbit around Earth, it is possible that the fault lines between Earth's tectonic plates – such as the great Ring of Fire that surrounds the Pacific – will ultimately settle down to constant seismic activity. *Constant.* I can't begin to imagine what that will mean for us, for humanity. No doubt devastating long-term impacts on the Earth's climate, all that volcanic dust and ash and heat being pumped into the air . . . When I look into the future now, the only rational reaction is dread and fear.'

'People need to see that we are hitting back,' Malenfant said. 'That we are *doing* something.'

'Perhaps. That is the American way. The myth of action. But does our action hero have to be *you*, Malenfant? And what happens when you crash up there, or die of starvation, or burn up on re-entry? How will *that* play in the polls?'

'Then you find another hero,' Malenfant said stonily. 'And you try again.'

'But even if you make it to the Moon, what will you find? You should know I've had several briefings in preparation for this meeting. One of them was with Dr Julia Corneille, from the Department of Anthropology at the American Museum of Natural History An old college friend, as it happens.'

'Anthropology?'

'Actually Julia's specialty is palaeoanthropology. Extinct homs, the lineage of human descent. You see the relevance.'

'Homs?'

'Hominids.' Della smiled. 'Sorry. Field slang. You can tell I spent some time with Julia . . . She told me something of her life, her work in the field. Mostly out in the desert heartlands of Kenya.'

'Looking for fossils,' Malenfant said.

'Looking for fossils. People don't leave many fossils, Malenfant. And they don't just lie around. It took Julia years before she learned to pick them out, tiny specks against the soil. It's a tough place to work, harsh, terribly dry, a place where all the bushes have thorns on them . . . Fascinating story.' She picked up the scrap of bone from her desk. 'This was the first significant find Julia made. She told me she was engaged on another dig. She was walking one day along the bed of a dried-out river, when she happened to glance down . . . Well. It is a fragment of skull. A trace of a woman, of a species called *Homo erectus*. The *Erectus* were an intermediate form of human. They arose perhaps two million years ago, and became extinct a quarter-million years ago. They had bodies close to modern humans, but smaller brains – perhaps twice the size of chimps'. But they were phenomenally successful. They migrated out of Africa and covered the Old World, reaching as far as Java.'

Malenfant said dryly, 'Fascinating, ma'am. And the significance –'

'The significance is that the homs who rained out of the sky, on the day you lost your wife, Malenfant, appear to have been *Homo erectus*. Or a very similar type.'

There was a brief silence.

'But if *Erectus* died out two hundred and fifty thousand years ago, what is he doing falling out of the sky?'

'That is what you must find out, Malenfant, if your mission is approved. Think of it. What if there *is* a link between the homs of the Wheel and ancestral *Erectus*? Well, how can that be? What does it tell us of human evolution?' Della fingered her skull fragment longingly. 'You know, we have spent billions seeking the aliens in the sky. But we were looking in the wrong place. The aliens aren't separated from us by distance, but by time. Here –' she said, holding out the bit of bone '– *here* is the alien, right here, calling to us from the past. But we have to infer everything about our ancestors from isolated bits of bone – the ancient homs' appearance, gait, behaviour, social structure, language, culture, tool-making ability – everything we know, or we think we know about them. We can't even tell how many species there were, let alone how they lived, how they *felt*. You, on the other hand, might be able to view them directly.' She smiled. 'Even *ask* them. Think what it would mean.'

Malenfant began to see the pattern of the meeting. In her odd mix of hard-nosed scepticism at his mission plans, and wide-eyed wonder at what he might find up there, Della was groping her way towards a decision. His best tactic was surely to play straight.

Nemoto had been listening coldly. She leaned forward. 'Madam Vice-President. You want this Dr Corneille to have a seat on the mission.'

Ah, Malenfant thought. Now we cut to the horse-trading.

Della sat back in her rocker, hands settling over her belly. 'Well, they sent geologists to the Moon on Apollo.'

'*One* geologist,' said Malenfant. 'Only after years of infighting. And Jack Schmitt was trained up for the job; he made sure he was, in fact. As far as I know there are no palaeoanthropologists in the Astronaut Office.'

'Would there be room for a passenger?'

Malenfant shook his head. 'You've seen our schematics.'

Della tapped her desk, and brought up computer-graphic images of booster rockets and spaceplanes. 'You are proposing to build a booster from Space Shuttle components.'

'Our Saturn V replacement, yes.'

'And you will glide down into the Red Moon's atmosphere in a – what is it?'

'An X-38. It is a lifting body, the crew evacuation vehicle used on the Space Station. We will fit it out to keep us alive for the three-day trip. On the surface we will rendezvous with a package of small jets and boosters for the return journey, sent up separately. The whole mission design is based around a two-person crew. Madam Vice-President, we just couldn't cram in anybody else.'

'Not on the way out,' Della said evenly. '*Two out, three back.* Isn't that your slogan, Malenfant?'

'That's the whole idea, ma'am. And those outbound two have to be astronauts. The best scientist in the world will be no use on the Red Moon dead.'

'The same argument was used to keep scientists off Apollo,' Della said.

'But it is still valid.'

Nemoto said coldly, 'The reality is that I must fly this mission because the Japanese funding depends on it. And Malenfant must fly the mission –'

'Because the American public longs for him to go,' Della sighed. 'You're right, of course. If this mission is approved, then it will be you two sorry jerks who fly it.'

If. Malenfant allowed himself a flicker of hope.

Nemoto seemed to be growing agitated. 'Madam Vice-President, *we must do this.* If I may –' She leaned forward and unrolled her softscreen on Della's desktop.

Della watched her blankly. Malenfant had no idea where this was leading.

'There is evidence that similar events have touched human history before, evidence buried deep in our history and myths. Consider the story of Ezekiel, from the Old Testament: *And when the living crea- tures went, the wheels went by them: and when the living creatures were lifted up from the Earth, the wheels were lifted up.* Or consider

95

a tale from the ancient Persian Gulf, about an *animal endowed with reason called Oannes, who used to converse with men but took no food . . . and he gave them an insight into letters and sciences and every kind of art –*'

Shit, Malenfant thought.

Della was keeping her face straight. 'So is this your justification for a billion-dollar space mission? UFOs from the Bible?'

Nemoto said, 'My point is that the irruption of the Red Moon is the greatest event in modern human history. It will surely shape our future – *as it has our past*. The emergence of the primitive hominids from Malenfant's portal tells us that. This one event is the pivot on which history turns.'

'I feel I have enough on my plate without assuming responsibility for all human history.'

Nemoto subsided, angry, baffled.

Della said bluntly, 'However I do need to know why you are trying to kill yourselves.'

Malenfant bridled. 'The mission profile –'

'– is a death-trap. Come on, Malenfant; I've studied space missions before.'

Malenfant sat up straight, Navy style. 'We don't have time not to buy the risks on this one, ma'am.'

'You're both obsessed enough to take those risks. That's clear enough. Nemoto I think I understand.'

'You do?'

Della smiled at Nemoto. 'Forgive me, dear. Malenfant, she may be an enigma to you, but that's because she's young. She lost her family, her home. She wants revenge.'

Nemoto did not react to this.

'But what about you, Malenfant?'

'I lost my wife,' he said angrily. 'That's motive enough. With respect, ma'am.'

She nodded. 'But you are grounded. Let me put it bluntly, because others will ask the same question many times before you get to the launch pad. Are you going back to space to find your wife? Or are you using Emma as a lever to get back into space?'

Malenfant kept his face blank, his bearing upright. He wasn't about to lose his temper with the Vice-President of the United States. 'I guess Joe Bridges has been talking to you.'

She drummed her fingers on her desk. 'Actually he is pushing you, Malenfant. He wants you to fly your mission.' She observed his surprise. 'You didn't know that. You really don't know much about people, do you, Malenfant?'

'Ma'am, with respect, does it matter? If I fly to the Red Moon, whatever my motives, I'll still serve your purposes.' He eyed her. 'Whatever they are.'

'Good answer.' She turned again to her softscreen. 'I'm going to sleep on this. Whether or not you bring back your wife, I do need you to bring us some good news, Malenfant. Oh, one more thing. Julia's ape-men falling from the sky . . . You should know there are a lot of people very angered at the interpretation that they might have anything to do with the origins of humankind.'

Malenfant grunted. 'The crowd who think Darwin was an asshole.'

Della shrugged. 'It's the times, Malenfant. Today only forty per cent of American schools teach evolution. I'm already coming under a lot of pressure from the religious groups over your mission, both from Washington and beyond.'

'Am I supposed to go to the Red Moon and convert the ape-men?'

She said sternly, 'Watch your public pronouncements. You will go with God, or not at all.' She fingered the bit of hominid skull on her desk. '*O ye dry bones, hear the word of the Lord.*'

'Pardon?'

'Our old friend Ezekiel. Chapter 37, verse 4. Good day.'

Emma Stoney:

There were bees that swarmed at sunset. Some of them stung, but you could brush them away, if you were careful. But there were other species which didn't sting, but which gathered at the corner of the mouth, or the eyes, or at the edge of wet wounds, apparently feeding on the fluids of the body.

You couldn't relax, not for a minute.

Uncounted days after her arrival, Emma woke to find an empty shelter.

She threw off her parachute silk and crawled out of the shelter's rough opening. The sun was low, but it was strong, its warmth welcome on her face.

Sally's hair was a tangled mess, her safari suit torn, bloody and filthy. Maxie clung to her leg. Sally was pointing towards the sun. 'They're leaving.'

The Runners were walking away. They moved in their usual disorganized way, scattered over the plain in little groups. They seemed to be empty-handed. They had abandoned everything, in fact: their shelters, their tools. Just up and walked away, off to the east. Why?

'They left us,' Maxie moaned.

A shadow passed over them, and Emma felt immediately cold. She glanced up at the deep sky. Cloud was driving over the sun.

A flake touched her cheek.

Something was falling out of the sky, drifting like very light snow. Maxie ran around, gurgling with delight. Emma held out her hand, letting a flake land there. It wasn't cold: in fact, it wasn't snow at all.

It was ash.

'We have to go, don't we?' Sally asked reluctantly.

'Yes, we have to go.'

'But if we leave here, how will they find us?'

They? What they? The question seemed almost comical to Emma. But she knew Sally took it very seriously. They had spent long hours draping Emma's parachute silk over rocks and in the tops of trees, hoping its bright colour might attract attention from the air, or even from orbit. And they had laboured to pull pale-coloured rocks into a vast rectangular sigil. None of it had done a damn bit of good.

There was, though, a certain logic to staying close to where they had emerged from the wheel-shaped portal. After all, who was to say the portal wouldn't reappear one day, as suddenly as it had disappeared, a magic door opening to take them home?

And beyond that, if they were to leave with the Runners – if they were to walk off in some unknown direction with these gangly, naked not-quite-humans – it would feel like giving up: a statement that they had thrown in their lot with the Runners, that they had accepted that *this* was their life now, a life of crude shelters and berries from the forest and, if they were lucky, scraps of half-chewed, red-raw meat: *this* was the way it would be for the rest of their lives.

But Emma didn't see what the hell else they could do.

They compromised. They spent a half-hour gathering the largest, brightest rocks they could carry, and arranging them into a great arrow that pointed away from the Runners' crude hearth, towards the east. Then they bundled up as much of their gear as they could carry in wads of parachute silk, and followed the Runners' tracks.

Emma made sure they stayed clear of a low heap of bones she saw scattered a little way away. She was glad it had never occurred to Sally to ask hard questions about what had become of her husband's body.

The days wore away.

Their track meandered around natural obstacles – a boggy marsh, a patch of dense forest, a treeless, arid expanse – but she could tell that their course remained roughly eastward, away from the looming volcanic cloud.

The Runners seemed to prefer grassy savannah with some scattered tree cover, and would divert to keep to such ground – and Emma admitted to herself that such park-like areas made her feel relatively comfortable too, more than either dense forest or unbroken plains. Maybe it was no coincidence that humans made parks that reminded them, on some deep level, of countryside like this. I guess we all carry a little Africa around with us, she thought.

She was no expert on botany, African or otherwise. It did seem to her there were a lot of fern-like trees and relatively few flowering plants, as if the flora here was more primitive than on Earth. A walk in the Jurassic, then.

As for the fauna, she glimpsed herds of antelope-like creatures: some of them were slim and agile, who would bolt as the Runners approached, but others were larger, clumsier, hairier, crossing the savannah in heavy-footed gangs. The animals kept their distance, and she was grateful for that. But again they didn't strike her as being characteristically *African*: she saw no elephants, no zebra or giraffes. (But then, she told herself, there were barely any elephants left in Africa anyhow.)

It was clear there were predators everywhere. Once Emma heard the throaty, echoing roar of what had to be a lion. A couple of times she spotted cats slinking through brush at the fringe of forests: leopards, perhaps.

And once they came across a herd – no, a *flock* – of huge, vicious-looking carnivorous birds.

The flightless creatures moved in a tight group with an odd nervousness, pecking at the ground with those savagely curved beaks, and scratching at their feathers and cheeks with claws like scimitars. Their behaviour was very bird-like, but unnerving in creatures so huge.

The Runners took cover in a patch of forests for a full half-day, until the flock had passed.

The Runners called them 'killing birds'. A wide-eyed Maxie called the birds 'dinosaurs'.

And they did look like dinosaurs, Emma thought. Birds had evolved from dinosaurs, of course; here, maybe, following some ecological logic, birds had lost their flight, had forgotten how to sing, but they had rediscovered their power and their pomp, becoming lords of the landscape once more.

The Runners' gait wasn't quite human. Their rib cages seemed high and somewhat conical, more like a chimp's than a human's, and their hips were very narrow, so that each Runner was a delicately balanced slim form with long striding legs.

Emma wondered what problems those narrow hips caused during childbirth. The heads of the Runners weren't that much smaller than her own. But there were no midwives here, and no epidurals either. Maybe the women helped each other.

Certainly each of them clearly knew her own children – unlike the men, who seemed to regard the children as small, irritating competitors.

The women even seemed to use sex to bond. Sometimes in the night, two women would lie together, touching and stroking, sharing gentle pleasures that would last much longer than the short, somewhat brutal physical encounters they had with the men.

By comparison, the men had no real community at all, just a brutish ladder of competition: they bickered and snapped amongst themselves, endlessly working out their pecking order. At that, Emma thought, this bunch of guys had a lot of common with every human mostly-male preserve she had ever come across, up to and including the NASA Astronaut Office.

Stone was the boss man; he used his fists and feet and teeth and hand-axes to keep the other men in their place, and to win access to the women. But he, and the other men, did not seek to injure or kill his own kind. It was all just a dominance game.

And Stone was not running a harem here. With all that fist-fighting he won himself more rolls in the hay than the other men, but the others got plenty too; all they had to do was wait until Stone was asleep, or looking the other way, or was off hunting, or just otherwise engaged. Emma had no idea why this should be so. Maybe you just couldn't run a harem in a highly mobile group like this; maybe you needed a place to hold your female quasi-prisoners, a fortress to defend your 'property' from other men.

It was what these people *lacked* that struck Emma most strongly. They had no art, no music, no song. They didn't even have language; their verbless jabber conveyed basic emotions – anger, fear, demands – but little information. They only 'talked' anyhow in social encounters, mating or grooming or fighting, never when they were working, making tools or hunting or even eating. She thought their 'talk' had more in common with the purring and yowling of cats than information-rich human conversation.

Certainly the Runners never discussed where they were going. It was clear, though, from the way they studied animal tracks, and fingered shrubs, and sniffed the wind, that they had a deep understanding of this land on which they lived, and knew how to find their way across it.

. . . Yes, but how did that knowledge get there, if not through talking, learning? Maybe a facility for tracking was hard-wired into their heads at birth, she speculated, as the ability to pick up language seemed to be born with human infants.

Whatever, it was a peculiar example of how the Runners could be as smart as any human in one domain – say, tracking – and yet be dumber than the smallest child in another – such as playing Maxie's games of hide-and-seek and catch. It was as if their minds were chambered, some rooms fully stocked, some empty, all of the chambers walled off from each other.

When the Runners stopped for the night, they would scavenge for rocks and bits of wood and quickly make any tools they needed: hand-axes, spears. But they carried nothing with them except chunks of food. In the morning, when it was time to move on, they would just drop their hand-axes in the dirt and walk away, sometimes leaving the tools in the mounds of spill they had made during their creation.

Emma saw it made sense. It only took a quarter-hour or so to make a reasonable hand-axe, and the Runners were smart at finding the raw materials they needed; they presumably wouldn't stop in a place that couldn't provide them in that way. To invest fifteen minutes in making a new axe was a lot better than spending all day carrying a lethally sharp blade in your bare hands.

All this shaped their lifestyle, in a way she found oddly pleasing. The Runners had no possessions. If they wanted to move to some new place they just abandoned everything they had, like walking out of a house full of furniture leaving the doors unlocked. When they got to where they were going they would just make more of whatever they needed, and within half a day they were probably as well-equipped as they had been before the move. There must be a deep satisfaction in this way of life, never weighed down by possessions and souvenirs and memories. A clean self-sufficiency.

But Sally was dismissive. 'Lions don't own anything either. Elephants don't. Chimps don't. Emma, these ape-men are animals, even if they are built like basketball players. The notion of possessing anything that doesn't go straight in their mouths has no more meaning to them than it would to my pet cat.'

Emma shook her head, troubled. The truth, she suspected, was deeper than that.

Anyhow, people or animals, the Runners walked, and walked, and walked. They were black shadows that glided over bright red ground, hooting and calling to each other, nude walking machines.

Soon Emma's socks were a ragged bloody mess, and where her boots didn't fit quite right they chafed at her skin. A major part of each new day was the foot ritual, as Emma and Sally lanced blisters and stuffed their battered boots with leaves and grass. And if she rolled up her trousers wet sores, pink on black, speckled her shins; Sally suffered similarly. They took turns carrying Maxie, but they were laden down with their parachute silk bundles, and a lot of the time he just had to walk as best he could, clinging to their hands, wailing protests.

During the long days of walking, Emma found herself inevitably spending more time than she liked with Sally.

Emma and Sally didn't much like each other. That was the blunt truth.

There was no reason why they should; they had after all been scooped at random from out of the sky, and just thrown together. At times, hungry or thirsty or frightened or bewildered, they would take it out on each other, bitching and arguing. But that would always pass. They were both smart enough to recognize how much they needed each other.

Still, Emma found herself looking down on Sally somewhat. Riding on her husband's high-flying career, Sally had gotten used to a grander style of life than Emma had ever enjoyed, or wanted. Emma had often berated herself for sacrificing her own aspirations to follow her husband's star, but it seemed to her that Sally had given up a lot more than she had ever been prepared to.

For the sake of good relations, she tried to keep such thoughts buried.

And Emma had to concede Sally's inner toughness. She had after all lost her husband, brutally slain before her eyes. Once she was through the shock of that dreadful arrival, Sally had shown herself to be a survivor, in this situation where a lot of people would surely have folded quickly.

Besides, she had achieved a lot of things Emma had never done. Not least raising kids. Maxie was as happy and healthy and sane as any kid his age Emma had ever encountered. And there turned out to be a girl, Sarah, twelve years old, left at home in Boston for the sake of her schooling while her parents enjoyed their extended African adventure.

Now, of course, this kid Sarah was left effectively orphaned. Sally told Emma that she knew that even if she didn't make it home her sister would take care of the girl, and that her husband's will and insurance cover would provide for the rest of her education and beyond. But it clearly broke her up to think that she couldn't tell Sarah what had become of her family.

It seemed odd to Emma to talk of wills and grieving relatives – as if they were corpses walking round up here on this unfamiliar Moon, too dumb to know they were dead – but she supposed the same thing must be happening in her family. *Her* will would have handed over all her assets to Malenfant, who must be dealing with her mother and sister and family, and her employers would probably by now be recruiting to fill an Emma-shaped hole in their personnel roster.

But somehow she never imagined Malenfant grieving for her. She pictured him working flat-out on some scheme, hare-brained or otherwise, to figure out what had happened to her, to send her a message, even get her home.

Don't give up, Malenfant; I'm right here waiting for you. And it is, after all, your fault that I'm stuck here.

One day at around noon, with the sun high in the south, the group stopped at a water hole.

The three humans sat in the shade of a broad oak-like tree, while the Runners ate, drank, worked at tools, played, screwed, slept, all uncoordinated, all in their random way. Maxie was playing with one child, a bubbly little girl with a mess of pale brown hair and a cute, disturbingly chimp-like face.

All around the Runners, a fine snow of volcano ash fell, peppering their dark skins white and grey.

The woman called Wood approached Emma and Sally shyly, her hand on her lower belly. Emma had noticed she had some kind of injury just above her pubis. She would cover it with her hand, and at night curl up around it, mewling softly.

Emma sat up. 'Do you think she wants us to help?' Maybe the Runners had taken notice of her treatment of the child with yaws after all.

'Even if she does, ignore her. We aren't the Red Cross.'

Emma stood and approached the woman cautiously. Wood backed away, startled. Emma made soothing noises. She got hold of the woman's arm, and, gently, pulled her hand away.

'Oh God,' she said softly.

She had exposed a raised, black mound of infection, as large as her palm. At its centre was a pit, deep enough for her to have put her fingertip inside, pink-rimmed. As Wood breathed the sides of the pit moved slightly.

Sally came to stand by her. 'That's an open ulcer. She's had it.'

Emma rummaged in their minuscule medical kit.

'Don't do it,' Sally said. 'We need that stuff.'

'We're out of dressings,' Emma murmured.

'That's because we already used them all up,' Sally said tightly.

Emma found a tube of Savlon. She got her penknife and cut off a strip of 'chute fabric. The ulcer stank, like bad fish. She squeezed Savlon into the hole, and wrapped the strip of fabric around the woman's waist.

Wood walked away, picking at the fabric, amazed, somehow pleased with herself. Emma found she had used up almost all the Savlon.

Sally glowered. 'Listen to me. While you play medicine woman with these flat-heads . . .' She made a visible effort to control her temper. 'I don't know how long I can keep this up. My feet are a bloody mass. Every joint aches.' She held up a wrist that protruded out of her grimy sleeve. 'We must be covering fifteen, twenty miles a day. It was bad enough living off raw meat and insects while we stayed in one place. Now we're burning ourselves up.'

Emma nodded. 'I know. But I don't see we have any choice. It's obvious the Runners are fleeing something: the volcanism maybe.

We have to assume they know, on some level anyhow, a lot more than we do.'

Sally glared at the hominids. '*They killed my husband.* Every day I wake up wondering if today is the day they will kill and butcher me, and my kid. Yes, we have to stick with these flat-heads. But I don't have to be comfortable with it. I don't have to *like* it.'

A Runner hunting party came striding across the plain. They brought chunks of some animal: limbs covered in orange hair, a bulky torso. Emma saw a paw on one of those limbs: not a paw, a *hand*, hairless, its skin pink and black, every bit as human as her own.

Nobody offered them a share of the meat, and she was grateful.

That night her sleep, out in the open, was disturbed by dreams of flashing teeth and the stink of raw red meat.

She thought she heard a soft padding, smelled a bloody breath. But when she opened her eyes she saw nothing but Fire's small blaze, and the bodies of the Runners, huddled together close to the fire's warmth.

She closed her eyes, cringing against the ground.

In the morning she was woken by a dreadful howl. She sat up, startled, her joints and muscles aching from the ground's hardness.

One of the women ran this way and that, pawing at the rust-red dirt. She even chased some of the children; when she caught them she inspected their faces, as if longing to recognize them.

Sally said, 'It was the little brown-haired kid. You remember? Yesterday she played with Maxie.'

'What about her?'

Sally pointed at the ground.

In the dust there were footprints, the marks of round feline paws, a few spots of blood. The scene of this silent crime was no more than yards from where Emma had slept.

After a time, in their disorganized way, the Runners prepared to resume their long march. The bereft mother walked with the others. But periodically she would run around among the people, searching, screaming, scrabbling at the ground. The others screeched back at her, or slapped and punched her.

This lasted three or four days. After that the woman's displays of loss became more infrequent and subdued. She seemed immersed in a mere vague unhappiness; she had lost something, but what it was, and what it had meant to her, were slipping out of her head.

Only Emma and Sally (and, for now, Maxie) remembered who the child had been. For the others, it was as if she had never existed, gone into the dark that had swallowed up every human life before history began.

Reid Malenfant:

As soon as Malenfant had landed the T-38 and gotten out of his flight suit, here was Frank Paulis, running across the tarmac in the harsh Pacific sunlight, round and fat, his bald head gleaming with sweat.

Paulis enclosed Malenfant's hand in two soft, moist palms. 'I can't tell you what a pleasure it is to meet you at last. It's a great honour to have you here.'

Malenfant extracted his hand warily. Paulis looked thirty-five, maybe a little older. His eyes shone with what Malenfant had come to recognize as hero worship.

That was why he was here at Vandenberg, after all: to scatter a little stardust on the overworked, underpaid legions of engineers and designers who were labouring to construct his Big Dumb Booster for him. But he hadn't expected it of a hard-headed entrepreneur type like Frank Paulis.

They clambered into an open-top car, Paulis and Malenfant side by side in the back. An aide, a trim young woman Paulis called Xenia, climbed into the driver's seat and cut in the SmartDrive. The car pulled smoothly away from the short airstrip.

They drove briskly along the empty roads here at the fringe of Vandenberg ASFB. To either side of the car there were low green shrubs speckled with bright yellow flowers. They were heading west, away from the sun and towards the ocean, and towards the launch facility.

Paulis immediately began to chatter about the work they were doing here, and his own involvement. 'I want you to meet my engine man, an old buzzard called George Hench, from out of the Air & Space Force. Of course he still calls it just the Air Force. He started working on missile programmes back in the 1950s . . .'

Malenfant sat back in the warm sunlight and listened to Paulis with half an ear. It was a skill he'd developed since the world's fascinated gaze had settled on him. Everybody seemed a lot more concerned to tell him what *they* felt and believed, rather than listen to whatever he had to say. It was as if they all needed to pour a little bit of their souls into the cranium of the man who was going to the Red Moon on their behalf.

Whatever. So long as they did their work.

They rose a slight incline and headed along a rise. Now Malenfant could see the ocean for the first time since landing. This was the Pacific coast of California, some hundred miles north of Los Angeles. The ocean was a heaving grey mass, its big waves growling. The ground was hilly, with crags and valleys along the waterline and low mountains in the background.

The area struck him as oddly beautiful. It wasn't Big Sur, but it was a lot prettier than Canaveral.

But the big Red Moon hung in the sky above the ocean, its parched desert face turned to the Earth, and its deep crimson colour made the water look red as blood, unnatural.

The coastline here had not been spared by the Tide; shore communities like Surf had been comprehensively obliterated. But little harm had come to this Air & Space Force base, a few miles inland. Canaveral, on the other hand, on Florida's Atlantic coast, had been severely damaged by the Tide. So Vandenberg had been the default choice to construct the launch facilities for Malenfant's unlikely steed.

The car slowed to a halt. They were in the foothills of the Casmalia Hills here. From this elevated vantage Malenfant could see a sweep of lowland speckled with concrete splashes linked by roadways: launch pads, many of them decommissioned.

Beyond that he made out blocky white structures. That was the Shuttle facility itself, the relic of grandiose 1970s Air Force dreams of pilots in space. The launch pad itself looked much like its siblings on the Atlantic coast: a gaunt service structure set over a vast flame pit, with gaping vents to deflect the smoke and flame of launch. The gantry was accompanied to either side by two large structures, boxy, white, open, both marked boldly with the USASF and NASA logos. The shelters were mounted on rails and could be moved in to enclose and protect the gantry itself.

It was nothing like Cape Canaveral. The place had the air of a construction site. There were trailers scattered over the desert, some sprouting antennae and telecommunications feeds. There weren't even any fuel tanks, just fleets of trailers, frost gleaming on their flanks. Engineers, most of them young, moved to and fro, their voices small in the desert's expanse, their hard hats gleaming like insect carapaces. There was an air of improvisation, of invention and urgency, about this pad being reborn after two decades under wraps.

'This has been a major launch centre since 1958,' Paulis said, sounding as proud as if he'd built the place himself. 'Many of them polar launches. Good site for safety: if you go south of here, the next landmass you hit is Antarctica . . . Slick-six – sorry, SLC-6 – is the southernmost launch facility here. It was originally built back in the 1960s to launch a spy-in-the-sky space station for the Air Force, which never flew. Then they modified it for the Air Force Shuttle programme. But Shuttle never flew from here either, and after *Challenger* the facility was left dormant.'

'I guess it took a lot of un-mothballing,' Malenfant said.

'You got that right.'

And now, right at the heart of the rust-grey industrial-looking equipment of the Shuttle facility, he made out a slim spire, brilliant white, nestling against its gantry as if for protection.

It looked something like the lower half of a Space Shuttle – two solid rocket boosters strapped to a fat, rust-brown external fuel tank – but there was no moth-shaped Shuttle orbiter clinging to the tank. Instead the tank was topped by a blunt-nosed payload cover almost as fat and wide as the tank itself. The stack vented vapour, and Malenfant could see ice glimmer on its unpainted flanks; evidently the engineers were running a fuelling test.

Malenfant felt the hairs on the back of his neck stand up.

It was he who had produced the first back-of-the-envelope sketch of a Big Dumb Booster like this, sketches to show how Shuttle technology could be warped and mutated to manufacture a heavy-lift launcher, a remote descendant of the Saturn V, for this one-shot project. With Nemoto's backers in place he had led the way in fleshing out the design, based on ancient, never-funded studies from the 1970s and 1980s. He had overseen the computer-graphic simulations, the models. His fingerprints were all over the whole damn project.

But it was not until now, this oddly mundane moment here on this hillside, in a cheap car with jabbering Paulis and taciturn Xenia, that he had actually set eyes on his BDB: his Big Dumb Booster, the spaceship whose destiny would shape the rest of this life, one way or the other.

But it was Paulis who had got the thing built.

Even after Malenfant had been given presidential approval, such strict limits had been placed on budget and schedule that the NASA brass had soon realized they would need input from the private sector. They had turned to Boeing, their long-term partners in running the Shuttle, but Paulis had been quick to thrust himself forward. Frank J. Paulis had made his fortune from scratch; unusually for his generation he had made most of it from heavy engineering, specifically aerospace. He had made promises of impressive funding and the use of his design, manufacture and test facilities around the country – in return for a senior management position on the BDB project.

NASA had predictably rebuffed him. Paulis had handed over his money and facilities anyhow.

But after a couple of months, when the first calamities had predictably hit the project and the schedule had begun to fall apart before it had properly started, NASA, under pressure from the White House, had turned to Paulis.

Paulis's first public act, in front of the cameras, had been to gather an immense heap of NASA documentation before the launch pad. 'This ain't Canaveral, and this is not the Shuttle programme,' he'd told his bemused workers. 'We can't afford to get tied up in a NASA paper trail. I invest the responsibility for quality in *you*, each and every one of you. I trust you to do your jobs. All I ask is that you do it right.' And he set the documentation heap alight with a flame-thrower.

There were some, raised all their careers in NASA's necessarily safety-obsessed bureaucracy, who couldn't hack it; Paulis had had a twenty per cent drop-out. But the rest had cheered him to the Pacific clouds.

After that, Paulis had proven himself something of a genius in raising public interest in the project. A goodly chunk of the booster when it lifted from its pad would be paid for by public subscriptions, raised every which way from Boy Scout lemonade stalls to major corporate sponsors; in fact when it finally took off the BDB's hide would be plastered with sponsors' logos. But Malenfant couldn't care less about that, as long as it *did* ultimately take off, with him aboard.

Paulis, remarkably, was still talking, a good five minutes since Malenfant had last spoken.

'. . . The stack is over three hundred feet tall. You have a boat-tail of four Space Shuttle main engines here, attached to the bottom of a modified Shuttle external tank, so the lower stage is powered by liquid oxygen and hydrogen. You'll immediately see one benefit over the standard Shuttle design, which is in-line propulsion; we have a much more robust stack here. The upper stage is built on one Shuttle main engine. Our performance to low Earth orbit –'

Malenfant touched his shoulder. 'Frank. I do know what we're building here.'

'. . . Yes.' Nervously, Paulis dug out a handkerchief and wiped sweat from his neck. 'I apologize.'

'Don't apologize.'

'It's just that I'm a little over-awed.'

'Don't be.' Malenfant was still studying the somewhat squat lines of the booster stack. 'Although I feel a little awe myself. I've come a long way from the first rocket I ever built.'

At age seventeen, Malenfant was already building and flying model airplanes. With some high-school friends he started out trying to make a liquid-fuelled rocket, like the BDB, but failed spectacularly, and so they switched to solid fuels. They bought some gunpowder and packed it inside a cardboard tube, hoping it would burn rather than explode. 'We propped it against a rock, stuck on some fins, and used a soda straw packed with powder for a fuse. We spent longer painting the damn thing than constructing it. I lit the fuse at a crouch and then ran for cover. The rocket went up fifty feet, whistling. Then it exploded with a bang –'

Paulis said, reverent, 'And Emma was watching from her bedroom window, right? But she was just seven years old.'

Malenfant was aware that the girl driver, Xenia, was watching him with a hooded, judgmental gaze.

Weeks back, in the course of his campaign to build support, he'd told the story of the toy rocket to one of his PR flacks, and she had added a few homely touches – of course Emma hadn't been watching; though she had been a neighbour at that time, at seven years old she had much more important things to do – and since then the damn anecdote had been copied around the planet.

His life story, suitably edited by the flacks, had become as well known as the Nativity story. His feelings of satisfaction at seeing the booster stack evaporated.

He really hadn't expected this kind of attention. But just as Nemoto had predicted, and just as Vice-President Della's political instincts had warned her, Malenfant and his brave, lunatic stunt had raised public spirits at a time when many people were suffering grievously. In the end it wouldn't matter *what* he did – people seemed to understand that there was no conceivable way he was going to 'solve' the problem of the Red Moon – but as long as he pursued his mission with courage and panache, he would be applauded; it was as if everybody was escaping the suffering Earth with him.

But the catch was they all wanted a piece of him.

Paulis was still talking. 'That thing in the sky changed everything. It didn't just deflect the tides. It deflected all our lives – mine included. When I woke up that first day, when I tuned my 'screens to the news and saw what it was doing to us, I felt – helpless. Swapping one jerkwater Moon for another is probably a trivial event, in a Galaxy of a hundred billion suns. Who the hell knows what else goes on out there? But I've never felt so small. I knew at that moment that my whole life could be shaped by events I can't control. Who knows what I might have become if not for *that*, knocking the world off of its axis? Who knows what I might have achieved?'

'Life is contingent,' the driver, Xenia, said unexpectedly. Her accent was vaguely east European. She reached back and covered Paulis's hand. 'All we can do is try our best for each other.'

'You're wise,' Malenfant said.

She sat gravely, not responding.

'On our behalf, please go kick ass, sir,' Frank Paulis said.

'I have less than twelve hours before I fly back out of here, Frank. Tell me who it is I have to meet.'

The car pulled away from the viewpoint and headed towards the sprawling base. Malenfant took a last long breath of the crisp ocean air, bracing himself to be immersed in the company of people once more.

Shadow:

Shadow huddled under a tree, alone.

Claw came stalking past, panting, carrying yellow fruit in his good hand. She cowered away from him, seeking to hide in the deep brown dark of the tree's thick trunk. He hooted and slapped her. Then he stalked on, teeth bared.

Flies clustered around her hand. The webbing between her thumb and forefinger had been split open. Her inner thighs were scratched and sore. Her belly and breasts were bruised, and a sharp pain lingered deep inside her.

Claw had used her again.

Her hands reached for food – a sucked-out fruit skin dropped by somebody high in the tree above her, a caterpillar she spotted on a leaf. But her mouth chewed without relish, and her stomach did not want the food. Agony shot upwards from her deepest belly to her throat. A thin, stinking bile spilled out of her mouth. She groaned and rolled over onto the ground, huddled over her wounded hand.

The light leaked out of the sky.

There was rustling and hooting as the people converged on the roosting site from wherever they had wandered during the day. The high-ranking women built their nests first, weaving branches together to make soft, springy beds, and settling down with their infants.

Somebody thumped Shadow's back, or kicked it. She didn't see who it was. She didn't care.

She stared at the dust. She did not eat. She did not drink. She did not climb the trees to build a nest. She only nursed the scarlet pain in her belly.

Just before the last sunlight faded, she heard screeching and crashing, far above her. Big Boss was making one last show of strength for the day, leaping from nest to nest, waking the women and throwing out the men.

The noises faded, like the light.

Something smelled bad.

She held up her hand in the blue-tinged dark. Something moved in the wound between thumb and forefinger, white and purposeful. She tucked the hand away from her face, deep under her belly.

She closed her eyes again.

Daylight.

She pushed at the ground. She sat up, and slumped back against the tree root.

The people were all around her, jostling, arguing, playing, eating. They didn't see her, here in her brown-green dark.

There was shit smeared on her fur. It was drying, but it smelled odd.

The man called Squat was trying to lead the people, to start the day. He was walking away from them, shaking a branch, stirring bright red dust that clung to his legs. He looked back at Big Boss, walked a little further, looked back again.

Big Boss followed, growling, his hair bristling all over his back. One by one the others followed, the adults feeding as they walked, the children playing with manic energy, as always.

Here was Little Boss. He squatted down on his haunches before Shadow. He was a big slab of hot, sweating muscle, bigger in height and weight than Big Boss himself. He picked up her damaged hand and turned it over. He poked at the edges of the wound, where pus oozed from broken flesh. He let go of the hand, so it fell into the dirt. He inspected her, wrinkling his nose.

He got up and walked a few paces away.

Then he turned. He ran back and, with all his momentum behind it, he kicked her, hard. She ducked her head out of the way, but the kick caught her shoulder and sent her sprawling.

Others came by: women, men, children. She received more slaps and kicks, and was confronted by teeth-baring displays of disgust. Shadow just lay in the dirt, where Little Boss's kick had thrown her.

But the beatings by the men were not severe today. They saved their energy for each other. Many of them jabbered and punched each other, in noisy, inconclusive bouts. The elaborate politics of the men was taking some new turn.

Then there were no more kicks or slaps. The people walked away, the rustle of their passing receding. Shadow was left alone. She dissolved, becoming only a mesh of crimson pain.

She knew herself only in relationship to other people: not through the place she lived, the skills she had. Ignored, it was as if she did not exist.

Now somebody crouched down before her. She smelled familiar warmth. She turned her head with difficulty; her neck was stiff. It was Termite, her mother. Beyond her Tumble, the infant, was playing with a lizard she had found, chasing it this way and that, picking it up by the tail and throwing it.

Termite, huge, strong, studied her daughter. Her face was twisted by uneasy disgust. But she probed at the scratches on Shadow's legs, dipped her fingers into the blood that had dried around Shadow's vagina, and tasted it. Then she inspected the ugly wound on Shadow's hand. Fly maggots were wriggling there.

Termite groomed carefully around the edge of the wound. She pulled out the maggots, squeezed out pus, and licked the edges of the wound. Then she gathered a handful of thick, dark green leaves. She chewed these up, spitting them out into a green mass that stank powerfully, and scraped it over the wound.

It hurt sharply. Shadow squealed and pulled her hand back. But her mother was strong. Termite grabbed her hand and continued to tend the wound, despite Shadow's struggles.

Tumble kept her distance. She would approach her mother, stare at Shadow and wrinkle her small nose, and retreat; then she would forget whatever she had smelled, and approach once more. She hovered a few paces away, attraction and repulsion balanced.

Later, Termite put her powerful arms under Shadow's armpits, hauled her upright by main force, and dragged her into the shade of a fat, tall palm. She brought her food: figs, leaves and shoots. Shadow tried to pull her face away. Termite grabbed her jaw and pinched the joints until Shadow opened her mouth. She forced the food between Shadow's lips, and pushed at her jaw until Shadow chewed and swallowed.

Shadow threw up.

Termite persisted.

By the time the roosting calls began to sound once more through the forest, Shadow was keeping down much of what she swallowed.

The people returned. The adults carried shaped cobbles, or bits of food. Some of the men had meat.

But there was much unrest. Squat and Little Boss were jabbering and throwing slaps at each other. Squat grabbed at a bloody animal leg Little Boss was carrying, trying to snatch it off him. Little Boss punched him hard in the nose, sending Squat flying back, and Little Boss took a defiant, bloody mouthful of his meat.

When the women started making their nests, Tumble climbed up her mother's legs and clung onto her shoulders and head.

Once again Termite tried to make Shadow stand, but Shadow fell back and sprawled in the dirt. So Termite leaned over and let Shadow fall across her shoulders. She stood straight with a grunt, and Shadow's arms and legs dangled at her back and belly.

With powerful gasps, Termite began to climb a palm, laden down by her infant and her nearly grown daughter.

Shadow's head dangled at Termite's back. She saw Termite's legs and rump, a dark slope before her, powerful muscles working. With every jolt, Shadow felt her innards clench, and bright red pain flowed through her. Tumble's small hands delivered stinging slaps to her unprotected backside.

High in a palm, Termite let Shadow slide into the crook of a branch. Sweating and panting, Termite quickly pulled branches together to make a nest. Then she grabbed Shadow by the armpits and pulled her into the nest.

Termite settled herself, curling around her daughter's back. Whimpering, Tumble settled down in the nest at her mother's back, on the far side from Shadow.

The light slid away. The world was black and grey.

Shadow closed her eyes. She slept, entering a deep dreamless sleep, with her mother's warmth around her.

When she woke, in the first pink light of day, she found her thumb in her mouth, as if she was an infant. Memories flooded into her head. Her illness was like a tunnel of blood red, leading back to greener days beyond.

Her back was cold. Termite wasn't there.

She sat up. Termite and Tumble were in the nest, on its far side. Termite was assiduously grooming her infant's fur. Tumble was picking through a lump of faeces, seeking undigested food.

Shadow inspected the wound in her hand. Green, chewed-up fibre clung to it. She licked away the green stuff. There was no sign of maggots or pus, and much of the damaged area was scabbed over, although the scabs cracked when she flexed her thumb.

She hooted and scrambled towards her mother.

Termite sat on the edge of the nest, her long arms wrapped around Tumble, watching Shadow with a hard, still face.

Shadow sat for long heartbeats in the centre of the nest. She picked up bits of fur from the nest and teased them through her fingers. The scent of her mother was still there, mixed with the green smells of the tree. But there was a sourness too.

The sourness was her own smell, Shadow's smell. Her mother, like her sister, could not bear to be with her, because of the smell. She ripped at her fur, screeching, and scattered handfuls of it around the disintegrating nest.

Termite watched impassively.

A stab of pain, lancing up from the depths of her gut, stopped Shadow dead.

She looked down at herself, her breasts and belly and legs. She felt a shiver of surprise that she was *here*, inside this body that stank so strangely.

The pain stabbed again, hot and white. She doubled over, and vomit surged from her, sour and yellow.

It was a hard time for them all. With Big Boss weakening, the social order of the group was breaking down, and anger washed among the people like froth on a turbulent stream.

It went hard for Shadow. Pushed even from her mother's protective circle, suddenly she was the lowest woman in the group. They all hated her, not just for her low place, but because of what she had become, this stinking, bleeding monster. She could not defend herself, from their beatings and the theft of her food.

But still she clung to the group. Still she made her nest each night, high in the trees, away from the cats and other predators, as close to the others as she dared approach. Much as she feared their fists, she was drawn back, for there was nowhere else to go.

And she was still ill. Her bleeding had stopped. She was afflicted by stomach cramps and pain deep in her back. Her breasts and belly started to swell. She was violently sick each morning. Her days were a blur of pain and loneliness. When she saw her shadow, of a hunched-over creature with hair ragged and filthy, she did not recognize herself.

But then, one day, she felt something squirm in her belly, a kicking foot.

Her head filled with memories, of blood and shit and milk. She remembered a woman lying on her back, legs askew, other women working to pull a pink, slick mass from her body, their hands sticky with blood.

Her loneliness sharpened into fear.

Again she ran to her mother, reaching for her sparse fur, trying to groom, to get close.

Since the illness had started, Termite had never once struck her daughter, not as the others did. But now, as her broad nostrils widened with the stink of Shadow's body, her fists clenched.

Shadow cowered, whimpering.

Claw came running by, hair bristling, hooting inanely. He was grinning, but blood ran from a gouge in the side of his face. He was running from a fight. As he passed Shadow he aimed a kick at her that caught her in the small of her back.

Shadow dragged herself to the shade of a big palm. There she slumped down, and vomited copiously.

Reid Malenfant:

The next time he woke, Malenfant found the light that soaked through his parachute-canopy tent was a little less bright, the air perhaps a fraction cooler.

Night was coming, at last, to the desert.

He tried to sit up. His head banged as if his brain was rattling around in his skull. His mouth was a sandbox, and he felt a burning dryness right through his throat and nose. It felt like the worst hangover of all time.

But you're built for heat, Malenfant. You've got a body adapted to function away from the shelter of the trees, to walk upright in the heat of the day. That's why you sweat and the chimps don't. Haven't you learned anything from those palaeo classes? . . .

He reached for his water flask and shook it. Still a quarter full, just as it had been before he slept. Deliberately he tucked it back under his blanket.

He got to his feet. He staggered, brushing his head against the hot, dusty canopy. The fabric rippled, and he heard sand hissing off it. He bent and found his broad stiff-brimmed hat, and jammed it on his bare scalp. Then, rubbing the stubble on his jaw, he stepped out of the makeshift tent.

Outside was like a dry sauna. He felt the moisture just suck straight out of his skin. The pain intensified around his temples and eyes, crumpling his forehead.

The world was elemental: nothing but sand, sky and gnarled Joshua trees, over which their 'chutes were draped.

This was the Mojave desert. He and Nemoto had been dumped here as a survival training exercise. During the day the heat was flat and crushing; they could do nothing but lie in their tent of 'chutes. And at night they foraged for food.

Nemoto was crouched over a low fire. She was heating some kind of thin broth in a pan she'd made out of aluminium foil. She had a spare T-shirt wrapped around her head. *To survive you don't need equipment,* the instructor had said. *All you need to pack is strength and ingenuity and determination. That, and a willingness to eat insects and lizards.*

Nemoto had proved ingenious at setting traps.

'I wonder –' His throat was so dry he had to start again. 'I wonder what's in the soup this time.'

Nemoto glanced up at him, and then looked back to her cooking. 'Your speech is slurred. Drink some water, Malenfant.'

He walked around their little campsite, stretching his legs. He could feel a tingling in his limbs, and the air felt thin. The horizon seemed blurred, perhaps by dust.

'I mean, why the hell are we here?' He lifted his arms and turned around. 'Whatever we find on the Red Moon, it won't be like this.'

'But on returning to Earth we might land in a desert area, and –'

He barked laughter, hurting his throat. 'Let's face it, Nemoto. The chances of our returning healthy enough to play wild man in the desert are too remote to think about.'

'Drink some water.'

He stalked away, vainly seeking cooler air.

As the project had grown, as all such projects did, it had acquired its own logic, much of it loaned from NASA – to Malenfant's chagrin, and against his better judgement. While the ship was being prepared, the booster assembled and tested, nobody seemed to know what to do with the astronauts, except train them to death and send them on goodwill tours, just as NASA always had.

Some of the training Malenfant could swallow. He had, after all, flown in space twice before, and Nemoto, on her single trip to Station, had logged up an impressive number of days on orbit. So they endured hours in classrooms and in hastily mocked-up simulators going over every aspect of their unlikely craft's systems, and the procedures they would have to follow at their mission's major stages.

The major problem with that turned out to be the very volatility of the design. As teams of engineers struggled to cram in everything they thought they needed, key systems went through major redesigns daily – and all of it impacted in the crew's interface with their craft. In the end Malenfant had grown tired of the simulation programmers' labouring efforts. He had shut down the sims, had a dummy cabin mocked up from plywood, and had blown-up layouts of their instrument panels cut out of paper and pasted over the wood. It wasn't too interactive, but it familiarized them with systems and procedures – and it was easy to upgrade each morning with bits of tape and sticky paper, as news of each redesign came through.

But the spacecraft-specific training was the easy stuff. The rest was more problematic. How, after all, do you train to face a completely unknown world?

Malenfant and Nemoto had undergone a lot of altitude training, for it was clear that the Red Moon's air would be thinner than Earth's. Likewise they had been taken to tropical jungles, for it was planned to bring them down in a vegetated region close to the Moon's equator.

But beyond that, all was uncertain. Nobody knew if they would find water fresh enough to drink. Nobody knew if they would be able to eat the vegetation – always assuming the grey-green swathes visible through telescopes were vegetation at all. Nobody knew if there would be animals to hunt – or if there were animals that might hunt two human astronauts. It wasn't even clear if the air could be breathed unfiltered.

The ship would be packed with three days' ground supplies, including air filters and water and compressed food. If the makeshift explorers found they couldn't live off the land in that time, they were just going to have to climb back in their lander and depart (always supposing they could find the return-journey rocket pack that was supposed to follow them to the Moon).

And then there was the mystery of the hominids who had come tumbling through the Wheel in the sky.

Malenfant and Nemoto had sat through hours of lectures by Julia Corneille and others, trying to absorb the best understanding of the evolution of mankind, watching one species after another parade through dimly realized computer animations – *Australopithecus*, *Homo habilis*, *Homo erectus*, archaic *Homo sapiens*, *Homo heidelbergensis*, *Homo neandertalensis* . . . It was a plethora of speculation as fragmentary, it seemed to Malenfant, as the bone scraps on which it was based. He had vaguely imagined that the newer evidence based on DNA variation might have cleared the picture, but it seemed only to have confused everybody further. Nobody knew where humanity was going, of course. It had startled Malenfant to find that if you dug deeper than pop science simplifications, nobody really knew where man had come from either.

The truth was that the sessions had been of little use. Malenfant had learned more than he wanted to know about archaeological techniques and dating methods and anatomical signifiers and all the rest. What he needed to know was how to handle a tribe of *Homo habilis*, alive, fighting and breeding, should he crest a hillside on the Red Moon and discover them – or vice versa. But

NASA's experts, curators of fragments all, simply weren't tuned to thinking that way. It was as if they could only see the bits of bone, and not the people that must once have lived to yield up these ancient treasures.

The only real consensus was that Malenfant and Nemoto should pack guns.

. . . He had lost his hat. He saw it on the ground.

There was a ringing in his ears. He ought to get his hat. He bent to reach it.

Next thing he knew, he was on his side. He lay there fuming.

The hat was too far away to reach, so he wriggled that way. Like a snake, he thought, cackling. When he had his hat he stuck it on the side of his head, so it shielded his face.

At least the palaeo training had been relevant, he thought. Too much of the rest of his time had been filled up with pointless exercises like this. They had even threatened to put him back in a centrifuge. 'I told them to stick the fucking centrifuge where the sun don't shine,' he muttered.

The sand was hot and soft. Its pressure seemed to ease the pain in his head. Maybe he would sleep awhile.

There were hands under his hips and shoulders, pushing him onto his back. A face above him blocked out the sky. It, she, was saying something. Nemoto, of course.

He said, 'Leave me alone.'

She leaned closer. 'Open your mouth.' She lifted a flask and poured in water.

He made to spit it out, but that would be even more stupid. He swallowed it. 'Stop that. We have to save it.'

'You're dehydrated, Malenfant. You know the drill. You drink what you have until it's gone, and if you have not been found by then, you die of thirst. Simple logic. Either way it does no good to ration your water.'

'Horse feathers,' he said. But he let her pour more water into his mouth. It was the most delicious thing he had ever tasted.

Emma Stoney:

They continued to work their way east. A range of mountains, low and eroded almost to shapelessness, began to loom above the horizon. Though their outlines and colours were softened to blurs by the murky air, Emma thought she made out bands of vegetation, forest perhaps, on their lower slopes.

After another day's walking, the Runners paused by a shallow, slow-running stream.

Sally threw herself flat on the ground. She seemed to go to sleep at once. Maxie, as ever full of life at precisely the wrong time, ran off to play with the Runner children.

Emma sat on dusty grass and eased off her boots. Maybe her feet were toughening up; at least she didn't have to pour any blood out of her boots today. She limped to the stream to drink, wash her face, bathe her feet. She found a stand of root plants, a little like potatoes, small enough to dig out of the ground. It was a pleasure for once to be able to provide for herself.

Emma watched the Runners. The descending sun had turned the western sky a tall orange-pink – volcano sunset, she thought – and peering through the dusty air was like looking into a tank of shining water, through which exotic creatures swam.

The stream had washed down a rich supply of volcanic pebbles, and many of the adults were knapping tools. They squatted on their haunches in the stream, their lithe bodies folded up like penknives, tapping one stone against another. The axes they made were flattened slabs of stone, easy to grip, with clean sharp edges. Stone axes and wooden spears: the only tools the Runners ever made, over and over, tools they turned to every task from butchering carcasses to shaving – even though their hands were clearly just as capable of fine manipulation as Emma's.

There were a lot of oddities, if you watched carefully.

The toolmakers worked in silence and isolation, as if the others didn't exist. Emma never saw a Runner pick up a tool dropped by somebody else and use it, not once. A few children and young adults sat beside their elders, watching, trying to copy them. Mostly the adults ignored their apprentices; only very rarely did Emma see examples of coaching, such as when one woman picked a rock from out of a boy's hand and turned it around so it served to flake the anvil stone better.

All the tools turned out by the women, so far as Emma could tell, were functional. But some of the men's were different. Take Stone, for example, the bullying alpha-male. Sometimes he would sit and labour for hours at an axe, knocking off a chip here, a flake there. It was as if he pursued some impossible dream of symmetry or fineness, working at his axe far beyond the point where he could be adding any value.

Or, more strangely, he would sit with a pile of stones and work feverishly, turning out axe after axe. But some of these 'axes' were mere flakes of rock the size of Emma's thumb – and some were great monsters that she could have held only in two hands, like a book opened for reading. These pathological designs seemed no use as tools; Stone would do no more than carry them around with him for a few hours, making sure everybody saw them, before dumping them, never used, their edges as sharp as the instant they were made.

Emma didn't know why Stone did this. Maybe it was a dim groping towards culture: hand-axe as art form. After all, the hand-axe was the only meaningful artefact they actually made, taking planning and vision and a significant skill; their other 'tools', like their termite-digging sticks or even their spears, were little more than broken-off bits of wood or bone, based on serendipitous discoveries of raw materials, scarcely finished. The hand-axe was the only way the Runners had to express themselves.

But if that was so, why didn't the women join in such 'artistic' activities as well?

Or maybe the useless hand-axes were about sex, not practicality or culture. After all to be able to make a decent axe showed a broad range of skills – planning, vision, manual skills, strength – essential for survival in this unforgiving wilderness. *Look at me, girls. I'm so fit and strong and full of food, I've got time to waste on these useless monsters and fingernail-sized scale models. Look at me!* When everybody around you had a body as drop-dead beautiful as any athlete's she had ever seen, you needed something to stand out from the crowd.

Could that be true? The Runners had to enjoy something like full humanity, in planning and vision and concentration, when making the axes. But could they then abandon that humanity and revert to some lower level of instinct, as the axes became a symbol of sexual prowess, as unconscious as a bird's bright plumage?

It was all another reminder to her that no matter how human these beautiful creatures looked and sometimes behaved, they were not human. Their small heads contained shards of humanity, she thought, floating on a sea of animal drives and instincts: humans sometimes, not other times . . .

Or maybe she was just being anthropomorphic. Maybe she shouldn't be comparing the Runners to herself, seeing how human they were, or weren't; the Runners were simply Runners, and they fit into their world as well as she fit into hers.

Though it was a full hour since they had abandoned the trek for the day, Fire was still wandering around with his hands clasped together. He couldn't drop his hot burden until the others had gathered kindling and fuel for him, and as long as the sun was up and the air was warm they had no interest in doing that – in fact it didn't even seem to occur to them – and so Fire was stuck.

But he had more than that on his mind. He was vainly pursuing one of the girls, Dig: a real knock-out, Emma thought, with crisp auburn hair, full, high breasts and hips to die for. Poor Fire seemed to have no idea how to get through to her; he just followed her around, holding out his handfuls of ash, and plaintively calling her name. 'Dig! Dig!'

Being the fire-carrier was obviously a key job, a cornerstone of this untidy little community. But as far as Emma could see his role didn't win Fire much respect from the other Runners, especially the men. Each night he would deliver his embers to the latest heap of kindling, and then would be pushed and slapped away. It was as if he was the runt of the litter. Certainly his handful of ashes just didn't get him the girls the way the hand-axes of the other boys and men did.

But this time, for once, Fire was getting closer to the object of his desire. She backed up against a tree, and he walked towards her, hands clasped, that ridiculous, tragic erection sticking out like a divining rod.

But a rock hit him hard in the side of the head.

The rock had been thrown by Stone.

Fire went down, toppling like a felled tree. He opened his hands to save himself before he hit the mud. His precious ashes scattered.

Runners ran forward. Dig and Blue got to their knees in the mud, and tried to scrape together the ashes and embers. But the embers were hissing, quickly extinguished in the mud.

Stone hadn't grasped the chain of events that led from his own hurled rock to the death of the fire, or else he just didn't want to know; either way he capered and howled, pressing the useless embers into the mud with his bare feet, and he aimed hefty kicks at Fire's ribs.

Fire curled up, arms wrapped over his head, whimpering in misery. Emma winced, but she knew better than to try to intervene.

After that, the daylight seemed to run out quickly. As the sun descended towards the horizon, the golden air turned to a dismal brown. The shadows of trees to the west lengthened, clutching at the cowering Runners like claws.

In the absence of a fire the Runners gathered more closely than usual, the women clutching their children, even the usually solitary men huddling close.

The first predators began to call.

Sally came to Emma. 'You have to use your spyglass,' she said. 'Make a fire. And you have to do it now, before we run out of sun.'

Emma sighed. 'I'm frightened of showing them too much of what we've got.'

'They aren't going to steal your glass and start using it all over the savannah,' Sally said. 'They don't *learn*.'

'It's not that. Right now they seem to think we are like them. If they think we're too strange, they might reject us.'

The shadow of a distant tree slid across Sally's face. 'Sister, I don't think it's the time for philosophical dilemmas. In a couple of hours the hyenas are going to be chomping on our bones. And anyhow these guys have attention spans that make Maxie look like Michelangelo. By the morning, they'll have forgotten it all. Come on, Emma. Just do it.'

'All right. Let's try to keep our tools out of their sight, though.'

'Agreed.'

They spent a few minutes gathering dry wood, and building a little tepee a couple of feet high. Then they scraped together dried leaves and tinder.

Emma crouched down on the ground, folded her magnifying glass out of her knife, and angled it until she caught the crimson light of the low sun. She moved it back and forth until she had focused a tight spot of light on a few bits of dry tinder. Then she waited, the cold of the ground seeping into her, her awkwardly angled arm growing stiff. She grumbled, 'I don't know why the hell the South African air force didn't just give me a box of matches.'

Some of the Runners came to watch what they were doing. They hooted excitedly, one woman even making rubbing-hands-warm motions. But when the tinder didn't catch light immediately, they became baffled and quickly lost interest.

Her spot of light disappeared. She looked up to see a small silhouetted figure, a grasping hand.

'Maxie's. Maxie's!'

Sally scooped him up. 'Get away, Maxie, for heaven's sake.' Maxie, denied the toy, began wailing.

Unnoticed, the tinder had started smoking.

Emma immediately dropped her glass. She cupped the thread of smoke with her hands and blew gently. The smoke trail billowed, nearly died.

She sat back and beckoned to Fire. 'Hey. Come over here. Come on. This is your job.'

Poor Fire sat squat on the ground, clutching his ribs, an immense lump forming on the side of his head.

'Umm, Fire smoke Fire. Fire Fire!'

At last he came forward, hobbling painfully. Shivering, he cupped his hands around the thread of smoke and blew, lips pursed.

It seemed to take him mere seconds to have a small flame going. With the precise motions of a surgeon, he began to feed the tiny red-yellow spot with bits of tinder.

When the smoke started to spread, the other Runners were drawn back. As the fire grew, they settled down around it, just as they did every night, and the men began to drag over heavy branches to make night logs.

Sally watched the Runners with cold contempt. 'Not a word, not a gesture of congratulation or apology. Or surprise. Or relief. They've already forgotten how Fire lost his embers ... The fire is just here, and they accept it. They really don't think like us, do they?'

Emma stretched stiff limbs. 'Right now, I couldn't care less. Just so long as the fire keeps away the bad guys with the teeth.'

As Emma fell into sleep, a rough hand grabbed her shoulder.

She froze. Her eyes snapped open. The sky, full of ash and smoke, retained a lingering purple-black glow, enough to show her a lithe, crouching silhouette. It, he, leaned over her. She was pushed onto her back. She could smell *Runner*: a thick, pungent, meaty smell of flesh that had never once been washed.

In the back of her mind she had rehearsed for this, from the first day here. Don't resist, she told herself. Don't cry out. She had seen the Runners copulate, every day. It would be fast, brutal, and over.

For a moment her assailant was still, his breath hot. She stiffened, expecting hands to claw at her clothing. But that didn't come. Instead a head, heavy, topped by tight curls, descended to her breast. She felt shuddering, a low moan.

Gingerly she reached up. She explored a flat skull, those extraordinary brow ridges like motorcycle goggles. And she touched a swollen mass on one temple. Her assailant flinched away.

It was Fire.

He was weeping. She remembered how he used to go to the old woman, Sing, for comfort, before she died. She wrapped one arm around his back. His muscles were hard sheets, his skin slick with dirt and sweat.

He reached up and grabbed her fingers. With a sharpness that made her yelp, he pulled her hand down towards his crotch. She found an erection as stiff as a piece of wood. She tried to pull away, but he pushed her hand back.

Gently, hesitantly, she wrapped her fingers around his hot penis. His hand took her wrist and pushed it back and forth.

She rubbed him once, twice. He came quickly, in a rapid gush against her leg. He sighed, released her wrist, and lay more heavily against her.

Half-crushed, barely able to breathe, she waited until his breathing was regular. Then, gingerly, she pushed at his shoulder. To her intense relief, he rolled away.

In the morning, Fire scooped up his embers and ash, and the Runners dispersed for their walk. It was as if none of the previous evening's events had ever happened.

Reid Malenfant:

In the last hours he had to endure a visit from an Apollo astronaut: a walker on a now-vanished Moon, eighty-five years old, ramrod straight and tanned like a movie star. 'You know, just before my flight we had a visit from Charles Lindbergh and his wife. He had figured that in the first second of my Saturn's flight, it would burn ten times more fuel than he had all the way to Paris. We laughed about that, I can tell you. Well, Lindbergh came to see me before I flew, and here I am come to see you before your flight. Passing on the torch, if you will . . .'

And so Malenfant, with a mixture of humility and embarrassment, shook the hand of a man who had shaken the hand of Lindbergh.

It was, at last, the night before launch.

At Vandenberg, he stood in the crisp Californian night air. The BDB's service structure was like an unfinished building, a steel cage containing catwalks and steps and elevators and enclosures. A dense tangle of pipes and ducts and tubing snaked through the metalwork. The slim booster itself was brilliantly lit, the sponsors' logos and NASA meatballs encrusting its hide shining brightly. Its main tanks were full of cryogenic propellants, and they spewed plumes of vapour into the air. No doubt in violation of a dozen safety rules, hard-hatted technicians, NASA and contractor grunts, scurried to and fro at the booster's base, and electric carts whirred by. It was a scene of industry, of competence, of achievement.

Malenfant stepped into an elevator and pushed the button for the service structure's crew level, three hundred feet high. He was escorted by a single tech, a Cape ape in clean-room regalia of a white one-piece coverall, latex gloves and puffy plastic hat. Malenfant had met the guy before, and they nodded, grinning; he was a somewhat grizzled veteran, long laid off by NASA but rehired for this project.

They rose vertically in the clanking, swaying steel cage. Beyond the cage flashed steel beams, cables and work platforms, mostly unattended now. And beyond *that* was the hide of the main tank itself: sleek, smooth, coated with ice where the cryogenic fuels had frozen the moisture out of the night air. It was such an immense cold mass that Malenfant felt the heat being drawn out of his own body, as if he were some speck of moisture that might end up glued to that glistening skin.

The elevator came to a stop. He stepped out, turned right, and walked over the access-arm catwalk. The walk was just a flimsy rail that spanned the rectilinear gulf between the tangled, rusted gantry, and the sleek hide of the booster. An ocean breeze picked up, laden with salt, and the catwalk creaked and swayed as if the gantry were mounted on springs. He grabbed a handrail for support. Through the chain-link fence he could see the lights of the base scattered in rectangles and straight lines over the darkened ground, and the more diffuse lights of the inland communities. The coast was black, of course, swept clean of habitation by the Tide.

This was a noisy place. The Pacific wind moaned through the complex, and the huge propellant pipes groaned and cracked as rivers of the super-cold fluids surged through them. Fuel and wind: it was a noise of power, of gathering strength, and the hairs on the back of his neck prickled.

He reached the end of the walk. He stepped through the white room, the cramped enclosure where he would be inspected one last time before the launch, and he faced the streamlined fairing that would protect the Moon lander during launch. There was a hatchway cut into the fairing. A small wooden step led up to the hatch, a touch of home-workshop mundanity amid all this shining hardware.

From here he could see into the cabin of the lander itself: small, crammed with supplies, and with two canvas-frame couches side by side. The light was a subdued green. Instrument panels on the wall glowed with softscreen displays and telltale lights. It was like looking into a small cave, he thought, an undersea cave crusted with jewels.

Malenfant had been through it all before. Every space project, as it developed, became entangled and complex beyond the understanding of any single human. But from the astronaut's point of view that proliferating tangle reached a certain maximum, until, after some indefinable point – as the booster stack crept forward through its integration schedule, as launch day approached – the whole thing began to simplify, to focus.

In the end, he thought, every mission reduces to this: human beings climbing into the mouth of a monster, to be hurled away from the Earth. And all the technicians and managers and fundraisers and cheerleaders and paper-chasers in the world can do nothing but watch.

Emma's mother and her sister's family were staying in apartments on the ASFB. They had invited Malenfant to join them for Mass, celebrated by the base's Catholic chaplain.

Blanche Stoney, the mother, was an intimidating seventy-year-old. She offered Malenfant her hand without getting out of her chair. The sister, Joan, a little younger than Emma, had raised four kids alone, and had looked exhausted every time Malenfant had met her. But the kids were all now young teenagers and, it seemed to Malenfant, remarkably well behaved.

The priest said Mass for the family in a cramped living room.

Malenfant, upright in his civilian suit, tanned walnut brown by the desert sun, felt as out of place as a spanner in a sewing basket. But he endured the ceremony, and took his bread and wine with the others. He tried to find some meaning and comfort in the young priest's familiar words, and the play of light on the scraps of ornate cloth, the small chalices and the ruby-red wine.

The priest had asked Joan's two eldest boys to serve as altar boys. They did fine except during the communion service, when the younger boy held the chalice upside down so that the hosts slid out and fell to the carpet, fluttering down one by one. In the background a softscreen showed live images of the preparation of the BDB. There were a lot of holds. Malenfant tried not to watch the *whole* time.

When it was done, the priest packed up and went home with promises to call during the mission.

Joan brought Malenfant a beer. 'I think we owe you this.'

Blanche, the mother, snapped, 'But you owed us your presence here tonight.'

'I don't deny that, Blanche.'

Malenfant spent some time trying to explain the technicalities of the mission to them – the countdown, the launch, the flight profile. Joan listened politely. At first the children seemed interested, but they drifted away.

In the end Malenfant was left alone with Blanche.

She skewered him with her gaze. 'You wish you were anywhere but here, don't you?'

'Either that or I had another beer.'

She laughed, clambered stiffly out of her chair, and, somewhat to his surprise, brought him a fresh can.

'I know you try,' she said. 'But you never really had much time for religion, did you? To you we're all just *ants on a log*, aren't we? I heard you say that on some 'cast or other.'

He winced at the over-familiar words. 'I think my wisdom has been spread a little thin recently.'

She leaned forward. 'Why are you going to the Red Moon? Is it really to find my daughter – or just vainglory? To prove you're not too old? I know what you flyboys are like. I know what really drives you. You have nobody here, do you? Nobody but Emma. So it's easy for you to leave.'

'That's what the Vice-President thinks.'

'Don't name-drop with me. What do *you* say?'

'Blanche, I'm going up there for Emma. I really and truly am.'

With sudden, savage intensity, she leaned forward and grabbed his hand. 'Why?'

'Blanche, I don't –'

'You destroyed her. You started doing that from the moment you set your sights on her. I remember what you used to say. *You bake the cakes, I'll fly the planes.* From the moment she met you, she had to start making sacrifices. It was the whole logic of your relationship. And in the end, you fulfilled that logic. *You killed her.* And now you want to kill yourself to get away from the guilt. Look me in the eyes, damn it, and deny that's true.'

For about the first time since it happened, he thought back to those final moments in the T-38, the clamour in that sun-drenched sky. He remembered the instant when he might have regained control, his sense of exhilaration as that huge disastrous Wheel approached.

He couldn't find words. Her rheumy eyes were like searchlights.

'I don't know, Blanche,' he said honestly. 'Maybe it's for me. Without her, I'm lonely. That's all.'

She snorted contempt. 'Every human being I know is lonely. I don't know why, but it's so. Children are consolation. You never let Emma have children, did you?'

'It was more complicated than that.'

'Religion is comfort for the loneliness. But you rejected that too, because we're just ants on a log.'

'Blanche – I don't know what you want me to say. I'm sorry.'

'No,' she said more softly. Then she rested her hand on his head, and he bowed. 'Don't say you're sorry. Just bring her back,' she said.

'Yes.'

'Where do you think she is now? What do you think she is going through?'

'I don't know,' he said, honestly.

Shadow:

Relations among the men worsened. Every day there were increasingly savage and unpredictable fights, and many of the women and infants, not just Shadow, suffered punches and kicks and bites as a consequence.

One day it all came to a head.

Big Boss was sitting cross-legged on the ground with his back to a small clearing, working assiduously at a cluster of nut-palm fruit. Shadow was in shade at the edge of the clearing, half-hidden as had become her custom.

Without warning Squat stalked into the clearing. All his hair stood on end, doubling his apparent bulk. He leaped up and grabbed branches, ripping them off the trees, shaking them and throwing them down before him. He picked up rocks and hurled them this way and that. His silence was eerie, but his lips were pursed tightly together, pulling his face into a harsh frown, his eyes fixed on Big Boss.

Big Boss ignored him. He kept on plucking at the fruit in his lap. Squat, and the other men, had made such displays before, and nothing had resulted.

But now Little Boss suddenly broke from the cover of the trees. Without warning or apparent provocation, he hurled himself on Big Boss.

Big Boss roared and faced his attacker, hair bristling. But Squat screeched and joined in. The three of them dissolved into a blur of flailing fists and thrashing limbs.

All around the clearing, other men ran to see what was happening. They circled the battlers, hooting and crying – but not one of them rushed to the aid of Big Boss.

Big Boss broke away. His eyes were round and white, and blood leaked over the side of his head, where one ear had been bitten so savagely it dangled by a thread of gristle. He ran towards the nearest tree, and tried to clamber into it. But he was limping, and Squat and

Little Boss easily caught him. They pulled him back and hurled him to the ground, and punched and kicked and bit him. Squat began to jump on Big Boss's back, slamming his heels again and again into ribs and spine.

Now more of the men joined in, screaming and yelling. Though they concentrated their attentions on Big Boss, they squabbled and fought amongst themselves, vying for their places in the new order.

At last Little Boss climbed up on Big Boss's back. He stood straight and roared. His mouth was bloody. He grabbed one of Big Boss's arms, as if Big Boss were no more than a monkey he had caught in the forest. Little Boss twisted the arm this way and that, and Shadow heard bones snap, muscle tear.

The women and children huddled together beneath the trees, clutching each other or grooming tensely, shrinking from the aggression.

The men ran off into the forest, tense and excited, hair bristling. Big Boss lay where he had fallen, a bloody heap on the ground.

Slowly the women emerged from their sheltered places. Cautiously they fed and groomed each other and their children. None of them went near the fallen Big Boss – none save an over-inquisitive child, who was hastily retrieved by his mother.

Only Shadow stayed in her pool of shade.

The day wore away. The shadows lengthened.

Big Boss raised his head, then let it fall flat again.

Then he got one arm under his body, and pushed himself upright. The other arm dangled. His flesh was ripped open, by teeth or chipped cobbles, so that flaps hung down from patches of gleaming gristle, and his skin was split by great gouges, crusted with dirt and half-dried blood. He had lost one ear completely, and one eye was a pit of blood from which a pale fluid leaked.

He opened his mouth. Spittle and blood looped between smashed teeth, and he moaned loudly.

The women and children ignored him.

Big Boss pulled his legs beneath him. He began to crawl towards the trees, one leg dragging, one arm dangling. Twice he fell flat. Twice he got himself up again, and continued to drag himself forward. Where he had been lying, the blood had soaked into the ground, leaving the dirt purple. And where he passed, he left a trail of sticky blood and spit and snot, like some huge snail.

When he got to the base of the tree, he twisted so he got his back against the bark of the trunk, and slumped back.

He was still for a long time. The sun, intermittently obscured by cloud, slid across the sky. Shadow thought Big Boss was dead.

But then he began to move again. Using the tree as a support, he pushed himself upright. He reached up with his less damaged arm to grab a low branch. He growled with pain. He got his chest over the branch, and fell forward, gasping. For a long time he was still once more, clinging to the branch. Then he carried on, hauling himself grimly from branch to branch, higher into the tree.

At last he reached a high point. Clinging to the tapering trunk with his legs, he pulled down branches with grim determination. Surrounded by clusters of yellow fruit, he slumped flat in this nest, the last he would ever make.

The women on the ground called, their panting hoots summoning each other and their children. The women climbed into the trees, infants clinging to their mothers' backs or chests. Shadow followed, keeping her distance. Soon she could see the women in their nests, clumpy shadows high in the trees, silhouetted against the deepening pink of the sky; here and there a limb stretched out, fingers working at a pelt or stroking a face.

Shadow glanced up at Big Boss's nest. One foot dangled in the air, toes clenching and unclenching. Until a new leader emerged, the ladder of rank was broken into chaos. The days to come would be stressful and trying for everyone.

As the last light seeped from the sky, the men returned. They swarmed around the bases of the trees. They were still squabbling, screeching and fighting. Some of them clambered up into the trees and began to harass the women and children, smashing open their nests and chasing them across the branches; the women fought back grimly.

Now two of the men started climbing into Shadow's own tree, peering up at her, whispering and showing their white teeth. Shadow could smell the blood on their fur.

Forces worked in Shadow's mind: a fear of the dark unknown, a fear of further punishment at the hands of the people, a chill urge to cradle the thing in her womb. At last the forces reached a new equilibrium.

She slid out of her nest. As silently as she could, enduring the feeble kicking of the child in her womb, she clambered from the branches of her tree into the next, and then the next.

She slipped, alone, into the arboreal dark. Soon the sounds of the squabbling, roosting people were far behind her.

Fire:

Here is Fire. Here are his legs walking. Here he is, keeping his hands closed together, cupping the hot embers and the ash.

The sun is hot. The light is in his eyes. His eyes hurt him. His head hurts him.

He remembers why. He is lying on the ground. His eyes see bits of light, Stone's feet swinging at his head and belly and chest. Once again Stone has driven him away from Dig.

Fire wants not to be here. But it is Fire who holds the embers, not his hands. Fire must be here to make his hands hold the hot embers.

The sky grows dark. The air grows cold. Fire looks up. The sky is covered over by cloud.

Something falls before Fire. It is a flake. It is white and soft. There are many flakes, falling slowly, all around him.

A flake settles on his chest. Another on his shoulders. His skin cannot feel them. More flakes settle around him, on the floor. His feet make footprints in the thickening grey cover. He stops. He looks back at the prints. He laughs. He steps backwards into the prints he has made. He steps forward into the prints.

The ground is growing grey. The people are grey. The trees are grey. Some of the people are afraid. Their fingers wipe grey from their eyes and scalps. The children with no names whimper. Their faces hide in their mothers' bellies.

Fire is not afraid. The grey is ash. Fire sees himself in the morning light. He sees his hands sweeping through ash, gathering embers. Now everything is ash. His head tips back. Ash falls into his mouth. His tongue tastes it. Fire is happy in this ash world. His legs run, and his mouth gibbers and hoots.

But now his head is wet.

His legs stop running. He lifts his head. He sees big fat raindrops fall from the sky, slowly sliding towards his face. They hit his mouth and his cheeks and his nose and his eyes. His eyes sting.

The rain makes little pits in the ash. His toes explore the pits. The wet ash turns to grey mud.

The other people trudge around him. Their hair is flat. The mud sticks to their feet in great heavy cakes. The rain turns the ash on their bodies to grey streaks.

The people reach a bank of trees. They stand there, baffled.

Stone steps forward. His great nostrils flare. 'River river river!' he cries. His legs march him into the trees. His arms push aside the foliage with great cracks and snaps.

Fire's legs carry him hurrying after Stone, into the forest.

The forest is green and dark and moist. Leaves and twigs clutch at Fire. His eyes look around fearfully, for Elf-folk, or worse. He sees nothing but people, like muddy shadows sliding through the bank of trees. He hears nothing but the crush of foliage by feet and hands, the soft breathing of the people.

Fire pushes out of the other side of the bank of trees.

The ground slopes down. There is rock here, purple-red, sticking out of the grass. Fire's feet carry him carefully over the slippery rocks.

He reaches water. The water is brown, and slides slowly past his feet. It is the river.

The people come down to the bank. Their hands splash water on their faces, washing away mud.

Fire does not touch the water. Fire's hands still hold the embers. Fire stands tall, and his eyes watch the river. To his left the river has scooped holes out from under the bank. A great lip of grass dangles towards the water. Fire sees that there is a gravel beach below the undercut, and deep dark openings behind it, caves.

'Fire Fire!' he cries. 'Fire Fire!'

Fire walks towards the caves, cupping the embers. Grass and Wood, the women, follow him. They build a pile of the branches they have carried. They find the driest moss they can.

Inside the cave, Fire lowers his embers reverently into the moss. It smokes, but soon a flame is there, licking at the moss. Fire blows on it carefully.

When the fire is rising, Emma and Sally and Maxie come into the cave. Things cling to their backs, things of blue skin. Emma and Sally make the clinging things slide to the floor. They come to the fire and hold up their hands to its warmth. Sally rubs Maxie's wet hair.

Fire grins. Emma grins back.

The flames are bright. Fire has a shadow. It stretches into the back of the cave, across a bumpy, mottled floor of rock. Fire follows his shadow. It grows longer, leading deeper into the dark.

There are animals at the back of the cave. Fire's eyes open wide. Fire's legs prepare to run.

His nose cannot smell animals. His nose smells people. He makes his legs walk forward.

The animals are sprawled flat against the wall. He makes his hand touch an animal. The fur is ragged and loose. He grabs it and pulls. The skin of the animal comes away from the wall.

There is no animal. There is only the skin of the animal. It was stretched out over branches. He pushes. The whole frame falls over with a clatter.

Behind the fallen frame he sees spears. He picks up a spear. Its tip is a different colour from the wood. His finger touches the tip. The tip is stone. It is an axe. No matter how hard he pulls, the stone wants to cling to its spear.

He drops the spear. He walks back along the cave, towards the light of the fire, the grey daylight.

People are gathered around the fire. Some children are sleeping. One woman sits in another's lap, gently cupping her breasts. A man and a woman are coupling noisily.

Emma and Sally and Maxie sit against a wall. Their eyes gaze at the fire, or out into the greyness beyond.

The people are not here, though their bodies are here. Emma and Sally and Maxie are here. They are always here.

Fire's body, warm and dry, wants to couple with Dig. His member stiffens quickly. He looks for Dig.

Dig is lying under Stone, on the floor. His hips thrust at her. Her eyes are closed.

Fire finds a rock on the floor. His fist closes around the rock and raises it, over Stone's head.

Fire thinks of Stone's anger, his fists and feet.

He drops the rock.

He walks out of the cave, to the river.

The rain is less now. It makes little grey pits on the surface of the water that come and go, come and go. He watches the pits.

For a time he is not there. There is only his body, only the water at his toes, the rain on his head, the pits on the water.

He squats down. The water is a cloudy, muddy brown. A fine grey scum floats on its surface. His eyes cannot see fish. But the water pools here, quietly. And he sees bubbles, bursting on the water.

He slides his hands into the water. His hands like the water. It is cool and soothes his scarred palms. He waits, knees on the ground, hands in the water, the last rain pattering on the back of his neck.

He is not there.

A cold softness brushes his hands.

His hands grab and lift. A fish flies over his head, wriggling, silvery. His ears hear it land with a thump on the grass behind him.

He slides his hands back into the water.

He is not there.

Reid Malenfant:

So here was Malenfant, for better or worse in space once again, flying ass-backwards towards the Moon – a Moon, anyhow.

Nemoto and Malenfant sat upright, side by side, in a rounded bulge at the rear of the cramped, coffin-like, gear-crammed capsule. They were each encased in the heavy folds of their garish orange launch-and-entry suits, and a rubbery wet-raincoat stink filled the air.

Malenfant gazed into the tiny, scuffed, oil-smeared rectangle of glass before his face, trying to make out the greater universe into which he had been thrust. There was no sense of space, of openness; surrounded by the womb-like ticking and purring of fans and pumps, immersed in the stench of rubber and metal, peering out through these tiny windows, it was like being stuck in a miniature submarine.

. . . But now Earth swam into view.

From the Station's low orbit Earth had always been immense to Malenfant, a vast glowing roof or floor to his world, ever present, dwarfing his petty craft. But now Earth was receding. First one precisely curved horizon slid into his window frame, and then the other, so that soon he could see the whole Earth, hanging like a Christmas-tree bauble in the velvet black, blue patches peeking out from beneath the white swirl of clouds, painted with the familiar continent-shapes. Malenfant could see Florida, Africa, Gibraltar and even much of South America, his single glance spanning the Atlantic Ocean. The planet slowly shifted position, drifting from the top of his window to the bottom, so he had to crane forward to see it. Even from here he could see the damage done by the Tide: smoke was smeared over a dozen coastal cities, and he saw the cold gleam of white-tops as angry waves continued to pound the land.

Malenfant had been somewhat relieved that the launch had gone through without significant hitches.

He had lain in his couch listening to the flexing of the tanks as they were laden with cryos, then the roar of propellants like a distant locomotive, the whine of the pumps, the waterfall shout of the pad's huge deluge system – and then the bursting roar of the engines. And he could think of nothing but the fact that this BDB booster stack on which he perched had never before flown in test, not even once – no time for that.

Anyhow they had gotten off the pad. The acceleration had been low at first. But as the engines far below had swivelled from side to side to adjust the direction of thrust, the two astronauts, stuck at the top of the stack, had been thrown back and forth, like ants clinging to the tip of a car antenna.

Then had come the violence of staging, as first the solid rocket boosters and then the big main engine cluster had cut out. Malenfant had been thrown forward against his harness, crashing his helmeted head against the curving bulkhead before him. After a heart-stopping moment of drift, the second stage had cut in, thrusting him back into his seat once more.

That second-stage burn had seemed to go on and on – six, seven, eight minutes, their craft growing lighter as fuel burned off, their velocity piling on. Not for Malenfant and Nemoto the old Apollo luxury of taking a couple of swings around the Earth to check out the systems; the BDB's last contribution had been to hurl them on a direct-ascent trajectory all the way out of Earth's gravity well without pausing.

Just ten minutes after leaving the pad at Vandenberg, the second stage finally cut out. Malenfant and Nemoto had listened to the clunk of the burnt-out stage disengaging itself from the lander, and the bull-snorts of nose-mounted attitude thrusters turning their little craft so it pointed nose-first to the Earth – ten minutes gone, and already Malenfant was bound irrevocably for the Moon.

Still the Earth shrank.

'There she goes,' he murmured. 'I feel as if I'm driving a car into a long, dark tunnel . . .'

It struck him that Nemoto hadn't said a single word since the pad rats had strapped them into their couches. Now, as they watched the Earth fall away, her small hand crept into his.

And then they broke. They began to work from panel to panel, throwing switches and checking dials, working through their post-insertion checklist, configuring the software that would run the craft's life support systems. Necessary work without which they would not survive, not even for an hour.

New Moon or old, Earth's satellite orbited just as far from the mother planet, and so it was going to take them three days to get there, just as it always had. But because they were flying backwards, they weren't going to be able to see the Red Moon itself. Not until they got there.

For the first few hours the abandoned BDB second stage trailed after them, following its own independent path. It was scheduled to sail past the Moon and fly into interplanetary space. The stage was a lumpy cylinder, shining bright in the intense sunlight. Malenfant could clearly see the details of the attachment mechanisms at its upper face, and how its thin walls had crumpled during the launch. But it was venting unburnt fuel from three or four places. The small thrust of the fuel vents was making it tumble, like a garden sprinkler, and it was surrounded by a cloud of frozen fuel droplets that glimmered like stars.

The stage's subtly modified path was bringing it closer to the lander than Malenfant would have liked, at one point no more than a few hundred feet away. He stayed strapped into his seat, watching this potential hazard, and weighing up options. But after a couple more hours the stage began to drift away of its own accord.

When the lander was alone in the emptiness, Malenfant felt an odd pang of loneliness, and almost wished the booster stage would come swimming back, like some great metal whale.

After six hours in space, twelve since they had been woken before the launch, they unbuckled.

Malenfant felt a surge of validating freedom as he found himself floating up from his couch. His treacherous stomach gave a warning growl, however. Throwing up in this confined space would be even more of a catastrophe than on Shuttle. He turned his back and popped a couple of tabs, trusting that the queasiness would pass.

Awkwardly, helping each other, they stripped out of their launch suits. Now they would wear lightweight jumpsuits and cloth bootees, all the way to the Red Moon.

The X-38, hastily modified from a Space Station bail-out craft, was just thirty feet long, an ungainly shape the pilots likened to a potato with fins. Malenfant and Nemoto had been given couches in the rounded bulge at the craft's rear. The craft, designed for a couple of hours' flight down to Earth from low orbit, had been crammed with gear to keep them alive for ten, eleven, twelve days, the time it would take to reach the Red Moon, and come straight back again, if the natives didn't look friendly. Much of its interior was too cramped for the crew even to sit upright – but then, in its primary bail-out mode carrying injured or even unconscious crew back to Earth, reclining couches would have sufficed.

To the rear end of the lander was fixed a liquid-rocket pack. The engine and propellants were based on the simple, reliable systems of the old Apollo Lunar Module. This engine would be used to decelerate them into lunar orbit, and then, if they chose to commit, to slow them further, until the lander began its long glide down into the atmosphere, shedding its heat of descent in a long series of aerodynamic manoeuvres, much like the Shuttle orbiter's entry to Earth's atmosphere.

During the last stages of the descent, a big blue and white parafoil, a steerable parachute a hundred and fifty feet wide, would blossom from the lander's rear compartment. That would be quite a ride. The parafoil, the largest steerable 'chute ever made, would be controlled by warping its wings, which was just the way the Wright brothers had steered their first ever manned flying machine. That seemed somehow appropriate. Anyhow, thus they would steer their way to a final descent, landing gently on skids.

In theory.

In fact *they* wouldn't be steering the craft anywhere. The whole descent was automated. This was something against which Malenfant had fought hard. To give up control of the rudders and flaps to some virus-ridden computer program went against every instinct he'd built up in thirty years of flying. But it was much easier and simpler for the engineers to devise a lander that could fly itself all the way down than to figure out how to give a pilot control. *Trust us, Malenfant. Trust the machine.*

The facilities were not glamorous, even compared to the Station and the Shuttle. To wash Malenfant had to strip to the buff and give himself a sponge-bath. It took longer to chase down floating droplets of water and soap than to bathe in the first place.

The toilet arrangements were even more basic. There was no lavatory compartment, as in the Shuttle and Station, so they were thrown back to arrangements no more advanced than those used on Apollo, and earlier. There were receptacles for their urine, which wasn't so bad as long as you avoided spillage, but for anything more serious you had to strip to the buff again and try to dump your load into plastic bags you clamped over your ass with your hands.

In this cramped environment they had, of course, absolutely no privacy from each other. But it never became a problem. Nemoto was twenty-five years old, with a fine, lithe figure; but Malenfant never found her distracting – and vice versa applied, so far as he could tell. Their relationship was prickly, but they were easy together, even intimate, but like siblings.

It was as if he had known this odd, quiet girl for a long time. In some other life, perhaps.

After eighteen hours awake, they prepared for sleep.

Malenfant had always had trouble sleeping on orbit. Every time his thoughts softened he seemed to drift up out of his couch, no matter how well he strapped himself down, and jerk himself to wakefulness, fearful of falling.

And on this trip it was even worse. He was acutely aware that he had travelled far from home this time – in particular, far beyond the invisible ceiling of Earth's magnetic field, which sheltered the world's inhabitants from the lethal radiation which permeated inter-planetary space. When Malenfant closed his eyes he would see flashes and sparks – trails left in the fluid of his eyeballs by bits of flying cosmic debris that had come fizzing out of some supernova a hundred thousand years ago, perhaps – and he folded over on himself, imagining what that cold rain was doing to his vulnerable human body.

After a couple of hours he prescribed himself a sleeping pill.

On the couch next to his, Nemoto lay very still, and didn't react when he moved; he couldn't tell if she was asleep or awake.

When he woke up, the pure oxygen of the cabin's atmosphere had made his nose irritable and runny, and his skin was starting to flake off, bits of it floating around him in the gentle breezes.

The nearest thing to navigation in space Malenfant had performed before had been the not-inconsiderable task of sliding a Shuttle orbiter into its correct low-Earth orbit, and then nudging two giant spacecraft, Space Station and orbiter, into a hair's-width precise docking and capture.

Flying to the Red Moon was a whole different ball game.

The X-38 had left a planet whose surface was moving at around 1,000 miles per hour. The craft was aiming to encounter a Moon moving at some 2,300 miles per hour relative to the Earth, with an orbital plane that differed from the spacecraft's. Furthermore the X-38 had to aim, not at where the Moon was at time of launch, but where it would be three days later. For the sake of the air-to-ground public-consumption transmissions they were forced to endure, Malenfant sought metaphors for what they were trying to achieve. 'It's like jumping from one moving train to another – and landing precisely in a top-price seat. No, more than that. Imagine jumping from a roller coaster car, and catching a bullet in your teeth as you fall . . .'

And the various computations had to be accurate to within one part in four *million*, or the X-38 would slam too steeply into the Red Moon's atmosphere and burn up, or else go flying past the Moon and become lost, irretrievably, in interplanetary space. If they got the navigation wrong, they were both dead. It was as simple as that.

It didn't console Malenfant at all to consider that this feat of translunar navigation had been achieved by manned missions before – nine times, in fact, if you included Apollo 13 – since here he was in an untried, utterly untested spacecraft, heading for an alien Moon, and everybody who had worked on those ancient missions was retired or dead.

So he laboured at his astronomical sightings, in-situ position recordings which backed up tracking from the ground. He had a navigational telescope and sextant, and he used these to peer through the grimy windows of the lander to take sightings of the Earth, the sun and the brighter stars. He kept checking the figures until he had 'all balls', nothing but zeroes in his discrepancy analysis.

Oddly, it was this work, when he was forced to concentrate on what lay beyond the cabin's cosy walls, that gave him his deepest sense of the vastness he had entered. There was Earth, for example, the stage for (almost) all of human history, now reduced to a tiny blue marble in all that blackness. Sometimes it was simply impossible to believe that this wasn't just another sim, that the darkness beyond wasn't just blacked-out walls, a few feet away, close enough for him to touch if he reached out a hand.

But sometimes he got it, and the animal inside him quailed.

Fire:

It is morning. The rain has stopped. The sky is grey.

Fire's eyes watch a branch drift down the river.

Blue wades into the water, waist-deep. He catches the branch. It is heavy. He sets his shoulders and pushes until the branch is resting against the bank.

Another branch comes. Blue grabs it, and hauls and pushes it against the first.

More people come, men and women. Some of them remember the river. Some of them don't, and are startled to see it. They wade into the water. They catch branches and shove them against Blue's crude, growing raft.

Children play, running up and down the bank, jabbering.

A crocodile sits in the deeper water. Fire sees the ridges on his back, his yellow eyes. The crocodile's eyes watch the people. Its teeth want the children.

Fire walks back to the cave. The fire is still burning. People have brought more wood. The damp stuff makes billows of smoke that linger under the roof of the cave.

Maxie is standing before the fire. Maxie's hands hold a fish. The fish is small and silver. A stick is jammed into the fish's mouth. Maxie throws the fish on a rock at the centre of the fire. The rock is hot. The fish's skin blisters. Its flesh spits and sizzles. There is a smell of fish and ash.

Sally helps Maxie get the fish out of the fire. '*Careful, Maxie. It's very hot.*'

Stone is watching Sally, his eyes hard and unblinking. His member stiffens. His hand strokes it.

Maxie blows on the fish noisily. His white teeth bite into the belly of the fish.

Stone strides to Sally. She stumbles back, alarmed. Stone tucks his leg behind Sally's. She falls on her back. He falls on top of her. She yells. His hand rips at her brown skin. It tears open. Fire sees her pink breast, a shadow of hair below her belly.

Sally's fingers scramble on the floor of the cave. They find a rock. '*Keep off me, you fucking ape!*' The rock slams into Stone's temple.

Stone grunts and slumps sideways.

Sally pulls herself out from under him. She scrambles away across the floor.

Stone's fingers touch his head. They come away bloody. He looks at Sally.

His hand locks around her ankle. She screams. He hauls at her leg. She is thrown across the floor, screaming. She slams hard against a rock wall.

Fire's ears hear bone snap. Sally is silent.

Stone grabs her ankles. She lies there, limp, one arm bent above the elbow. He prises her legs apart. His strong fingers rip at brown skin.

Maxie is pressed against the wall. His mouth is wide open.

Emma has come into the cave. She runs to Stone. Her hand drags at his shoulder. '*Leave her alone!*'

Stone ignores her. Fire knows he cannot hear Emma. Stone is not in his ears and his head, but in his penis, his balls.

Fire thinks of Maxie, manipulating the fish in the fire. Maxie is smart. Maxie remembers. Maxie has hands to make good axes. Sally is Maxie's mother. Stone wants more babies like Maxie.

Stone is doing what is right for his people.

All this shimmers in Fire's head, like raindrop splashes on the water. But then it breaks up, like the splashes, and all he sees is an elemental logic: Stone with Sally, Fire with Dig.

Fire smiles.

Emma goes limp. She is sobbing. '*For God's sake.*'

A rock flies past Fire's shoulder. It strikes Stone's arm. Stone roars. Blood spurts. He falls away from Sally. Sally lies limp. Fire sees he has not entered her.

Another rock flies in from the mouth of the cave. Stone drops flat. The rock flies over his head.

Fire faces the mouth of the cave. A person is standing there.

Not a person. Fire sees a short, stocky body draped with animal skins, a heavy, protruding face, a brow ridge as thick as a person's, straight black hair. One hand holds an axe. The other hand holds a spear.

It is not a person. It is a Ham. The Ham says, '*My home, Runner.*'

Fire's hands ram into the Ham's belly.

The Ham falls back. Fire runs out of the cave.

People run this way and that, making for the river, screaming from fear or anger. Shadows flicker along the top of the undercut, flicker between caves. Spears stab, stone-tipped, so fast Fire can barely see them. Voices call. '*U-lu-lu-lu-lu!*'

A Ham drives a spear into the chest of the woman, Wood. She is knocked onto her back. The spear breaks and twists as she falls. Her body rips and spills. She cries out.

Fire is terrified, awed.

'*Help me. Fire, please.*'

It is Emma. She has dragged Sally to her feet. Sally is lolling, unconscious. Sally's arm dangles, blood soaking into the brown skin over it.

Fire remembers the river. Fire remembers the raft. Fire's legs want to be on the raft, away from this blizzard of jabbing spears and shadows.

Fire's hands grab Sally by the waist. He hurls her over his shoulder. She cries out as her broken arm is jarred against his hip. He feels the cool flesh of her belly and breast against his shoulder. Emma has picked up Maxie. Her legs are running.

Stones hail around them, sticking into the ground. The people's legs run from the stones and the Hams' yells. '*U-lu-lu-lu-lu!*'

The people run splashing into the water. There is nowhere else to go. They scramble onto the raft. It is just a mass of floating branches, roughly pushed together. The raft is too small. The people fall off, or climb on each other's backs. As their legs and arms scrabble at the branches the raft drifts apart, in big floating chunks. The people call out and grab at each other's hands and ankles.

Fire runs onto the raft. His foot plunges through the soaked foliage and he falls forward. Sally falls off his shoulders and lands on a wriggling pile of children. The children push her away.

Emma is on the raft. Her hands slap at the children. '*Leave her alone!*'

Maxie sits by his mother, his hands clutching leaves and branches, wailing.

The raft is drifting away from the bank, into the deeper river. It twists, slowly. The people yell and sprawl, their hands clinging to the branches.

Stone comes running down the bank. His eyes are white. Hams pursue him. Stone hurls himself into the water. He goes under. His head comes up. He is coughing. Blue reaches out and grabs Stone. Stone clings to a branch, his body dangling in the water. Fire sees blood seep from Stone's shoulder.

The Hams run up and down the bank, yelling, hurling stones. '*U-lu-lu-lu-lu!*' The stones fall harmlessly into the water.

The raft drifts towards the middle of the river, away from the bank with the undercut, the capering Hams.

Fire's shoulder stings. He looks around. Emma has slapped him. '*Help me.*'

Emma's small axe cuts away Sally's brown, bloody skin. Underneath is more skin. It is pink, but it is mottled purple and black. Emma's hands run up and down the skin.

'*Good. The skin isn't broken. But I have no idea how to set a broken bone. Damn, damn.*' She produces a small gleaming thing. Water pours out over Sally's arm. No, not water: it stinks, like rotten fish. Her hands pull a chunk of branch from the raft. Fire can see water rippling underneath. Emma holds the branch against Sally's arm. '*Hold this,*' she says. '*Fire hold. Hold it, damn it.*' Her hands wrap his around Sally's arm. His hands hold the branch against the arm. Emma takes a sheet of skin from around her neck. Her hands move over Sally's arm, very fast. When she pulls away her hands, the skin is wrapped around Sally's arm.

Fire stares and stares.

Emma lifts Sally's head and places it on her lap.

Maxie says, '*Is mommy going to be all right?*'

'*Yes. Yes, I hope so, Maxie.*'

'*She needs a hospital.*'

Emma laughs, but it is like a sob. '*Yes, Maxie. Yes, she needs a hospital.*'

The raft is in the middle of the river, slowly turning. The banks to either side are far away, just lines of green and brown. The raft is small, and the river is large.

There is a scream.

Fire sees ridges. Yellow eyes. Teeth.

Stone roars. His arms lift his body. His bulk comes crashing down on the raft.

The whole raft shakes. People scream, clinging to each other. Branches splinter and separate. A child falls into the water, wailing.

Yellow eyes gleam. The crocodile's vast mouth opens.

The child's eyes are white. They stare at the people on the raft.

The mouth snaps shut.

The child is gone, forgotten.

146

The raft drifts down the river, slowly turning. The people cling to it in silence, locked inside their heads.

Reid Malenfant:

Ten minutes before lunar orbit insertion the cabin grew subtly darker. Gradually, as his eyes dark-adapted, Malenfant caught his first true view of the stars, a rich spangling carpet of them, glowing clear and steady.

They had fallen into the shadow of the Red Moon.

Malenfant and Nemoto were both strapped into their couches. They had a checklist to work through, and settings on their various softscreen displays to confirm, just as if they were real pilots, like Borman and Anders, Armstrong and Collins. But the insertion sequence was completely automated, it either worked or it didn't, and there wasn't a damn thing Malenfant could do about it – nothing save slam his fist into the fat red abort button that would change the engine's firing sequence to send them straight home again. He would do that only in the event of a catastrophic control failure. Or, he mused, if somebody down there started shooting . . .

He glanced up at his window. There was a disc of darkness spreading across the stars, like an unwelcome tide.

It was, of course, the Red Moon. His heart thumped.

What were you thinking, Malenfant? Are you surprised to find that this huge object, this vast new Moon, is in fact real?

Well, maybe he was. Maybe he had spent too long in Shuttles and the Station, going around and around, boring a hole in the sky. He had become conditioned to believing that spaceflight wasn't about *going* anywhere.

Passing behind the alien Moon, they abruptly lost the signal from Houston. For the first time since launch day, they were alone.

The cabin was warm – over eighty degrees – but his skin was cold where his clothes touched him.

Emma Stoney:

The river's broad body ran from west to east, so that the setting sun glimmered above its upstream sections, making the water shine like greasy tarmac. Thick black volcanic clouds streaked the glowing sky. And when she looked downstream, she saw the Earth, nearly full, hanging low over the horizon, directly above the dark water, as if the river were a great road leading her home.

The raft drifted over the brown, lazily swelling water, rotating slowly, heading roughly east. In fact it was scarcely a raft, Emma thought, just a jammed-together collection of branches, held together by no more than the tangle of the branches and twigs, and the powerful fingers of the Runners. Every so often a chunk of foliage would come loose and drift away, diminishing the raft further, and the Runners would huddle closer together, fearful. And the raft drifted: just that, with no oars or rudder or sail, completely out of any conscious control.

The Runners did not speak to each other, of course. Where humans would have been shouting, crying, yelling, debating what to do, comforting or blaming each other, the Runners just clung to the branches and to each other, silent, eyes wide and staring. Each Runner was locked in her own silent fear, almost as isolated as if she were physically alone. Emma was frightened too, but at least she understood the fix they were in, and her head whirred busily seeking plans and options. All the Runners could do was wait passively while fate, and the river, took them where it would.

Emma, surrounded by naked, powerful, trembling bodies, had never been so forcefully struck by the Runners' limitations.

And meanwhile those 'Hams' had looked for all the world to her like picture-book Neandertals. What was going on here? . . .

The river crowded through a section of swamp-forest. Here the trees were low, and the purple spikes of flowering water-hyacinths crowded close to the oily black water. They passed an inlet crowded with water-lilies, their white flowers cupped half-closed. Their leaves were oval, with serrated edges bright green on top and red-brown underneath. As Emma watched dully, a red-brown body of a bird unfolded from its well-concealed place at the base of one lily-pad.

Its neck and collar were white and gold, and it unfolded long legs and spindly toes, watching them suspiciously.

. . . Not a bird. A bat, apparently incubating its young on nests built on these floating weeds. She had never heard of bats behaving like that. As the Runner raft passed, the bat stepped with a surgical precision across the lily-pads, its leathery wings rustling. Then it scuttled back to its nest of weed, settling with an air of irritation.

Though the meal of the lost child seemed to have satisfied the huge creature that had first stalked them, Emma glimpsed ridges of skin and yellow eyes everywhere. The crocodiles watched as the raft eroded, inevitably approaching the point where it would dump all its hapless inhabitants in the water.

Sally turned her head. With a cough, she threw up. Pale yellow bile splashed over Emma's lap, stinking.

'Shit, oh shit.' She got hold of Sally's leg, behind the knee, and strove to pull her over on her side.

The raft rocked, its component branches rippling, and the Runners hooted and snapped.

Emma ignored them. At last she got Sally on her side. She pushed Sally's good arm under her head, with her broken arm on top of her torso, and one knee bent over so she wouldn't roll back. She tipped Sally's head back, hoping to ensure she wouldn't choke, and was rewarded with another gush of vomit that splashed over her hands.

And now she became aware of another problem: a fresh stink, a spreading patch of moisture over Sally's behind. Diarrhoea, obviously.

Fire hooted and held his hands over his prominent nose.

There wasn't anything Emma could do about it, not for now. But it sure wasn't a good sign. Perhaps it was blood poisoning: one touch of a filthy Runner finger in a wound, one splash of river water, might have done the damage. Or it might be something worse, some disease such as hepatitis or cholera or typhoid, or even some virulent nasty native to this ugly little world; she didn't know enough about the symptoms of such things to be able to diagnose, one way or another.

And even if she did know what Sally was suffering from, what could she do about it? Her pocket-sized medical kit was gone, lost with the rest of her meagre kit as they had fled from the huge skin-clad creatures called Hams. She began to go through the pockets of her ragged, filthy flight suit, hoping to find even a single antibiotic tablet that had gone astray.

Sally convulsed again, and her vomit turned more clear, just a thin, stringy fluid.

Maxie, squatting with the other children, watched all this in wide-eyed dismay. He had been silent since they had left the shore, and now he watched Emma wrestle with Sally as if she were a side of beef, no doubt storing up more problems in that tousled, bewildered head. Later, Emma; one patient at a time.

After an hour of random drifting, the raft began to approach the river's far shore. Shallow beaches strewn with purple-black pebbles slid by. More by chance than design, the Runners were completing the crossing of this huge, sluggish waterway.

Sand glimmered rust-red, a few feet beneath the surface, and it was snagging the raft's branches. The raft creaked and spun. It began to break up, its component branches drifting apart. The Runners cried out. One skinny woman fell into the water with a fearful hoot.

'Emma!' Maxie came stumbling to her, his little feet plunging into brown river water. He threw himself into her arms, and she clutched him close.

More of the Runners fell into the water, or leapt away from the raft towards the shore, splashing noisily and yelling with fear. They seemed to have a lot of difficulty swimming, and Emma wondered if their heavily muscled bodies were denser than humans'. Wading clumsily, grabbing onto each other and their children, they began to flop out of the water and onto the beach, where they lay like sleek, muscular seals. They shook their heads to rid their tightly curled hair of water; droplets fell back to the river with eerie low-gravity slowness.

Emma felt cold water seeping into the legs of her track suit. Maxie cried out and squirmed higher up her body.

There was simply no way Emma was going to be able to get both Maxie and his mother across those few yards of deeper water.

Fire was one of the last to leave the raft. He actually stood upright on the raft, precariously, and its branches cracked and parted under his feet. Then, hooting, he leapt feet-first into the water. He staggered as his feet sank into the mud, but kept his balance. He looked down at the water lapping around his waist, as if amazed.

Emma called, 'Fire! Help us, Fire. Fire Fire Emma Maxie!'

He looked around dully.

Emma held Maxie up above her head. The kid squealed and

kicked; Emma wasn't going to be able to hold him like this for long. She cried, 'Fire Fire!'

Fire reached out with a liquid motion. With one hand he grabbed Maxie under his armpit and lifted him away from Emma, as if the child was as light as balsa wood. Then he turned and began splashing his way to the shore, holding Maxie high.

Without allowing herself to think about it – without even looking out for crocs – Emma pushed away the last branches, the last of the raft, and let herself and Sally slide into the water. Sally lay face-down in the water, passive, but Emma managed to roll her onto her back. The makeshift sling was filthy, stained by blood and the muddy river water. Emma got the inert woman's head against her belly, and cupped her fingers under Sally's chin. Then, working with her feet and her one free arm, she began to swim backwards, towing Sally's floating form.

She was soon exhausted. Her soaked clothes were heavy and clinging, and her boots made her feet feel as if they were encased in concrete. It seemed an age before her kicking feet began to sink into a steeply rising river bottom. She stood up, gasping.

Sally was still floating, so Emma grabbed a handful of cloth at her shoulder and, still supporting her head, began to drag her out of the water. Nobody came to her assistance – nobody but Maxie, and he was more hindrance than help.

At last she got Sally out of the river, far enough that her feet were free of the lapping, muddy brown water, and she fell on her back with exhaustion.

On this side of the river, there was less evidence of the ash falls that had plagued the Runners for days. But beyond the narrow, pebble-strewn beach, the shore was heavily wooded. The Runners huddled together in suspicious silence, peering at the dense green banks above them.

Night was coming.

With barely a word exchanged, some of the Runners crept cautiously into the woods. Others walked down the beach, tentatively exploring, and Fire and a couple of the women began to drag branches from the edge of the forest, building a fire. Fire cast shy glances at Emma; evidently he remembered, in some dim way, how she had managed to start a fire even when he had lost his treasured handful of embers, probably a key moment in his tortured young life.

First things first, she thought.

She pulled Sally further up the beach. She turned Sally over once more to the recovery position, unzipped Sally's trousers and with some difficulty wrestled them off her, followed by her panties. The clothes were filthy, of course, from faeces and river mud, and they clung to her flesh; but Emma was reluctant to use her knife – this was Sally's only set of clothing in the whole world, after all. When she had the pants off she used handfuls of leaves to clean Sally up as best she could, and covered her with her own T-shirt, briskly stripped off.

Then, leaving Maxie with his mother, she walked briskly down the beach. After fifty paces she came to a small stream, decanting from some source in the forest. It had cut itself a shallow, braided valley. Two of the children were playing here, splashing and wrestling. Emma walked a little way upstream of them and began to rinse out Sally's trousers and underwear in the shallow, sluggish water. When she was done she cleaned off her arms and hands, splashed cold water over her face, and took a deep drink. Then she dug her plastic bag out of her pocket – one of the few artefacts she had yet to lose – and dipped it to the stream to fill it with water.

More barely remembered medical lore came back to her. Diarrhoea and vomiting led to dehydration, which you ought to treat with sugar and salt, a teaspoon of each to a litre of water, if she remembered right. Fine, save that she had no sugar or salt, and no teaspoon for that matter . . .

She glanced up the beach.

Stone was squatting beside Sally. He had removed the T-shirt from her lower body, and was running his hands up her thigh. Maxie had cowered back to the edge of the woods, watching the huge man grope his mother.

Emma put down the water, straightened up, and began to walk back to Sally. She felt around her neck for her Swiss Army knife. She got to within a foot of Stone without him noticing she was there.

So where are you going to stick your blade, Emma? In his cheek, his rock-hard penis, his back? What makes you think this tiny little bee-sting blade will do more than goad him anyhow? He'll kill you, then do what he wants with Sally anyhow.

She pulled out the foldaway lens and lifted it up. She angled it so she caught the sun, and focused a bright spot on the back of Stone's broad neck. He howled, slapping his neck, and jumped up, whirling, his penis flopping. As calmly as she could she tilted back the lens so the spot of light shone in his eyes. He raised his hands, dazzled. She said, 'Keep away from her, Stone, you asshole, or I will bring down the sun on you. Stone sun Stone sun! Understand?'

He growled, but still the light shone in his eyes. He stumbled away, his penis wilting.

Trembling, trying to give an impression of command, Emma walked back along the beach, picked up her bag of water, and hurried back to Sally.

Sally still lay on her side, her head resting on her good arm, eyes closed, mouth open. There was a bubble of saliva at her mouth. That bubble of saliva popped, abruptly.

'Oh shit,' Emma said. She grabbed Sally and pushed her on her back. Sally sighed once, and then was still. Emma pinched Sally's cheeks until her lips parted. The skin was cool and waxy. She dug her fingers in Sally's mouth, and scooped out gobbets of vomit and flung it on the sand. Then she placed one hand under Sally's chin and tilted her head back. She could hear no breath, not a whisper.

She ran her hands over Sally's torso, seeking the end of the breastbone. Then she pulled her hands to the middle of her chest, placed the heel of her hand a little higher, and began to press down. 'One-and-two-and . . .'

A child leapt out of the woods, a lithe hairy child, its face twisted into a snarl. Maxie scrambled away, screaming. Emma shrank back from Sally, gasping with terror.

. . . No, not a child. It was an ape, an adult – a female, in fact, with two small empty dugs, a skinny, naked body covered in spiky black-brown hair. She was maybe three feet tall. She had the face of a chimp, with lowering eyes gazing out of ridged sockets, and a protruding mouth with thick wrinkled lips covering angular teeth. Emma could have cupped her brain pan in one hand. But she walked and ran upright, human-style, like a clumsy mannequin – her feet were more human than not – and in one curved, bony hand, dangling below her knees, she clutched what looked like a shaped pebble.

She was a caricature, a shrunken, shrivelled, spellbound mix of ape and human, a dwarfish sprite: an Elf, just as the Runners called her kind. This ape-woman ran up to Emma and capered before her.

Emma picked up a handful of sand and hurled it in the Elf's face.

The Elf howled and staggered back, rubbing her eyes.

Fire came running out of the forest's shade. With a single, almost graceful swipe, he slammed a rock against the side of the Elf's head.

She fell sprawled on the beach, unconscious or dying, half her face crushed.

Now there was screaming and yelling. All along the beach, Elf-folk were boiling out of the forest. They ran along the shore, rocks and sticks in their hands.

But the Runners fought back hard. Mothers grabbed their children and ran into the sea, where the Elf-folk seemed reluctant to follow. Men and women threw rocks at the scampering Elf-folk, and swung at them with their fists and feet.

But there were many, many of the Elf-folk, and they fought with a mindless intensity that seemed to overwhelm even the Runners.

Emma, trying to ignore this hideous drama, threw herself back at Sally.

After fifteen compressions Emma pinched Sally's nose, clamped her mouth on Sally's, and breathed hard and deep. She tasted vomit and blood. She pulled her head away, let Sally's chest deflate, and tried again. After two breaths she searched again for a pulse, found none, and slammed the heel of her hand into Sally's chest once more.

The conflict went on, crude, animal-like.

It's not my battle, Emma told herself. These aren't people. If they are humans at all they are some kind of predecessor species. Really, they are just two breeds of animals fighting for space. But one breed was at least hollering simple words – 'Stone!' 'Stone, Blue, Blue!' 'Away, away!' – and she couldn't help a deep sense of gratification every time one of those spindly Elf bodies went down, under Runner fists and feet.

Now Stone broke out of the squabbling pack. He had two Elves clinging to his back. One had its teeth sunk into his shoulder, and the other had torn off part of his scalp and a section of his right ear. Stone was howling, and blood poured over him from the glistening crimson wound in his head. More Elves swarmed over him, scratching, biting and beating. Stone went down, and rolled over into the water.

Emma heard an anguished scream. A woman burst out of the squabbling pack. It was Grass. Some of the Elves had closed in a pack around something that struggled, yelling, brown limbs flashing. It was a Runner child – perhaps Grass's child. Grass threw herself at the Elves' backs. They drove her off easily, but she came back for more, twice, three times, until at last a chipped rock was slammed against the side of her head, and she fell to her knees, grunting.

The Elf-folk slid into the forest with their prize, their screeching cries of triumph sounding like laughter.

. . . And still Emma could find no pulse. She sat back, arms hurting, lungs aching. She was aware of Maxie watching her, a little pillar of desolation, ominously silent. 'Oh, Maxie, I'm sorry.'

Stone was still in the water, on all fours, head lolling, his hair soaked, the water swirling crimson-brown under him.

Fire stood over him. He was holding a boulder, Emma saw, a slab of worn basaltic rock as big as his head.

Stone looked up, blood congealing over one eye. He raised a hand to Fire, reaching up for help.

Fire slammed the rock down on the crown of Stone's skull. There was a sound like a crunching apple.

Stone slumped. Thick red-black blood diffused in the water.

Fire stood staring at the body. Then he turned to Emma. His gait and eyes held a glittering hardness she had not seen before. She shrank back, scrambling over the ground, away from Sally's body.

Fire squatted down before her. His powerful, bloody fingers brushed her neck. She shuddered at his touch, feeling the burn scars on his palms. He pushed his hand inside her flight suit, and his hand closed around the Swiss Army knife. The lens was open. He snapped off the lens attachment as if breaking a matchstick.

Fire looked at the lens, and at Sally's body, and at Emma. Then he backed away from her, stinking of blood.

Maxie was a few feet away, backed up against a tree. His gaze was sliding over Runners, blood-stained sand, the river.

Emma stood, cautiously. Keeping her eyes on Fire, she reached out for Maxie. 'Come on, Maxie. This is no place for us, not any more. It never was . . .'

'No!' Maxie pulled away from her, his face twisted.

She thought, Now I'm the woman who killed his mother. Nevertheless, I'm all he's got. She made a grab for him.

He ran along the beach.

'Maxie!'

Before she had taken a couple of strides after him he had joined the Runners, who were clustered together, fingering their wounds. She caught one last glimpse of his small face, hard resentful eyes peering back at her. He seemed to be pulling off his clothes.

Then he was lost.

There was a cry, a grisly, high-pitched cry, a child's cry, eloquent of unbearable pain. The woman, Grass, stood and peered mournfully into the forest.

Emma slid into the gloom of the forest, for she had no other place to go.

Reid Malenfant:

Events unfolded quickly now, faster than they had for the Apollo astronauts. The Red Moon's gravity, stronger than Luna's, was pulling hard at their falling spaceship, dragging it into a curve that would all but skim the atmosphere.

Nemoto murmured to herself, still working through her tasks as calmly as if they were in just another simulator in Houston.

Malenfant tried to focus on his checklist. But he kept looking up at the strange, shifting diorama beyond the window.

Suddenly he saw the dawn.

Light seeped into the edge of the great disc of blackness. At first it was a deep red, spreading smoothly out around the curve of this small world. Then the band of light began to thicken, growing orange-yellow, and finally shading into blue. The light was coalescing at its brightest point, as if gathering to give birth to the disc of sun itself. And now Malenfant saw shadows of low clouds in the atmosphere; they drew clear dark lines hundreds of miles long over deeper air layers. The surface began to pick up the first of the light – it was an ocean, dark and smooth and sleek, glowing a deep bloody red. And still the light continued to leak into the sky, diffusing higher and higher.

This was a sunrise, not on airless Luna, but on a world with an atmosphere actually deeper than Earth's – and an atmosphere left laden with dust by a chain of great stratovolcanoes. It was a startling, full-blooded dawn, somehow unexpected so far from home.

For the first time Malenfant's thoughts swivelled from Earth, his departure point, and turned with a rush to the world he was approaching. Suddenly he was eager to be down on the ground, to be sinking his fingers into the soil of a new world, and drinking in its air.

Emma Stoney:

The light seeped away, and the shadows turned a deeper green.

She moved as silently as she could. But still she was aware of every leaf she crushed, every twig that cracked. And each time she heard a rustle or snap, she expected an Elf to leap out at her.

She didn't know where she was going, what the hell she was doing. But she knew she had to get away from that beach.

The screaming began again, startling her. It was very close, very loud. She crouched down in the bush, staring, listening, too frightened to move.

And she glimpsed movement, through a screen of trees to her right. Smart, Emma. You walked right in on them.

They were the Elf-folk, of course. They had the Runner child spreadeagled against a bare patch of ground. His eyes were wide and staring. Elf teeth closed on the boy's upper thigh, and came away bloody, huge ape lips wrapped around a handful of meat.

The boy thrashed. Emma saw how his eyes turned white. And he screamed, and screamed, and screamed.

After that – as Emma watched, frozen in place by her fear of detection – the boy was steadily dismembered: the drinking of blood, the biting-off of genitals, the startlingly efficient twisting-off of an arm. And through all of this the boy was still alive, still screaming.

. . . There was a hand on her shoulder.

She gasped, swivelled, fell back in the bush with a soft crash. Someone was standing over her, a shadowy figure.

It was not an Elf, or a Runner. It was a woman. She was wearing a loose tunic of skin, bound around her waist with what looked like a rope plaited from greenery. There were tools stuck in the belt, tools of bone and wood. Her body looked shorter, stockier than a Runner's. Her face protruded. She had no chin. Her skull was large, larger than a Runner's, but she sported a thick ridge of bone over her eyes, and there were prominent crests of bones at her cheeks and over the crown of her head.

Not a human, then. This was one of the powerful, shadowy creatures the Runners had called a 'Ham'. Emma felt savage disappointment, renewed fear.

But the other beckoned, an unmistakably human gesture.

Still Emma hesitated. Somewhere on this brutal world were the people who had taught the Runners to speak English. If she couldn't get back to Earth, then if her destiny lay anywhere, it was there – and not with this Ham.

But now she glanced back at the Elves. They had pulled open the boy's rib cage, and the child gave a final, exhausted moan as his heart was torn out.

You're kind of short of choices, Emma.

She followed the Ham.

The Ham glided away through the forest, pointing to the footsteps she made in the dead brush on the ground. When Emma stepped there, she made no sound.

Reid Malenfant:

Nemoto said laconically, 'Three, two, one.'

The booster pack fired, and Malenfant was pushed deep into his seat.

The light of their rockets illuminated the deserts and forests of the Red Moon. All over the little world, eyes were raised to the sky, curious and incurious.

3

HOMINIDS

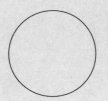

Manekatopokanemahedo:

Manekato lingered on the threshold of the room, held back by a mixture of respect and dread.

Her mother, Nekatopo, was dying.

Nekatopo, breathing evenly, gazed at the soft-glowing ceiling. A slim Worker waited beside the bed for her commands, as still as a polished rock.

Nekatopo's room was a hexagonal chamber whose form was the basis of the design of the House, indeed of the Farm itself. This room had been occupied by matriarchs throughout the deep history of the Lineage, and so it was Nekatopo's now – and would be Manekato's soon. But the room was stark. The ceiling was tall and the walls bare panels, glowing softly pink. The only piece of furniture was the bed on which Nekatopo lay, itself hexagonal.

Manekato remembered how her grandmother had decorated these same walls with exuberant fruits. But her daughter had stripped away all of that. 'I honour my mother's memory,' she had said. 'But these walls are of Adjusted Space; they are not material. They do not tarnish or erode. They have a beauty beyond space and time, as our ancestors intended. Why deface them with transience? . . .'

But Manekato found the unreal simplicity as overwhelming, in its way, as the happy clutter of her grandmother. When this room was hers, Manekato would find a middle way: her own way, as all the matriarchs had done – and she felt a sudden flush of shame, for her mother was not yet dead, and here she was calculating how she would use her room.

Now she saw that salty tears leaked over Nekatopo's cheeks, soaking the sparse hair, and trickled into her flat nose.

Manekato was troubled to her core. Her mother had never cried – not even on hearing the news of her imminent death – not even on the day when she had had to send away her only son, Babo,

Mapping him to his marriage on a Farm on the other side of the world.

Manekato fled, hoping her mother had not noticed she had been here.

She walked alone, along the path that led to the ocean. The Wind was gentle today, comparatively; she was barely aware of the way it ruffled the thick black hair on her back, and shivered over the trees that clung to the ground nearby.

To a human she would have looked something like a gorilla: stocky, powerful, all of eight feet tall, she knuckle-walked elegantly. She pressed her knuckles into the crushed gravel of the path with gentleness, even reverence. Every speck of land on the Farm was precious to her, like an extension of her own heart. Even this humble path served its purpose with quiet dignity, and had borne the weight of her mother and her mother's mother, deep into the roots of time, as it bore her weight now.

Quiet dignity, she thought. That is what I must strive for, in the difficult days ahead.

The path ended at a shallow cliff top that overlooked the sea. The sea was grey and cloudy, laden with silt, and tall waves, generated by a storm raging far over the horizon, crashed with exorbitant violence on the heavily eroded shore. Manekato glimpsed the rectangular gridwork that covered the ocean floor – the boundary of the undersea Farms – a shining mesh that disappeared into the murk of the cloudy water.

The tides were shallow on this moonless Earth, so the beach was narrow and battered by waves. But still huge birds plummeted from the sky, their muscular wings folded, stabbing after the unwary fish and crabs who clung to life at this thin, inhospitable margin. Manekato swivelled her ears to hear the calls of the birds, deep-pitched and throaty to penetrate the unceasing roar of the Wind.

Manekato turned and looked back the way she had come, resting her weight easily on her knuckles. The Farm sprawled over a low hill – in fact it was the core of a volcano, Wind-eroded to a snub long before her Lineage had begun to work this land. The Farm was dominated by the low, streamlined House that sat at the crest of the hill, its prow facing the direction of the prevailing Wind like a beached ship. Around the House sprawled a glowing gridwork of light, in the hexagonal pattern that was the signature of the Poka Lineage. Each of the fields marked out by the grid bore a different crop, ranging from the most advanced self-recursive Worker designs – even from here she could see nubs of heads and stubby limbs pushing out of the ground – all the way back to the Lineage's first harvest, a fat-trunked, ground-hugging willow whose bark still provided some of the best tea available anywhere.

But the land itself was only a cross-section of the greater Farm. There were more cultivated layers stacked deep beneath her feet, fed by light piped from the surface, and mines for the water and hydrocarbons locked in the ground's deeper rocks, and even one mighty borehole that punched through the planet's crust and into the mantle, sipping at Earth's core heat. There were more ducts that pumped heat and carbon dioxide and other waste products back into the ground, of course, as the Poka Lineage contributed to the husbandry of the world.

Even above the ground the Farm's activities extended. Manekato could see engineered birds wheeling over the main House, snapping Wind-blown debris from the sky. The birds were restricted to the Farm's perimeter, and Manekato could see how they flocked in a great wedge-shaped slice of sky that projected up from the ground, so high that the uppermost birds were mere dots against the banded, rippling clouds that were the province of the Sky Farmers.

From the core of the Earth to the bellies of the clouds: that was the extent of the Poka Farm, every scrap of it worked and reworked, every speck of dirt, every molecule of air and water functional, every bacterium and insect and animal and bird with a well-designed role to play in the managed ecology.

There was not a patch of this world that was not similarly cultivated, cherished by its Lineage.

And the Farm would soon belong to Manekato, all of it – even though she was just eight years old: still a young adult, little more than a third of her life gone.

Even though she didn't want it.

Now Manekato heard a faint cry. She swivelled her parabolic ears towards the House, and picked out the voice of her mother, calling her name.

She hurried up the path, back sloping, powerful legs working, levering herself forward on her knuckles. As she passed, immature Workers called out to her, tinny voices piping from ill-formed mouths, already seeking to serve; and willow leaves swivelled frantically in her shadow as they strove to drink in all the light of the eight-hour day.

She returned to her mother's room, at the heart of the Farm. Unhappily she stepped forward, approaching the bed.

Her mother's bed looked like a simple hexagonal nest, woven of leafy branches. It was in fact a cluster of semi-sentient Workers, designed to mimic the nests of willow and birch branches that children learned to make for themselves from an early age. It had been manufactured to Manekato's design by Worker artisans, twelve generations removed from the crude self-recursive creatures budding in the fields outside.

The floor of the room was a pit filled with hard-compacted white dust. The dust was the ground-up bones of her ancestors. One day Nekatopo's bones would be added to the pit, and, not many years after that, Manekato's too. Nobody knew how deep the dust pit extended. Manekato could feel the soft grittiness of the dust, but not a grain of it clung to her feet.

Nekatopo opened her eyes.

'. . . Mother?'

'Oh, Mane, Mane.' It was a childish diminutive she had not used since Manekato was a baby. She reached up, her great arms withered and weak.

Manekato embraced her, feeling the tears soak into the hairs in her own chest.

'Oh, Mane, I'm so sorry. But you must go to the Market.'

Manekato frowned. She knew that no woman had travelled to the Market since her grandmother's day. Manekato herself had never left the boundary of the Farm, and the prospect of travelling so far filled her with dread. 'Why?'

Nekatopo struggled to sit up, and wiped her face with the back of her hand. 'I don't even know how to tell you this. *We are going to lose the Farm.*'

Manekato felt her mouth fall open. A change in the possession of a Farm occurred only when a Lineage became extinct, or when some member of a Lineage had committed a grave crime.

'I don't understand.'

'I know you don't. Oh dear, dear Mane! It is the Astrologers. They have news for us which – well, it has gone around and around in my head, like the Astrologers' own wretched stars wheeling around the world. *The Farm is to be destroyed.* A great catastrophe is to befall the world – so say the Astrologers.'

Manekato could not take in any of this. 'Storms can be averted, waves tamed –'

'You must believe the Astrologers,' Nekatopo whispered, insistent. 'I'm sorry, Manekato. You must go to the Market and meet them.'

Manekato pulled away from her frail mother, frightened, resentful. 'Why? If all this is true, what use is talk?'

'Go to them,' Nekatopo sighed, subsiding back into the arms of the semi-sentient branches.

Manekato walked to the door. Then – torn by shock, uncertainty, shame, doubt – she hesitated. 'Nekatopo – if the Farm dies – what will become of me?'

Nekatopo lay on her bed, a dark brown bundle, breathing softly. She did not reply – but Manekato knew there was only one possible answer. If the Farm died, then the Lineage must die with it.

She burned with confusion, resentment.

But still she hesitated. It struck her that whatever the fate of the Farm, if she travelled to the Market, her mother might not be able to welcome her home again.

So, softly, she began to recite her true name. 'Manekatopokanemahedo . . .'

Manekato's true name consisted of nearly fifty thousand syllables – one syllable more than her mother's name, two more than her grandmother's – one syllable added for each generation of the Lineage, back to the beginning, when members of a very different species, led by a matriarch called Ka, and her daughter called Poka, had first scratched at the unpromising slopes of the eroded hills here.

Manekato's people had farmed this scrap of land for fifty thousand generations, for more than a million years.

Nekatopo listened to this child-like performance, unmoving, but Manekato sensed her wistful pleasure.

Joshua:

Joshua crouched by a bubbling stream. His nostrils were filled by the musky smell of the hunters' skins, the soft green scent of grass.

The giant horse had become separated from its herd. It snorted, stamping a leg that seemed a little lame. Forgetting its peril in the foolish way of all horses, it nibbled at grass.

The Ham hunters crept forward. Most of them were men. There was no cover, here on the open plain, but they hunkered down in the long grass, and the drab brown skins they wore helped them blend into the background. They were patient. They worked towards the horse step by silent step, staying resolutely downwind of the animal. Lame or not, the heavy old stallion could still outrun any of them – or punish them with its hooves should they fail to trap it properly.

This small drama took place on a plain that stretched from the foot of a cliff. To the east, beyond a stretch of coarsely grassed dunes, the sea glimmered, a band of grey steel. And to the north a great river decanted into the sea via a broad, sluggish delta system. The plain was wet and scrubby, littered by pools. At the base of the cliff itself, a broad lake was fed by springs that sprouted from the cliff's rocks.

The coastal plain, with its caves and streams and pools and migrant herds, was the home of Joshua's people. They called themselves the People of the Grey Earth. Others called them Hams. They had lived here for two thousand generations.

To Joshua, the landscape was a blur, marked out by the position of the other hunters, as if they glowed brightly – and by the horse, the centre of their attention.

A soft call came. Abel was waving his arm, indicating they should approach the horse a little closer. Abel was Joshua's older brother.

Joshua crouched lower and moved through the grass, towards the incurious horse.

But now his questing fingers found something new, lying hidden in the grass. It was a stick, long and straight. No, it was a *spear*, with a stone tip fixed to the wood by some black, hard substance; he could see where twigs had been sheared away from it by a stone knife. He picked up the spear and hefted it, testing its weight. It was light and flimsy; it would surely break easily on a single thrust. Its shaft was oddly carved, into fine, baffling shapes.

A bear.

He dropped the spear, crying out, and stumbled back. Suddenly a bear had been looking at him, from out of the shaped wood in his hands.

A massive hand clamped over his mouth and he was pushed to the ground.

Abel loomed over him. His skins, of horse and antelope, were tightly bound about his body by lengths of rawhide thread. His eyes were dark pools under his bony brow. 'Th' horse,' he hissed.

'Bear,' Joshua said, panting. 'Saw bear.'

Abel frowned and cast around, seeking the bear. Then he saw the broken spear. He picked it up, briefly fingering its dense carving, then hurled it from him with loathing. 'Zealots,' he said. 'Or En'lish. Skinny-folk.'

Yes, Joshua thought uneasily. Skinnies must have made the little spear. But nevertheless there had been, briefly, a bear glaring at him from out of the carved wood.

'Ho!' It was Saul, another of the Ham hunters. 'Horse breakin'!'

Abel and Joshua struggled to their feet. The horse, startled, was coming straight towards the brothers, a mountain of meat and muscle, a giant as large as a carthorse.

Joshua grabbed a cobble, and Abel raised his thrusting spear. They grinned at each other in anticipation.

Joshua ran straight into the animal's mighty chest.

He was knocked flying, and he landed in the dirt in a tangle of loosened furs. Winded, he got straight up, and ran back towards the fray.

He saw that his brother had grabbed the horse around its neck. The horse was bucking, still running, and it carried Abel with it; but Abel was stabbing at the horse's throat with his spear. The spear was a short solid pillar of wood, stained deep with the blood of many kills. It was a weapon of strength and utility, without carving or decoration of any kind.

The slender spear of the Skinny-folk was meant to be thrown, so that an animal could be brought down from a distance, sparing such hard labour; the Hams had no such technology, and never would.

In a moment Abel's thrusts had reached some essential organ, and the animal crashed to the dust. The other men closed, yelling, hurling themselves on the animal to subdue it before it died. With a gleeful howl, ignoring the pain of his bruised chest and back, Joshua joined in. Before the animal was overpowered they all suffered bruises and cuts; one man broke a finger.

When the horse was dead, the butchery began.

Joshua found a flat cobble. He sat on the ground with one leg folded under him, tucked a flap of antelope skin over each hand, and began to work the cobble with fast, precise motions.

With fast blows of a pebble, he knocked away bits of stone, working around the cobble until he had left a series of thin ridges on a domed surface. After twenty or thirty strokes, with bits of stone littering the ground around him, he pulled a bone hammer from the cord around his waist. The hammer was a bit of antelope thigh bone, broken, discoloured, heavily worn with use. With care, he struck one of the ridges. A thin, teardrop-shaped flake fell away. He picked it up and inspected it; it was fine and sharp, good enough for use without further work. He returned to his cobble and knocked out a series of flakes, with one confident blow after another, until the core had been returned to convexity. Then he began to prepare the core to make further flakes.

Joshua was good at working stone. It was a high art because each nodule of stone had its own unique properties; the toolmaker had to find a path through the stone to the tools he or she wanted. It was a question of seeing the tools in the raw stone. Men and women alike would watch his fast, precise movements, seeking to copy him. The women pushed their children towards him, making them watch. Nobody asked him about it, of course; people didn't *talk* about tool-making.

Making such tools was the thing Joshua did best, the thing for which he was most valued, the thing for which he valued himself. And yet it set him aside from the others.

He tucked his bone hammer back in his rawhide belt and took his flakes to the horse. He began work on a leg. With a series of swipes he cut down the skin on the inside of the limb, pulling it away from the muscle. Some of the horse's thick brown hair stuck to the edge of the tool. Then he moved to the belly, opening up the hide. He grasped the open skin and pulled it sideways. Where membranes clung to the skin, he swiped at them gently with his flake, holding the stone at its centre between his fingers. The membranes parted easily. There was no blood, no mess.

When the horse was skinned, it was easily dismembered. Joshua cut away the meat of the neck. It fell open and was pulled away. He turned his axe over and over, seeking to use all its edge. When he was done he moved to the rib cage, and sliced down it with a crunch.

The people talked softly, steadily. They talked boastfully about their own and each other's prowess in the hunt of the horse, the people waiting for them at the hut – especially young Mary, whose breasts and hips were beginning to fill out, making her a centre of intense interest among the men, and amusement for the women. Their attention was filled with each other; the horse, now it had turned to a mere mine of meat, had receded.

But even here, as the people worked together on the fallen horse, they sat a little away from Joshua. They were reluctant to look at him directly, and did not respond to what he said, as they responded to others.

Joshua was short, robust, heavily built. He was barrel-chested, and his arms and short, massive-boned legs were slightly bowed. His feet were broad, his toes fat and bony. His massive hands, with their long powerful thumbs, were scarred from stone chips. His skull, under a thatch of dark brown hair, was long and low with a pronounced bulge at the rear. His face was pulled forward into a great prow fronted by his massive, fleshy nose; his cheeks swept back as if streamlined, but his jaw, though chinless, was massive and thrust forward. Over each of his eyes a great ridge of bone thrust forward, masking his eyes. There was a pronounced dip above the brow ridges, before his shallow forehead led back into a tangle of hair.

He looked powerful, ferocious. But in his pale brown eyes there was uncertainty and confusion.

Joshua was twenty-five years old. Already he was one of the senior members of the group; only a handful of men and women were older than he was. And yet he still felt something of an outsider, as he had all his life.

The problem was his tool-making. He would always be valued for it. But others were suspicious of what lay at the centre of that profound skill: his ability to see the tools in the stone.

It was uncomfortably like what the Zealots did, and the English. Skinny-folk spoke to the sky and the ground as if they were people. Their tools were carved and painted in ways that, sometimes, made even Joshua see people or animals that weren't really there.

Just as the knives and burins and scrapers he saw in the cobbles weren't really there either, not until he dug them out. The others sensed that his head was full of strangeness, and that was why there was a barrier around him, a barrier that never broke down.

Now the hunters had completed their butchery, and the meat lay scattered around them in neat crimson piles. Joshua dropped his stone flakes, and soon forgot them. The hunters picked up cobbles and smashed open the bones. They would bring the meat back to their hut at the base of the cliffs. But first they would enjoy the warm, greasy, delicious marrow, the privilege of successful hunters. There was a mood of contentment. They knew that they need not hunt again for several days, that the women and children would welcome their return with joy, and that the evening would be filled with good food, companionship, and sex.

And, while the men lolled contentedly, Abel began to talk of the Grey Earth.

The Grey Earth was the home of the people.

The Hams had fallen, baffled, to this strange place of red dirt and grass. They lived here, but it was not as the Grey Earth had been. On the Grey Earth, the animals ran past the people's caves like great rivers of meat. On the Grey Earth, there were no skinny Zealots or English or troublesome Elf-folk; on the Grey Earth there were only Hams, the people of the Grey Earth.

The men listened. The Grey Earth lay two thousand generations in the past, and now it made the people's only legend, relayed from one generation to the next, utterly unchanging and unembroidered; they were a people conservative even in their story-telling.

But Joshua looked up into the sky. The sun was fading now, and the earth shone brightly. This earth was not the Grey Earth, for it was not grey, but a bright, watery blue.

The Hams lived in an unchanging present. Joshua's sense of his life was of a series of days more or less like today, stretching ahead of and behind him like images in a hall of mirrors, reaching from his dimly recalled days as a toddler begging scraps from his mother, all the way to no-longer-remote times when he would become as toothless and broken-down as old Jacob, back in the hut, again helpless and dependent on the kindness of others. The Hams knew of life and death and the cycle of their lives. But of the world beyond themselves they knew of no change.

. . . No change but one, Joshua reflected: in the past, they had lived on the Grey Earth, and now they did not.

Joshua looked at his companions as they rested, lolling against the ground, licking marrow from their fingertips, listening amiably to Abel's loose legends. He knew that not one of them would share his thoughts, of past and future and change, of knives buried in rocks.

Joshua kept silent, and peered up at the earth's cool loveliness.

The hut was in the overhang of the cliff, close to the lake. It was built of beech saplings stuck in the ground, bent over and tied at the top. Skins of horses and antelopes had been laid loosely over the frame, weighted down with rocks. More massive rocks had been dragged to the rim of the hut. The area around was scattered with debris, animal bones, abandoned tools, cobbles scooped from the hut floor, and handfuls of ashes.

As the hunters returned with their haul of meat, Joshua saw that smoke was already rising from rents in the roof. Only a few children were outside, playing with the scattered cobbles and bits of skin. Joshua saw bats pecking hopefully at the abandoned bones.

The children ran to the hunters, and playfully grabbed at their meat.

Inside the hut the air was smoky, but the fires in their shallow hearths gave off a yellow-red glow that sent long flickering shadows over the dome of skin above. Beside the hearths, many of the women and children were already eating. The women had been hunting too. Impeded by their children and infants, women mostly did not tackle the huge game taken on by the men, but the steady flow of smaller game they returned, like beavers and rabbits and bats, provided more than half the group's provisions.

Joshua began to shuck off his skins, loosening or cutting rawhide ropes and letting the skins fall where they might. In the hot, stuffy air of the hut he began to scrape dirt and sweat from his skin with a bit of antelope jaw bone.

Soon everybody was naked. Men and women alike were muscular and stocky, as were all but the very youngest children, so that the hut was filled with brawny, glistening bodies, moving to and fro with slabs of meat and bits of stone and bone and skin, comparing fresh injuries and wounds. The Hams lived lives of constant exertion and physical stress, and injuries were common.

Nobody knew their fathers here. But people were tied by loyalty to their mothers and siblings, and couples were more or less monogamous while they stayed together. So the horse meat was distributed through the group, fairly evenly.

Joshua, with his own slab of meat, found a place on the fringe of the hearth built by Ruth, who coupled with Abel. The low fire was surrounded by heaps of dried seaweed, to be used as bedding. Abel sat with Ruth, and two small children settled down before them, noisily tearing at rabbit legs, blood running down their chins.

One of the younger men approached the pubescent girl Mary, but she huddled close to her mother.

Joshua ate his meat raw, tearing at it with his shovel-shaped teeth and cutting it with a flake knife; every so often he scraped his teeth with the knife. And as his powerful jaw ground at the meat, great muscles worked in his cheeks.

On the fringe of the firelight he sat alone, speaking to nobody.

He had had only brief relationships with some of the women. Abel, by comparison, had shared a hearth with this one woman, Ruth, for many seasons. Like the men and even some of the children, the women saw too much strangeness in Joshua.

In one corner of the hut sat old Jacob. He was sitting on a patch of cobbles, flat sides up, laid over a damp place on the floor. He watched the others, waiting without complaint.

Now Abel, his own hunger sated, sat beside the older man. He gossiped to him gently of the day, of who had said and done what to whom, and he tore at meat, cutting off strips with a small knife. But the old man had trouble chewing; he complained loudly about the pain of the pulpy stumps of his smashed teeth. So Abel chewed the meat himself, pulling at it until it was soft, and pushed it into Jacob's mouth as if feeding an infant. Jacob accepted it without comment or shame.

Jacob's body showed the traces of a long life's relentless work. A charge by an enraged horse had left him with smashed teeth, a shattered arm, a crushed left side and a sprained leg that stubbornly refused to heal. The suite of injuries had left him incapable of participating in the hunt, or even joining in the easier tasks of the hut, like building the fires or making tools.

Joshua recalled how a healthier Jacob had once helped Joshua tend Miriam, Joshua's mother, when she lay dying of an illness that had made her belly swell and caused her to cough blood. And now Abel tended Jacob. It was the way of things, accepted without question.

Jacob was the oldest individual in the group, at thirty-nine years old.

As the evening drew in the adults gathered in loose knots. Joshua joined a loose circle, saying little, cutting at a stick of fire-hardened wood to make a new thrusting spear. Ruth scraped at the skin of the horse to remove its fur, and dragged it through her teeth. Others settled into similar quiet chores.

Like the others Joshua listened intently to the talk, absorbing every detail of rumours, of promises made, romances broken, children praised or disciplined, injuries healed or acquired. His hands worked at the stick, but it was a simple, ancient task, so deeply ingrained by generations of practice that it was almost as unconscious as breathing. It was as if all that existed in the world was the circle of faces, orbiting the light of the fires. All they talked of was each other, never of the tools they made; those were things of doing, not talking.

As the last of the daylight seeped out of the bits of sky visible through the smoke vents, people drifted apart. Abel took Ruth's hand and led her to a dark corner of the hut, close to where toothless Jacob snored noisily.

Joshua lay down alone, close to the fire Ruth had built, on a rough pallet of seaweed. He stared into the fire, and he thought he saw creatures capering in the flames, Skinny-people like the Zealots or the English. But though the dancing creatures amused him, they disturbed him too, for there were only flames, no people or animals here.

It seemed to Joshua that he woke to hear a soft gasp, like surprise, from Jacob, and then silence. But Joshua ignored this, and fell deeper into sleep.

In the morning they found Jacob lying dead, slumped over on his damaged arm.

They would bury Jacob just outside the hut's main entrance.

Joshua swept away rubbish, picked-over animal bones and flakes of worked rock, and began to dig, using bare hands and stone scrapers, powerful muscles working.

When the grave was done it was about half Joshua's height in length, and so shallow that when he stood in it, its lip barely came up to his knees. Even so the diggers had disturbed other bones, yellow and brown from their immersion in the ground, the bones of people long forgotten.

Abel carried Jacob's corpse in his arms. The ruined body, toothless mouth gaping, was light, for it had been some time since Jacob could eat properly. Abel was weeping, for he had been fond of Jacob, who was now gone. Abel put the body on the ground. He tried to fold it up into a foetal position, knees tucked against the chest, head resting on a forearm. But the body was already too stiff. So Abel and others were forced to haul at the body until its joints cracked, and it folded as required. Then Abel bound up the wrists and ankles with rawhide thong.

Children watched wide-eyed.

Abel set the body into the grave among the yellowed bones of deeper, nameless ancestors. Then he used his broad feet to scuff dirt back into the hole.

Others joined in, with hands and feet, kicking at the piles of dirt around the grave. When the grave was roughly filled, Abel stamped on it to level it, and allowed the children to run over it.

People wept openly. Many of them had loved Jacob. But now Jacob was gone.

If the world of the Hams was unchanging, it was also a world of limits. If too many children were born, then they would starve, for the land afforded only so much food. No animal could be hunted save those small or old or weak enough to be brought down by the strength of a combination of hunters at close quarters. Every person went through life limited by their strength and their health and the richness of the land and the vagaries of the weather. Nobody, not even Joshua, could make a *new* tool, of a type that had not been made before.

And here was the ultimate limit, the limit of death. Jacob was *gone*, no more existent than in the days before he was born, beyond hope and pain and love. For now the people grieved, and they would speak of him as if he were alive. But soon those who remembered him would die in their turn, and even his name would fade from the world.

Absently Joshua looked up to the sky, his thick neck stiff, seeking the Blue Earth.

And that was when he saw it: a thing like a bat that sailed across the sky, black and white like a gull – and yet it was not a bat. Its wings were stiff, and it was huge and fat, and it drifted beneath a huge blue and white skin, suspended there by threads.

It sailed out of Joshua's sight, beyond the line of the cliffs. He watched, open-mouthed, noting where the extraordinary bat-creature fell.

Shadow:

Shadow didn't want to wake up. In her sleep she was warm and cushioned by the woven branches, dreaming arboreal dreams five million years old.

It was the baby that dispelled her dreams, with a bout of savage kicking that led to a stabbing stomach cramp.

Her green mood shattered in a hail of red. She rolled over, groaning, and her gullet flexed, as if she were about to vomit. But it was a dry retch; her stomach was empty.

She sat up, rubbing the base of her belly. Slowly the cramps eased. The sun was already above the horizon, the sky tinged subtly pink by the air's dust.

She inspected this tree to which she had fled in the dark. Elf-folk had been here. The branches were twisted and torn where they had been pulled together for nests, and much of the green fruit of the tree was missing.

She had not come far. She was still within the range of the people. The sun was already high, glimmering down through the canopy. The people woke with the dawn. They might be close already.

She grabbed a handful of fruit and pushed it into her mouth.

The people. As she did every time she woke, she remembered in grim red shards what had happened to her, Claw and Big Boss and Little Boss and the rejection by her mother. The fragmentary, terrified images broke up into a wash of green and red and blue. She hooted in alarm, as if some predator had come wheeling out of her own head to threaten her.

She abandoned her nest and scurried down the tree to the ground. She crashed through the undergrowth, twisting aside small branches and shrubs without a thought for the noise she was making. She saw no people, and did not hear them.

And she did not stop until she was in a place she did not know.

For the first time in her life, she was in a place without the guidance of her elders, who had known the position of every fruiting tree, every bubbling stream. *Everything was new*: the trees, the rocks, the subtle crimson shades of the dust, even the way the sun lanced down through the canopy. She had no way to figure out a path through this new landscape, a way to survive. Her kind did not see patterns in the natural world; they learned the features of the environment around them – the dangers, the sources of food and water – by rote.

Panic struck her. She longed to run back the way she had come. She thought of Claw.

One of the trees had a hole in its trunk, a little above her eye level. Suddenly she was thirsty. She probed at the hole with one finger. She was rewarded with cool dampness. She pulled out her finger and licked it. Hastily she gathered leaves, chewed them to a spongy mass, and stuck them in the hole. When she pulled out the leaf mass it was dripping wet, and she sucked the water gratefully.

Her stomach clenched abruptly. She squatted on her haunches and briskly, painfully, passed watery shit. She took some soft, crumbling wood from a rotting tree trunk, mashed it up to a wool, and used it to wipe her backside clean of the sour-smelling stuff.

She heard a distant hooting, an answering scream. It was the Elf-folk.

As soon as she was able, she got to her feet and walked on, feeding on whatever fruit and shoots she found, heading resolutely away from the noises of her people.

But soon, very soon, she ran out of forest. She stood on the fringe of the open savannah, clinging to the forest's green shade.

And a bat came drifting across the sky, a great black and white bat with blue wings.

She howled and lunged back into the green mouth of the forest.

Emma Stoney:

After getting away from Fire's Runner group, Emma had followed the beckoning Ham woman into the forest. It was an arduous trek, through increasingly dense foliage. But after perhaps a mile they came to a small clearing.

There were shelters here, made of skins stretched out over saplings driven into the ground. There was an overpowering stench, of people, of sweat, wood smoke, excrement and burning fur. Even the walls of the huts stank, she found, a musty, disagreeable odour of a kind she associated with the clothing of old people who didn't wash or change enough.

But, stench or not, it was a kind of village.

A Ham village.

A village of Neandertals.

She approached cautiously, following the Ham who had found her.

The Hams barely seemed to notice her. They were utterly wrapped up in each other. Some of the children plucked at her clothing with their intimidating, strong fingers. But otherwise the Hams stepped around her, their eyes sliding away.

But however coolly the Hams greeted Emma, they did not expel her.

She dug out her own hearth and built a fire.

Nobody shared food with her that first night. But the next day she managed to catch a rabbit with a home-made snare, and she brought the meat back to the camp and cooked it, even sharing a little with the adults. They took the meat, sniffing the burned stuff gingerly, but ignored her.

So it went on.

There were many of them, she soon learned, perhaps eighty or ninety, in shelters that faded into the dense green forest background.

With their hulking bodies and broad bony faces the Hams seemed like extras in some dreadful old movie to Emma, wrapped up in their animal skins, knocking their crude tools out of the rock. Everything they did, from cracking open a bone to bouncing a child in the air, was suffused with strength – they seemed much more powerful even than the Runners – and Emma quailed before their brute power. But it was apparent that such strength was not always wisely applied, for she saw evidence of a large number of injuries, bone fractures and crushing injuries and scarred skin.

They were humans, of a sort, but humans who made a living about the hardest way she could imagine. Their favoured hunting technique, for example, even for the largest prey, was to wrestle it to the ground. It was like living with a troupe of rodeo riders.

But they cared for their children, and for their ill and elderly.

And they spoke English, just like Fire's people, the Runners. Who could have taught them? That central mystery nagged at her – and she sensed her own destiny lay in unravelling it.

The forest, like the savannah, was full of predators: cats and bears and dogs, not to mention snakes and insects, some of them giant-sized, that she didn't trust at all.

But the most dangerous creatures of all were the people.

There seemed to be many types of hominids wandering around this globe. She knew there were Hams and Runners and Elf-folk and Nutcracker-folk, and presumably others. The vegetarian Nut-crackers seemed content to chew on bamboo and nuts in the depths of the forest, following a sleepy, untroubled, almost mindless lifestyle that Emma sometimes envied. The Runners conversely generally stuck to the plains.

The forest-dwelling Elf-folk – three or four feet high, like upright, savage chimps – were, for Emma, the most dangerous factor in the landscape. Having glimpsed what that troupe of Elf-folk had done to the Runner child, to finish her life as a living food source in the hands of Elf-men remained her abiding nightmare.

But everybody pretty much left the Hams alone.

For one thing, with their clothing and comparatively elaborate tool kit and distorted English they were a lot smarter than the rest. And they were beefy besides, even the women and children, more than a match for any Elf.

For all the Hams jabbered their broken English, Emma knew she could never become part of this inward-looking, deeply conservative community. But she also knew she was a lot safer here than wander-ing around, alone in the forest.

And so she stayed, inhabiting a rough lean-to on the edge of the community, bit by bit building up her own survival skills and recovering her strength, and waiting for something to turn up.

The Hams' technology was more advanced than the Runners', but still, considering those big brain pans, remarkably limited. They had more advanced knapping techniques, manufacturing a range of flakes and points and burins in addition to the ubiquitous hand-axes. They fitted stone tips to their thick thrusting-spears.

But that was about it. They had no piece of technology with more than two or three components. They didn't have innovations even Emma could think of, such as spear-throwers and bows.

Other gaps. If they weren't interested in something – a type of plant, for instance, which had no use for food or medicine or tools, nor carried any threat as a poison – they simply ignored it. If it didn't matter, it was as if it didn't even exist; as far as she could tell there were whole categories of such 'useless' objects and phenomena which had no names.

There were no books here, of course – there was nothing like writing of any kind. And no art: no paintings on animal skins, no tattoos, not so much as a dab of crushed rock on a child's face.

Indeed, the Hams seemed to loathe symbology of any kind. The Hams tolerated the odd colours of Emma's skin and hair, her slimness of build, the way she spoke, even the garish blue of her clothes – but they could not bear the South African air force logo that adorned the breast of her flight suit, and she had to cut it out with a stone knife. (Loath to throw away anything that had come from home, she had tucked the patch into a pocket on her sleeve.)

She came to suspect that what disturbed them wasn't the symbols themselves as much as the response of herself to them – and other *Skinny-folk*, a class which seemed to include herself and the mysterious 'Zealots' and 'En'lish'. The Hams would jabber about how Skinnies saw *people in the rock*, as if the symbols themselves were somehow sentient.

As a result, the Hams' world was a startlingly drab place, lacking art and religion and story – save, of course, for their one great central myth of the Grey Earth, where they had come from. They didn't tell jokes. The children played only as baby chimps might, exercising their muscles and testing their animal reactions against each other.

And to them, death appeared to be a genuine termination, a singularity beyond which an individual, leaving no trace, had no meaning. To the Hams, today was everything, yesterday a minor issue – and if you weren't here tomorrow, you wouldn't matter.

In many ways, they were like the Runners, then. But, unlike the Runners, they talked and talked and talked. They seemed to have a wide vocabulary, much of it English, and they would hold long, complex conversations around their fires.

But it was only gossip. They never talked about how to make a better tool. Just about each other.

Emma thought she had gotten used to the Runners, who were a strange mixture of human and animal. If these Hams were still not quite human as she was, nevertheless they had their own gaps in their heads, barriers between the rooms. As she watched them jabbering of who was screwing whom while their hands worked at one tool or another, apparently independently, she found it hard to imagine how it must be to *be* a Ham.

Sometimes she envied them, however.

To her, a beautiful sunset was a comforting reminder of home, a symbol of renewal, of hope for a better day tomorrow. The Hams would watch such displays as intently as she did. But to them, she believed, a sunset was just a sunset, like the sound of some instrument lacking any overtones, a simple pure tone – but a tone with a beauty and purity which they experienced directly and without complication, as if it was the first sunset they had ever seen.

Day succeeded empty day.

At first, on arriving here, she dreamed of physical luxuries: running hot water, clean, well-prepared food, a soft bed. But as time wore on, it was as if her soul had been eroded down. She had simpler needs now: to sleep in the open on a bower of leaves no longer troubled her; to have her skin coated in slippery grime was barely noticeable.

But she longed for security, to be able to settle down to sleep without wondering if she would be alive to see the morning, to live without the brutality and death that permeated the forest.

And she longed for the sight of another human face. It didn't have to be Malenfant. Anybody.

One day her wish was granted.

They had been men, pushing their way through the forest, pursuing some project of their own. They wore clothing of animal skin, but it was carefully stitched – a long way beyond the crude wraps the Hams tied around their bodies – and they spoke English, with a strong, twisted accent.

Emma was electrified. She gazed on their thin, somewhat pinched faces with longing, as intently as one Ham might gaze at another. Were they the source of the Hams' and Runners' language? Her impulse was to call out to them, approach them.

But she saw that the Hams cowered from these *Zealots*, as they called them, a label Emma found less than encouraging. So she, too, slipped back into the forest with her Hams.

Sometimes she raged inwardly. Or she worked through imaginary conversations with Malenfant – who had, after all, been flying the plane when she got stuck here, and so was the only person she could think of to blame.

But when the Hams saw her stalking around the forest lashing at branches and lianas, or, worse, muttering to herself, they became disturbed.

So she learned not to look inwards.

She watched the Hams as they shambled about their various

tasks, their brute bodies wrapped up in tied-on animal skins like Christmas parcels. One day at a time: that was how the Hams lived, with no significant thought for tomorrow – for they appeared simply to assume that tomorrow would be much like today, and like yesterday, and the day before that.

She did not abandon her shining thread of hope that someday she would get out of here – without that she would have feared for her sanity – but she tried to emulate the Hams in their focus on the now. One day at a time. It was almost comforting. She tried to accept the notion that the best prospect for *the rest of her life* might be to dwell on the fringes of a group like this: physically safe, but excluded, utterly ignored, the only representative of a different, and uninteresting species.

The future stretched out in front of her, a long dark hall empty of hope.

Until she sighted the lander.

Reid Malenfant:

Malenfant took a tentative step away from the lander. Encumbered by his escape suit, breathing canned air, he peered out of a sealed-up helmet. His heavy black boots crunched on dead leaves and sparse grass, all of it overlaid on a ruddy, dusty soil. But he could barely hear the noise of his footsteps, and could not smell the grass or the leaves.

All around this little clearing, dense forest sprouted: a darkness through which green shadows flitted. He tipped back on his heels and peered up into a tall, washed-out sky. The Earth sailed there, fat and blue, the outline of a continent dimly visible.

So here was Reid Malenfant walking on the surface of a new world: a boyhood dream, realized at last. But he sure hadn't expected it to be like this.

Maybe he was unimaginative – it was something Emma had accused him of many times – maybe he had focused too much on the battle to assemble the mission in the first place, and the thrilling details of the three-day flight across space to get here. Maybe, somehow, he had been expecting this wandering Red Moon would be content to serve as no more than a passive stage for his designs. Now, for the first time, on some deep, gut level, he realized that this was a *whole world* he was dealing with here – complex in its own right, with its own character and issues and dangers.

And his scheme to rescue Emma seemed as absurd and quixotic as many of his opponents at home had argued.

But what else could he have done but come here and try?

Nemoto was walking around the clearing experimentally, slim despite the bulky orange escape suit and the parachute pack still strapped to her back. Her gait was something like a Moonwalk, halfway between a walk and a run. 'Fascinating,' she said. 'Walking is a pendulum-like motion, an interchange between the body's gravitational potential energy and the forward kinetic energy. The body, seeking to minimize mechanical energy spent, aims for an optimal form of gait – walking or running – at any given speed. But the lower the gravity, the lower the speed at which walking breaks into running. It's all a question of scaling laws. The Froude number –'

'Give me a break, Nemoto.'

She stopped, coming to stand beside him. And, before he could stop her, she unlocked her helmet and removed it.

She grinned at him. She looked green about the gills, but then she always did. And she hadn't dropped dead yet.

Malenfant lifted his own helmet over his head. He kept his hand on the green-apple pull that would activate his suit's emergency oxygen supply. His Snoopy-hat comms unit felt heavy, incongruous in this back-to-nature environment.

He took a deep breath.

The air was thin. But he'd anticipated as much, and the altitude training he'd gone through reduced the ache in his chest to a distant nuisance. (But Emma, he remembered, had had no altitude training; this thin air must have hurt her.) The air was moist, faintly cold, what he would describe as bracing. He could smell green, growing things – the autumn smell of dead leaves, a denser green scent that came from the forest.

And he could smell ash.

Nemoto was inspecting a small portable analyser. 'No unanticipated toxins,' she said. 'Thin but breathable.' She stripped off her Snoopy hat, and started to shuck off her orange pressure suit. 'In fact,' she said, 'the air here is healthier than in most locations on Earth.'

After their three days in space cooped up in a volume no larger than the interior of a family car, Malenfant was no longer shy of Nemoto. But he felt oddly self-conscious getting naked, out here in the open, where who-knew-what eyes might be watching. But he began to unzip his suit anyhow. 'I can smell ash.'

'That is probably the Bullseye,' Nemoto said. The big volcano had been observed to erupt more or less continuously since the Red Moon's arrival in Earth orbit, perhaps induced by the tides exerted by the Earth on its new Moon. 'You should welcome the ash, Malenfant. This is a small world, with no tectonic activity. Weathering here is a one-way process, and without a restorative mechanism all the air would eventually get locked up in the rocks, with no way to recycle it.'

'Like Mars.'

'And yet not like Mars. We don't yet understand the geological and biological cycles on the Red Moon. Perhaps we never will. But the injection of gases into the air by the Bullseye surely serves to keep the atmosphere replenished. What else do you notice?'

He raised his head, sniffed, listened.

'Birdsong,' Nemoto said. 'An absence rather than a presence.'

'No birds? It ought to be easier for them to fly here, in the lower gravity.'

'But the air is less dense. Wings would have less lift than on Earth. The bird would require more muscle power, respiration . . . We may see gliders, and flightless birds. But we cannot expect the diversity we see on Earth.'

A pity, Malenfant thought.

Malenfant donned T-shirt, shorts, a thin sweater, and a bright blue coverall, and then pulled his boots back on. He was glad of the warmth of the clothes; the air here was damp and cold, though the sun's heat was sharp. Nemoto dressed the same way. They tucked their heavy Gore-Tex escape suits back into the lander, against the time when they would be needed during the return to Earth – an eventuality Malenfant was finding increasingly hard to visualize.

Malenfant settled his comms pack on his shoulder. This was a specialized piece of gear manufactured for them by technicians at the Johnson Space Center. On top of a small but powerful transceiver package sat a tiny, jewel-like camera. Antennae were built into their coveralls, and the signals were relayed by small comsats orbiting low around the Red Moon. The deal was that save for emergency the controllers would keep their mouths shut during the surface stay (which they insisted on calling an extra-vehicular activity, with, to Malenfant's mind, an absurd emphasis on the vehicle they had arrived in, as opposed to the place they had come to). But in return the ground had control of the cameras.

Soon the little camera on Malenfant's shoulder was swivelling back and forth with a minute whirring noise. 'Good grief,' he said. 'I feel like Long John Silver.'

Nemoto laughed, as she usually did when she detected one of his jokes. He wasn't sure whether she understood the reference or not.

With her own camera working, she walked across the flattened clearing. She began to load small sample bags with fast, random selections of the vegetation and the underlying crimson soil; these were contingency samples, to be lodged in the loader against the event that they had to leave here in a hurry. She found a shallow puddle, covered with a greenish scum, and she pushed the probe of her sensor pack into it. 'Water,' she said. 'Though I wouldn't recommend you drink it.'

Malenfant, his own camera peering here and there, turned to face the way the lander had come down, from the west. The route was somewhat easy to spot. The lander, suspended beneath its blue parafoil, had come bellying down out of the sky, crashing through the trees with abandon, and had left a clear trail of its glide-down in snapped trunks, crushed branches and ripped-up bits of parafoil. The trail terminated in this small clearing, where shattered tree trunks clustered close around the lander's incongruous black and white carcass.

Malenfant stalked around the lander, inspecting the damage. The whole underside was scored, crushed and gouged. Heat-resistant tiles had been plucked away and scattered through the forest, and all the aerosurfaces were scarred and crumpled.

The only good thing you could say about that landing was that it wasn't his fault.

After scouting out the Red Moon from orbit for a few days, the crew and the mission planners on the ground had settled on the largest settlement they had spotted as a suitable target for the landing. (Not that they could tell who or what had built that settlement . . .) It was close to the delta where the great continental river completed its long journey to the ocean. The plan had been to come down on a reasonably flat, open plain a few miles to the west of the Beltway, the thick belt of forest at the continent's eastern coast, close enough to that big settlement for Malenfant and Nemoto to complete their journey on foot. Later, the follow-up rocket pack would rendezvous with the lander on the ground.

That was the plan. The Red Moon hadn't proven quite so cooperative.

As soon as the lander had ducked into the thicker layers of this little world's surprising deep atmosphere, strong winds had gripped it. The mission planners had expected the unexpected; there had been no time or resources to model the Red Moon's meteorology in detail. But none of that had helped ease Malenfant's mind as he lay helpless in his bucket seat, buffeted like a toy in the hands of a careless child, watching their landing ellipse whip away beneath the lander's prow.

The lander's autonomous systems had looked actively for an alternative site suitable for a safe and controlled landing. But another gust stranded the lander over the Beltway itself. When it realized that it was running out of altitude – and that soon it would reach a line of cliffs, beyond which there was only ocean – the lander had taken a metaphorical deep breath and dumped itself in the forest.

'The trees appear to be predominantly spruce,' Nemoto said. 'The growths are tall, somewhat spindly. If we had come down in a forest more typical of Earth –'

'I know,' Malenfant growled. 'We'd have crumpled like a cardboard box. You know, that path we cut through the trees reminds me of Star City. Moscow. Yuri Gagarin's jet trainer came down into forest, and cut its way through the trees just like that. Ever since, they have cropped the trees to preserve the path. Gagarin's last walk from the sky.'

'But our landing was not so terminal,' Nemoto said dryly. 'Not yet anyhow.'

The sturdy little craft could never make another descent – but that didn't matter, for it didn't need to. The plan for the return to Earth was that Malenfant and Nemoto would fit a rocket pack to the lander's rear end, raise the assembly upright, and take off vertically. And since the lander's shell, sheltering its crew, hadn't crumpled or broken or otherwise lost its integrity, the return flight might still be possible. All Malenfant had to do to get home, then, was to find the rocket pack when it came floating down from the sky after its separate journey from Earth – completing its lunar surface rendezvous, as the mission planners had called it – fit it and launch.

Oh, and find Emma.

Malenfant turned away from the lander and walked tentatively towards the edge of the forest. The gravity was indeed eerie, and it was hard not to break into a run.

The trunks of the trees at the edge of the clearing were laden with parasites. Here a single snake-like liana wound around a trunk; here a rough-barked tree was covered by mosses and lichens; a third tree was a riot of ferns, orchids and other plants. From a bole in one aged trunk, an eye peered out at him. It was steady, unblinking, like an owl's. He backed away, cautiously.

He found a tall, palm-like tree, with dead brown fronds piled at its base. He crouched down and rummaged in the litter until he had reached crimson dirt. It was dry and sandy, evidently poor in nutrients. When he touched it to his lips, it tasted sharply of blood, or iron. He spat out the grains. The dust seemed to drift slowly to the ground.

He picked out yellow fruit from the debris of fronds. With a sideways glance at his shoulder camera, he said, 'Here's some fruit that seems to have fallen from the tree up there. You can see it is shaped like a bent cylinder. It is yellow, and its skin is smooth and soft to the touch –'

A small brown ball unrolled from the middle of the nest of fronds. Malenfant yelped, stumbling back. The ball sprouted four stubby legs and shot out into the clearing. Malenfant had glimpsed beady black eyes, a spiky hide, for all the world like a hedgehog.

Nemoto walked up to him, her camera tracking the small creature.

'The double-domes said there would be no small animals here,' he grumbled. 'Thin air, fast metabolism –'

'A pinch of observation is worth a mountain of hypothesis, Malenfant. Perhaps our small friend evolved greater lung surfaces through a novel strategy like folding, or even a fractal design. Perhaps she conserves energy by spending periods dormant, like some reptiles. We are here to learn, after all.' She grabbed the fruit. 'Your description of this banana was acute.' She peeled it briskly, exposing soft white flesh, and bit into it. 'But it is a banana. A little stringy, the taste thin, but definitely *Musa sapientum*. And, of course, the thinness of the taste might be an artefact of the body fluid redistribution we have both suffered as a result of our spaceflight.'

Malenfant took another banana, peeled it and bit into it savagely. 'You're a real smart ass, Nemoto, you know that?'

'Malenfant, all the species here should be familiar, more or less. We have the hominid samples who fell through the portals to the Earth. Although their species is uncertain, their DNA sequencing was close to yours and mine . . .'

A shadow moved through the forest behind Nemoto: black on green, utterly silent, fluid.

'Holy shit,' Malenfant said.

The shadow moved forward, resolved, stepped into the light.

It was a woman. And yet it was not.

She must have been six feet tall, as tall as Malenfant. Her eyes locked on Malenfant's, she bent, picked up the banana Nemoto had dropped, and popped it into her mouth, skin and all.

She was naked, hairless save for a dark triangle at her crotch and a tangle of tight curls on her head. She held nothing in her hands, wore no belt, carried no bag. She had the body of a nineteen-year-old tennis player, Malenfant thought, or a heptathlete: good muscles, high breasts. Perhaps her chest was a little enlarged, the ribs prominent, affording room for the larger lungs the theorists had anticipated, like an inhabitant of a 1950s dream of Mars. There was a liquid grace in her movements, a profound thoughtfulness in her stillness.

But over this wonderful body, and a small, child-like face, was the skull of a chimp. That was Malenfant's first impression anyhow. there were ridges of bone over the eyes, a forehead that sloped sharply back. Not a chimp, no, but not human either.

Her eyes were blue and human.

'*Homo erectus*,' Nemoto was muttering nervously. 'Or *H. ergaster*. Or some other species we never discovered. Or something unrelated to any hominid that ever evolved on Earth . . . And even if descended from some archaic stock, this is not a true *Erectus*, of course, but a descendant of that lineage shaped by hundreds of thousands of years of evolution – just as a chimp is not like our common ancestor, but a fully evolved species in its own right.'

'You talk too much, Nemoto.'

'Yes . . . We have seen the reconstructions, inspected the bodies ejected from the Wheel. But to confront her alive, *moving*, is eerie.'

The hominid girl studied Malenfant with the direct, uncomplicated gaze of a child, without calculation or fear.

He stepped forward. He could *smell* the girl: unwashed, not like an animal, an intense locker-room smell. He felt a deep charge, pulling him to her. At first he thought it was an erotic attraction – and that was present too; the combination of that clear animal gaze and the beautiful, fully human body was undeniably compelling, even if he sensed those stringy arms could break his back if she chose. But what he felt was deeper than that. It was a kind of recognition, he thought.

'I know you,' he said.

The girl stared back at him.

Nemoto fidgeted behind him. 'Malenfant, we were given protocols for encounters like this.'

He murmured, 'I should offer her a candy and show her a picture card?' He returned his attention to the girl. '*I know you*,' he repeated.

I know who you are. We evolved together. Once my grandmother and yours ran around the echoing plains of Africa, side by side.

This is a first contact, it struck him suddenly: a first contact between humanity and an alien intelligent species – for the intelligence in those eyes could not be denied, despite the absence of tools and clothing.

. . . Or rather, this is a contact renewed. How strange to think that buried deep in man's past was a *last* contact, a last time we met one of these cousins of ours: perhaps a final encounter between one of my own ancestors and a girl like this in the plains of Asia, or a dying Neandertal on the fringe of the Atlantic, when we left them no place else to go.

The girl held her hands out, palms up. 'Banana,' she said, thickly, clearly.

Malenfant's jaw dropped. 'Holy shit.'

'English,' Nemoto breathed. 'She speaks English.'

'En'lish,' the girl said.

Now Malenfant's heart hammered. 'That must mean Emma is here. She is near, and she survived.'

Nemoto said cautiously, 'We know very little, Malenfant; there is a whole world around us, a world of secrets.'

There was a crackle behind Malenfant: a twig breaking, a footfall. He whirled.

There were more of the ape-people, eight or ten of them, male and female, all adults. They were as naked as the girl, though not all as handsome; some of them sported scars, gashes and even burns, and some had hair streaked with grey. They were standing in a line, neatly fencing off Malenfant and Nemoto from the lander, and they were all gazing hard at the two of them.

'These do not seem quite so friendly,' Nemoto murmured.

'Oh, really? You think now's a good time to start the sign-language classes?'

'Malenfant, where are the guns?'

'. . . In the lander.' *Shit.*

The silence stretched. The ape-people stood like statues.

'I am loath to abandon the lander,' Nemoto hissed. 'We have not even packed the contingency samples.'

Malenfant suppressed a foolish laugh. 'There go our science bonuses.'

One of the ape-people stepped forward. Straggles of beard clung to his chin, though the longer strands seemed to have been cut, crudely. He opened his mouth and hissed. Malenfant thought his teeth were stained red.

Nemoto said, 'Malenfant, I think –'

'Yeah. I think he's about to take a sample of *us*.'

The big man raised his arm. Too late, Malenfant saw he was holding a stone in his fist. Malenfant ducked sideways. The stone missed his head, but it sliced through the layers of cloth over his shoulder, and nicked the flesh.

'Plan B,' he gasped.

The two of them broke and ran for the forest. They pushed past the girl, who made a half-hearted effort to grab them. For a heartbeat Malenfant nursed a hope that he had made some connection, that she had on some level decided to let them go.

But then he was plunging into the green mouth of the forest after Nemoto, and there was no time for reflection.

The forest, away from the sunlight, was suffused by a clinging cloudy moistness that seemed to linger around every bush, and made every tree trunk slippery under Malenfant's palms. Soon they were both shivering.

And it was almost impossible to walk. Malenfant had done a little jungle survival training during his induction into the Shuttle programme. But this forest was almost impassable, so deeply layered were the tangled roots, branches, leaves and moss over the uneven ground. Malenfant was acutely aware that this was not a place for humans.

Still they blundered on, slipping, crashing, blundering, falling, making a noise that must have echoed off the flanks of the Bullseye itself.

He imagined the frantic activity in the back rooms of Mission Control in Houston, the buzzing calls to palaeontologists and anthropologists and evolutionary psychologists. For once in his life he would have been glad to hear the tinny voices from the ground. But, though there was a hiss of static from the tiny speaker built into his shoulder pack, he could make out no voices.

Once he thought he confronted one of the ape-people. He caught a glimpse of someone – some *thing* – in the dense green gloom ahead of him, upright like an ape-person, but smaller, chimp-sized, maybe hairy. It jabbered at him, reached up its long arms, and slipped out of sight into the forest canopy above.

After that, Malenfant found himself looking for possible threats upwards as well as side to side.

At length, breathing hard in the thin air, shivering, they came to a halt, crouching close to the ground by a fat, fungus-laden tree trunk. Malenfant's face was slick with sweat and forest dew.

Nemoto's eyes were wide in the gloom, glancing this way and that, like a cornered animal.

'We haven't been too smart, have we?' he whispered.

'We were not expecting to come under immediate attack by a troupe of *Homo erectus*.'

'Yeah, but it's taken us a bare half-hour after opening the hatch to lose the lander, our supplies, and our weapons. I'm not even sure which way we're running.'

'We will recover the lander.'

'How do you know?'

'Because we must,' Nemoto said simply.

A shadow slid across his field of view. It was subtle, difficult to distinguish from the swaying motion of a branch, the shifting coins of dappled sunlight that lay over the forest floor.

The camera on his shoulder swivelled to look into his face, and he forced a grin. 'If you guys have any suggestions, now would be a good time . . .'

Eight, nine, ten shadows moved, all around them, shadows that coalesced into ape-people.

'The *Erectus*. They have been hunting us,' Nemoto said. 'Their intelligence is advanced enough for that, at least.' She seemed calm, beyond fear.

The ape-people advanced. Some of them were grinning, and one of the men, perhaps excited by the prospect of a kill, sported an impressive erection.

Malenfant stood up slowly. The camera on his shoulder swivelled back and forth, whirring, somehow the most distracting object in his universe. He said, 'I think –'

A vast, heavy creature came running out of the depths of the wood. It hurled itself at the largest ape-man. They rolled on the floor, wrestling.

The ape-men gathered around the combatants, hooting and hollering, their teeth showing between drawn-back lips – perhaps a rictus of fear – and they slapped ineffectually at the rolling figures.

Nemoto clutched Malenfant's arm, and they backed away.

Nemoto said, 'I thought it was a bear.'

'No,' Malenfant said grimly.

No, not a bear: a *man* – yet another sort of man, shorter than his naked opponent, but much more heavily muscled, and dressed in animal skins that were tied to his body with bits of red-black rope. Though the ape-man on the ground was a formidable opponent – surely more than a match for any human in hand-to-hand combat – the bear-man was stronger yet, and soon he had the ape-man pinned to the ground by sitting on his chest.

The bear-man snarled, 'Enough?'

Once again the use of English, distorted but clear enough, startled Malenfant. Was it really credible that Emma could have taught the use of English to not one but *two* species of other-men? But if not, what was going on?

The man on the ground snapped at the hand that slapped him, but it was clear that the fight had gone out of him. The bear-man sat back and let him up.

The ape-man rejoined his companions and, his defiance momentarily sparking, he growled at the bear-man. 'Ham! Eat Ham good eat!'

The bear-man – the 'Ham' – opened his huge mouth wide, exposing a row of flat brown teeth. He ran at the ape-people, making them scatter, and with a broad, bare foot he aimed a heavy kick at the naked rump of the last man.

Then the bear-man walked up to Malenfant and Nemoto. He was a good head shorter than Malenfant – no more than five five, five six – but he was broad as a barn door. Under the skins which wrapped him loosely, Malenfant could see muscles moving. His walk was somewhat ungainly, as if his legs were bowed, or his balance not quite perfect. His skull was long and flat, with a bulge at the back that showed beneath a sprawl of thick black hair. He had a vast cavernous nose, and brown eyes glinted beneath bony brows like two caves. Sweat had pooled in a hollow between the brow ridges and his low forehead.

'Neandertal,' Nemoto muttered. 'Or possibly *Homo heidelbergensis*. Most probably *Neandertalensis*, of the so-called classic variant. Or rather a lineage evolved from Neandertal stock, in this unique place.'

Malenfant could smell beer on the Neandertal's breath. 'Holy shit,' he said. *Beer?*

The Neandertal – or bear-man, or Ham – grinned at them. 'Stupi' Runners,' he said. 'Scare easy.' He stuck his tongue out and lunged forward. *'Boo!'*

Both Malenfant and Nemoto took a step back. The bear-man's voice was gravelly and thick, and his vowel sounds slurred one into the other. 'But,' Malenfant said, 'he speaks better than I do after a couple of hours at the Outpost.'

Now there was a crashing from the forest that resolved itself into clumsy, unconcealed footsteps. A new voice called, 'What the devil is going on, Thomas?'

Malenfant frowned, trying to place the accent. English, of course – a British accent, maybe – but twisted in a way he didn't recognize.

The bear-man called, 'Here, Baas. Runners. Chase off.'

A man walked out of the shadows towards them – a human this time, a stocky man, white, aged maybe fifty, with a grubby walrus moustache. He was dressed in a buckskin suit, and he had a kind of crossbow over his shoulder. What looked like a long-legged rabbit hung from his belt.

When he saw Malenfant and Nemoto, he stopped dead, mouth a perfect circle.

Malenfant spread his hands wide. 'We're from America. NASA.'

The man frowned. 'From where? . . . *Have you come to rescue us?*' Malenfant saw hope spark in his eyes, sudden, intense. He walked towards Malenfant, hand extended. 'McCann. Hugh McCann. Oh, it has been so long in this place! Are you here to take us home?'

Malenfant felt a light touch on his shoulder, a soft crunch. When he looked, the camera he had worn there had gone, disappeared into the paw of the Neandertal.

Emma Stoney:

The spaceship had been quite unmistakable as it drifted out of the sky, heading east, Shuttle-orbiter black and white under a glowing blue and white canopy. Her eyes weren't what they used to be, but she'd swear she made out the round blue NASA meatball logo on its flank.

Malenfant. Who else?

She knew immediately she had to follow it. She couldn't stay with the Ham troupe any more. She couldn't rely on whoever had drifted down from the sky to come find her. Her destiny had been in her own hands since the moment she had fallen out of the sky of Earth into this strange place, and it was no different now. She had to get herself to that lander.

She gathered up her gear. She equipped herself with stone tools and spears from the Ham encampment – without guilt, for the Hams seemed to make most of their tools as they needed them and then abandoned them. With her hat of woven grasses and her poncho of animal skin, all draped over the remnants of her air force coverall, she must look like the wild woman of the woods, she thought.

She attempted to say goodbye to the Ham who had first found her, and to some of the others she had gotten to know. But she was met with only blankness or bafflement.

After all, since nobody ever went anywhere, nobody said *goodbye* in a Ham community – except maybe at death.

She slipped into the forest.

Shadow:

Thanks to extended pulses of volcanism, this small world was steadily warming, and temperate forests were shrinking back in favour of more open grasslands. The range of Shadow's family group was only a little smaller than the remnant of forest to which they clung; with invisible, unconscious skill, Shadow's elders had always guided her away from the exposed fringes of the forest.

But now her people had turned on Shadow. And to escape them she would have to leave her forest home.

Emerging from the trees, she found herself at the foot of a shallow forest-covered slope, a foothill of taller mountains which reared up behind her. She faced a wide plain, a range of open, park-like savannah, grasslands punctuated by stands of trees. To the right of the plain a broad river ran, sluggish and brown. Away to the left a range of more rocky hills rose, their lower slopes coated with a thick carpet of forest. The hills marched away in a subtly curving ring; they were the rim mountains of a small crater.

She longed to slink back into the dark cool womb of the woods behind her.

She looked again at that smudge of green covering the crater wall. *Forest*: the only other patch of it in her vision. She thought of food and water, nests high in the trees.

She took a step out into the open.

The sun's heat was like a warm hand on her scalp. She saw her shadow at her feet, shrunken by the height of the sun. The forest behind her tugged at her heart like the call of her mother. But she did not turn back.

She ran forward, alone, her footsteps singing in the grass.

She was soon hot, panting, dreadfully thirsty. Her thick fur trapped the heat of the sun. Her feet ached as they pounded the ground. Her arms dangled uselessly at her side; she longed to grasp, to climb. But there was nothing here to climb. She ran on, clumsy, determined, over ground that shone red through sparse yellow grass.

But as she ran she turned this way and that, fearing predators. A cat or a hyena would have little difficulty outrunning her, and still less in bringing her down. And she watched those remote woods. To her dismay they seemed to come no closer, no matter how hard she ran.

She came to a clear, shallow stream.

Unbearably thirsty, panting, she waded straight into the water. The stream was deliciously cool. The bed was of cobbles, laced with green growing things that streamed in the water. At its deepest the stream came up a little way beyond her knees.

She slid forward until she was on all fours. She rolled on her back, letting the water soak into her fur. She raised handfuls of water to her mouth. The water, leaking from her fingers, had a greenish tinge, and it was a little sour, but it was cold. She drank deeply, letting the water wash away the dust in her mouth and nose. She saw a thin trail of dust and blood seeping away from her.

A thin mucus clung to her wet hand. She saw that it contained tiny, almost transparent shrimps. She scraped the shrimps off her palm and popped them in her mouth. Their taste was sharp and creamy and delicious.

She stood up. With her gravid belly stroking the surface of the stream, she put her hands in the water, open like a scoop. She watched carefully as the water trickled through her fingers, and when the little crustaceans struck her palm she closed her hands around them.

Her thoughts dissolved, becoming pink and blue, like the sky, like the shrimp.

When she had had her fill of shrimp she clambered out of the stream, her fur dripping. She reclined on the bank. She folded her legs and inspected her feet. They were bruised and cut, and a big blister had swollen up on one toe. She washed her feet clean of the last of the grit between her toes, and then inspected the blister curiously; when she poked it with a fingernail the clear liquid in it moved around, accompanied by a sharp pain.

She heard a distant growl.

Startled, she tucked her feet underneath her, resting her knuckles on the ground. She peered around at the open plain.

The shadows, of rocks and isolated trees, had grown long. She had forgotten where she was: while she had played in the water, the day had worn away. She mewled and wrapped her long arms around her torso. She did not want to return to the running. But every instinct in her screamed that she must get off the ground before night fell.

She climbed out of the stream and began running towards the crater rim hills.

The light faded, terribly rapidly. Her shadow stretched out before her, and then dissolved into greyness.

Her face began to itch, as if some insect was working its way into her skin. She scratched her cheeks and brow. She looked for someone to groom her. But there was nobody here, and the itch wouldn't go away.

Still she ran, thirsty, dusty, exhausted.

And still those growls came, echoing across the savannah: the voices of predators calling to each other, marking out the territory they claimed.

*   *   *

It grew darker. The earth climbed in the sky. The land became drenched in a silvery blueness.

There was a growl, right in front of her. She glimpsed yellow eyes, like two miniature suns.

She screamed. She picked up handfuls of dirt and threw them at the yellow eyes. There was a howl.

She turned and ran, not caring where she went. But her gait was waddling and stiff, her feet broken and sore.

She could hear steady, purposeful footsteps behind her.

Memories clattered through her mind: of a bite that had crushed the skull of a child in a moment, of the remains of a predator's feast, bloody limbs and carcass, of the screams of a victim taken live to a nest, where cubs had fed long into the night. She screamed and ran and ran.

There was light ahead of her.

She ran towards the light, panting and hooting. She thought of daybreak in a safe tree top, her nest warm under her, her mother's massive body close by.

The light was yellow, and it flickered, and shadows moved before it. A fire.

She heard those scampering footsteps. There was a hot, panting breath on her neck.

A stone zinged through the air, past her head. It clattered against a rock, harmlessly. Now another stone flew. It caught her in the chest, knocking her flat on her back.

Behind her, the chasing cat yelped and yowled. When she sat up and turned, she saw its lithe silhouette sliding across the blue, glittering grass.

'Elf Elf away.'

She yelled and scrabbled in the dirt.

She found herself looking up at a tall figure – a woman, perhaps twice as tall as she was, taller even than Big Boss had been, her torso long and ugly. She had small flat breasts. She was hairless, save for knots of hair on her head and between her legs. She had a small face and wide nose, and she carried a stick that she was pointing at Shadow.

She was a Runner.

Cautiously Shadow got to her feet. She jabbered at the woman, a series of intense pants, hoots, screeches and cries. She expected the woman to respond. They would chatter together, sounds without words, their cries slowly matching in pitch and intensity as they greeted each other.

But the woman jabbed with the stick, coming close to piercing Shadow's skin. 'Elf Elf away!'

Shadow feared the stick. But before her was the yellow fire. She could hear the fire pop and crackle, and she could smell food, the sharpness of leaves and burned meat. Many people were there – all tall and skinny and hairless like this stretched-out woman, but people nevertheless. Behind her there was only the darkness of the savannah, like a vast black mouth waiting to swallow her.

She took a pace towards the woman, hands outstretched. She tried to groom her, reaching for the hair on the woman's head.

The sharp stick jabbed in her shoulder. Again Shadow was thrown back into the dirt. She poked a finger in her latest wound; blood seeped slowly from it, soaking her fur. She whimpered in misery. The sharp noses of the cats would soon detect the blood.

Still the woman stood over her, arms akimbo, stick poised for another thrust.

Shadow tried to stand. A searing pain clamped around her stomach, making her stumble to the crimson dirt. She cried out, and beat her fists on her betraying belly. She looked up at the threatening, curious woman. She whimpered. She held out her feet, and flexed her toes. Helpless, she was reduced to the gestures of an infant.

The woman lowered the stick. She crouched down. Clear eyes looked into Shadow's. She reached out with her hand and stroked Shadow's fur. She touched the wounded shoulder, and the hand came away bloody; the woman wiped it in the dirt at her feet. Then she ran a curious hand over the bump in Shadow's belly.

Again Shadow reached for the woman's scalp and crotch to groom her. But the woman flinched back.

Shadow dropped her head, her energy exhausted. She lay in the dirt, on her back, her arms and legs splayed; Shadow was beaten.

The woman stared at her a while longer. Then she walked away, towards the fire.

Shadow curled over on her side.

Something hit her chest. She flinched back.

It was a piece of meat. It lay on the ground before her. She saw it had been cut from an animal – perhaps an antelope – by a sharp-edged stone. And people had bitten into it already; she saw where it had been ripped and torn by teeth. But still it was meat, a piece as big as her hand. She crammed it into her mouth, tearing at it with hands and teeth.

When she was done she lay down once more. The ground was hard and dusty, and she longed for the springy platform of a nest. But her arm made a pillow for her head.

Suspended between black night and the flickering fire light, she sank into redness.

Reid Malenfant:

On the walk through the forest with McCann, this oddball English guy, Malenfant got fixated on McCann's crossbow.

The crossbow, made purely of wood, was heavy. There was a long underslung trigger that neatly lifted a bowstring out of the notch. The trigger mechanism worked smoothly. The string itself was made of twisted vine, very fine, very strong. But there was no groove to direct the bolt. And the bolts themselves seemed crude to Malenfant: about as long as a pencil, but a lot thinner, and with a flight made from a single leaf, tucked into a slice in the wooden bolt, just one plane. It was hard to see how you could make an accurate shot with such a thing. But as they walked McCann did just that, over and over, apparently pleased to have an audience.

Nemoto's silent contempt for all this was obvious. Malenfant didn't care. His mind was tired of all the strangeness; to play with a gadget for a while was therapy.

It was getting dark by the time the Englishman led them to a fortress in the jungle. The two of them, bruised and bewildered, were led into the compound, taking in little. Surrounded by a tough-looking stockade, it turned out to be a place of straight lines and right angles, the huts lined up like ranks of soldiers, the line of the stockade walls as perfect as a geometrical demonstration.

'Shit,' murmured Malenfant. 'I can feel my anus clench just standing here.'

Nemoto said, 'They are very frightened, Malenfant. That much is clear.'

Malenfant glimpsed people moving to and fro in the gathering dark. No, not quite people. He shuddered.

McCann showed them hospitality, including food and generous draughts of some home-brew beer, thick and strong.

The hours passed in a blur.

*   *   *

He found himself in a sod hut, with Nemoto. His bed was a boxy frame containing a mattress of some vegetable fabric. It didn't look too clean.

They were both fried. They hadn't slept in around thirty-six hours. They had been through the landing, the assault by the *Erectus* types, the march through the jungle. And, frankly, the beer hadn't helped. At least here, against all expectations, they had found what seemed like a haven. But still Malenfant inspected his lumpy bed suspiciously.

'I know what to do,' Malenfant said. 'Always turn your mattress. Then the body lice have to work their way back up to get to you.' He lifted the corner of his mattress out of its wooden box.

'I would not do that,' Nemoto said; but it was too late.

There was the sound of fingernails on wood, a smell like a poultry shed. Cockroaches poured out of the box, a steady stream of them, each the size of a mouse.

'Shit,' Malenfant said. 'There are thousands in there.' He stamped on one, briskly killing it.

'It's best to leave them,' Nemoto said evenly. 'They have glands on their backs. They only stink when disturbed.'

Malenfant cautiously picked up a cockroach. Its antenna and palps hung limp, and it had a pale pink band over its head and thorax.

'Very ancient creatures, Malenfant,' Nemoto said. 'You find traces of them in Carboniferous strata, three hundred million years deep.'

'Doesn't mean I want to share my bed with one,' Malenfant said. Carefully, as if handling a piece of jewellery, he set the cockroach on the floor. It scuttled out of sight under his bed frame.

Malenfant finally lowered his head to the pillow.

'Just think,' Nemoto said from the darkness. 'When you sleep with that pillow, you sleep with all the people who used it before.'

Malenfant thought about that for a while. Then he dumped the pillow on the floor, rolled up his coverall, and stuck that under his head.

Later than night Malenfant was disturbed by a howl, like a lost child. Peering out, he spotted a small creature high in a palm tree, about the size of a squirrel.

'A hyrax,' Nemoto murmured. 'Close to the common ancestor of elephants, hippos, rhinos, tapirs and horses.'

'Another ancient critter, crying in the night. I feel like I've been lost in this jungle since God was a boy.'

'I suspect we are very far from God. Try to get some sleep, Malenfant.'

Shadow:

Pain stabbed savagely in her lower belly. It awoke her from a crimson dream of teeth and claws. She sat up screaming.

There was no cat. In the grey-pink light of dawn, she was sitting in the dirt. She was immediately startled to find herself on the ground, and not high in a tree.

Before her she could see skinny people walking around, pissing, children tumbling sleepily. Some of them turned to stare at her with their oddly flat faces.

But now more pain came, great waves of it that tore at her as if her whole body was clenched in some huge mouth.

Something gushed from between her legs. She looked down, parting her fur. She saw bloody water, seeping into the ground. She screamed again.

She scrabbled at the ground, seeking to find a tree, her mother, seeking to get away from this dreadful, wrenching agony. But the pain came with her. Her belly flexed and convulsed, like huge stones moving around inside her, and she fell back once more.

Now there was a face over hers: smooth and flat, shadowed against the pinkish sky. Strong hands pressed at her shoulders, pushing her back against the dirt. She lashed out, trying to scratch this creature who was attacking her. But she was feeble, and her blows were easily brushed aside. She could feel more hands on her ankles, prising her legs apart, and she thought of Claw, and screamed again. But the pressure, though gentle, was insistent, and kick as she might she could not free herself of these grasping, controlling hands.

Now the pain pulsed again, a red surge that overwhelmed her.

No more than half-conscious, she barely glimpsed what followed: the strong, skilful hands of the Runner women as they levered the baby from its birth canal, fingers clearing a plug of mucus from its mouth, the brisk slicing of the umbilical with a stone axe. All that Shadow perceived was the pain, the way it washed over her over and over, receding at last as the baby was taken from her – to be followed by a final agonizing pulse as the afterbirth emerged.

When it was done, Shadow struggled to prop herself up on her elbows. Her hair was matted with dust and blood. The ground between her legs was a mess of blood and mucus, drying in the gathering sunlight.

There were women around her, tall like tree trunks, their shadows long.

One of them – older, with silvery hair – was holding the afterbirth, which steamed gently. The old woman nibbled at it cautiously, and then, with a glance at Shadow, she ran away towards the smoking fire with her stolen treat.

The other women stared at Shadow's face. Their small, protruding noses wrinkled. Now that the greater pain was ebbing, Shadow became aware of an itching that had spread across her cheeks and forehead and nose; she scratched it absently.

A woman stood before her. She held the baby, her long fingers clamped around its waist. It had large pink ears, small, pursed lips, and wrinkled, bluish-black skin. Its head was swollen, like a pepper. It – he – opened his mouth and wailed.

He smelled strange.

The skinny woman thrust the baby at Shadow, letting him drop on her belly. Feebly the baby grasped at her fur, mouth opening and closing with a pop.

With hesitant hands, Shadow picked him up around the waist. He wriggled feebly. She turned him around so his face was towards her, and pressed his face against her chest. Soon his mouth had found her nipple, and she felt a warm white gush course through her body.

But the baby smelled wrong. She could hardly bear even to hold him.

The Running-folk let her stay the rest of the day, and through the night. But they gave her no more food. And when dawn came, they drove her away with stones and yells.

Her baby clamped to her chest, its big awkward head dangling, Shadow walked unsteadily across the savannah, towards the wooded crater wall.

Reid Malenfant:

Malenfant woke to the scent of bacon.

He surfaced slowly. The smell took him back to Emma and the home they had made in Clear Lake, Houston, and even deeper back than that, to his parents, the sunlit mornings of his childhood.

But he wasn't at home, in Clear Lake or anywhere else.

When he opened his eyes he found walls of smoothed-over turf all around him, a roof of crudely cut planking, the whole covered in a patina of smoke and age. Light streamed in through unglazed windows, just holes cut in the sod covered by animal skin scraped thin. Under the smell of the bacon he could detect the cool green earthy scent of forest.

The day felt hot already. Thin air, Malenfant: hot days, cold nights, like living at altitude.

Nemoto's pallet was empty.

When he tried to sit up, pushing back the blankets of crudely woven fibre, his shoulder twinged sharply: injured, he was reminded, where a *Homo erectus* had thrown a stone at him, prior to trying to eat him.

He swung his legs out of bed. He was in his underwear, including his socks, and his boots were set neatly behind the hut's small door. He could feel the ache of a faint hangover, and his mouth felt leathery. He remembered the beer he had consumed the night before, a rough, chewy ferment of some local vegetation, sluiced down from wooden cups.

The door opened, creaking on rope hinges. A woman walked in.

Malenfant snatched back the blankets, covering himself.

She was short, squat, dressed in a blouse and skirt dyed a bright, almost comical yellow. Her face protruded beneath a heavy brow, but her hair was tied back neatly and adorned with flowers.

She looked like a pro wrestler in drag. She curtsied neatly.

She was carrying Malenfant's coverall, which had been cleaned and patched at the shoulder. She put the coverall on his bed, and crossed to a small dresser, evidently home-made. There was a wooden bowl of dried flowers on top of the dresser. She scooped out the flowers and replaced them with a handful of pressed yellow blooms – marigolds, perhaps – that she drew from a pouch in her skirt. Her feet were bare, he saw, great spade-shaped toes protruding from under the skirt.

She curtsied again. 'Breakfas', Baas,' she said, her voice a gruff rasp. She had not once met his eyes. She turned to go out the door.

'Wait,' he said.

She stopped. He thought he saw apprehension in her stance, though she must have been twice his weight, and certainly had nothing to fear from him.

'What's your name?'

'Julia.' It was difficult for her to make the 'J' sound; it came out as a harsh squirt. *Choo-li-a.*

'Thanks for looking after me.'

She curtsied once again and walked stolidly out of the room, her big feet padding on the wooden floor.

The settlement consisted of a dozen huts, of cut sod or stacked logs, with roofs of thick green blankets of turf. The huts were a uniform size and laid out like a miniature suburban street. The central roadway was crimson dust beaten flat by the passage of many feet, and lined with heavy rocks. Around each of the huts a small area was cordoned off by more lines of rocks. Some of the rocks were painted white. In the 'gardens' plants grew, vegetables and flowers, in orderly rows.

Crude-looking carts were parked in the shadow of one wall, and other bits of equipment – what looked like spades, hoes, crossbows – were stacked in neat piles under bits of treated skin. There was even a neat, orderly latrine system: trenches topped by little cubicles and wooden seats.

The effect was oddly formal, like a barracks, a small piece of a peculiarly ordered civilization carved out of the jungle, which proliferated beyond the tall stockade that surrounded the huts. Last night McCann had been apologetic about the settlement's crudity, but with its vegetable-fibre clothing and carts and tools of wood and stone, it struck Malenfant as a remarkable effort by a group of stranded survivors to carve out of this unpromising jungle something of the civilization they had left behind.

But the huts' sod walls were eroded and heavily patched by mud. And several of the huts appeared abandoned, their walls in disrepair, their tiny gardens desiccated back to crimson dust.

There was nobody about – no humans, anyhow.

A man dressed in skins crossed the compound's little street, barefoot, passing from one hut to another. He was broad, stocky, like Julia. A Neandertal, perhaps.

In one corner of the compound two men worked at a pile of rocks, steadily smashing them one against the other, as if trying to reduce them to gravel. The men were naked, powerful. Malenfant could immediately see they were the *Homo erectus* types. They were restrained by heavy ropes on their ankles, and they didn't seem aware of his presence. The display of their strength, unaccompanied by the control of minds, disturbed him.

But he could still smell bacon. Comparative anthropology could wait.

He followed his nose to a hut at the centre of the compound. Within, a table had been set with wooden plates and cups and cutlery, and in a small kitchen area another Neandertal-type woman, older then Julia, was frying bacon on slabs of rock heated by a fire. In the circumstances, it seemed incredibly domesticated.

Nemoto was sitting at the table, chewing her way steadily through a slab of meat. She looked at him as he entered, and raised an eyebrow.

'. . . Malenfant. Good morning.'

Malenfant turned at the voice, and his hand was grasped firmly.

Hugh McCann was wearing a suit, Malenfant was startled to see, with a collared shirt and even a tie. But the suit and shirt were threadbare, and Malenfant saw how McCann's belt dug into his belly.

McCann saw him looking. He said ruefully, 'I never was much of a hand with the needle. And our bar-bar friends make fine cooks, but they don't have much instinct for tailoring, I fear.'

Malenfant was fuddled by the scent of the food. 'Bar-bars?'

'For *barbarians*,' Nemoto said, her mouth full. 'The Neandertals.'

'They call themselves Hams,' McCann said. 'A Biblical reference, of course. But bar-bars they were to me as a boy, and bar-bars they will always remain, I fear.' His accent was clearly British, but of a peculiarly strangulated type Malenfant hadn't encountered outside of World War II movies. And he gave Malenfant's name a strong French pronunciation. He took Malenfant's elbow and guided him towards the kitchen area. 'What can we offer you? The bacon comes from the local breed of hog, and is fairly authentic, but the bird who laid those eggs was no barnyard chicken: rather some dreadful

flightless thing like a bush turkey. Still, the eggs are pretty tasty.'
He flashed a smile at the Ham cook, showing decayed teeth.

First things first. Malenfant grabbed a plate and began to ladle
it full of food. The wooden utensils were crude, but easy to use.
He took his plate to the table, and sat with Nemoto, who was still
eating silently. Malenfant sliced into his bacon. The well-cooked
meat fell apart easily.

After a moment McCann joined them. 'I expect last night is all a
bit of a blur. You did rather go on a bust, Malenfant.'

'Body fluid redistribution,' Nemoto said dryly. 'Low oxygen content. You just could not take it, Malenfant.'

'I'll know better next time.'

'Runners,' Nemoto said.

'What?'

'The *Erectus/Ergaster* breed. Mr McCann calls them Runners –
Running Men, Running-folk.'

'Quite a danger in the wild,' McCann said around a mouthful of
bacon. 'That scrog of wood where we found you was hotching with
them. But once broken they are harmless enough. And useful. A
body strong enough for labour, hands deft enough to handle tools,
and yet without the will or wit to oppose a man's commands – if
backed up by a light touch of the *sjambok* from time to time . . .'

Nemoto leaned forward. 'Mr McCann. You said that when you
were a boy you called the Neandertals – that is, the Hams – bar-bars.
So were there Hams in, umm, in the world you came from?'

McCann dug a fork into his scrambled egg, considering the question. He seemed more comfortable talking to Malenfant than to
Nemoto, and he directed his remarks to him. 'Look here,' he said.
'I don't know who you are or where you're from, not yet. But I'm
going to be honest with you from the start. I don't mind telling
you that yours are the first white faces we've seen since we've
come here. Aside from those dreadful Zealot types, of course, but
they're no help to us, and beyond the pale anyhow . . . Yes,' he said.
'Yes, there are Hams where I come from. There. That's a straight
answer to a straight question, and I trust you'll treat me with the
same courtesy.'

'Where?' Nemoto pressed. 'Where are your Hams? In Europe,
Asia –'

'Yes. Well, they are now. But not by origin, of course. The Hams
came originally from the New World.'

Nemoto asked, 'America?'

McCann frowned. 'I don't know that name.'

Malenfant eyed Nemoto. 'What are you thinking?'

'An alternate Earth,' Nemoto said simply.

Yes, he thought. McCann had come from an Earth, a different Earth, a world where Neandertals had survived to the present – a world where pre-European America had been in the occupation, not of a branch of *Homo sapiens*, but of another species of humankind altogether, a different flesh . . . What an adventure that must have been, Malenfant thought, for a different Columbus.

Nemoto said softly, 'I think we may be dealing with a whole sheaf of worlds here, Malenfant. And all linked by this peculiar wandering Red Moon.'

McCann was listening intently. Malenfant saw how deeply cut were the lines in his face; he might have been fifty, but he looked older, careworn, intense, lit by a kind of desperation. He said, 'You believe we come from different worlds.'

'Different versions of Earth,' Nemoto said.

He nodded. 'And in this Earth of yours, there are no Hams?'

'No,' Nemoto said steadily.

'Well, we have no Runners. The Runners may be native to this place, perhaps.' He eyed them sharply. 'And what about the others, the Elf-folk and the Nutcrackers . . .'

Malenfant said, 'If you mean other breeds of hominids, or pre-hominids – no. Nothing between us and the chimps. The chimpanzees.'

McCann's eyes opened wider. 'How remarkable. How – lonely.'

The Neandertal woman, with a bulky grace, came to the table and began to gather up their dishes.

They walked around the compound.

There was very little metal here: a few knives, bowls, shears. These tools, it seemed, had been cut from the wreck of the ship that had brought McCann and his colleagues here: like Nemoto and Malenfant, the English had got here under their own power. So the tools were irreplaceable and priceless – and they were a target for steady theft, by Hams within and without the compound. McCann said the Hams did not use the tools; they seemed to destroy them or bury them, removing this trace of novelty from the world.

There were many Hams, working as servants. And there appeared to be several of the so-called Runners, kept under control at all times, apparently domiciled outside the main stockade. He tried to put aside judgement. He was not the one who had battled to survive here for so long; and it was evident that this McCann and his companions came from a very different world from his.

And besides, McCann appeared to believe that he treated 'his' hominids well.

They met one other of the English, a bloated-looking red-faced man with a Santa Claus beard and an immense pot belly that protruded from the grimy, much-patched remnant of a shirt. He was riding in a cart drawn by two of the Runners, harnessed with strips of leather like pack animals. Santa Claus glared at Malenfant and Nemoto as he passed them, and then went riding out of the stockade through gates smoothly pulled back by Hams.

'There goes Crawford in his Cape cart,' whispered McCann conspiratorially. 'Something of an oddball, between you and me. Well, we all are, I suppose, after all this time. I fear he's too much set in his ways to deal with you. Of course if he suspected you were French he'd shoot you where you stand! . . . Martyr to his lumbago, poor chap. And I fear he may have a touch of the black-water.'

McCann talked quickly and fluently, as if he had been too long alone.

There had been twelve of them, it seemed – all men, all British, from an Empire that had thrived longer than in Malenfant's world. Their rocket ship had been driven by something called a Darwin engine.

McCann struggled to describe the history of his world, his nation. After bombarding them with a lot of detail, names of wars and kings and generals and politicians that meant nothing to Malenfant, he settled on a blunt summary.

'We are engaged in a sort of global war,' McCann said. 'That's been the shape of it for a couple of centuries now. Our forefathers struck out for new lands, in Asia and Africa and Australia – even the New World – as much out of rivalry as for expectations of gain.'

But the ultimate 'new land' had always hovered in the sky. Before the Red Moon had appeared in McCann's sky, a Moon had sailed there – not tiny Luna, but a much fatter world, a world of water-carved canyons and aquifers and dust storms, a world that sounded oddly like Mars. Drawn by that Moon, the great nations of this other Earth had launched themselves into a space race as soon as the technology was available, decades before Malenfant's history had caught up.

Malenfant, battered by strangeness, found room for a twinge of nostalgia. He'd have exchanged McCann's fat Moon for Luna any time. If only a world like Mars had been found to orbit the Earth, instead of poor desiccated Luna – a world with ice and air, just waiting for an explorer's tread! With such a world as a lure, just three days away from Earth, how different history might have been. And how differently his own life, and Emma's, might have turned out.

'The lure of the Moon was everything, of course,' McCann said. 'From times before memory it has floated in the sky, fat and round and huge, with storms and ice caps and even, perhaps, traces of vegetation, visible with the naked eye. You could see it was another world in the sky, waiting for the tread of man, for the flag of empire, the ploughs of farmers . . . It was quite a chase. Got to stop the other chap getting there first, you see.'

Malenfant was getting confused again. 'Other chap? You mean the Americans?'

Nemoto said gently, 'There are no Americans in his world, Malenfant.'

'The French, of course,' said McCann. 'The blooming French!'

Colonies on this bounteous Moon had been founded in what sounded like the equivalent of the first half of the twentieth century. Since then wars had already been fought, wars on the Moon waged between spreading mini-empires of Brits and French and Germans.

But then, in McCann's universe, the Mars-Moon had disappeared, to be replaced by this peculiar, wandering Red Moon, with its own cargo of oceans and life. Once the world had gotten over its bewilderment – once the last hope of contacting the lost colonies on Mars-Moon was gone – a new race had begun to plant a flag in the Red Moon.

'. . . Or *Lemuria*, as we call it,' McCann said.

Nemoto said, 'A lost continent beneath the Indian Ocean, once thought to have been the cradle of mankind.'

McCann talked on: of how the dozen men had travelled here; of a disastrous landing that had wrecked their ship and killed three of them; of how they had sent heliograph and radio signals home and waited for rescue – and of how their Earth had flickered out of the sky, to be replaced by another, and another.

'A sheaf of worlds,' murmured Nemoto, gazing at McCann.

When it was clear that no rescue was to come, some of the exploratory party had submitted to despair. One committed suicide. Another handed himself over to a party of Elf-folk for a hideous and protracted death.

The survivors had recruited local Hams, and used their muscles and Runner labour to construct this little township. They had found no others of their kind, save for the sinister-sounding Zealots, of whom McCann was reluctant to speak, who lived some distance from the compound.

It seemed that it had been the mysterious Zealots who had taught the indigenes their broken English – if inadvertently, through escaped slaves returning to their host populations. The Zealots had been here for centuries, McCann seemed to believe.

'Not much of a life,' McCann said grimly. 'No women, you see. Some of us sought relief with the Hams, even with Runners. But they aren't *women*. And there were certainly no children to follow.' He smiled stoically. 'Without women and children, you can't make a colony, can you? After a time you wonder why you bother to shave every day.'

One by one the Englishmen had died, their neat little huts falling into disrepair.

McCann showed them a row of graves, outside the stockade gate, marked by bits of stone. The last to die had been a man called Jordan – 'dead of paralytic shock', McCann said. McCann appeared especially moved to be at Jordan's grave side. Malenfant wondered if these withdrawn, lonely men, locked in civility and their memories of a forever lost home, had in the end sought consolation in each other.

But McCann, in a gruesome effort to play the good host, talked brightly of better times. 'We had a life of sorts. We played cards – until they wore out – and we made chess sets, carving pieces from bits of balsa. We had no books, but we would spin each other yarns, recounting the contents of novels as best we remembered them. I dare say the shades of a few authors are restless at the liberties we took. Once or twice we even put on a play or two. Marlowe comedies mostly: *Much Ado About Nothing*, that kind of thing. Just to amuse ourselves, of course.

'We used to play sports. Your average Ham can't kick a soccer ball to save his life, but he's a formidable rugby player. As for the Runners, they can't grasp the simplest principle of rules or sportsmanship. But, my, can they run! We would organize races. The record we got was under six seconds for the hundred-yard dash. *That* fellow was rewarded with plenty of bananas and beer . . .'

McCann spoke of how the survivors, just four of them, had become withdrawn, even one from the other, as they waited gloomily for death. Crawford would disappear into the forest for days on end with squads of Hams, 'fossicking around', as McCann put it. The others would rarely even leave their huts.

'And you?' Nemoto asked. 'What is your eccentricity, Mr McCann?'

'A longing for company,' he said immediately, smiling with self-deprecation. 'That's always been my weakness, I'm afraid.'

'Then it must have been hard for you here,' Malenfant said.

'Indeed. But when my companions withdrew into themselves, I sought out the company of the lesser folk: the Hams, even the Runners at times. My companions took to calling me *Mowgli*. Perhaps you know the reference. I have attempted to civilize them, teach them skills – more advanced tool-making, even reading. With little success, I am afraid. Your bar-bar is smarter than your Runner, and these pre-sapients are smarter in turn than the pongid species, the Elves and Nutcrackers. Your bar-bar can be taught to use a new tool, you know – to *use* it but never to make it. They can make things work but never understand *how* they work, rather like human infants. And, like your Kaffir, your bar-bar can see the first stage of a thing, and maybe the second, but no more.

'And that, of course, is the difference between man and pre-sapient. Wherever there are sub-men, who live only for the day and their own bellies, we must rule. But the work shapes one. The responsibility. It has made me pitiful and kindly, I would say, as I have learned something of their strange, twisted reasoning.' He leaned towards them. 'They have no chins, you see, none of them. And everybody knows that a weak chin generally denotes a weak race.'

When evening came again, fires were built within the palm-thatched huts, and smoke rose through the roofs and the crude chimneys that pierced them. Malenfant saw a pair of bats, flapping uncertainly between the turbulent columns of smoke. They were big, as big as crows, with broad, rounded wings.

'Leaf-nose bats,' Nemoto murmured.

'Don't tell me. Prehistoric bats.'

Nemoto shrugged. 'Perhaps. There are many bats here. They have occupied some of the niches never taken by the birds.'

Malenfant watched the bats' slow, ungainly flapping. 'They sure look unevolved.'

'Ah, but they were the peak of aerial engineering when they hunted flies and mosquitoes over lakes full of dinosaurs, Malenfant. You should have a little more respect.'

'I guess I should.'

Nemoto whispered conspiratorially, 'It all hangs together, Malenfant.'

'What does?'

'McCann's account of his alternate Earth. A much larger Moon would raise immense tides. The oceans would not be navigable. McCann's America must once have been linked to Eurasia by land bridges, as ours was, for otherwise the Hams presumably couldn't have reached it. But when the land bridges were submerged, the Americas were effectively cut off – until iron-hulled ships and aeroplanes emerged, in the equivalent of our own twentieth century. Malenfant, it may have been easier to fly to the Moon than to reach America. Think of that.'

'What does all this mean, Nemoto?'

'I am working on it,' she said seriously. 'Consider this, though. We are alone on our Earth, our closest relatives terribly distant. But McCann's world has a spectrum of hominid types – as it was on our own Earth, long ago. McCann's Earth may in some senses be more *typical* than ours.'

A party of Runners, supervised by a Ham, brought in a couple of deer, slung between them, half-butchered.

'Look at that,' muttered Nemoto. 'I think that one is a mouse deer.' It was small, the size of a dog, its coat yellow-brown spotted with white, and it had tusks in its upper jaw. 'You see them in Africa. Actually it isn't really a deer at all. It is midway between pigs and deer, and more primitive than either. It climbs trees. It catches fish in the streams. Probably unchanged across thirty million years. Older than grass, Malenfant.'

'And the other?'

This was a little larger than the mouse deer, with a black stripe down its back, and powerful hind legs: a creature evolved for the undergrowth, Malenfant thought.

'A duiker, I think,' Nemoto said. 'Another primitive form, the oldest of the antelopes. Sometimes hunts birds and feeds on carrion. Maybe here it eats bats. Everything is ancient here.' Now she seemed agitated. 'Perhaps these forms were brought here by the same mechanism that imported hominids. What do you think?'

'Take it easy.'

Her small, thin face worked in the gathering gloom. 'This is wrong, Malenfant.'

'Wrong? What's wrong with it?'

'The ecology is – out of tune. Like a misfiring engine. It is a jumble of species and micro-ecologies, a mixed-up place, fragments thrown together. Though many of the fragments are very ancient, there has been no time for these plants and animals to evolve together, to find an equilibrium. Periodically something disturbs this world, Malenfant, over and over, stirring it up.'

Malenfant grunted. 'Guess you can't go wandering across the reality lines without a little confusion.'

But Nemoto would not take the matter lightly. 'This is not right, Malenfant. All this *mixing*. There is a *reason* the primitive hominids became extinct, a reason why the mouse deer's descendants evolved new forms. An ecology is like a machine, where all parts work together, interlocking. You see?'

Malenfant said, amused, 'These deer and antelopes seem to have been prospering before they ran into some hunter's crossbow bolt.'

'It shouldn't be this way, Malenfant. To meddle with ecologies, to short-circuit them, is irresponsible.'

Malenfant shrugged. 'Sure. And we cut down the forests to build shopping malls.' He was feeling restless; maybe his first shock was wearing off. He'd had enough of McCann; he was eager to get out of here, get back to the lander – and progress his primary mission, which was to find Emma.

But when he expressed this to Nemoto she laughed harshly. 'Malenfant, we barely managed to survive our first few minutes after landing. Here we are safe. Have patience.'

He seethed. But without her support, he didn't see what he could do about it.

Manekatopokanemahedo:

When she was Mapped to the Market – when the information that comprised her had been squeezed through cracks in the quantum foam that underlay all space and time – she was no longer, quite, herself, and that disturbed her greatly.

Manekato was used to Mapping. The Farm was large enough that walking, or transport by Workers, was not always rapid enough. But Mappings covering such a short distance were brief and isomorphic: she felt the same coming out of the destination station as entering it (just as, of course, principles of the identity of indiscernible objects predicted she should).

A Mapping spanning continents was altogether more challenging. To compensate for differences in latitude and altitude and seasons – early summer *there*, falling into autumn *here* – and to adjust for momentum differences – people on the far side of the spinning Earth were moving in the opposite direction to her – such a Mapping could be no more than homomorphic. What came out looked like her, felt like her. But it was not indiscernible from the original; it could not *be* her.

Still, despite these philosophical drawbacks, the process was painless, and when she walked off the Mapping platform, her knuckles tentatively touching new ground, she found herself comfortable. The air was hot, humid, but caused her no distress, and even its thinness at this higher altitude did not give her any discomfort.

And the air was still. *There was no Wind.* Thanks to the Air Wall wrapped around it, the Market was the only place on Earth from which the perpetual Wind was excluded. She had been prepared for this intellectually, of course. But to stand here in this pond of still air – not to feel the caressing shove of the Wind on her back – was utterly strange.

This crowded Mapping station was full of strangers. She peered around, feeling conspicuous, bewildered. Some of the people here were small, some tall, some squat, some thin; some were coated with hair that was red or black or brown, and some had no hair at all; some crawled close to the ground, and some almost walked upright, like their most distant ancestors, their hands barely brushing the ground. Manekato, who had spent her whole life on a Farm where everybody looked alike, tried to mask her shock and revulsion at so much *difference*.

She was met outside the station by a Worker, a runner from the Astrologers. She slid easily onto its broad back, wrapping her long arms around its chest, and allowed herself to be carried away.

Her first impression of the Market was of waste. The streets were broad, the buildings an inefficient variety of designs, and she could spot immediately places where heat would leak or dust gather, or where the layout must prevent optimally short journeys from being concluded.

All of this jarred with her instinct. The goal for every Farmer was to squeeze the maximum effectiveness and efficiency from every last atom – and beyond, to the infinitesimal. The mastery of matter at the subatomic level, resulting in such everyday wonders as Mapping and Workers, had brought that ultimate dream a little closer.

But, she reminded herself, this was the Market, not a Farm.

In the deepest past there had been a multitude of markets, where Farmers traded goods and information and wisdom. The transient population of the markets had always been predominantly male. Women were more tightly bound to the land, locked into the matriarchal Lineages that had owned the land since the times almost before history; men were itinerant, sent to other Farms for the purpose of trade, and marriage.

But as technology had advanced and the Farms had become increasingly self-sufficient, the primary function of the markets had dwindled. One by one they had fallen into disuse. But the role of the markets as centres of innovation had been recognized – and, perhaps, their purpose in providing an alternate destiny for rootless men and boys. So some of the markets had been preserved.

At last only one Market remained: the grandest and most famous, perched here on the eroded peak of its equatorial mountain, supported now by tithes from Farms around the world. Here men, and a few women, dreamed their dreams of how differently things might be – and enough of those innovative dreams bore fruit that it was worth preserving.

It had been this way for two hundred thousand years.

The Worker carried her away from the Market's crowded centre towards its fringe. The crowds thinned out, and Manekato felt a calming relief to be alone. Alongside an impossibly tall building the Worker paused and hunched down, letting her slip to the ground.

A door dilated in the side of the building. She glanced into the interior; it was filled with darkness.

Reluctant to enter immediately, she loped further along the gleaming, dust-free road. Not far beyond the building the ground fell away. She was approaching the rim of the summit plateau, worn smooth by the feet and hands of visitors. She leaned forward curiously. The mountain's shallow flanks fell away into thicker, murky air; far below she glimpsed green growing things.

And she saw the Air Wall.

It was like a bank of windblown cloud, moving swiftly, grey and boiling. But this cloud bank hung vertically from the sky, and the clouds streamed horizontally past her. Now that it was not masked by the buildings she could see how the great Wall curved around the mountain-top, enclosing it neatly. It stretched down like a curtain to the ground below, where dust storms perpetually beat against the struggling vegetation, and it stretched up towards the sky.

It was not easy for her to look up, for her back tilted forward, and her neck was thick, heavily muscled, adapted to fight the Wind. Besides, at home there was generally nothing to see but a lid of streaked, scudding cloud. But now she tipped back awkwardly, raising her chinless jaw.

It was like peering up into a tunnel, lined by scraps of hurrying cloud. And at the very end of the tunnel there was a patch of clear blue.

She had never before seen the sky beyond the clouds.

She shuddered. She hurried inside the building.

And there she met her brother.

Reid Malenfant:

While he waited for an opportunity to progress his mission, Malenfant ate and drank as much as he could, and after the first day put his body through some gentle exercise. He stretched and pushed up and pounded around the red dust of the neat little stockade in his vest and shorts, while Ham servants watched with a kind of absent curiosity, and Runners hooted and shook their shackling ropes. The low gravity made him feel stronger, but conversely the reduced oxygen content of the low-pressure air weakened him. If he over-exerted himself he would soon run out of air; his chest would ache, and, in the worst cases, black spots would gather around his vision.

But he would adapt. And for now, it did no harm to test his limits.

McCann took him for tourist-guide jaunts around the compound, and even beyond. He seemed childishly eager to show off what he and his companions had built here.

McCann said the English had tried to mine mudstone – a kind of natural brick – so as to build better houses. 'We have the raw muscle, among the Runners and the Hams,' McCann said. 'That's fine for hauling, lifting and dragging. But they can't be set to fine work, Malenfant; not without a man's constant supervision. You certainly can't send off a party even of the Hams to a mudstone seam and expect them to return with anything but a jumble of gouged-out, misshapen rocks – nothing like *bricks*, you see – that's if they bring back anything at all.'

There were a lot of pleasurable knick-knacks to inspect, constructed over long hours by the ingenious hands of these bored Englishmen. Malenfant, a gadget fan, pored over wooden locks, clocks and slide rules, all made entirely of wood.

McCann had even maintained a crude calendar system – though it was little more than marks on wood. 'Like a rune staff,' McCann said, grimacing. 'How far we have fallen. But we haven't quite mastered the knack of paper-making, you see; needs must. And besides this wandering world has a damnably irregular sky. Even the stars swim about sometimes, you know. But we try to impose order. We do try.'

Everything was made of wood, or stone, or bone, or material manufactured from vegetable products. You could make rope, for instance, from birch bark, pine roots or willow. Ham women baked pine bread made from phloem, the soft white flesh just inside the tree's bark. You could drink the sap of birch trees, if you had to. And there were medicinal products: spruce resin to ease gut ache. And so on.

McCann said, 'This benighted world is bereft of metals, you see – of sizeable ore lodes, anyhow, so far as we could find. Of course the very dust is iron oxide – hematite, I think – but we have notably failed to establish a workable extraction regime . . . It was an early disappointment, and all the more severe for that. And we were reluctant to mine the only source of refined metals here – I mean our ship, of course. As long as we clung to hope that we might escape this jungle world, we were reluctant to turn our only vessel into pots and pans. All seems a little foolish now, doesn't it? And so ours is an economy of stone and wood. We have become like our woad-wearing forebears. Amusing, isn't it?'

They came to a hut where a Ham woman, somewhat bent, was ladling water from a wooden bucket at her feet. Malenfant, glimpsing machinery, poked his head inside the hut, and allowed his eyes to adjust to the shade.

A big wooden container sat on a stand above a smouldering fire. There was some kind of mash inside the container: the woman showed him, though she had to remove a lid sealed with some kind of wax to do it. Two narrow bamboo pipes led down from the container. Condenser pipes, Malenfant thought. The pipes finished in v-notches that tipped their contents neatly into gourds . . .

'It's a still,' Malenfant breathed. 'Holy shit. Hillbilly stuff. Just the way Jack Daniels started. God, I love this stuff.'

McCann preened, inordinately proud; briefly Malenfant was taken back to his pre-launch inspections at Vandenberg and elsewhere.

Immediately outside the stockade the forest seemed sparse. The leaves were a pale green, lighter than usual, and lianas tangled everywhere, irregular. Though there were sudden patches of shade, much of the ground was open to the sun; there was no solid canopy here.

This area had been cleared, Malenfant realized – twenty, thirty years ago? – and then abandoned. And now, oblivious to the failed ambitions of the stranded English, the forest was claiming back the land. He gazed at the ground, and thought he discerned the straight-line edges of forgotten fields, like Roman ruins.

But even out here there were signs of rudimentary industry. A charcoal pile had been constructed: just a heap of logs with earth piled over the top, steadily burning. And there was a tar pit, a hole in the ground filled with pine logs, buried under a layer of earth. The logs burned steadily, and crude wooden guttering brought out the tar.

They came to a stand of small oil-palm trees that clung to the banks of a stream. They were slim and upright with scruffy green fronds, holding onto the slope with prop-roots, like down-turned fingers curling out from the base of their pale grey trunks. Under the direction of one or two of the Hams, Runner workers gathered oil from the flesh of the nut and the kernel of the seeds, and sap from shallow cuts near the trees' bases.

'You cook with the oil, or you make soap with it,' McCann said. 'And if you were to hang a bucket under that cut in the trunk you'd be rewarded by ready-made palm wine, Malenfant. Nature is bountiful sometimes, even here. Though it takes human ingenuity to exploit it to the full, of course.'

McCann even showed Malenfant the poignant ruin of a windmill. Crudely constructed, it was a box of wood already overgrown by vegetation and with daylight showing through cracks in its panels. Later McCann showed him elaborate drawings, crammed into the blank pages of yellowing log books. There had been ambitious schemes for different designs of mills – 'magpie mills' with a tail to turn into the wind, and even a water mill – none of them realized. 'We never had the labour, you see. Your Ham or your Runner is strong as an ox. But you can't teach him to build, or to maintain, anything more complex than a hand-axe or a spear. He will go where you tell him, do what you tell him, but no more; he has no initiative or advanced skill, not a scrap. One had to oversee everything, every hand turned to the work. After a time – well, and with no hope for the future – one rather became disheartened.'

McCann was obviously desperate for company, and it was hard to blame him. He challenged Malenfant to a game of chess – which Malenfant refused, never having grasped the game. Despite this McCann set out crudely carved wooden pieces, and moved them around the board in fast, well-practised openings. 'I played a lot with old Crawford before he lost his wits. I do miss the game. I even tried to teach the bar-bars to play! – but though they appear capable of remembering the moves of the pieces, not even the brightest of them, even Julia, could grasp its essence, the *purpose*. Still, I would have Julia or another sit where you are sitting, Malenfant, and serve as a sort of token companion as I played out solitary games . . .'

As he pushed the pieces around the board McCann bombarded Malenfant with anecdotes and memories, of his time here on the Red Moon and on his own lost version of Earth.

But the talk was unsatisfactory. They were exiles from different versions of parallel Earths. They could compare notes on geography and the broad sweep of history, but they had no *detail* in common. None of the historical figures in their worlds seemed to map across to each other. Although McCann seemed to follow a variant of Christianity – something like Calvinism, so far as Malenfant could determine – his 'Christ' was not Jesus, but a man called John; 'Christian' translated, roughly, to 'Johannen'.

No doubt all this was fascinating as a study of historical inevitability. But it made for lousy small talk. McCann strove to mask his profound disappointment that Malenfant was not from the home where he had left a wife and child, a family from whom he had not heard since their world had disappeared from the sky.

Conversely Malenfant told McCann what he could of Emma, and asked if anyone like her had shown up, here on the Red Moon. But McCann seemed to know little of what went on beyond the limits of the stockade, and the scrap of Red Moon he and his colleagues controlled. Malenfant, frustrated, realized afresh he was going to have to find Emma alone.

McCann said now, 'Solitary, seeking diversion, I discovered the intricate delights of the knight's tour.' He swept the board empty of pieces, save for a solitary knight, which he made hop in its disturbingly asymmetrical fashion from square to square. 'The knight must move from square to square over an empty board, touching all the cells, but each only once. An old schoolboy puzzle ... I quickly discovered that a three-by-four board is the smallest on which such a tour can be made. I have discovered many tours on the standard chessboard, many of which have fascinating properties. A closed tour, for example, starts and ends at the same cell.' The knight moved around the board with bewildering rapidity. 'I do not know how many tours are possible. I suspect the number may be infinite.' He became aware of Malenfant's uncomfortable silence.

Malenfant tried to soften his look – how sane would *you* be after so many decades alone on Neandertal Planet, Malenfant?

Embarrassed, McCann swept the pieces into a wooden box. 'Rather like our situation here, don't you think?' he said, forcing a smile. 'We move from world to world with knight's hops, forward a bit and sideways. We must hope our tours are closed too, eh?'

After the first night McCann gave the two of them separate huts. In this dwindling colony there was plenty of room.

Malenfant found it impossible to sleep. Lying in his battered sod hut, he gazed through his window as the night progressed.

He heard the calls of the predators as the last light faded. Then there was an utter stillness, as if the world were holding its breath – and then a breath of wind and a coolness that marked the approaching dawn.

Malenfant wasn't used to living so close to nature. He felt as if he were trapped within some vast machine.

His head rattled with one abortive scheme after another. He was a man who was used to taking control of a situation, of bulling his way through, of pushing until something gave. This wasn't his world, and he had arrived here woefully ill-equipped; he still couldn't see any way forward more promising than just pushing into the forest on foot, at random. He had to wait, to figure out the situation, to find an option with a reasonable chance of success. But still his enforced passivity was burning him up.

The door opened.

The Neandertal girl came into his hut. She was carrying a bowl of water that steamed softly, a fresh towel, a jug that might hold nettle tea.

He said softly, 'Julia.'

She stood still in the grey dawn light, the glow from the window picking out the powerful contours of her face. 'Here, Baas.'

'Do you know what's going on here?'

She waited.

He waved a hand. 'All of this. The Red Moon. Different worlds.'

'Ask Ol' Ones,' she said softly.

'Who?'

'Th' Ol' Ones. As' them wha' for.'

'The Old Ones? Where do they live?'

She shrugged, her shoulders moving volcanically. 'In th' ol'est place.'

He frowned. 'What about you, Julia?'

'Baas?'

'What do you want?'

'Home,' she said immediately.

'Home? Where is home?'

She pointed into the sky. 'Grey Earth.'

'Does Mr McCann know you want to go home?'

She shrugged again. 'Born here.'

'What?'

She pointed to herself. 'Born here. Mother. Moth' born here.'

'Then this is your home, with Mr McCann.'

She shook her head, a very human gesture. She pointed again to the forest, and the sky.

Then she said, 'You, Baas? What you wan'?'

He hesitated. 'I came looking for my wife.'

Her face remained expressionless. But she said, 'Fam'ly.'

'Yes. I guess so. Emma is my family. I came here looking for her.'

'Lon' way.'

'Yes. Yes, it was a long way. And I ain't there yet.'

She walked towards him, rummaging in the pouch of her skirt. 'Thomas,' she said.

'I know him. He found me.'

'Took off of Runner in fores'.' She held out something in the dark, something small and jewel-like that glittered in her palm.

He took it, held it up to the light of the window. It was a hand-lens, badly scuffed, snapped off at its mount. It was marked with the monogram of the South African air force.

'*Emma*,' he breathed. He was electrified. So there were indeed things McCann didn't know, even about the Hams of his own household. 'Julia, where –'

But she had gone.

Manekatopokanemahedo:

'I have three wives and six children. That is how it is done in my new home . . .' Babo was talking fast, nervously, and his knuckles rattled as he walked with her through the tall dark halls of the building. His body hair was plaited and coloured in a fashion that repelled Mane's simple Poka tastes. 'The Farm is fine, Mane, and bigger than that of the Poka Lineage, but its design is based on the triangle: plane-covering, of course, but cramped and cluttered compared to Poka's clean-lined hexagons.'

'You always were an aesthete,' she said dryly.

This whole building, she realized slowly, was a store of records piled up high from the lowest room to the highest. Physically, some of the records were stored in twinkling cubes that held bits of the quantum foam, minuscule wormholes frozen into patterns of meaning; and some were scraped onto parchment and animal skin.

'Some of these pieces are very ancient indeed,' Babo said. 'Dating back half a million years or more. And the Air Wall, you know, is a controlled storm. It is like a hurricane, but trapped in one place by subtle forces. It has raged here, impotent, for fifty thousand years – so that for all that time the Market has been in the eye of the storm – an eye that reveals the sky beyond the clouds, a sky opened for the study of the Astrologers . . .'

She stopped and glared at him. 'Oh, Babo, I don't want to know about Air Walls or records! I never thought I would see you again – I didn't know you had become an Astrologer.'

He sighed, ruminatively picking his nose. 'I am no Astrologer. But the Astrologers sent for me. When I was younger I did spend some time here, working informally, before I reached the home of my wives. Many boys do, Mane. You matriarchs run the world, but there is much you do not know, even about those who sire your children!'

'*Why are you here,* Babo?'

He wrapped his big hands over his head. 'Because the Astrologers thought it would be *kinder* that way. Kinder if your brother told you the news, rather than a stranger . . .'

'What news?'

He grabbed her hand, pulling her. 'Come see the sky with me. Then I'll tell you everything.'

Reluctantly, she followed.

The building was tall, and they had a long way to ascend. At first they used simple short-range isomorphic Mappers, but soon they came to more primitive parts of the building, and they had to climb, using rungs stapled to walls of crude bricks.

Babo led the way. 'A remarkable thing,' he called down to her. 'We find climbing easy; our arms are strong, our feet well adapted to grasping. But it appears that our climbing ancestors evolved into creatures that, for a time, walked upright, on their hind feet. You can see certain features of the position of the pelvis – well. But we have given that up too; now, once more, we walk on all fours, using our knuckles, clinging to the ground.'

'If you tried to walk upright you would be knocked over by the Wind.'

'Of course, of course – but then *why* is it we carry traces of a bipedal ancestry? We are creatures of anomaly, Mane. We are not closely related to any of the animals on this Earth of ours – not one, not above a certain basic biochemical equivalence of course, without which we could not eat our food and would quickly starve to death. We can trace evolutionary relationships among all the world's creatures, one related to the other in a hierarchy of families and phyla – *except us*. We seem to be unique, as if we fell out of the sky. We have no evolutionary forebears, no bones in the ground that might mark the passing of those who came before us.

'Is it possible *we evolved somewhere else*? – a place where the Wind did not blow so strongly, where it was possible to walk upright?'

'What sort of place? And how could we have got here from there?'

'I don't know. Nobody knows. But the pattern of the bones, the biochemistry, is unmistakable.'

'Idle speculation, Babo, won't germinate a single seed.'

'A Farmer's practical reply,' he said sadly. 'But we are surrounded by mystery, Manekato. The Astrologers hope that your mission will settle some of these fundamental quandaries. Oh, please keep climbing, dear Mane! We are soon there, and I will tell you everything.'

With bad grace, clinging to the rungs with feet and hands, she continued her ascent.

They reached a platform, open to the sky. But there was no breeze, and the air felt as warm as it had inside the tower.

Babo walked around nervously, peering into the sky. 'It is darkling already. Our days are short, because the planet spins quickly – did you ever reflect on that, Mane? It didn't have to be so. Earth could spin more slowly, and we would have leisurely days, and – oh, look!' He pointed with a long stabbing finger. 'Look, a star!'

She peered up awkwardly. There was a single bright star, close to the zenith, set against the deepening blue of the sky.

'How strange,' Babo breathed, 'that before the first tentative Mappings no human eye saw a star.'

Manekato grunted. 'What of it? Stars are trivial. You don't need to *see* them.'

That was true, of course. Every child was expected to figure out the stars.

When Manekato was two years old she had been shut in a room with a number of other children, and a handful of objects: a grain of sand, a rock crystal, a bowl of water, a bellows, a leaf, other things. And the children were told to deduce the nature of the universe from the contents of the room.

Of course the results of such trials varied – in fact the variations were often interesting, offering insights into scientific understanding, the nature of reality, the psychology of the developing mind. But most children, working by native logic, quickly converged on a universe of planets and stars and galaxies. Even though they had never seen a single star.

Stars were trivial mechanisms, after all, compared to the simplest bacterium.

'Ah, but the detail is everything,' Babo said, 'and that you can never predict, of course. That and the *beauty*. That was quite unexpected, to me. Oh, and one other thing. The *emptiness* of the universe . . .'

Manekato's childhood cohort, like most others, had concluded – groping with an intuition of uniformity – that if *this* world was inhabited, and the universe was *large* – well, then, there must be many inhabited planets. She recalled what a great and unwelcome surprise it had been to learn that that was not true: that, as far as could be discerned, the universe was empty of the organization that would have marked the work of intelligence.

'It is a deep, ancient mystery,' Babo said. 'Why do we see no Farms in the sky? Of course we are a sedentary species, content to cultivate our Farms. But not every species need have the same imperatives as us. Imagine an *acquisitive* species, that covets the territory of others.'

She thought it through quickly. 'That is outlandish and unlikely. Such a species would surely destroy itself in fratricidal battles, as the illogic of its nature worked itself out.'

'Perhaps. But wouldn't we see the flaring of the wars, the mighty ruins they left behind? We should *see* them, Mane.'

She snapped, 'Babo, get to the point.'

He sighed and came to squat before her. Gently he groomed her, picking imaginary insects from her coat, as he had when they were children. 'Mane, dear Mane, the Astrologers have read the stars . . .'

The word 'astrology', in Manekato's ancient, rich language, derived from older roots meaning 'the word of the stars'. Here astrology had absorbed astronomy and physics and other disciplines; here astrology was no superstition, no foolishness, but one of the fundamental sciences. For if the universe was empty of mind save for humans, then the courses of the stars could have no meaning – save for their role in the affairs of humanity.

And now, Babo said, the Astrologers, peering into the sky and poring over records dozens of millennia deep, had discerned a looming threat.

Joshua:

Mary was in oestrus. The scent of her seemed to fill the air of the hut, and the head of every man.

Joshua longed for the time of her blood to pass, and she and the other women could recede to the grey periphery of his awareness. For the deep ache aroused by Mary distracted him from the great conundrum which plagued him.

Over and over he thought of the great blue wings he had seen falling from the sky, bearing that fat black and white seed to its unknown fate in the forest at the top of the cliff. He had never seen such a thing before. *What was it?*

Joshua's was a world that did not countenance change. And yet, a stubborn awareness told him, there *was* change. Once the people had lived on the Grey Earth. Now they lived here. So the past contained a change. And now the black and white seed had fallen from the sky, and whatever grew from it surely marked change to come in the future as well.

Change in the past, change in the future.

Joshua, helplessly conservative himself, had an instinctive grasp of parsimony: his world contained two extraordinary events – Grey Earth and sky seed – and surely they must be linked. But how? The elements of the conundrum revolved in his head.

Joshua had solved puzzles before.

Once, as a boy, he had found a place where Abel, his older brother, had knapped out a burin. It was just a patch of dune where stone flakes were scattered, in a rough triangle that showed where Abel had sat. Joshua had picked over the debris, curious. Later, in the hut, he had found the discarded burin itself. It was a fine piece of work, slender and sharp, and yet fitting easily into Joshua's small hand. And he remembered the spall outside.

He sat where his brother had sat – one leg outstretched, the other tucked underneath. He reached for bits of the spall, and tried to fit them back onto the finished tool. One after another he found flakes that nestled closely into the hollows and valleys of the tool, and then more flakes which clustered around them.

Soon there were more flakes than he could hold in his hands, so he put down his assemblage carefully, and climbed a little way up the cliff behind the hut. He found a young tree sprouting from a hollow, and bled it of sap. With the sticky stuff cradled in his hands he ran back to his workplace, and began to fix the flakes to the tool with dabs of the sap. The sap clung to his fingers, and soon the whole thing was a sticky mess. But he persisted, ignoring the sun that climbed steadily into the sky.

At last he had used up almost all the large flakes he could find on the ground, and there was nothing left there but a little dust. And he had almost reassembled the cobble from which the burin had been carved.

Shouting with excitement he ran into the hut, cradling his reconstruction. But he had received a baffled response. Abel had picked at the sticky assemblage of flakes, saying, 'What, what?'

A cobble was a cobble, until it was turned into a tool, and then the cobble no longer existed. Just as Jacob had been a man until he died, and then there was only a mass of meat and bones, soon to be devoured by the worms. To turn a tool back into a cobble was almost as strange to the people as if Joshua had tried to turn Jacob's bones back into the man himself.

Eventually Abel crushed the little stone jigsaw. The gummy flakes stuck to his hand, and he brushed them off on the dusty ground, growling irritably.

But in some corner of his spacious cranium Joshua had never forgotten how he had solved the puzzle of the shattered cobble. Now, as he pondered the puzzle of the multiple earths and the falling seed, Joshua found that long-ago jigsaw cobble pricking his memory.

And when a second seed fell from the sky – another fat black and white bundle suspended under a blue canopy, landing where the first had lodged at the top of the cliffs – he knew that he could not rest until he had seen for himself what mighty tree might sprout from those strange seeds.

Joshua approached Abel and Saul and other men to accompany him on his jaunt up the cliff face. But there was no purpose to his mission – no game to be hunted, no useful rock, no foraging save for the huge enigmatic seeds which had slid silently over the surface of everybody else's mind.

And besides, everybody knew there was danger at the top of the cliff. The camp of the Zealots was there, in the centre of a great clearing hacked crudely out of the forest. The Zealots were Skinny-folk. They were easily bested if you could ever get one engaged in close quarters. But the Zealots were cunning, and their heads were full of madness: they could baffle the most powerful of the Hams. They were best avoided.

Joshua tried to go alone. He set foot on the rough goat trail that led by gully and switchback turn up to that cliff-crest forest.

The trail was easy enough, but he soon turned back. The isolation worked on him, soon making him feel as if he didn't exist at all. The People of the Grey Earth needed nothing in life so much as each other.

But word of his project permeated the gossip-ridden hut. A few days later, to his surprise, he was approached by the young girl Mary, who asked him about the cliff, and the forest, and the strange sky seed.

And a day after that, to his greater surprise, she accompanied him on the trail.

She gossiped all the way to the top of the cliff. '. . . Ruth say Abel skinny as an En'lish. An' Ruth tell tha' to Miriam. An' Miriam tell Caleb, an' Caleb tell Abel. An' Abel throw rocks and skins all over th' hut. So Abel couple Miriam, and he tell Caleb about tha', and he tell Ruth. And Ruth say . . .'

Unlike himself she was no loner. She was immersed in her little society. By comparison it was as if he couldn't even see or hear the vibrant, engaged people she described.

All of which made it still stranger that she should choose to accompany him on this purposeless jaunt. But Mary was at a key moment in her life, and a certain wanderlust was in her blood right now. Soon she would have to leave the security of the hearths her mother built, and share her life with the men, and with the children who would follow. To cross from one side of a skin hut to the other was an immense journey for someone like Mary. And as nervous courage empowered her for that great adventure, she seemed ready, for the time being, to take on much more outlandish quests.

She was not in oestrus, to Joshua's great relief. As he made his careful way up the cliff face he was pleased not to have the distraction of his own singing blood.

They reached the top of the cliff. Here they found a shrub laden with bright yellow fruit, and they sat side by side at the cliff's edge, plucking the fruit, their broad feet dangling in the air. They gazed out in silence towards the east, and the sea.

The sun was still rising, and its light glimmered from the sea's steel-grey, wrinkled hide. The distinct curve of the world was reflected in layers of scattered purple clouds which hovered over the sea. Joshua could see the grassy plain where he lived, sweeping towards the ocean, terminating in dune fields and pale sand. Near the squat brown shape of the hut itself, people moved to and fro, tiny and clear. He followed streams, shining lines of silver that led towards the sea.

A small group of antelopes picked their way through the morning grass. One of them looked up, as if staring directly at him.

Joshua felt himself dissolve, out from the centre of his head, to the periphery of the world. There was no barrier around him, no layer of interpretation or analogy or nostalgia; for now he *was* the plain and the sea and the clouds, and he was the slim doe that looked up at the cliff, just as he was the stocky, quiet man who gazed down from it. For a time he was immersed in the world's beauty in a way no human could have shared.

Then, by unspoken consent, Joshua and Mary folded their legs under them and stood. Side by side, they walked into the forest that crowded close to the cliff.

The green dark was a strong contrast to the bright sea vista. It was not a comfortable place to be.

Washed by the salty air off the sea, the forest was chill, thick with a clammy moisture that settled into Joshua's bones. And as they penetrated deeper the ground was covered in a tangled mass of roots, branches, leaves and moss, so that in some places Joshua couldn't see the actual surface at all. He slipped, stumbled and crashed over the undergrowth, making a huge amount of noise.

Mary started to shiver and complain, growing increasingly fearful. But Joshua pulled his skin wraps tighter around him and shoved his way deeper into the forest.

A shadow slid through the wood, just a little way ahead, utterly silent.

Joshua and Mary both froze. Joshua bunched his fists. Was it a Zealot?

The shadow slowed to a halt, and Joshua made out a squat, stocky body, with short legs and immensely long arms, the whole covered by a dark brown layer of hair. A hand reached out and grabbed a bamboo tree. The tree was pulled down until it cracked, and drawn towards a gaping mouth.

It was a Nutcracker-man. Joshua relaxed.

Mary stumbled closer to Joshua, making a cracking noise.

The Nutcracker-man turned his great head with its sculpted skull ridge and giant cheekbones. Perhaps he saw them; if he did he showed no concern. He pulled his bamboo towards his mouth and bit sideways at the trunk, seeking the pithy interior. As he chewed, the heavy muscles that worked his jaw expanded and contracted, making his entire head move.

Though slow and foolish and easily trapped, the Nutcrackers' muscles made them formidable opponents. But the Nutcrackers rarely ventured from their forests, and when they did they showed no instinct for aggression against the Hams. Likewise the Hams did not eat people. The two kinds of people had little in common and nothing to fight about, and simply avoided each other.

After a short time the Nutcracker-man finished his bamboo. He slid effortlessly away into the green, placing his hands and feet slowly and methodically, but he moved rapidly and almost noiselessly, soon outstripping any effort Joshua might have made to catch him.

Out of curiosity Joshua and Mary tried the bamboo. It took both of them to crack a trunk as thick as the one the Nutcracker had pulled over with one hand, and when he tried to bite into it Joshua's teeth slid off the trunk's glossy casing.

They moved deeper into the forest. The sun, showing in glittering fragments through the dense canopy, was now high. But Joshua caught occasional glimpses of the sea, and he kept it to his right, so that he knew he was working roughly the way the floating black and white seed had fallen. Mary kept close behind him. Her biceps showed, hard and massive, beneath the tight skins wrapped around her arms.

And now there was another shadow passing through the forest ahead. But this time there was much more noise. Maybe it was a bear, careless of who or what heard it. They both crouched down in a dense patch of tangled branches, and peered out fearfully.

The shadow was small, even slender.

It was just a man, and a feeble-looking man at that, with nothing like the bulk of a Ham, still less a Nutcracker. He was a Skinny: surely a Zealot. He wore skins wrapped closely around his limbs and torso, and he carried a length of bamboo tube. His face was covered by an ugly mass of black beard, and he was muttering to himself as he blundered noisily through the forest.

With some care he selected a broad-trunked tree. He sat down beneath it. He reached into his trousers to scratch his testicles, and emitted a long, luxurious fart. Then he raised the bamboo to his lips. To Joshua's astonishment, a foamy liquid gushed from the bamboo into the man's mouth. '*Up your arse, Praisegod Michael.*' He raised the flask, and drank again. Soon he began to wail. '*There is a lady, sweet and kind . . .*'

Mary clapped her hand over her mouth to keep from laughing. The Zealot was squealing like a sickly child.

Joshua was fascinated by the bamboo flask, by the way the murky liquid poured out into the man's mouth and down his bearded chin.

The Zealot finished off the contents of his flask. He settled further back against his tree trunk, tucking his arms into his sleeves. He had a broad-rimmed hat on his head, and as he reclined it tipped down over his eyes, hiding his face. His mouth popped open, and soon rattling snores issued from it.

Joshua and Mary crept forward until they stood over the sleeping Zealot. Joshua bent to pick up the bamboo. He tipped it upside down. A little foamy fluid dripped onto his palm. He licked it curiously. The taste was sour, but seemed to fill his head with sharpness.

He inspected the bamboo more closely. Its end had been stopped by a plug of wood, and a loop of leather attached another plug that, with some experimentation, Joshua managed to fit into the open end of the tube, sealing it. Joshua's people carried their water in their hands, or sometimes plaited leaves or hollowed-out fruit. Though they would have been capable of it, it had never occurred to them to make anything like the Zealot's bamboo flask.

Mary, meanwhile, was crouching over the Zealot. She was studying his clothing. Joshua saw that it had been cut from finely treated skin. The skin had been heavily modified, with whorls and zigzag lines and crosses scratched into it and coloured with some white mineral. The edges of the various pieces of skin had been punctured. Then a length of vegetable twine had been pushed through the puncture holes, to hold the bits of skin together. Mary picked at the seams and hems with her blunt fingers; she had never seen anything like it.

Joshua found the patterns on the skins deeply disturbing. He had seen their like before, on other Zealot artefacts. To Joshua the patterns made by the markings were at the limit of his awareness, neither there nor not there, flickering like ghosts between the rooms of his mind.

Now Mary's searching fingers found something dangling around the man's neck on a piece of thread. It was a bit of bone, that was all, but it had been shaped, more finely than Abel's best tools.

Joshua studied the bone. Suddenly a man surged out of the carving: his face contorted, his hands outstretched, and his chest ripped open to reveal his heart.

Joshua screamed. He grabbed the bit of bone and yanked it so the thread around the Skinny's neck broke, and he hurled it away into the forest.

The Skinny woke with a gulping snore. He sat up abruptly, and his hat fell off his head. Seeing the two hulking Hams, he raised his hands to the sky and began to yell. '*Oh, Heaven help me! By God's wounds, help me!*'

Mary looked up into the sky, trying to see who he was speaking to. But of course there was nobody there. The Skinny-folk were immersed in madness: they would talk to the sky, the trees, the patterns on their clothes or ornaments, as if those things were people, but they were not.

So Mary sat on the Zealot's chest, crushing him to the ground; he gasped under her weight. 'Stop talkin' sky! Stop!'

The bearded Zealot howled.

She slapped him across the face. The Zealot's head was jerked sideways, and he instantly became limp.

Mary backed away. 'Dead?'

Joshua, reluctantly, bent closer. The Zealot had fouled himself, perhaps when Mary had leapt on him; a thin slime of filthy piss trickled from his trouser legs. But his chest rose and fell steadily. 'No' dead.'

Mary, her eyes wide under her lowering brow ridges, said, 'Kill?'

Joshua grimaced. 'Bad meat. Leave for th' bears.'

'Yes,' Mary said doubtfully. 'Leave for th' bears.'

They wiped their hands clean of the Zealot's filth on handfuls of leaves. Then they turned and pushed on, heading steadily north.

After a time, Joshua stepped cautiously into a clearing.

The trees here were battered and twisted. When he looked to the west, he saw how they had been smashed down and broken back to make a great gully through the forest.

And to the east, at the tip of this gully, was the seed from the sky.

He gazed at the blocky shape at the end of the huge trench, excitement warring with apprehension. It was a mound of black and white, half-concealed by smashed foliage. It was surrounded by bits of blue skin – or not skin; a bit of it fluttered against his leg, a membrane finer than any skin he had ever seen.

It was so strange he could barely even make it out.

Mary, nervous, had stayed back in the fringe of the forest. ''Ware,' she said. 'Zealots.'

Joshua knew it was true. He could smell the smoke of their hearths, their burned meat. They were now very close to the Zealots' camp.

But the lure of the sky seed was irresistible. He began to work his way around the edge of the clearing, stepping over fallen tree trunks, shoving aside smashed branches, ready to duck back into the forest's green shadows.

The sky seed was big, bigger than any animal, perhaps as big as the hut where the people lived. He saw that the thing had fallen here after crashing through the trees, almost reaching the point where the forest gave out at the edge of the cliff itself.

But that was all the sense he could make of it.

He had no words to describe it, no experience against which to map it. Even the touch of it was unfamiliar: glossy black or white, the patches separated by clear straight lines, the soft surface neither hot nor cold, neither skin nor stone nor wood. It was difficult for him even to *see* the thing. He would study some part of it – like the small neat puncture-holes on one part of its hide, surrounded by scorch-marks – but then his gaze would slide away from the strangeness, seeking some point of familiarity and finding none.

'Back,' Mary hissed to Joshua.

He made out the telltale signs that Skinny-folk had been here: the narrow footmarks in the raw dirt, the remains of the burnt rolls of leaves they liked to carry in their mouths. The Zealots had indeed been here too, inspecting the sky seed, just as he was.

But, despite the imminence of danger, he could not abandon this sky seed. It repelled him – yet it attracted him, like the carving on a Skinny-folk spear. Drawn close, driven away, he hovered.

He came to a sudden decision.

He bent and applied his shoulder to the blunt rear of the sky seed. It was lighter than it looked, and it ground forward through the dirt. But soon he was coming up against the resistance of the last battered trees at the cliff's edge.

'Joshua!' Mary hissed.

'Help push.' And he applied himself again.

She tried to make him give up his self-appointed task, wheedling and plucking at his skins. But when she saw he wouldn't come away, she joined him at the back of the sky seed. She was not yet fully grown, but her strength was already immense, enough to drive the sky seed forward, crunching through the spindly cliff-edge trees.

With a screeching scrape, the sky seed pitched over the raw rock lip of the cliff and lurched out of sight. After a last tortured groan, silence fell.

Manekatopokanemahedo:

'Soon, something will appear in the sky,' Babo said. 'A satellite, like those of the outer planets. *Earth will have a Moon*, for the first time in its history.'

Manekato scratched her head. 'How? By some gravitational deflection?'

'No. Like a Mapping, I think. But not a Mapping. The truth is nobody knows, Mane. But the Astrologers can see it is approaching, in the shivers of the starlight.'

'It must be artificial, this moving of a Moon. A contrivance.'

'Yes, of course. It is a deliberate act. But we do not know the agents or their motive.'

Manekato thought through the implications. 'There will be tides,' she said. 'Earthquakes. Great waves.'

'Yes. And *that* is the danger posed to our Farm, and some others.'

Suddenly she was filled with hope. 'Is that why I am here? Is it possible to avert this Moon – to save the Farm?'

'No,' he said, sadly but firmly.

She pulled away from him. 'You talked of my mission. What mission, if the Farm is doomed?'

'You must travel to the Moon,' said Babo.

'Impossible,' she spanned. 'No Mapping has ever been attempted over such a distance.'

'Nevertheless you must make it possible,' Babo said. 'You must use the resources of the Farm to achieve it.'

'And if I reach the Moon?'

'Then you must find those responsible for sending this rogue here. You must make them remove it, and have them assure you it will not return.' He forced a smile. 'We are a species good at negotiation, Mane. The Lineages could not have survived otherwise. You are all but a matriarch, the matriarch of Poka Lineage. You will find a way. Go to the Moon, Mane – take this chance. I will be with you, if you wish. If you succeed, Poka will be granted new land. We have pledges . . .'

'And if I fail – or refuse?'

He stiffened. 'Then our Lineage will die with us. Of course.'

'Of course –'

There was a fizz of purple light, a stink of ozone. A Worker fell from the sky and landed in the centre of the room. Semi-sentient, it raised a sketchy face and peered at them. Recognizing Manekato, it gave her the doleful news it had brought, its voice flat and unengaged.

Orphaned, brother and sister clung to each other as they wept.

Reid Malenfant:

After days of pressure from Malenfant, McCann agreed to lead them in an orderly expedition back to the crash site of the lander. Malenfant felt a vast relief, as if he was being let out of gaol: at last, some progress.

First, McCann inspected them critically. 'I'll have Julia fit you both with buckskin. One must go cannily. You'll stand out a mile in those sky-blue nursery rompers.'

The buckskin gear turned out to be old and musty – presumably manufactured, with much labour, for deceased inhabitants of this place. And McCann loaned Malenfant and Nemoto calf-length leather boots, to keep out the snakes and the bugs. The boots were ill-fitting, and much worn. The gear was heavy, stiff and hot to wear, and its rough interior scratched Malenfant's skin. But it was substantial, feeling like a suit of armour, and was obscurely comforting.

McCann wore a suit of sewn skin and a Davy Crocket hat; he had a crossbow on his back, and a belt of flechettes over his shoulder. He looked capable, tough and well-adapted.

Malenfant wrapped up his coverall and other bits of gear in a skin pack that he wore on his back. He insisted Nemoto do the same; he wanted to be sure they didn't have to return here if they got the chance to get away.

A party of six Hams was gathered in the courtyard. They were all squat, burly men. The Hams wore their peculiar wrappings of skin, tied in place by bits of thong or vegetable rope, not shaped or sewn. They carried weapons, spears and clubs on loops of rope or tucked into their belts, and their broad elliptical heads were shaded by hats of woven grass.

One of them was Thomas, the man who had rescued Malenfant and Nemoto from the wild Runners in the first place.

Malenfant couldn't figure out why the Hams had gotten the lens to him (or come to that how they knew he would be interested). Maybe they just like the story, Malenfant thought, the guy who flies to another world in search of his wife. Just like the American taxpayer. Or maybe there are aspects of these quasi-people none of us will ever understand.

When Malenfant approached to thank him, Thomas shook his hand, an oddly delicate gesture he must have learned from the stranded English, taking care not to crush Malenfant's bones. But, when Malenfant questioned him away from the others, he would say nothing of where he had found Emma's lens.

Two Hams opened the gates of the stockade, and the little party formed up. McCann was to ride in a kind of litter – 'What a Portugoose would call a *machila*, I'm told.' The litter, just a platform of wood, was to be borne by two Hams, and McCann had offered the same to Malenfant and Nemoto.

Malenfant had refused.

Nemoto had been sceptical. 'You are sentimental, Malenfant. After a few hours you may long for a ride. And besides, the Hams are well capable of bearing our weight. They are treated well –'

'That's not the point.'

'Survival is the point. What else?'

Anyhow, with the sun still climbing – with McCann's litter in the van, Malenfant and Nemoto walking in the centre with Hams beside and behind them – the little party set off.

McCann said they would take a roundabout route to the lander. It would take longer, but would avoid the densest forest and so would be less problematic.

They walked through the forest. The air was laden with moisture and without a breath of wind. The sweat was soon dripping from Malenfant's scalp into his eyes, and his buckskin was clinging to his back as if glued there.

The Hams walked barefoot along a trail that was invisible to Malenfant, with their feet splayed at wide angles, making fast, short steps, almost delicate. Malenfant tried to keep up. But the brown sheets of dead leaves on top of wet mud made him slip, or he would walk into thorny lianas, or trip over the surface roots that splayed out from the boles of the largest trees. As the feet and legs of the Ham in front began to blur, he realized he was going to have to imitate the Ham's small movements, but he lost further ground as he tried to master the oddly precise mincing motions.

McCann walked alongside Malenfant, musing. 'Hear how quiet it is. One does miss birdsong. Africa is full of birds, of course: parrots and plovers, kingfishers and skimmers. How sad a world without the song of birds, Malenfant.'

Here was a canthium tree: a massive straight black trunk, branches spreading high above the palms. 'Keep away from it,' McCann said. 'The flowers stink like corpses – to attract flies, you see, which carry its pollen. The pre-sapients keep away from it. The trunk is covered in biting ants –' He froze, and held Malenfant's arm. 'Look there. *An Elf.*' He dropped to all fours and crawled forward, hiding behind a tree.

Malenfant followed suit. The two of them finished lying in cold mud, side by side, peering through a brush of greenery.

A man sat on a bough, a few feet off the ground – a dwarfish, naked, hairy man with a face like a chimp's, and no forehead to speak of. He had long legs like a human, long arms like an ape. He pulled twigs towards his face and bit off leaves, with thick, active lips. His face was black, his eyes brown, sheltered by a thick brow of bone. He moved slowly, thoughtfully.

A twig cracked.

The Elf stopped eating. He leaned forward, rocked from side to side to see better. He urinated, a stream of acrid piss that splashed to the floor not feet from Malenfant's face.

Then he turned away and called. *'Oo-hah!'*

Suddenly there were more of them, more Elves, shadowy figures with glinting eyes and empty hands. They had black faces and palms and soles. If they had crouched like chimpanzees it would have been okay, but they didn't; they stood eerily upright, as if their bodies had been distorted in some hideous lab. They were *wrong*, and Malenfant shivered.

'There are ways to trap them,' McCann whispered. 'Though their more robust cousins the Nutcrackers provide better meat. You hunt with special spears, twelve feet long. Then you goad the Nutcracker-man, until he charges onto your spear point . . .'

The first Elf man stood up straight on his bough. He opened his mouth wide, revealing pink gums and impressive canines, and let out a series of short, piercing barks. He slapped the tree trunk and rattled a branch.

The others joined in, whooping with rage. Their hair was suddenly erect, which made them look twice the size, and they stamped and shook branches in a frenzy. It was quite a display, Malenfant thought, a mass of noise and movement.

Then the man in the tree turned, bent over and let out an explosion of faeces that showered over Malenfant and McCann.

Malenfant brushed gloopy shit off his head. 'Jesus. What a situation.'

McCann was laughing.

Now McCann's Hams stood up. They yelled and banged their spears together, or against logs and tree trunks.

The Elves turned and ran, melting into the green shadows as fast as they had appeared.

Malenfant was relieved when they broke out of the forest, just as McCann had promised, and he found himself walking through a more open country, a kind of parkland of grass and scattered clumps of trees.

Nemoto trudged sourly beside him, her small face hidden by a broad straw hat.

There were herbs in the grass, and when they were crushed by bare Neandertal feet they sent up a rich aroma. The sun was strong on Malenfant's face, and the blue Earth rode high in the sky. Malenfant felt lifted, exhilarated – even giddy, he thought, anoxic perhaps, and he made sure he kept his breathing deep and even, making the most of the thin air.

McCann noticed Malenfant's mood. With a touch of the stubby whip he called a *sjambok*, he directed his Ham bearers to carry him closer to Malenfant. 'Quite a day, isn't it, Malenfant? You know, I believe that with a knight's move of that mopani tree over *here* one might take that kopje, with the thicket of wild banana, over *there*.'

Malenfant forced a laugh. 'Remember, I'm a checkers man.'

McCann was clutching a battered Gladstone bag on his lap, from which he extracted water and ointments to dab on his face, neck and wrists. He looked sideways at Malenfant, as if apologetically. 'I fear I may have come across as something less than a man to you, on our first meetings.'

'Not at all.'

'It's just that one is so desperate for company. But you mustn't think that I am protesting my lot. I draw strength from the teachings of my father – I grew up in a kirk on the Scottish borders – which took a grip on my mind from early days. My father made me a fatalist in creed: man is but a playing-piece in the hands of the Maker. Chess again, eh? And so it was foreordained that I should be brought to this distant shore. But I admit to a great deal of pleasure in my new home on a day like today. Much of it is familiar. In my time here I've spotted wildebeest, kudu, impala. There are few birds in flight, but you'll find flightless, clucking versions of quail, partridge, pheasant . . .'

'But it isn't your true home,' Malenfant said gently. 'Nor mine. It's not even from the right universe. Just as it isn't home for these Hams, is it?'

McCann eyed him sharply. 'You've been talking to the fragrant Julia – their legend of the Grey Earth, the place in the sky from which they stumbled. Yes?' He laughed. 'Well, it might even be true. Perhaps a party of bar-bars did fall through a shining portal, just as you say your wife did. But it was a blooming long time ago, Malenfant.

'Listen. Once upon a time old Crawford got it into his head that there might be something of value in the ground here – gold, diamonds, even hidden treasure of obscure origin, perhaps laid down by some race of supermen. And he went digging – especially in the hearths and caves of the bar-bars. He had to turf out a few of them to do that, for they will cling to their domiciles. He found no treasure. But what he did find was more bar-bars, or anyhow traces of them, their buried bones mixed in with those peculiar knobkerries and assegais they favour in the wild. There was layer upon layer of bone, said old Crawford, in every place he dug.

'Well, the meaning is obvious. These bar-bars have endured a long stretch on this exotic little world: they must surely have been here for hundreds of generations, thousands of years, or more. And in all that time they have clung to their dreams of home.' He considered Malenfant. 'You may think I am harsh with the bar-bars, Malenfant, or uncaring. I am not. Inferior they may be. But what memory lies buried in those deep skulls of theirs! – don't you think?'

The country began to rise. The little party grew strung out. The grass grew thinner, the underlying crimson soil more densely packed.

They reached the crest of a ridge and took a break. The ground was hard-packed here, covered thinly by bracken and little bushes like hazels. The party, drinking water from a pannikin handed around by a Ham, was surrounded by a thin, subsiding cloud of red dust.

Malenfant stepped forward. The ground fell away before him, and he saw that this ridge curved around, making a neat circle. It was a bowl of greenery. A few improbably tall trees sprouted, but much of the basin was covered by grass that was littered with colour, the yellow and white of marigolds and lilies. Pools glistened on the uneven floor, ringed by lush primeval-looking ferns.

It was a crater, a classic impact formation a couple of miles across. Standing here, Malenfant heard distant calls and hoots. They were the cries of hominids, cousins to mankind, patrolling this forested crater. It was a startling, uplifting, utterly alien prospect.

McCann was standing beside him. 'Here we stand, men born on different worlds, confronting a third. Do you know your Plutarch, Malenfant? *Alexander wept when he heard from Anaxarchus that there was an infinite number of worlds* ... *"Do you not think it lamentable that with such a vast multitude of worlds, we have not yet conquered one?"'* He pointed with imperious confidence into the bowl of the crater. 'There lies our *Redoubtable* – or at least her corpse. Come, you men.'

Brushing a walking stick before him, he strode off down the flank of the crater. Malenfant and Nemoto, and the Hams with their litter, hurried to follow.

Malenfant came first on a rib of metal, heavily corroded, that arched into the air above him. Its smooth circular shape was a startling contrast to the fractal profusion of the greenery all around. He stepped under the rib, onto twisted and rusted metallic remnants that groaned under his weight. He found he was in a long cylindrical chamber, its walls extensively broken and corroded, open to the sky. When it was intact this tank must have been six or seven yards in diameter.

Thorn bushes pushed through the base of the cylinder, and creepers curled over its sides; above, a thick canopy turned the light dim, moist and green. The ship had been a long time dead, and the vegetation had grown over and through it, concealing its remains.

McCann walked in alongside him, followed by Nemoto. The Hams lingered on the fringe of the deeper forest, leaning on the litter and sipping water. Thomas kept an eye on McCann, but his gaze slid over the lines of the ship, as if it were a thing of mists and shadows, not really there.

'This was the propellant tank,' McCann said. He pointed with his stick. 'You can see the bulkheads to either end, or what's left of 'em.' McCann pushed on through mazes of piping and cables. Malenfant and Nemoto followed more cautiously, taking care of the sharp edges of twisted metal under their feet.

McCann's figure was stocky and competent, and swathed in his treated animal skins he looked somehow right against the background of the fallen, smashed-open ship; Malenfant wondered how often he visited this relic of home.

They passed through a ripped-open dome into another cylindrical tank. 'Here we stored oxidants. Though of course much of the oxidant was drawn from the air.'

'A ramjet,' Malenfant said to Nemoto.

McCann came to a tangle of what looked like crude electrical equipment, valves and relays, so badly corroded it was an inseparable mass. 'Control gear,' he said. 'For the pumps and valves and so forth.' They passed through a more solid bulkhead, supported by heavy ribs, and arrived in what appeared to have been habitable quarters. There had been several decks, separated by two or three yards – but now tipped over, so the floors and ceilings had become walls. A fireman's pole ran along the length of this section, passing neatly through holes in the floors, horizontal now.

McCann pointed out highlights with his stick. 'Stores.' Malenfant saw the crumpled remnants of bulky machines, perhaps recycling and cleansing devices for air and water, and refrigerated stores for food, but damaged by fire and gutted; they lay in the dark of the rocket's hull like foetuses in unhatched dinosaur eggs. 'Infirmary, galley, sleeping quarters and such.' Little was left here save a bare frame that might have held bunk beds, a heavy table bolted to the tilted-over floor and fitted with leather restraints, perhaps intended for surgery, and the nubs of pipes and flues showed where galley equipment had been ripped out or salvaged.

'And the bridge.' At the nub of the ship, this had been lined with polished oak panels, now scuffed, broken and covered by lichen and moss. Brass portholes bore only fragments of the thick glass that had once lined them. There were heavy couch frames bolted to the floor, long since stripped of their soft coverings. Malenfant could make little of what must once have been instrument panels; now they were just rectangular hollows in the fascia, though he glimpsed tangles of wires behind.

McCann saw him looking. 'Once we realized the old lady wasn't serviceable we stripped out what we could. We built a succession of radio transmitters and heliographs. We got replies, of course, as long as the Earth – I mean, *my* Earth – still hovered in the sky. That, and promises of rescue, which assurances I have no doubt would have been fulfilled. We kept on trying even after Earth had gone, until the last generator seized up. Powered by a bicycling Runner, incidentally.'

'I'm sorry,' Malenfant said. 'She must have been a beautiful ship.'

'Oh, she was. Help me.' Leaning on Malenfant's arm, he clambered stiffly up the hull wall, using gaping porthole sockets as hand- and footholds.

Malenfant followed him. Soon the two of them stood side by side on the outer hull of the habitable section, surrounded by gashes and treacherous-looking rents. But McCann was confident in his step.

From here Malenfant could make out the full sweep of the ship's length, a slim spear that must have been two hundred yards long. Its lovely back was broken; and green tendrils clutched at the ship, as if pulling it into the belly of the Moon that had killed it. But still a solitary fin poked out of the greenery, crumpled but defiant. The fin bore a faded roundel that reminded Malenfant of the logo of the Royal Air Force.

The Ham man, Thomas, walked beside the ship close to McCann, keeping his eyes on the Englishman.

'He is loyal,' said Malenfant. 'He looks out for you all the time.'

'He knows I have done my best to improve the lot of his people.'

Even if it didn't need improving, Malenfant thought. 'But he seems to be having trouble looking at the rocket.'

'The bar-bar mind is rigid, Malenfant. Conservative beyond imagining, they are utterly resistant to the new. At the beginning we had a devil of a battle to keep them from destroying our gear – even when tamed, a bar-bar still harbours destructive tendencies.'

Malenfant recalled the fate of his shoulder camera. He said, 'That almost seems superstitious.'

'Oh, not that. There is no superstition among the bar-bars: there is no magic in their world, no sense of the numinous. To them the surface of the world is everything; they do not see hidden meanings, nor seek deeper explanations.'

'They have no gods, then.'

'Nor can they even conceive of the possibility.' McCann smiled. 'And what a loss that is. I am sure they are well spared propitiations to the savage and bloody gods of the jungle. But they cannot know the Mercy of the one true God. You understand, it is not merely that they do not know Him – they *cannot*. And without God, there is no order to their lives, no meaning – save what *we* provide.' He tapped Malenfant on the chest with the worn head of his walking stick. 'I know you are uncomfortable with our relationship to these barbarians, Malenfant. I see it in your eyes. I've seen it in Africa, when men of conscience go among the Kaffirs there. But can't you see it is our duty to provide them with a Johannen way of life – even if they can't comprehend its meaning? – just as the philosophers and theologians have been proposing since the first steel clippers found these bar-bars' cousins running wild in the New World.'

Malenfant studied Thomas's face, but could see no hint of reaction to McCann's sermonizing.

McCann began to talk briskly about the horsepower generated by the 'Darwin engines' that had once powered the ship. 'I know your little tub came gliding in like a bat. We applied a little more brute force. In the last stages of its descent the *Redoubtable* was intended to land upright on Earth or Moon, standing on its rocket exhaust. And it should have taken off in the same manner.'

'Direct ascent,' Malenfant said. It was a mode that had been considered for Apollo's lunar landings, a whole ship traversing back and forth between Earth and Moon. But aside from the greater expense compared to the final Lunar Module design, landing such a giant ship with rockets would have posed stability problems, like an ICBM landing on its tail.

From McCann's descriptions, it sounded as if that had been the downfall of the *Redoubtable*.

'She was a veteran,' McCann said softly. 'She had done the Earth–Moon round trip a dozen times or more. But now we were dealing with a new Moon, you see. Well, we hastily modified her for her new mission. She landed on her fins well enough on the fields at Cosford, but this crater floor is no tarmacadam strip in Shropshire. She was top-heavy, and –' He fell silent, studying the ruined carcass of the ship. 'I was navigator; I must share responsibility for the disaster that followed. Most of us got out, by the Mercy of God.' He clapped Malenfant on the back, forcing a laugh. 'And since then our lovely ship has been scavenged to make cooking pots.'

'Erasmus Darwin,' Nemoto called.

Malenfant looked down.

Nemoto was standing in the ruins of the habitable compartment, peering up at him. Her face was like a brown coin in the gloom. 'The

Darwin drive,' she said. 'Grandfather of Charles, who is probably the Darwin you're thinking of, Malenfant. In the 1770s he sketched a simple liquid-fuel rocket engine, along with a ramjet. In our world, the sketch languished unnoticed in his notebooks until the 1990s. But in Mr McCann's world –'

McCann nodded. 'The design was the seed around which a new generation of rockets and missiles grew. After the pioneering work of Congreve, the Brunels, father and son, became involved in the development of craft capable of carrying heavy loads into the atmosphere. The first dummy load was orbited around the Earth before the death of Victoria, Empress of the Moon, and the first manned flight beyond the atmosphere was launched from Ceylon in 1920 . . . Ah, but none of this happened in your world, did it, Malenfant? It is a divergence of history. In your world Darwin was ignored or forgotten, his ideas no doubt rediscovered by some other, more vigorous nation.'

'Something like that.'

Nemoto moved on, working her way through the ship's gloomy interior.

McCann watched her, then leaned closer to Malenfant. 'Always watching, thinking, *recording*, your little Oriental friend – eh, Malenfant?'

'That's her way,' Malenfant said cautiously. 'And it's our mission. Part of it, anyhow.'

'And quite the fount of knowledge about obscure British philosophers two centuries dead.' McCann's eyes narrowed. 'I have observed the gadget she carries.'

Malenfant saw no point in lying. 'It's called a softscreen.'

'Its working is no doubt beyond my comprehension, but its purpose is clear enough. It is a repository of knowledge, from which Madam Nemoto sips as she requires. I am a man of this dismal jungle now, Malenfant, but you need not think me a fool.'

'Take it easy, McCann.'

McCann frowned, as if decoding the colloquialism. 'Without my shelter you would both surely be "taking it easy" beneath the crimson dust by now. Remember that.' When Malenfant did not answer, McCann clapped him on the shoulder again. 'Enough of one beached vessel; let us seek another. Come.' McCann began to clamber down to the ground, into the helpful arms of the Ham who served him.

* * *

It took another two hours to reach the clearing dug out by the lander on its way down.

The lander was gone.

This was the place he remembered: the Gagarin avenue cut through the trees, the scattered bushes and branches – and even bits of blue parafoil, grimy, damp, still clinging to the damaged foliage. But the lander was gone.

McCann stalked over the grass, inspecting ripped-up bushes, scattered trees. 'You're sure this is the place?'

'It can't be.'

Nemoto approached him. 'Malenfant, you are not a man who has trouble remembering where he parked the car.'

Malenfant wanted to believe the lander was sitting someplace else, where it had fallen, as battered and crumpled and precious as when he and Nemoto had so foolishly become parted from it – a key part of the technological ladder that would take him, and Emma, home. But there could be no doubt.

'*We're stranded*, Nemoto,' he blurted. 'As stranded as these damn English.'

'Perhaps we always were,' she said evenly.

He hitched his pack of tied-up skin, containing all his belongings, all that was left of Earth. 'We're a pretty pathetic expeditionary force.'

She shrugged. 'We still have the most important tools: our minds, and our hands, and our knowledge.' She eyed him. 'What do you intend to do now?'

'Let's get out of here. We have to find the lander. There's nothing more we can achieve with these English. I hate to be a bad guest, but I'm not sure how well McCann will take our leaving.'

'Not well, I fear,' Nemoto said dryly. And she stepped back.

A hand clamped on Malenfant's arm. It was a Ham, not Thomas.

McCann came walking up, leaning on his stick, his broad face red and grim. 'Thank you, Madam Nemoto,' he said. 'He has behaved just as you predicted.'

Malenfant glared at Nemoto, disbelieving. 'You betrayed me. You warned him I'd try something.'

'You are very predictable, Malenfant.' She sighed, impatient, her face expressionless. 'You should not make the mistake of believing we share the same agenda, Malenfant. This new Moon, this Red Moon, is the greatest mystery in recorded history – a mystery that deepens with every day that passes, everything we learn.

Unless we discover the truth behind it, we will have accomplished nothing.'

'And you believe you can achieve that by staying here, with McCann?'

'We need a base, Malenfant. We need resources. We can't spend our whole lives looking over our shoulders for the next stone axe to fall, or grubbing around in the forest for food. These British have all that.'

'*And what of Emma?*'

Nemoto said nothing, but McCann said smoothly, 'Our scouts and hunters range far and wide, Malenfant. If she is here, we will find her for you.'

If your Ham scouts tell you everything they see, Malenfant thought. He fingered the little lens in his pocket.

'Let's look at the matter in a sensible light,' McCann said now. 'I know you think little of me, Malenfant. But once again I assure you I am not a fool. I desire more than a chess partner; I desire escape from this place – what man wouldn't? Now you have fallen from the sky into my lap, and only a fool would let you go, for surely your *Americans* will come looking for you from that blue Earth of yours. And when they do, they will find me.'

'My world isn't your world,' Malenfant snarled.

'But my world is lost,' McCann said wistfully. 'And I know you have an England. Perhaps I will find a place there.' His face hardened, and Malenfant perceived a new toughness. This was, Malenfant remembered, a representative of a breed who had carved out a global empire – and on a much more hostile planet than Earth. 'Providence has given me my chance and I must take it. I believe that in keeping you now, in following the promptings of my own infallible heart, I see the workings of Omnipotence. Is this moral arrogance? But without such beliefs man would never have left the trees and the caves, and remained like our pre-sapient and pongid cousins.' He glanced at Nemoto. 'As for your companion's slight treachery – perhaps she is destined to betray you, over and over, on all Anaxarchus's infinity of worlds. What do you think?' And he brayed laughter.

The little column formed up for the homeward journey. The big Ham called Thomas took his place beside Malenfant.

And he winked broadly.

Emma Stoney:

A day after leaving the first troupe, Emma found another group of Hams, women and a few infants foraging for berries and fruit. They had regarded her blankly, but then, seeing she was no threat – and, as not *one of them*, of no conceivable interest – they had turned away and continued their gathering.

Emma waited patiently until they were done. Then she followed them back to their encampment.

She stayed here a couple of days, and then moved on, seeking another troupe.

And then on again.

Hams were basically the same, wherever she found them. Their tool-making, for instance. Though each group varied its kit a little according to circumstances, like the availability of different types of stone – and perhaps, she speculated, some slight cultural tradition – still, if something was not in their tool-making repertoire, which was evidently very ancient and fixed, no Ham was interested.

They didn't even talk about their tool-making, even while they jabbered endlessly about their intricate social lives. It was as if they were conscious while they were interacting with each other, but not while they were making tools, or even hunting.

After a time Emma began to get used to it. She reasoned that *she* did many things she wasn't aware of, like breathing, and keeping her heart pumping. And she could think of times when she had performed quite complex tasks requiring skill, judgement and the focus on a specific goal without knowing about it – such as driving all the way to work with her mind on some stunt of Malenfant's, only to 'wake up' when she found herself in the car lot. Or she thought of her father, able to carve fine furniture from wood in his hobby workshop, but never able to tell her how it was done; all he could do was show her.

With the Hams, that circle of unawareness spread a little further, that was all. Or maybe it was just that you could get used to anything, given time.

Anyhow it didn't matter. She wasn't here to run experiments in hominid cognition. It was enough that she was able to use her fish and rabbits and other hunting produce as subtle bribes to gain favour – or at least as a hedge against exclusion.

Thus she worked her way through the forest, moving from one Ham group to the next, using them as stepping stones of comparative safety, one way or another travelling steadily east, day after day, seeking Malenfant.

But sometimes she glimpsed faces in the forest, just at the limit of her vision: hominid faces, watchful, like no species she had yet encountered. It seemed she had barely glimpsed the extent of her kin, on this strange world.

Reid Malenfant:

The details of the regime that would govern Malenfant's life coalesced with startling speed and efficiency – such speed, in fact, that Malenfant wondered who else McCann or the others had had cause to imprison.

Malenfant was free to come and go, within the stockade. But there was always a burly male Ham at his elbow, even sleeping outside his hut during the night.

He took to prowling around the perimeter fence. It was tall, and its ferocious spikes were daubed with a sticky, tar-like substance. For the first time it struck him that the fence was just as effective at keeping him in as keeping out the undesirables of the wilds beyond. And anyhow every time Malenfant tried to approach the fence too closely, he was immobilized by his Ham guard – as simple as that; one of those massive hands would clamp on his shoulder or elbow or even his head, exerting a strength he couldn't hope to match.

He tested his cage in other ways.

He spoke to Thomas, asking for his help. But Thomas would say nothing, giving no hint that he was prepared to follow up on that reassuring wink in the forest.

One night Malenfant tried climbing out of his hut's window. But though it was unglazed the window was small and high. By the time he had dropped clumsily to the ground his Ham keeper was standing over him, silhouetted by blue Earthlight, solid and silent as a rock.

He considered making other protests – going on a hunger strike, maybe. But he sensed McCann might simply let him starve; the steel he had glimpsed in the soul of this other-world Brit did not encourage him to seek for weakness or pity. Alternatively McCann might have his Ham servants force-feed Malenfant, not a prospect he relished, since the Hams were muscled a little too heavily to be good nurses.

Anyhow he needed to build his strength for the days to come, and the search for Emma he confidently expected to be progressing sooner rather than later.

So, after a couple of days, Malenfant began to engage with McCann once more: eating with him, even walking around the compound, conversing. It was a peculiar arrangement, in which both of them clearly knew their relative positions of power and yet did not speak of it, as if they were engaged in some formal game.

Malenfant tried to find out as much as he could about this world from McCann. But the British had done little exploring more than a few days' travel away from their stockade. Their main business here had, after all, been ensuring their survival. And McCann's mind seemed peculiarly closed to Malenfant. The purpose of McCann's original mission had not been exploration, and still less science, but economic and political gain for his Empire; he was more like a prospector than a surveyor. But sometimes he spoke again of the deeper mission he felt he had taken on: to bring the word of his God, and his Christ-figure John, to the barbarian hominids of the Red Moon.

McCann was a man with a head full of agendas. It seemed to Malenfant he was barely able to see the Red Moon and its exotic inhabitants for what they were – just as the Hams had seemed unable to look directly at the wreckage of the *Redoubtable*.

Maybe every hominid species had such blind spots, mused Malenfant. He wondered what his own were.

For his part McCann pressed Malenfant about rescue.

Malenfant tried to describe the politics and economics of his home world. He knew it was extremely unlikely that the will to mount a further mission could be assembled on Tide-ravaged Earth – even though the NASA support teams knew where the lander had come down, and had received those few minutes of footage to show he and Nemoto had survived, at least for a time.

McCann showed Malenfant the transceiver gear he and his companions had scavenged from the wreck of the *Redoubtable*. It was a formidable array of antique-type parts, huge glass valves and mica capacitors and big clattering relays. For years the British had nursed it, for instance keeping it continually powered to save the valves from the thermal shock of being switched on and off. But at last too many of the valves had failed, and other parts were corroded and damaged from prolonged exposure to the damp air. Malenfant tinkered with the gear, but he had less idea than McCann how to fix it.

In his own mind Malenfant's primary mission remained clear: to find Emma, and get the hell off this Moon. If he could help McCann on the way, fine; if Nemoto wanted to come home or stay here, it was up to her. But they were side issues. To Malenfant, only home and Emma mattered.

So they worked through their days. But as time passed it seemed to Malenfant that McCann grew steadily more anxious. Periodically he would peer up into the sky, as if seeking to reassure himself that Earth was still there.

And Malenfant barely saw Nemoto.

One morning, maybe a week into his captivity, he was woken as usual by Julia, with her wooden bowl of hot water and a fresh stone blade for him to shave. Dressed in her blouse and long skirt of sewn skin, with her muscled body moving powerfully, she looked absurd, like a chimpanzee in a child's dress.

She picked up his covered slop bucket, curtsied at him – 'Baas' – and made to leave.

'Help me,' Malenfant blurted.

She stopped by the door. Malenfant could see the shadow of a burly Ham male outside the door.

'Baas?'

'You know I'm being kept here against my will – umm, Boss McCann won't let me go. You helped me before. You gave me the lens – the clear stone. You know it came from Emma. I want to get out of here and find her, Julia. I don't want to hurt anybody, not Boss McCann, not anybody. I just want to get to Emma.'

She shrugged, her mountainous shoulders rippling. 'Breakfas',' she said.

Frustrated, he snapped, 'Why do you stay here? Any one of you could take on McCann and his cronies. Even their crossbows couldn't hold you back if you put your mind to it.'

She looked at him reproachfully. 'Tired ol' men,' she said, as if that was explanation enough. Then she turned and walked out, the slop pail carried effortlessly in one huge hand.

Manekatopokanemahedo:

The great Mapping, across a distance unprecedented in recorded history, could be regarded as a technological triumph. But to Manekato it had been like the working out of an intricate mathematical theorem, a theorem that proved the identity of certain points of space and time with certain other points. The fact that those other points were placed close to the surface of a world which had not even existed as the proof was developed scarcely added to the complexity of the procedure. And once the proof was established, the journey itself would be a mere corollary, of little interest save as an exercise for the young.

The proof had not been trivial, but it had not been over-demanding. Most adults, with a little effort, could have achieved the same result. Manekato had worked at the Mapping with part of her mind, with the rest consumed by her grief for her mother and her concerns over her own future.

On Mane's Earth, anybody could develop a space programme in their spare time.

With her brother Babo and the woman who called herself Without-Name, Manekato stood on the crushed bones of her ancestors. The eternal Wind blasted over the rock, unnoticed. Above her hovered a great rippling lens of star-filled sky, as if a hole had been cut in the clouds: thanks to simple Mapping techniques it was as if she was suspended in orbit, far above the clouds of Earth. But the three of them barely glanced up; it was a minor, uninteresting miracle.

This eroded volcanic core, once the heart of the Farm, was bare now. After her mother had died, Manekato had ordered the deletion of the great House. The walls of Adjusted Space had disappeared like a bursting bubble, as if fifty millennia of sturdy existence had been but a dream. Manekato had welcomed the simple geologic clarity of the mountain's eroded summit: she knew she could never live in the House, and it served no purpose save to preserve memories of unhappiness.

But she had retained the pit containing the ashes of her grandmothers, and to it she had added the last remains of Nekatopo.

Without-Name stalked around the perimeter of the ash pit, her knuckles pressing disrespectfully into the sealed-in dirt, leaving impressions of her hands and feet. A Worker followed this ill-mannered guest, restoring the pit's smoothness. 'Destroy the pit,' Without-Name told Manekato. 'Fill it in. Delete it. It serves no purpose.'

'The pit is the memory of my Lineage,' said Manekato evenly.

Without-Name bared her teeth and growled. 'This pit is not a memory. It is a hole filled with dust.'

Babo protested, 'The practice of adding oneself to the Farm's ground at the end of one's life is as old as our species. It derives from the sensible desire to use every resource to enrich the ground for one's descendants. Today the practice is symbolic, of course, but –'

'Symbolism. Pah! Symbolism is for fools.'

Babo looked shocked.

If Without-Name enjoyed goading Manekato, she positively relished taunting Babo. 'Only children chatter of an afterlife. We are nothing but transient dissipative structures. In your cherishing the bone dust of the dead you are seeking to deny the basic truth of existence: that when we die, we are gone.'

Babo said defiantly, 'I have visited the Rano Lineage and I saw the pit of your ancestors. You are a hypocrite. You say one thing and practise the other.'

She raised herself to her hind feet and towered over him. She wore her body hair plucked clean in great patches over her body, and where hair remained it had been stiffened into great bristling spikes. It was a fashion from the other side of the world that made her seem oddly savage to Manekato. 'Not any more,' she hissed. 'I salute death. I salute the cleansing it brings. There is only life – all that matters is the here and the now – and what can be achieved in the moment.'

Manekato held back her emotions.

This Without-Name's preferred diminutive actually was – had been – Renemenagota. But she insisted she had abandoned her true name. 'My land is to be destroyed,' she had said. 'And so is my Lineage. What purpose does a fossilized name serve?' Even the contradiction in her position – for *Without-Name* was itself a name, of course, so that she was trapped in an oxymoron – seemed only to please her perversely. Manekato knew she must work with this woman, who was a refugee as she was, to study the rogue Moon and its fabricators; that had been the directive of the Astrologers. But Manekato felt that she had been the target of Without-Name's bitterness and discourtesy from the moment they had been thrown together . . .

There was a dazzling electric-blue flash, gone in an instant.

A shift in the Wind touched Manekato's face. She looked into the tunnel of stars.

'If you embrace experience,' she said, 'then you must embrace *that*.'

Without-Name lifted her head awkwardly, and fell forward onto her knuckles.

Babo was already gazing at the sky, open-mouthed. Even the Workers were backing away, small visual sensors protruding from their hides, peering up at the dangerous sky.

Suddenly the Red Moon swam there, complete, huge.

Reid Malenfant:

Nemoto said in a monotone, 'We are dealing with multiple universes. That much is clear. We have seen for ourselves multiple Moons. And we have hints of multiple Earths. The Earth of Hugh McCann is clearly quite different from our Earth – even if his history is interestingly convergent with ours. And the Hams talk of a Grey Earth, a third place where conditions may be different again . . .'

In the hut Malenfant had come to think of as the dining hall, Nemoto and Malenfant faced each other at either end of the long table. The table's wooden surface, polished to darkness by decades of use, was bare. An elderly Ham woman was preparing lunch.

It had taken days before Malenfant had been able to face Nemoto, such was his anger at her betrayal. But she was his only companion from home, and if he was ever going to get out of here he might need her help. As for Nemoto, it was as if the incident of the betrayal had simply been a step in some grand plan, which any rational person would accept as justified.

But she was changing, Malenfant saw: becoming more with-drawn, hollow-eyed – dangerously detached from the texture of the world around her, obsessed instead with huge ideas of origins and destinies.

So Malenfant listened coldly, as Nemoto described alternate realities.

'Malenfant, perhaps there are a cluster of alternate universes with identical histories up to the moment of some key event in the evolution of humanity – and differing after that only in the details of that event, and its consequences.' Nemoto waved her hands vaguely, as if trying to indicate three-dimensional space around her. 'Imagine the possible universes arrayed around us in a kind of probability space, Malenfant. Do you see that universes differing *only* in the details of the evolution of mankind must somehow be *close* to ours in that graph?'

'And you're saying this is what we're experiencing – a crossover between possible universes? Well, maybe. But it's just talk. What I don't see is how you can hop from one cosmos to the next.'

Nemoto smiled coldly. 'I do not know how that is possible, Malenfant. And what is more important is that I do not know *why* anybody should wish to make it happen.'

'*Why* . . . You think all of this is deliberate – somehow artificial?'

'Your Wheel in Africa looked artificial to me, Malenfant. Perhaps the Hams' Old Ones, if they exist, will be able to tell us what they intended.'

'And you're going to ask them, I suppose.'

'If they exist. If I can find them. What else is there to do? Malenfant, there is something else. I have raised with McCann the question of whether other life forms exist beyond the Earth – *his* Earth, I mean. His scientists have looked for evidence, as ours have. They have found none. Philosophers there have propounded something similar to our Fermi Paradox to crystallize this observation.'

'Why is this important?'

'I don't know yet. But it does appear odd that such a profound contradiction is to be found in both universes . . .'

Light flickered, startlingly blue, beyond the door frame. Malenfant gasped. The colour had tugged at his heart – for it was the colour of the flash from within the Wheel that had consumed Emma.

They hurried outside. There was something in the sky.

Manekatopokanemahedo:

In her first stunned glance Manekato made out a single vast continent, scorched red, and a blue-grey ocean from which the sun cast a single blunt highlight. The disc, almost full, was surrounded by a thin layer of blurred softness. An atmosphere, then. But no lights shone in the darkened, shadowed crescent.

The Wind buffeted Manekato, turbulent, suddenly uneven. Already it begins, she thought.

Small Workers, no larger than insects, hovered around Babo's head, defying the shifting breeze; she saw their light play over his face, dense with information. 'Its gross parameters are as we anticipated,' he said. 'A Moon, a world, two-thirds of Earth's diameter, a quarter of its mass. It has an atmosphere –'

'It is not Farmed,' Without-Name hissed. 'Your jabber of numbers is meaningless, you fool. Look at it: *it is not Farmed*. This Moon is primordial.'

Without-Name was right. Even without magnification Manekato could see great expanses where nothing lived: that ugly red scar of a continent, the naked oceans, those crude caps of ice. It was a world of waste, of unawakened resources.

Wild.

'Wild, yes,' growled Without-Name. 'Consider the comparison with our Earth. For two million years we have cherished every atom. We have carefully sustained the diversity of species. We have even sacrificed ourselves – billions of years of lost lives – refusing longevity in order to maintain the balance of the world.'

Mane murmured, 'An ecology consisting of a single species would not be sustainable.'

Without-Name laughed. 'You quote childish slogans. Think, Manekato! Our species has been shaped, even as we have shaped our world. But *nothing* about that ugly Moon has been managed. We will have no place. We will have to fight to achieve our purposes, perhaps even to survive.'

Mane was troubled by that perception, though she acknowledged it might contain a grain of truth.

'But,' Babo said, an edge in his voice, 'the Red Moon cannot be primordial – it must contain mind – *for it would not be here otherwise*.'

Yes, Mane thought. Yes. And for that she was afraid of this monstrous Moon. It was a deep fear, of a type she had never suffered before, a fear suffused by a sense of powerlessness. She had to search deep into the recesses of her memory, poring through the most ancient roots of the million-year-old language with which all children were born, to find an ancient, obsolete word that suited what she felt:

Superstition.

Babo rattled more statistics of the Moon's composition, describing a ball of silicate rock and a small iron core. But as his courage grew his thinking seemed to clear. '*Earth*,' he said. 'That wandering Moon is made of the same material as Earth's outer layers. How can that be?'

The three of them began to talk rapidly, their minds developing and sharing hypotheses.

'Given the identity of substances this body cannot have formed elsewhere in the Solar System.' 'Could it have budded off an Earth while the planet was accreting from the primordial cloud of dust and ice?' 'No, for then its proportions should resemble Earth's global composition, and this body shows a deficiency of iron and other heavy elements. It is more like a piece of the Earth's mantle, its outer layers, ripped up and wadded together and thrown into the sky.' 'Then an Earth must have formed, differentiated so the iron-rich rocks sank to the core, before the material to assemble this Moon was detached from the outer layers. But how would it happen?' 'A vast volcanic event? But surely that would not be sufficiently violent –' 'A collision. A rogue planetesimal, a giant, or even a planet. Such a collision might cause a splash of ejecta which could accrete into this Moon . . .'

Within seconds, then, they had unravelled the mystery of the Moon's origin, a deduction that had taken humans two centuries of geological science.

All around the Earth, other witnesses must be coming to a similar conclusion, and Manekato imagined a growing consensus of understanding whispering in Babo's ear.

'But,' Manekato said, 'if this Red Moon was born from Earth, it was not *our* Earth.'

'No,' Babo said sombrely. 'For our Earth never suffered a catastrophic collision of that magnitude. We would see the results today, for example in the composition of the planet's core. And if our world had enjoyed the company of such a Moon everything would have been different in its evolution: much of the primordial atmosphere would have been stripped off in the collision, leaving thinner air less rich in carbon dioxide; there would have been many subtle effects on tides and the world's spin . . .'

'On such a world,' Manekato said, 'one would not need a Mapping to see the stars. And in such a sky a Moon like this would ride. But such is not our world.'

'Not our universe,' said Without-Name bluntly. 'Tell me then, Babo: what do your Astrologers have to say of a power which can Map a Moon, not merely from planet to planet, but *between universes?*'

'They have little to say,' he said evenly. 'That is why we must go there . . . There is something more.' He uttered a soft command to his Workers.

A new Mapping was made, showing them a vision from a large Farm that straddled the equator of the planet.

A giant blue circle, hovering above the ground, was sweeping over the Farm's cultivated ground, upright and improbably tall. People stood and watched as it passed. Workers backed away before it. Children ran alongside it, laughing, levering themselves forward on their knuckles in their excitement.

And there were people falling out of the circle's empty disc.

No, not people, Manekato saw: *like* people, naked hominids, some tall and hairless, some short and squat and covered in fine black hair. They flopped and gasped for breath like stranded fish, and their flimsy bodies were buffeted this way and that by the Wind.

'What does it mean, Babo?'

'One can predict the broad outline of events. But chaos is in the detail . . .' He waved his hand, banishing the image.

A gust of Wind howled across the bare, eroded plateau, powerful enough to make Manekato stagger.

Babo stepped forward. 'It is time.'

Manekato and Without-Name took his hands and each other's, so the three of them were locked together in a ring.

At the last moment Manekato asked, 'Must it be so?'

Babo shrugged regretfully. 'The predictions are exact, Mane. The focusing effect of the shoreline's shape here, the gradient of the ocean floor, the precise positioning of the new Moon in the sky: all of these have conspired to doom our Farm, and the Poka line with it.'

Without-Name tipped back her head and laughed, the spikes that covered her body bristling and twisting. 'And for all our vaunted power we can do nothing about it. This is a moment that separates past from future. It is a little death. My friends, welcome the cleansing!'

Manekato uttered a soft command.

The three of them rose into the air, through a body's height. The Mapping had begun.

Mane . . .

Surprised to hear her name called, Manekato looked down. One of the Workers, a battered old gadget from a long-forgotten crop, was peering up at her with a glinting lens. It was clinging to the ground with long stabilizing suckers, but the Wind battered at it, and its purple-black hide glistened with rain.

Memory stirred. There had been a Worker like this when she had clambered from her mother's womb, chattering excitedly, full of energy and curiosity. In those first days and weeks that Worker had fed her, instructed her, kept her from harm, and comforted her when she was afraid. She had not seen the old gadget for years, and had thought little of it. Could this be the same Worker? Why should it seek her now, as it was about to be destroyed?

A wall of rain swept over the mountain-top. The three of them were immediately soaked, and Manekato laboured to breathe the harshly gusting air.

When the rain gust passed, the mountain-top had been swept bare; all the Workers were gone, surely destroyed. Manekato felt an odd, distracting pang – regret, perhaps?

But this was no time to dwell on the past; the nameless one was right about that.

The three of them ascended without effort.

She was still clothed in her body, her legs dangling, her hair soaked. But of course this body was a mere symmorph: differing from her original self in form, but representing the same idea. (And in fact, as she had been through hundreds of previous Mappings, that 'original' body had itself been nothing but a symmorph, a copy of a copy reworked to suit temporary needs, though one tailored to remain as close to her primary biological form as possible.)

But such a morphology was no longer appropriate. With a soundless word, she discarded the symmorph, and accepted another form.

Now she was smeared around Earth, immersing it in her awareness, as if it were a speck that floated in her eyeball.

The great Farms glittered over the planet: from pole to pole, around the equator, even on the floor and surface of the oceans, and in the clouds. It was as if the planet were encrusted with jewels of light and life and order. There were no barren red deserts, no frozen ice caps *here*.

But already, as the Red Moon began its subtle gravitational work, the first changes were visible. Huge ocean storms were unravelling the delicate ocean-floor and water-borne Farms. A vast line of earth-quakes and ugly volcanism was unstitching an eastern continent. And, from an ocean which was sloshing like water in a disturbed bath, a train of immense tsunamis marched towards the land.

Soon the Poka Farm was covered – extinguished, scoured clear, even the bedrock shattered, the bone dust of her ancestors scattered and lost, beyond memory.

The jewel-like lights were failing, all over the world. There was nothing for her here.

She gazed at her destination, the new, wandering Moon.

Reid Malenfant:

Malenfant's world was stratified into layers of varying incomprehensibility.

At the base of it all was the stockade, the familiar sturdy fence and the huts of mud and wood: the physical infrastructure of the world, solid, imperturbable.

And then there were the people.

Hugh McCann was standing alone at the centre of the colony's little street, hands dangling at his sides, gazing up at a corner of the sky. His mouth was open, and his cheeks glistening, as if he was weeping. Nemoto was shielding her eyes, so that she couldn't so much as glimpse the sky above.

He saw Julia and Thomas, close together near the gate. The Hams didn't seem disturbed by the fiery sky. They were stripping off their neat, sewn-together garments, revealing bodies that were ungainly slabs of corded muscle. They pulled on much cruder skin wraps, of the kind Malenfant had seen Thomas wear out in the bush, tying them up with thongs. More Hams were coming in through the open gate (*the gate is open, Malenfant!*), and they picked up the discarded English-type clothing and started to pull it on.

A shift change, he thought, wondering. As if the settlement was a factory maintained by a pool of labour beyond the stockade walls.

And in the sky . . .

You can't put off thinking about it any longer, Malenfant.

Start with the basics. There is the white sun, the yellow Earth (*yellow?*). There are the clouds, stringy cirrus today, littered over the sky's dome. And beyond the clouds, in the spaces between sun and Earth –

What, Malenfant?

He saw bars, circles, lines, patterns that seemed to congeal and then disappear. If he stared fixedly at one point of the sky he would make out a fragment of texture, as if something was sliding by, something huge, beyond the roof of the world. But it never stayed stable in his vision – like an optical illusion, a form that oscillated between two interpretations, a bubble that flipped into a crater. And no matter how he tried he would find his eyes sliding away to the familiar, to the huts, the red dust of the ground.

'Why can't I see it?'

Nemoto kept her head down. 'It's too far beyond your experience, Malenfant. Or above it. You think of your eyes as little cameras, your ears as microphones, giving you some objective impression of the true world. They are not. Everything you think you see is a kind of virtual-reality projection, based on sensory input, framed by prejudice about what the brain imagines *ought* to be out there. Remember, we evolved as plain-dwelling hunter-gatherers, and our sensoriums are conditioned to the hundred-mile scale of Earth landscapes. Malenfant, you just aren't programmed to see –'

'The scaffolding in the sky.'

'Whatever it is.'

'Like the Hams. When we went to the wreck of the *Redoubtable*. It was as if they couldn't see it at all.'

'Do you find the thought disturbing, Malenfant? To find you have the same limitations as Neandertals?'

'What's happening, Nemoto? What is coming down on us?'

'I could not begin even to guess.'

McCann was standing alone, still weeping.

As Malenfant approached, McCann used his sleeve to wipe away the dampness on his cheeks, the dribble of mucus that had dangled from his nose. 'Malenfant. You bear yourself well. The first Change I witnessed threw me into a cold grue of terror. But you have a stiff back; I could see that about you from the start.'

'What are you talking about?'

'Can't you see?' And he stabbed a finger at the sky, at the Earth.

The new Earth.

The planet was a ball of yellow-white cloud, very bright. It was banded by water-colour streaks of varying colours. There were dark knots in the bands, perhaps giant storms. It reminded Malenfant of nothing so much as spaceprobe images of Jupiter or Saturn. It was a Banded Earth.

Deep unease settled into his gut. 'What happened to the Earth?'

'Nothing, Malenfant,' Nemoto said, her voice expressionless. 'It's gone. Or rather, we have. The Red Moon has moved on a fresh universe, another of the vast ensemble of possibilities –'

'And it has taken us with it,' McCann said bitterly. 'We have suffered another knight's move between possibilities. Now do you see why I weep? It is unmanly, perhaps – but now that the Red Moon has moved on from your world, any chance of rescue by your people is gone with it.' He laughed, an ugly sound. 'I have seen a whole succession of worlds skip through that dismal sky, Malenfant, each of them as bleak as the last – save only for yours, where I could see the glint of cities on the night side. And then your squat glider came floating down from the sky, and I allowed myself to hope, you see – a fool's mistake. But now hope is gone, and you are as stranded as I am – both of you – all of us in this Purgatory . . .'

Malenfant saw it in that instant; it was as if the world swivelled around him, taking on new, and unwelcome, configurations. The Red Moon had moved on. He was indeed stranded, beyond the reach of any help from those who knew him – *stranded in another universe*, to which he had somehow been transported.

In a corner of his mind he wondered if poor impoverished Luna had been restored to the skies of Earth.

As the light show faded the Hams – the 'new shift' – were moving slowly around the stockade, picking up brooms and tools, heading for the huts. Beginning their work.

Malenfant said, 'Why do they come here?'

McCann held up his hands, plucked at his threadbare jacket. 'Look at me. I am old and fat and tired – and at that I am perhaps the best functioning of those who survived the crash of the *Redoubtable*. And now look at the bar-bars.' He faced Malenfant. 'You think I am some slave-keeper. How could I keep these people, if they did not wish to stay? Or – if I keep slaves, *where are the children*? Where are the old, the lame?' He pointed beyond the gate. 'There is a troupe of them out there. We keep up a certain trade, I suppose you'd call it. They sustain this little township with their labour, as you have seen. And in return, there are things we have which they covet: certain foodstuffs – and beer, Malenfant, your bar-bar gentleman likes his beer!'

Nemoto said levelly to Julia, 'Why do you keep these English alive?'

Julia grinned, showing a row of tombstone teeth. 'Tired ol' men,' she said.

McCann eyed Malenfant ruefully. 'Pity, you see; the pity of animals. They saw we had no women or children, that we were slowly dying. They regard us as pets, these Hams. *That* is what we are reduced to.'

'And all your talk of educating them in a Christian, umm, Johannen life –'

'A man does not welcome too much reality . . .'

That gate was still open. You're wasting time, Malenfant.

He found Julia. She was dressed in her native skins; no trace of her guise as a maid for the English remained. He pointed towards the open gate. He said, 'Emma.'

She nodded.

He went back to the others. 'I'm out of here, McCann. Will you try to stop me?'

McCann laughed. 'What difference does it make now? But what will you do?'

'What I came to do,' Malenfant said bluntly.

'Ah – Emma. I wish I had the comfort of such a goal.' McCann looked at Nemoto. 'And you, Madam Nemoto? Will you stay with a beaten old man?'

Nemoto raised her face to the sky; flickering light reflected from her skin. 'I will seek answers.'

'Answers?' McCann snorted. 'Of what use are answers? Can you eat answers, sleep under them, use them to ward off the Runners, the Elves?'

She shrugged. 'I am not content to subsist, like you, like these Hams.'

Malenfant felt reluctant to lose her, even though she had betrayed him. And besides, she was scarcely street-wise: he imagined her dreaming of sheaves of parallel universes as a shaped cobble stove in her skull . . . 'Come with me.'

She appraised him coolly. 'We have always had different agendas, Malenfant.'

McCann looked from one to the other. Impulsively he said, 'I have been sedentary too long. Let me accompany you, Malenfant. I dare say I have a few tricks, born of long experience, which might yet save your hide.'

Malenfant glanced at Julia, who had no reaction. 'What about Crawford and the others?'

McCann clapped Thomas on his broad shoulder. 'I see no reason why our friends should fail to look after three as well as they have looked after four.'

Thomas nodded curtly.

Malenfant faced Nemoto. 'I hope you find what you are looking for.'

'I will see you again,' she said.

'No,' he said, flooded by a sudden certainty. 'No, you won't. We'll never meet again.'

She stared at him. Then she turned away.

Manekatopokanemahedo:

She was standing on a shining, smooth surface of Adjusted Space, bright yellow, softly warm under her bare feet. Babo and Without-Name still clung to her hands; she released them.

On the Red Moon, there was no Wind. She relished the luxury of not having to fight against the air's power, enjoying the ease with which she took each breath.

Around them were a dozen more people – more exiles from one ruined Farm or another, their symmorphs adorned with a startling variety of colours and stylings of skin and hair – and perhaps a hundred times as many Workers: Workers tall and slim, short and squat, Workers that flew and crawled and rolled and walked. As was customary, the people's new symmorphs were as close as possible in appearance to the shells they had abandoned on Earth.

The Mapping had taken account of the different physical conditions. Thus Manekato felt no discomfort as her lungs drank in the thin, oxygen-depleted air of this small world, and her new body would suffer no ill-effects from the relative lack of carbon dioxide. But she had taken care not to engineer out all of the Red Moon's experiential differences; for if she had there would scarcely be a purpose in coming here at all. Thus the air was cold and damp and laden with a thousand powerful, unfamiliar scents – and thus the lower gravity, just two-thirds of Earth's, tugged only feebly at her limbs.

Manekato loped through the crowd of gazing people and scuttling Workers. Her gait felt oddly clumsy in the low gravity, as if her muscles were suddenly over-powered. The yellow floor was perhaps a hundred paces across. It was a neatly circular disc of Adjusted Space, its smoothness comforting. She reached the rim of the disc. Tiny Workers streamed past her into the green world beyond, recording, interpreting, transmitting.

Beyond the platform was a wall of forest, concealing a dense green gloom. The trees were tall here: great spindly structures of wood, very different from the ground-hugging species of Wind-blasted Earth. Shadows flitted through that green dark. She thought she saw eyes peering out at her, eyes like a mirror of her own.

Babo ran past her with a gurgled cry. He ran straight into the forest and clambered into the lowest branches of a tree, clumsily, but with enthusiasm and strength.

Manekato peered down. In the Moon's red dust grass grew, sprinkled with small flowers, white and yellow. She leaned forward, supporting her weight on one fist, and touched the grass. The blades were coarse, and other plants and moss crowded around, fighting over each scrap of soil. She saw leaves protruding from beneath the disc, crushed, bent back; some of the living things of this world had already died because of her presence.

The land here had never been Farmed: not once, not in all the billions of years this world had existed. Even this patch of grass-covered land, where billions of living things fought for life in every scrap, was disturbing, enthralling proof of that.

In front of the forest fringe she made out a small, brown-furred Worker – no, not a Worker, an *animal*, its species probably unmodified by conscious design. It had a short, slim body, and four spindly legs; it bent a graceful neck, and a small mouth nibbled at the grass. It moved gracefully, but with a startling slowness, an unhurried languor that contrasted with the frantic scuttling of the people and the Workers. By the look of the genitalia between its back legs its kind must reproduce in a mammalian fashion, rather than be nurtured directly from the ground . . .

Nobody had nurtured this creature, she reminded herself; there had been no conscious process. It had been born in blood and pain and mucus, without the supervision of any human, and it found food to sustain its growth in this wild, unmanaged, undisciplined place.

On her world, there had been no parks or zoos for nine hundred millennia. Though the richness of the ecology was well understood and managed minutely – including the place of people within that ecology – there were no creatures save those that served a conscious purpose, no aspect of nature that was not thought through and controlled. Not so much as a stomach bacterium.

Manekato had known that this new Moon would be wild, but that its ecology would function none the less. But it was one thing to have a theoretical anticipation and another to be confronted with the fact. She felt as if she had entered the workings of some vast intricate machine, all the more remarkable for lacking a conscious designer or a controlling intelligence.

Now Babo came hurrying back from the forest. He clutched something in his arms that wriggled sluggishly.

Babo's legs were covered in scrapings of green moss, and his hair was dishevelled and dirty. But his eyes were bright, and he was breathing hard. 'My arms are strong,' he told his sister. 'I can *climb*. It is as if this body of mine remembers its deepest past, many millions of years lost, even though the trees on Earth are mere wind-blown stubs compared to these mighty pillars . . .'

Without-Name asked, 'What is it you carry?'

He held it out carefully. It had a slim body and a small head. Its legs were short and somewhat bowed, but Manekato could see immediately that this creature was designed – no, had *evolved* – to walk bipedally. It was perhaps half of Babo's height, and much slimmer.

'It is a hominid,' she said wonderingly.

'I found it in the tree,' Babo said. 'It is quite strong, but moves slowly. It was easy to catch.'

Manekato reached to touch the creature's face.

The hominid whipped its head sideways and sank its teeth into Manekato's finger.

Manekato fell back with a small cry. Miniature Workers in her bloodstream caused the ripped flesh to close immediately.

'*Ha!*' the creature yelled. '*Elf strong Elf good hurt stupid Ham hah!*'

This jabber meant nothing to Manekato.

Without-Name took the creature from an unresisting Babo. She held it up by its head. Dangling, the hominid hooted and thrashed, scratching at Manekato's arm with its legs and fists, but its motions were slow and feeble.

With a single, harsh motion Without-Name crushed the hominid's skull. The body shuddered once, and was limp. Without-Name let the body fall to the ground, its head a bloody pulp. A Worker scuttled close and swept up the tiny corpse.

Babo looked at Without-Name, his face empty of expression. 'Why did you do that?'

'There was no mind,' said Without-Name. 'There was no utility. Therefore there was no right to life. I have been dispossessed by this Moon. I will not rest until I have made the Moon my possession in turn.'

Manekato suppressed her anger. 'We did not come here to kill. We came to learn – to learn and negotiate.'

Without-Name spat a gobbet of thick phlegm out onto the grass. 'We all have our reasons to be here, Manekatopokanemahedo. You follow the foolish dreams of the Astrologers. *I* am a Farmer.'

'And,' Manekato said slowly, 'is that your ambition here? To subdue a new world, to turn it all into your dominion?'

'What higher ambition could there be?'

'But we have yet to find those who moved this world. *They* were more powerful than these blades of grass, that wretched hominid. Remember that, Renemenagota, when you boast of what you will conquer.'

Now Manekato saw that two burly Workers had brought another hominid for their inspection. It was taller, heavier than the last, but it was scrawny, filthy, hollow-eyed.

Again Without-Name picked up the specimen by its skull and lifted it easily off the ground. The creature cried and struggled, clearly in distress, but its movements were still more sluggish than the first's, and it made no attempt to injure Without-Name.

'Let it go,' Manekato said evenly.

Without-Name studied her. 'You are not of my Lineage. You do not have authority over me.'

'Look at it, Renemenagota. *It is wearing clothes.*'

Babo breathed deeply. 'Do it,' he said. 'Or I will have the Workers stop you. *I* have the authority for that, nameless one, thanks to the Astrologers you despise.'

Without-Name growled her protest. But she released the hominid, which fell into a heap on the floor, and stalked away.

Manekato and Babo huddled over the hominid. It had curled into a foetal position; as gently as they could they turned it on its back and prised open its limbs.

'I think it is female,' Babo said. 'Its head is badly bruised, as is its neck, and it struggles to breathe. Without-Name has damaged it.'

'Perhaps the Workers can repair it.'

The hominid coughed and struggled to sit up. Babo helped it with a lift from a powerful hand.

'*My name*,' the hominid said, '*is Nemoto.*'

Shadow:

The antelope had got separated from its herd. It was running awkwardly, perhaps hampered by age or injury.

With fluid grace, the lion leapt onto the antelope's back, forcing it to the ground in a cloud of crimson dust. The antelope kicked and struggled, its back and haunches already horribly ripped. Then the lion inflicted a final, almost graceful bite to its throat. As its blood poured onto the dust of the savannah, Shadow saw surprise in the antelope's eyes.

More lions came loping up to feed.

Shadow remained huddled behind her rock – exposed on the open savannah, but downwind of the kill. She kept her baby quiet by cradling its big, deformed head tightly against her stomach.

The lions pushed their faces into the fallen antelope's carcass, digging into the entrails and the easily accessible meat of the fleshy areas. Soon their muzzles were crimson with blood, and their growls of contentment were loud. Shadow was overwhelmed by the iron stink of blood, and the sharp burning scent of the lion's fur – and by hunger; her mouth pooled with saliva.

Her face itched, and she scratched it.

At last the lions' purring growls receded.

Already more scavengers were approaching the carcass. Hyenas loped hungrily towards it in a jostling pack, and overhead the first bats were wheeling, huge carrion-eating bats, their wings black stripes against the sky.

And, from the crater's wooded rim, people emerged: Elf-folk like Shadow, men, women and infants, melting out of the green shelter of the woods, their black pelts stark against the green and crimson of the plain. They eyed the carcass hungrily, and they carried sticks and cobbles.

But the hyenas were hungry too, and in a moment they were on the antelope, burying their muzzles inside the great rips made by the lions' jaws, already fighting amongst themselves. Their lithe bodies clustered over the carcass, tails high in the air, from a distance like maggots working a wound.

The people moved in, yelling and waving their sticks and throwing their stones. Some of the dogs were hit by hurled cobbles. One man, a squat, manic creature with one eye closed by a huge scar, got close enough to pound one animal with a fat branch, causing the dog to yelp and stumble. But the dogs did not back away. A few of them tore themselves away from the meat long enough to rush at the hominids, barking and snapping, before hurling themselves back into the feast. Most simply ignored the people, gouging out as much meat as they could before being forced away by a dog bigger and stronger.

So it went, a web of complex but unconscious calculations: each hyena's dilemma over whether to attack the hominids, or whether to gamble that another dog would, leaving it free to take more meat; the hominids' estimation of the strength and determination of the hyenas versus their own hunger and the value of the meat.

This time, at least, the hyenas were too strong.

The Elf-folk troupe backed away sullenly. They found a place in the shade of the trees at the forest edge, staring with undisguised envy at the rich meat being devoured by the dogs.

At last the hyenas started to disperse. They had taken most of the meat, and the antelope was reduced to scattered bones and bits of flesh on a blood-stained patch of ground, as if it had exploded. Again the people came forward, and their stones and sticks drove away the last of the dogs.

There was little meat to be had. But there was still a rich resource here, which hominid tools could reach. The adults took the antelope's bones and, with brisk, skilful strikes of their shaped stones, they cracked them open. Soon many of the people were sucking marrow greedily. Children fought over scraps of flesh and cartilage.

Huge bats flapped down, their leathery wings black, vulture-like. They pecked at outlying bits of the carcass, bloodying their fur. The people tolerated them. But if the bats came too close they would be greeted by a stick wielded by a hooting hominid.

Shadow came out from behind her rock.

A child came up to her, curious, a bit of gristle dangling from her chin. But as Shadow neared, the child wrinkled her nose and stared hard at Shadow's face. Then she turned and ran for the security of her mother.

As Shadow approached the group, the people moved their children away from her, or growled, or even threw stones. But they did not try to drive her away.

Shadow saw a big older woman, the hair of her back oddly streaked with silver. This woman – Silverneck – was working assiduously at the remnant of a thigh bone. Shadow sat close to Silverneck, not asking for food, content not to be rejected.

The sun wheeled across the sky, and the people worked at the carcass.

At length Silverneck hurled away the last fragments of bone. She lay on her back, legs crossed, and crooked an arm behind her head. She belched, picked bits of marrow and bone from her teeth, and thrust a finger into one nostril with every sign of contentment.

Cautiously, her baby clinging to her back, Shadow crept closer. She started to groom Silverneck, picking gently through the hairs of Silverneck's shoulders. The older woman, reclining stiffly, submitted to this in silence, eyes closed as if asleep.

Shadow knew what she must do to win a place here. In her home forest she had watched women seeking favour with their seniors. Still cautious, Shadow moved towards Silverneck's waist and reached out to stroke the older woman's genitals, just as she had seen others do before.

A hand grasped her wrist, gentle but strong. Silverneck's face, worn almost bald by grooming, was a mass of wrinkles. And it showed disgust. She pulled her legs under her, and pushed Shadow away.

Shadow sat still, baffled, disturbed.

After a time Shadow again reached out to groom Silverneck. Again Silverneck submitted. This time Shadow did not try to cross the boundary to sexual contact, and Silverneck did not push her away.

As the shadows lengthened across the plain, the carrion-eating bats clustered closer around the remnants of the carcass. One by one the people started to drift back to the forest. The first roosting calls began to sound from the tree tops.

At last the old woman stretched and yawned loudly, bones popping. Then she got to her feet and ambled back towards the forest's edge.

Shadow sat where she was, waiting.

Silverneck looked back once, thoughtfully. Then she turned and moved on.

Shadow got to her feet, her baby clinging to her back. Hastily she rummaged through the carcass, but the marrow and meat had been chewed or sucked off every bone. Cramming bits of greasy skin into her mouth, she hurried after Silverneck into the forest.

Manekatopokanemahedo:

With a wave of his hand Babo conjured an image of the Red Moon – but it was not an image, rather a limited injective-recursive Mapping of the Moon into itself. The Moon turned for their benefit, a great hovering globe twice Babo's height. Manekato gazed at searing red desert-continent and steel ocean.

The little hominid who called herself Nemoto stood close to Manekato, her eyes wide, her smooth face bearing some unreadable expression.

'Your work is proceeding well,' Manekato said to her brother.

'It is a routine application of familiar techniques; merely a question of gathering sufficient data . . . But already the key to this world's mysteries is clear.'

'Ah.' Manekato said sombrely. She reached up and pointed at the huge volcano that dominated the western side of the rust-red continent. 'You mean *that*.'

'Yes, the volcanic anomaly,' Babo said. 'Which in turn must derive from some magmatic feature, a plume arising deep within the belly of this world.'

'*You talk of the Bullseye?*' Nemoto was watching them, straining to hear, turning her little head this way and that in order to position her small immobile ears.

Babo watched Nemoto uneasily. 'Do you think she can follow us?'

'I have taught her a few words,' said Manekato. 'But our speech is too rapid for her to grasp; like all the creatures here on this oxygen-starved world, she is sluggish and slow-witted. I have had more success in decoding her own language. It is a little like the nonsense argots you used to make up for my amusement as a child, Babo.'

Babo was still watching Nemoto. 'She imitates your behaviour well. Look how she gazes at the volcano! It's almost as if she can understand what she is seeing.'

Manekato grunted. 'Do not underestimate her, brother. I believe she is intelligent, to a degree. Consider the clothes she wears, her speech with its limited grammar, the tools she deploys – even her writing of symbols into her blocks of bound paper. Why, she claims to have come here, not through the blue portals, but in a spacecraft designed by others of her kind. And that she came to this Moon from *curiosity*. I found this as hard to believe as you, but she drew sketches which convinced me she is telling the truth.'

'But even the making of clothes may be no more than the outcome of instinct, Mane,' Babo said gently. 'There is a kind of aquatic spider that makes diving-bells from its webbing, and nobody would argue that *it* is intelligent. Perhaps some day we will discover a species, utterly without mind, which makes starships. Why not? And nor is symbol-making sufficient to demonstrate intelligence; there are social ants which –'

Manekato raised a hand to quiet him. 'I am aware of the dangers of anthropomorphism. You think I have found a pet, here in this dismal place – that I am seeking intelligence where all I see is a reflection of my own self.'

Babo rubbed her back affectionately. 'Well, isn't that true?'

'Perhaps. But I strive to discount it. And meanwhile I have come to the belief that Nemoto and her kind may be – not merely intelligent – but *self-aware*.'

Babo laughed. 'Come now, Mane. Let us show her a mirror, and together we will watch her seek the hominid behind the glass.'

'I already tried that test,' Manekato said. 'She was very insulted.'

'If she is too proud to be tested, why does she follow you around?'

'For protection,' Manekato said promptly. 'You saw how Without-Name treated her when she first found her. Nemoto shows great fear of her.'

Babo grunted. He crouched down before the hominid, Nemoto; his huge body was like a wall before her slim frame.

Nemoto returned his gaze calmly.

'. . . Intelligent, Mane? But the size of the cranium, the limited expanse of the frontal lobes – *the dullness of those eyes*. I do not get a sense of a person looking back out at me.'

Manekato snapped, 'And you can assess a creature's intelligence merely by looking at it?' She said, '*Nemoto.*'

The hominid looked up at her.

'*You remember what I told you of the Mapping.*' Manekato strove to slow down her speech, and to pronounce each word of Nemoto's limited language clearly and distinctly.

Nemoto was frowning, concentrating hard. '*I remember. You defined a mathematical function to map the components of your body to material of the Moon.*' Her words, like her actions, were slow, drawn-out. '*The domain of this function was yourselves and your equipment, the range a subset of the Moon. When you had defined the Mapping . . .*'

'Yes?'

Nemoto struggled, but failed to find the words. '*I have much to learn.*'

Babo grunted. 'It is impressive that she knows there are limits to her knowledge. Perhaps that indicates some degree of self-awareness after all.'

Manekato said, 'Then I am winning the argument.'

Babo grumbled good-naturedly. 'Just remember we are here to study the Moon, and those who sent it spinning between the universes – not to converse with these brutish hominids, who were certainly not responsible.'

Manekato studied Nemoto. The little creature was watching her with empty, serious eyes. '*Come,*' said Manekato, and she held out her hand.

Nemoto took it with some reluctance.

Babo turned back to the refinement of his Mapping.

Manekato led Nemoto across the Mapped-in floor of the compound. They passed between structures that had been conjured out of Adjusted Space to shelter the people. Rounded yellow forms, to Mane's taste over-ornate, they made the compound look like a plate set before a giant, loaded with exotic shapes – and with insect-like humans, Workers and hominids scuttling across it.

'*You must not let my brother upset you,*' Manekato said evenly, striving to express herself correctly in the narrow confines of Nemoto's limited tongue.

'*He has no imagination,*' said Nemoto.

Manekato barked laughter, and Nemoto flinched. '*I'll tell him you said that! . . . But he means you no harm.*'

'Unlike Without-Name, who does mean harm, and who has far too much imagination.'

'That is insightful, and neatly phrased.' She snapped her fingers and a Worker came scuttling. 'Well done, Nemoto. You deserve a banana.'

Nemoto regarded the yellow fruit proffered by the Worker with loathing.

Manekato shrugged. She popped the banana into her mouth and swallowed it whole, skin and all.

Nemoto said cautiously, 'I think your world has no Moon – none but this unwanted arrival.'

Manekato, interested, said, 'And what of it?'

'Our scientists have speculated how the destiny of my world might have differed if it had been born without a Moon.'

'Really?' Manekato wondered briefly if 'scientists' was correctly translated.

Nemoto took a deep breath. 'Our Moon was born in a giant impact, in the final stage of the violent formation of the Solar System. The effects on Earth were profound . . .'

Manekato was fascinated by all this – not so much by the content, which seemed trivially obvious, but by the fact that Nemoto was able to spin together such a coherent statement at all – even if it was delivered in a maddeningly slow drawl. But Nemoto seemed desperate to retain Manekato's attention, to win her understanding – and perhaps her approval.

'And what difference would all this make to the evolution of life?'

Nemoto said, 'You come from a world that spins fast. There must be winds there – persistent, strong. Perhaps you were once bipeds, but now you walk on all fours; probably I could not stand upright on your world. Your trees must hug the ground. And so on. Your air, derived from a primordial atmosphere never stripped off by impact, is thicker than mine, richer in carbon dioxide, probably richer in oxygen. You think fast, move fast, fuelled by the oxygen-rich air.' She hesitated. 'And perhaps you die fast. Mane, I can expect to live for seventy years – years measured on your Earth, or mine. And you?'

'Twenty-five,' Manekato breathed. 'Or less.' She was stunned by Nemoto's sudden acuity – but then the hominid had been observing her for days now, learning about Manekato as Manekato had learned about her; she had simply saved up her conclusions – as a good scientist should.

'The evolution of life must have been quite different,' Nemoto said now. 'With lower tides your oceans must be less enriched of silt washed down from the continents. And there must be less global ocean movement. I would expect a significantly different biota.

'As for humans, I believe that our evolutionary paths diverged at the stage we call the "Australopithecine", Manekato. But the environment was different on our worlds, evoking a different adaptation. I would hazard that hunting is not a viable strategy for hominids on your world. Probably your short days were simply not long enough. You call yourself "Farmers". Perhaps your world encouraged the early development of agriculture.'

' "Australopithecines". I don't know that word.'

'The hominids called Nutcrackers and Elves here seem to be surviving specimens. From that root stock your kind took one path; mine took another.'

'But, Nemoto – why do such divergent worlds have people at all? Why would hominid forms evolve on world after world –'

'Your kind did not originate on your Earth,' Nemoto said bluntly. 'Your scientists must have deduced that much.'

Manekato bristled. She tried to put aside her annoyance at being patronized by this monkey-thing. 'You are right. That much is evident. People share the same biochemical substrate as other living things, but are linked to no animal alive or of the past by any clear evolutionary path.'

'But on my Earth there is a clear evolutionary path to be traced from humans back into the past.'

'So you are saying my line originated on your Earth? And how did my Australopithecine grandmothers get delivered to "my Earth"?'

Nemoto shrugged. 'Perhaps by this Red Moon, and its blue-ring scoops.'

It was a startling vision – especially coming from the mouth of this small-brained biped – but it had a certain cogency. Manekato was aware her mouth was dangling open; she shut it with a snap of her great teeth. 'Who would have devised such a mechanism? And why?'

Nemoto's face pulled tight in the grimace Manekato had come to recognize as a smile. 'The Hams have a legend of the Old Ones, who built the world. I am hoping you will find them.'

Manekato glared at Nemoto: she was profoundly impressed by Nemoto's acuity, yet she was embarrassed at her own condescension towards the hominid. It was not a comfortable mixture. '*We will talk of this further.*'

'*We must,*' said Nemoto.

Reid Malenfant:

Malenfant counted them. Sixteen, seventeen, eighteen Runners: eighteen powerful, languid bodies relaxing on the barren ground. The band seemed to be settling here for the night. The three of them – Julia, Malenfant, Hugh McCann – hunkered down in the dirt. The grass beneath Malenfant's scuffed boots was sparse, and the Mars-red dust of the world showed through, crimson-bright where it caught the light of the setting sun.

This swathe of scrubby grassland was at the western border of the coastal forest strip NASA cartographers had christened the Beltway. Further west of this point, beyond a range of eroded mountains, there was only the arid, baked interior of the great continent, hundreds of miles of red desert, an Australia in the sky. No doubt it was stocked with its own unique ecology exquisitely evolved to maximize the use of the available resources, Malenfant thought sourly, but it was an unremittingly hostile place for a middle-aged American – and of no interest to him whatsoever, unless it held Emma in its barren heart.

McCann moved closer to Malenfant, his buckskin clothes creaking softly. 'How strange these pongids are,' he said. 'How very obviously ante-human. See the way they have made their crude camp. They have built a fire, you see, probably from a hot coal carried for tens of miles by some horny-handed wretch. They even have a rudimentary sense of the hearth and home: look at that big buck voiding his bowels, off beyond the group – what an immense straining – everything these fellows do is mighty!

'But that is about the extent of their humanity. They have no tools, save the pebbles they pluck from the ground to be shaped; they carry nothing for sentiment – nothing at all, so their nakedness is deeper than ever yours or mine could be. And though they gather in little clusters, of mothers with infants, a few younger siblings, there is no community there.

'If you look into the eyes of a Runner, Malenfant, you see a bright primal presence, you see cleverness – but you do not see a *mind*. There is only the now, and that is all there will ever be. Whatever dim spark of awareness resides behind those deceptive eyes is trapped forever in a cage of inarticulacy . . . One must pity them, even as one admires them for their animal grace.'

Malenfant grimaced. 'Another lecture, Hugh?'

McCann sighed. 'I have been effectively alone here too long, my reflections on the strange lost creatures who inhabit this place rattling around in my head. Would I were as conservative with my words as dear Julia, who, like the rest of her kind, speaks only when necessary!'

Or maybe, Malenfant thought, she just hasn't got much to say to you, or me. He'd observed the Hams chattering among themselves, when they thought no human was watching them. For all his bush craft, McCann's understanding of the creatures around him was obviously shallow.

Without a word, Julia stood up and began to walk across the sparse scrub towards the Running-folk. McCann and Malenfant stayed crouched in the dirt.

The Runners turned to watch her approach. They were silent, still, like wary prey animals.

Julia got as far as the Runners' fire. She hunkered down there, making sure she didn't sit close to the meat. The Runners were still wary – one burly man bared his teeth at Julia, which she calmly ignored – but they didn't try to drive her away.

After a time an infant came up to her, bright eyes over a lithe little body. Julia reached out her massive hand, but its mother instantly snatched the child back.

Malenfant suppressed a sigh. Sometimes Julia would win the Runners' confidence quickly; other times it took longer. Tonight it looked as if Julia would have to spend the night in the Runners' rough camp before they could make any further progress.

As the days had worn on, Malenfant had lost count of the number of Runner groups they had tracked down. Julia was always given the lead, hoping to establish a basis of trust, and then Malenfant and McCann would follow up. Malenfant would produce his precious South African air force lens, his one indubitable trace of Emma, hoping for some spark of recognition in those bright animal eyes.

It hadn't worked so far, and Malenfant, despite his own grim determination, was gradually losing hope. But he didn't have any better ideas.

As Julia sat quietly with the Runners, the light leaked out of the sky. The predators began to call, their eerie howls carrying far on the still evening air.

Briskly, without speaking, Malenfant and McCann built a fire. They used dry grass for tinder, and had brought bundles of wood from the Beltway for fuel.

Malenfant's supper was a few mouthfuls of raw fish. The Runners used their fires primarily for warmth, not cooking. If McCann or Malenfant were to throw this tough, salty fish onto the fire, the smell of burned flesh would spook the Runners and quickly drive them away.

After that it was foot-maintenance time. Malenfant eased off his boots and inspected the latest damage. There was a kind of flea that laid eggs under your toenail, and naturally it was Malenfant who was infected. When the critters started to grow in the soft flesh under there, feeding off his damn toe cheese, McCann said Julia would dig them out with her stone knives. Malenfant backed off from that, sterilized his pocket knife in the fire, and did it himself. But, Christ, it hurt, unreasonably so, and it made a bloody mess of his toes; for the next few days he had had a *lot* of trouble walking.

When he was done with his feet, Malenfant started making pemmican. It was one of his long-term projects. You took congealed fat from cooked fish, and softened it in your hands. Then you used one of Julia's stone knives to grate the cooked flesh into powdery pieces and mixed it with the fat. You added some salt and berries and maybe a little grated nutmeg from McCann's pack, and then pulled the mess apart into lumps the size of a golf ball. You rolled the balls into cocktail-sausage shapes, and put them in the sun, to set hard.

He had already done the same with a haunch of antelope. It was simple stuff, dredged up from his memories of his astronaut survival training. But the treatment ought to make these bits of fish and meat last months.

McCann sat and watched him. He was nursing a wooden bowl filled with a tea made of crushed green needles from a spruce tree. Malenfant had been sceptical of what he saw as an English affectation, but the tea was oddly refreshing; Malenfant suspected the needles were full of Vitamin C. But the tea was strongly flavoured and full of sharp bits of needle (which he had learned to strain out through a sock).

McCann said, 'Malenfant, you are a man of silence and unswerving intent. Your preparations are admirable and thorough. But to enter the desert is foolhardy, no matter how many pemmican cakes you make. Even if you could find your way through the mountains, there is only aridity beyond.'

Malenfant growled, 'We have this conversation roughly once a day, Hugh. We must have found all the Runner groups who work this area, and have come up blank. On the other hand, we know a lot of them work deeper into the desert.' He squinted, peering into the harsh flat light of the arid western lands. 'There could be dozens more tribes out there. We have to go find them.'

McCann pulled a face and sipped his tea. 'And seek out traces of your Emma.'

Malenfant kept kneading his pemmican. 'You've come this far, and I'm grateful. But if you don't want to follow me any further that's okay by me.'

McCann smiled, tired. 'I suppose I have attached myself to you – become a squire to your chessboard knight. On this desolate Red Moon we are all lost, you see, Malenfant – not just your Emma. And we all seek purpose.'

Malenfant grunted, uncomfortable. 'I'm grateful for your company. But why the hell you're doing it is your business, not mine. I never cared much for psychoanalysis.'

McCann frowned at the term, but seemed to puzzle out its meaning. 'You always look outward, don't you? – but perhaps it would serve you to look inward, from time to time.'

'What is that supposed to mean?'

'For a man with such a powerful drive – a drive to a goal for which he is clearly prepared to give his life – you seem little interested in the origin of that drive.' McCann raised a finger. 'I predict you will puzzle it out in the end – though it may require you to find Emma herself before you do so.'

They would take turns to stand watch: McCann first, then Malenfant.

Malenfant cleaned his teeth with a bit of twig. Then he settled down for his first sleep.

The nights here were always cold. Malenfant zipped up his jumpsuit, placed a bag of underwear under his hips to soften the hardness of the ground, and pulled a couple of layers of 'chute cloth over his body. He set his head on the pack in which he carried the remnant of his NASA coverall, his real-world underwear and the rest of his few luxuries, and he put spare underwear under his hip for a mattress. Though he had gotten used to his suit of deerskin –

it had softened with use, and after the first few days he suspected it stank more of him than its original owner – he clung to the few items he had salvaged from the ludicrous wreck of his mission as a kind of message to himself, a reminder that he hadn't been born in these circumstances, and maybe he wouldn't have to die in them either.

As usual he had trouble settling.

'I don't like to complain,' he said at length.

'Of course not.'

'This ground is like rock. I can't turn over without dislocating a hip.'

'Then don't turn over.'

So it went.

After three hours it was Malenfant's turn to stand watch. McCann shook Malenfant awake, pitching him into a cold, star-littered night. Malenfant shook out his blanket and went to take a leak. Sign of age, Malenfant.

Beyond the circle of light from their hearth, the desert was deep and dark, its emptiness broken only by the ragged glow of the Runners' fire.

Sometimes it scared him to think of what a wilderness it was that had claimed him. There were no cop cars cruising through that darkness, no watching choppers or surveillance satellites, nobody out there to help him – no law operating save the savagely impartial rule of nature.

And yet every day he was struck by the strange *orderliness* of the place. Decaying animal corpses did not litter the ground, save for a handful of bleached bones here and there; it was rare to walk into so much as a heap of dung. There was death here, yes, there was blood and pain – but it was as if every creature, including the hominids, was a cog in some vaster machine, that served to sustain all their lives. And every creature, presumably unconsciously, accepted its place and the sacrifices that came with it.

All save one species of hominid, it seemed: *Homo sap* himself, who was forever seeking to tear up the world around him.

The final time he woke that night, he found Julia looming over him. She was a vast silhouette whose disturbing scent of *other* was enough to kick Malenfant's hind brain into wakefulness. He sat up, rubbing his eyes. His 'chute-silk blanket fell away, and all his warmth was lost to the cool, moist air. It was a little after dawn, and the world was drenched with a blue-grey light that turned the crimson sand purple.

The Runners had gone. He could just make them out, slim dark figures against the purple-grey desert, running easily and silently, far away into the desert.

He hadn't even gotten to show them his lens.

Manekatopokanemahedo:

There was a call from Babo, who was standing beneath his beautiful spinning globe. Manekato hurried to her brother, and Nemoto jogged after her.

The great rotating Moon-projection had been rendered semi-transparent. And there was a hole in its very heart.

Something lurked there, blocky, enclosed – clearly artificial, very large. It was connected to the surface by a long, thread-like tube: not entirely straight, bending like a reed as it passed through the Moon's layers of core, thick mantle and deep, hard lithosphere, so much thicker on this small cold world than the crustal layers of the Earth. The tube terminated in what looked like a small, compact crater, not far from the eastern shore of the world-spanning continent not far from the location of the compound, in fact.

Manekato reached inside the Map. The misty layers of mantle and core resisted her gently, as if her fingers were pushing through some viscous liquid. She wrapped her fingers around the knot of machinery at the Map's centre. It was dense and complex and well-anchored.

Nemoto watched her carefully.

'It is the world engine,' said Babo.

Studying the globe as a whole, Manekato saw that the surface crater was diametrically opposite the summit of the great volcanic mountain, at the peak of the huge region of uplift that so distorted the figure of the world. Looking more closely she could see detail in the Map's misty outer layers: a disturbance in the core, a great plume in the deep-buried mantle, hot magmatic material working its way up through cracks in the mighty lithosphere towards that antipodal bulge.

'I cannot believe that such asymmetry is deliberate,' Babo said.

'No,' Manekato said. 'The internal disturbances must be a result of the poor control of the Moon as it lurches from universe to universe. Perhaps the Moon is not meant to plummet about the cosmic manifold like this. The mechanism is poorly designed . . .'

'Or faulty. If it has been sweeping up hominids since early in our evolution, Mane, it must have been operating for millions of years.'

'Perhaps even the great machines of the Old Ones are subject to failure.'

'Quantum tunnelling,' said Babo. 'That's how they do it. That's how this thing in the core sends this Moon from universe to universe.'

Manekato said, 'Tell me what you mean, brother.'

'You understand the concept. An electron, say, does not have a precise position or velocity; rather it is embedded in a spreading cloud of probability. Given a measurement of its position, there is a small but finite chance that the electron will next be found – not close to the last position – but far away, outside any cage you care to throw around it – or at the heart of the sun – or in orbit around a distant star . . .'

'Yes, yes. *Or even another universe.* Is that your point?'

He scratched his head absently. 'Well, we know that quantum tunnelling can cause the nucleation of a new universe. The vacuum sustains a series of energy levels. A bubble of "our" vacuum can tunnel to an otherwise empty spacetime at a lower energy state, and there expand and become causally disconnected from our own . . .'

'We are talking of moving not an electron, but a world.'

Babo shrugged. 'I think we have the pieces of the puzzle now, at least; perhaps understanding will follow.'

'In any case, our next object is clear,' Manekato said. She pressed a finger into the crater at the top of the tube from the core; she could barely feel the feather-touch of its tiny rim. 'We must go to this strange crater, learn all we can – and, perhaps, seek a way to direct the future course of this rogue Moon.'

'*The manifold is a sheaf of possible universes,*' Nemoto said.

Babo grimaced. 'What did she say?'

Nemoto went on, '*I understand some of what you say. Perhaps the manifold universes were nucleated from a single primal universe by some such mechanism as quantum tunnelling. Perhaps the nucleation of the universes was deliberate. Perhaps the Old Ones lived in the primal universe . . .*'

Babo bared his teeth at her, and Nemoto fell silent.

Manekato said dryly, 'What's wrong?'

'She sees so much,' Babo said. 'Much further than I imagined. If she sees so much, will she not see that the achievements of the Old Ones are as far beyond us as . . .'

'As our Farms and our Maps are beyond her poor grasp?' She touched his shoulder, mock-grooming, seeking to calm him. 'But would that be so bad? Would it hurt us to learn some of her humility?'

'I don't think she is so humble, Mane. Look at the defiance in that small face. It is unnatural. It is like being challenged by a Worker.'

A cry rent the air.

Nemoto turned sharply. Manekato felt her ears swivel. It had been a cry of pain and despair – an animal's cry, but desolating none the less.

Nemoto began to run towards the place the cry had come from.

After a moment's hesitation, Manekato hurried after her pet.

'*Oh, let me up; I beg you, Madam Daemon, by the blood of Christ, let me up!*'

It was Without-Name, of course. She had caught another hominid. She had him sprawled on the smooth floor of the compound with her massive foot in the small of the back, so that he could do little but flop like a fish. He was wearing clothes of a cruder design than Nemoto's – scraps of skin sewn together with bits of hide, as if he had clambered inside the gruesome reconstruction of a dead animal. It seemed his capture had not been without incident. Blood leaked from a filthy wound on his forehead, and his right foot was dangling at an awkward angle, just a mass of blood, badly pulped. His blood and snot and sweat, even his urine, had spilled over the floor of Adjusted Spacetime.

Others stood around the gruesome little tableau. Manekato was dismayed to see fascination on several faces, as if the blood-soaked allure of this world was seeping into more than one soul.

She rested a hand on Nemoto's shoulder. '*He is a member of your troupe? That is why you are distressed.*'

'No. I have never seen him before. And we don't have "troupes". But he is human, and he is suffering.'

Babo challenged Without-Name. 'What new savagery is this, Renemenagota of Rano?'

'Am I the savage? Then what is this under my foot? We are not

281

at home now, Manekato – we are not even on Earth. And if we wish to progress our inquiries we must abandon the techniques we would apply on the Earth.'

'I don't understand.'

'You gaze at a pretty Map while the real world is all around you – vibrant, primal.' She slapped at the floor of Adjusted Space. 'You even separate yourselves from the dirt. Have you stepped off this platform, Manekato, even once? I tell you, this is not a place for logic and Maps. It is a place of red and green, of life and blood and death – a place for the heart, not the head.'

'And your heart tells you to torment this helpless wretch,' Babo said.

'But not without a purpose,' Without-Name said. 'He comes from a troupe of hominids to the north of here. They live in crude shelters of wood and mud, and they call themselves *Zealots*. They are as intelligent as your pet, Manekato – but they are utterly insane, driven by dreams of a God they cannot see.' She bellowed laughter, and applied more pressure with her heel to the Zealot's back; he groaned, his eyes rolling, as bones cracked. 'These Zealots have been here for centuries. With their feeble eyes, their dim brains, they have seen this world which you are too frightened to touch. *They have seen the workings of the Old Ones*, for they have been dragged from one cosmos to the next by their meddling. And they have formulated their own ambition in response: to spit in the face of the sky itself.' She looked down at the sprawled, twitching hominid. 'It is absurd. But in its way, it is magnificent. Hah! *These* are the creatures of this world. I want to see what they see, know what they know. That way I will learn the truth about the Old Ones – and what must be done to defeat them.'

Others growled assent behind her.

Manekato, deeply disturbed, stepped closer to Without-Name. 'We did not come here to inflict pain.'

'There is no pain here,' Without-Name said easily. 'For there is no sentience. You see only reflex, as a leaf follows the sunlight.'

'No.' It was Nemoto. She stepped forward, evading the clutching hand of Manekato.

The nameless one gaped at her, briefly too startled to react.

'*I know that you understand me. I believe your species has superior cognition to my own. But nevertheless we have cognition. This man is aware of himself, of his pain. And he is terrified, for he is aware that you plan to kill him, Renemenagota.*'

Without-Name reared up on her hind legs, and the man in the dust howled. '*You will not use my name.*'

'*Let him go.*' Nemoto held out her arms, her hands empty.

The moment stretched. Without-Name towered over the slim form of the hominid.

Then Without-Name stepped off the fallen man and pushed him away with her foot. She dropped to her knuckles and laughed. 'Your pet has an amusing defiance, Manekato. Nevertheless I tell you that these creatures of the Moon are the key to our strategy here. The key!' And she knuckle-walked away towards the forest, where she blended into the shadows of the trees.

Where she had shoved him, the fallen Zealot had left a trail of urine and blood. Workers hurried forward to tend him, and to clean the mess he had made.

Manekato approached the trembling hominid. '*Nemoto – I am sorry –*'

Nemoto shrugged off her touch. '*So you understand, at last. Let me reward you with a banana.*' And she stalked away, her anger visible in every step, every gesture.

Reid Malenfant:

'About the desert,' McCann said. He took a half-burned twig and started to scrape at the red dust, sketching out a map. 'Here is the Congo – I mean, the great river which rises in the foothills of the great volcano you call the Bullseye, the river that winds its way through the interior of the continent to debouche into the ocean beyond the forests. For much of its length the river's flow is confined to a series of ancient canyons, where the stream is fed by a series of underground tributaries. The north bank is very arid. But on its south bank – *here*, for example – there are flood plains where the vegetation grows a little more thickly.

'Here is what I propose. We will cut across the plain, meeting the river valley at *this* point, where there is a crossing place to the south bank, which is the greener. We will follow the river, heading steadily west, following it upstream as it works its way through the mountains, and using the vegetation and its inhabitants as our base resource. Thus we will seek out these shy Runner bands of yours. And if we fail to find your Emma before the character of the country changes – well, we will think of something else.'

Malenfant felt tempted to argue with this strategy. But he had no better ideas of how to explore a continent-wide desert, in search of a single person. And there might be a logic to it: whatever she was doing, whoever she was with, Emma surely couldn't be anywhere else but close to water.

The river, then. He nodded curtly. McCann grinned and scuffed over his map with the sole of his boot.

They heard a cry.

It was Julia. She was hunting a lame deer. She had stripped naked and was running flat out towards it; baffled by a rock outcropping, the animal turned the wrong way, and Julia fell on the animal's neck and wrestled it to the ground.

'Dinner is served,' McCann said dryly.

'There must be an easier way to make a living,' Malenfant said.

McCann shrugged. 'You don't find much to admire about these non-human humans, do you, Malenfant? Don't you envy Julia her brutal strength, her immersion in the bloody moment, her uncomplicated heart?'

'No,' Malenfant said quietly.

They entered the desert.

Malenfant sacrificed more parafoil silk to make a hat and a scarf for his neck, and he added a little of a silvered survival blanket to the top of his hat to deflect the sunlight. After the first couple of days his eyes hurt badly in the powerful light. In his pack was a small chemical-film camera; he broke this open with a rock, and tied the fogged film over his eyes with a length of 'chute cord.

McCann fared a little better. His ancient suit of skin, well-worn and much-used, had a hood he could pull over his head, and various ingenious flaps he could open to make the suit more or less porous.

Julia's squat bow-legged frame was made for short bursts of extreme energy, not for the steady slog of a desert hike. She struggled as her feet sank into the soft, stingingly hot sand. But she kept on, grinning, self-deprecating, her tongue lolling from her open mouth, her sparse hair plastered to the top of her head.

Anyhow it wasn't a desert, Malenfant supposed; not strictly. Life flourished, after a fashion. In the red dust shrubs and cacti battled for space with the ubiquitous stands of spiky spinifex grass. Lizards of species he couldn't identify scuttled after insects. He spotted a kind of mouse hopping by like a tiny kangaroo. He had no idea how such a creature could survive here; maybe it had some way of manufacturing its own water from the plants it chewed on.

Not a desert, then. Probably a climatologist would call it a temperate semi-desert. But it was dry as toast, and hot enough for Malenfant.

It was a relief to them all when they reached the river.

Malenfant and Julia pulled off their clothes and ran with howls of relief into the sluggish water. McCann was a little more decorous, but he stripped down to his trousers and paddled cautiously. Malenfant splashed silty-brown liquid into his face, and watched improbably large droplets hover around him; he felt as if his skin were sucking in the water directly through his pores.

Great islands floated past, natural rafts of reed and water-hyacinth, emissaries from the continent's far interior, a startling procession of vegetation on its way to the sea. It was a reminder that this single mighty stream drained an area the size of India.

The river flowed sluggishly between yellow sandstone cliffs streaked with white and black. Here and there he saw sandbars strewn with black or brown boulders – mudstones and shales, said McCann, laid down in ancient swamps. The sedimentary strata here were all but horizontal, undisturbed: these were rocks that had remained stable for a great length of time, for a thousand million years and more. This Moon was a small, static world.

Life flourished close to the river. The bank was crowded with plants that craved the direct sunlight, bushes and lianas competing for space. Even behind them the first rank of trees was draped with lianas, ferns and orchids, overshadowed only by the occasional climbing palm. Wispy manioc shrubs grew on the lower slopes. Speckled toads croaked all along the river bank, and fireflies the size of earwigs, each of them making a spark of green light, danced and darted in the tangled shadows of the trees.

A vast spider-web stretched between two relatively bare tree trunks. It was heavy with moisture, and glistened silver-white, like strings of pearls. Looking closer, Malenfant saw that many spiders, maybe a hundred or more, inhabited the web. A social species of spider?

Objects hung from the higher branches of the palms, like pendulous fruit, leathery and dark brown, each maybe a foot long.

'They are bats,' McCann murmured. 'They have wing spans of a yard or more. Those are males. At night they call for the attention of females.' He rammed his fingers into his nostrils, and cried, 'Kwok! Kwok! And the females fly up and down the line for hours, selecting the male who sings the most sweetly . . .'

After a time Julia clambered out of the water. She took a handful of palm oil from a wooden gourd in McCann's pack, and worked it into her skin, paying attention to every crease and the spaces between her fingers and toes. When she stood, her skin shone, lustrous. She was silent, beautiful.

McCann went fishing. He found a spot where the bank curved, cupping a still, shallow patch of water, thick with reeds. He took leaves from a pretty little bush with white flowers shaped like bells. He scattered the flowers in the river, over the still spot.

Above the shallower water, by the reed-beds, dragonflies hovered and zigzagged, big scarlet creatures the size of small birds. Sometimes they dipped their abdomens into the river, breaking the sluggish, oily surface of the water. Perhaps they were laying eggs, Malenfant mused, wishing he knew more natural history; when you got down to it he knew very little about his own world, let alone this exotic new one.

To Malenfant's surprise, fish started coming to the surface in front of McCann, their fins breaking the oily meniscus, their mouths popping. Evidently they couldn't breathe. McCann, stocky, determined, splashed into the water and started grabbing the fish, holding their tails and slamming their heads against rocks on the bank.

Malenfant thought he saw something move through the water. He scrambled out fast.

It had been bigger than any fish, but not the distinctive shape of a croc or an alligator – something that must have been at least his size, and covered with sleek hair, like a seal. But neither of the others noticed anything, so he didn't mention it.

They spent a day at the side of the river, and replenished their stock of fish, then moved on, heading steadily west.

By noon the following day they had come to a place which showed signs of habitation. A small beach close to the river was littered with blackened scars, perhaps the marks of hearths, and neat rings of holes showed in the ground. When Malenfant walked here his boots crunched over a litter of stone tools.

Julia cowered, her huge arms wrapped around her torso.

Malenfant asked, 'What is it? A Runners' camp?'

McCann's face was grim. 'Runners are not so permanent as this – and nor do they make such structures. See these holes? They are for the wooden supports of tents and the like . . . But see the scattering of the fires, the heaps of discarded tools. Men do not conduct themselves so, Malenfant; we would build a single fire; we would take our tools with us. This is a Ham settlement – or was. And, look, the great thickness of the debris tells of a long occupation, which is of course typical of these dogged, infinitely patient Hams. But it was an occupation that was ended bloodily. Here, and here . . .' Stains on rocks, that might have been dried blood. 'They are recent. It is the Zealots, Malenfant. We must be alert for their scouts.'

Julia was clearly distressed here. They moved on quickly.

After that, another day's hike took them to the spot McCann had picked out as a possible crossing place. On the far side of the river, just as he had promised, the land was flatter and less rocky, and there was more life: a few shrubs, some straggling trees, even patches of green grass.

And, stretched between the banks, tied firmly to a rock on either side, there was a rope.

Malenfant and McCann inspected the rope dubiously. It seemed to be of vegetable fibre, woven tightly together into a thick cord.

McCann picked at the rope. 'Look at this. I think this material has been worked by teeth.'

'It isn't human, is it?'

McCann smiled. 'Certainly this is not what our hands would make – but we have never observed the Hams or the Runners use ropes on such a scale, or to have the imaginative intellect to make a bridge – and still less the Elves or Nutcrackers.' He looked around coolly. 'Perhaps there are others here, other pre-sapient types we have yet to encounter.'

Malenfant grunted. 'Well, whoever they are, I'm glad they came this way.'

Malenfant crossed first. He went naked. He probed at the river bed with a wooden pole as he inched forward, and he dragged another rope, a length of 'chute cord, tied around his waist. The water never came higher than his ribs.

Once he was across, he and McCann started to transfer their packs of clothes and food. They used a karabiner clip from Malenfant's NASA jumpsuit to attach each pack to the ropes, then pulled at the 'chute cord to jiggle the packs across.

Julia came next. She entered the water with a dogged determination that overcame her obvious reluctance – which wasn't surprising, as her stocky frame was too densely packed for her to float; whatever else they were capable of, Neandertals couldn't swim. McCann fixed a loop of cord around her waist and clipped her to the 'chute line with the karabiner clip. Then he and Malenfant kept a tight hold of the 'chute line as she crossed – though whether they could have retrieved her great weight from the water if something had gone wrong Malenfant wasn't sure.

It took no more than an hour for them all to get across. They spread out their gear to dry, and rested. Cleansed by the water, lying on warm rocks, Malenfant found he enjoyed the touch of the sun on his face, the arid breeze that blew off the desert.

Julia grunted, pointing at the river. There were creatures in the water.

They were sleek swimmers, their hair long and slicked down, their bodies streamlined. Their hands and feet were clearly webbed – but those hands had five fingers, and the small-brained heads had recognizable eyes and noses and mouths. They were churning in the water, clambering over each other like mackerel in a net. Oblivious of Malenfant and the others, they seemed to be lunging at the sky, their round eyes shining.

They were hominids.

'Swimmers,' said McCann morosely. 'Sometimes they'll steal fish off your line . . . The Hams have stories of how a Swimmer will aid you if you get yourself into trouble in the water, but I've never observed such a thing. And, do you know, they appear to sleep with only one eye shut at a time; perhaps they need to keep conscious enough to control their breathing . . .'

Malenfant imagined a troupe of Australopithecines, perhaps, scooped from some quasi-African plain a couple of million years ago, and dumped by the merciless working of the electric-blue portals on an isolated outcrop of rock on some watery Earth. Ninety-nine out of a hundred such colonies would surely have starved quickly – even if they hadn't drowned first. But a few survived, and learned to use the water, seeking fish and vegetation – and, in time, they left the land behind altogether . . .

And now here were their descendants, scooped up by another Wheel, stranded once again on the Red Moon.

Hominids like dolphins. How strange, Malenfant thought.

Something immense collided with the back of his head.

*   *   *

He was on the ground. He felt something pushing down on his back. A foot, maybe. One eye was pressed into the ground, but the other was exposed, and could see.

That fat new Earth still swam in the sky.

He heard a commotion. Maybe Julia was putting up a fight. A face – runtish, filthy – eclipsed the Banded Earth.

Once again the back of his head was struck, very hard, and he could think no more.

Shadow:

Shadow learned day by day how to live with these new people, here on the slope of the crater wall.

One morning she brought a bundle of ginger leaves she had collected from the forest. She approached the group of women that was, as usual, centred on Silverneck. She sat next to Silverneck, offering the leaves.

A woman called Hairless – left almost totally bald in her upper body by over-grooming – immediately grabbed all the leaves. She passed some to Silverneck and the others. When Shadow tried to get back some of her leaves, Hairless slapped her away.

So Shadow came up behind Hairless and began to groom her. Though Hairless flinched away at first, she submitted.

But now Hairless spotted the baby, clinging to Shadow's neck. She reached out and plucked the baby off Shadow, as if picking a fruit off a branch. Shadow did not resist. Hairless poked her finger in the baby's mouth and fingered his genitals. The baby squirmed, his huge head lolling.

While Hairless probed at her baby, Shadow stole back some leaves.

But Hairless developed a sudden disgust for the malformed infant. She thrust the child back at Shadow, jabbering.

Shadow retreated to the fringe of the group, chewing quietly on her prize.

Shadow was the lowest of the women here. She made her nests on the periphery of the group, and she kept as quiet as possible. Though she clung to Silverneck as much as she could, she was subject to abuse, violence, and theft of her food from men and women alike.

But this community was different from that of Termite and Big Boss. Here, sex was everything.

During some rough-and-tumble play between older infants, a chase and wrestle involved a boy taking the penis of another in his mouth. Soon the wrestling had dissolved into a bout of oral sex and other erotic games, after which the chasing began again.

One day two of the more powerful men came into conflict. One of them was Stripe, the dominant man, a tall, robust man with a stripe of grey hair down one side of his head. The other was One-eye, the shorter, more manic man who had taken it on himself to attack the pack of hyenas with a stick on the day Shadow had joined this new group. The fight, caused when One-eye didn't respond submissively enough to an early-morning show of power by Stripe, escalated from yelling and hair-bristling to a show of shoving and punching. At last one firm kick from Stripe put One-eye on his back.

The smaller man got up, confronting Stripe again. Both men's fur bristled, as if full of electricity – and both had erections. After another bout of shouting, they grew quieter, and One-eye, hesitantly, reached out and took Stripe's erection, rubbing it gently. After a time Stripe's bristling hair subsided, and he briskly cupped One-eye's scrotum.

The contact was quickly over. Neither man reached an orgasm, but orgasms were usually not the point.

Sex was everything. Couplings between men and women, and the older children, were frequent, both belly-to-back and belly-to-belly. Infants became excited during couplings, jumping over the adults involved and sometimes pressing their own genitals against the adults'. But contact between members of the same sex was common too.

It was a lesson Shadow learned quickly. She learned how to avert a male fist by grasping a penis or scrotum, or taking it in her mouth, or allowing a brief copulation. She earned toleration by groups of women as they fed or groomed by rubbing breasts and genitals, or allowing herself to be touched in turn.

But still, things went badly for her, no matter how hard she worked. She was surrounded by hostility and disgust. The women would push her and her baby away, the men would hit her, and children would stare, wrinkle their noses at her and throw stones or sticks.

There was something wrong, with herself and her baby. The wrongness began to be embedded in her, so that she accepted it as part of her life.

That was why she submitted to the attentions of One-eye without resisting.

Many of the men, at one time or another, initiated sexual contact with Shadow. She was young, and, save for the lingering *wrongness*, healthy and attractive. But the contacts rarely led to ejaculation; the man, after being lost briefly in pleasure, would look at her, and his face would change, and he would push her away. After a time most of her contacts came from boys, eager to experiment with a mature woman, and men who for some reason were frustrated elsewhere; she learned to submit to their immature or angry fumblings, and the blows that came with them.

But One-eye was different. Of all the men, One-eye alone developed an obsession with Shadow.

At first his approaches to her were conventional. He would come to her with legs splayed and erection showing, sometimes shaking branches and leaves. She would submit, as she had learned to submit to any demand made of her, and he would take her into the shade of a tree.

But from the beginning his coupling was rough, leaving her breasts pinched and bitten, her thighs scratched and bruised.

After a time his demands became cruder. He would drop the formalities of the invitation and simply take her, wherever and whenever he felt like it – even if she was feeding, or suckling her child, or sleeping in her nest. He seemed to find her exciting and would quickly reach orgasm. But the speed of the couplings did not reduce their violence.

The other women rejected One-eye. If he approached them they would turn away, or run to the protection of the powerful women. His intent, manic strength repelled the women. And so he was forced to prey on the very old and young and weak, who were unable to defend themselves – them, and Shadow, for Shadow got no protection from the other women, not even Silverneck.

Bruised and bloodied, she submitted to his attentions, over and again, and the sex became harsher.

One day Shadow caught a glimpse of one reason why she continued to be shunned.

One-eye had used her particularly hard that day, and some old wounds had been opened by his roughness; she wanted to clear the dirt and blood from the injuries before they began to stink. Deep in the forest, high on the wall of the crater, she found a small, still pool. She leaned over the pool, reaching for the water.

A reflection peered back out at her.

She leapt back, jabbering in alarm. Her infant, feebly crawling in the leaves, fell on her belly and mewled.

Cautiously Shadow crept back to the pond. A face peered out at her, a face made grotesque with a bulbous nose and lumpy protrusions on its cheekbones and brow. The face was alarming and threatening – but of course it was her own face.

Screeching, she dug her fingernails into her face, the swellings there, and tried to rip it off, longing to throw it far away from her. But she succeeded only in making her face bleed, and great crimson drops splashed into the little pool that had betrayed her.

By now, Shadow had no memory of the infected stream from which she had drunk when she crossed the plain, and had no understanding of the fungus infection she had contracted.

She lay down in the leaves, thumb jammed in her mouth. Her child began to sneeze, loudly and liquidly.

Shadow uncurled. She rolled over and picked up her infant. She inspected the child's dribbling nose, then she plucked some leaves and wiped away the snot and dirt. Then she took the softly weeping child to her breast.

Far away she heard a hooting. It was the cry of One-eye, seeking to use her body once more. She curled tighter around her child.

The infant's cold grew steadily worse, developing into a fever that kept him awake during the night.

Shadow quickly grew exhausted, without energy enough even to feed herself, or keep herself properly clean. The swellings on her face now itched constantly. They hurt badly when struck. And they continued to grow, to the point where she could see the fleshy masses framing her eye sockets and cheekbones.

Even in the midst of all this, she was not spared One-eye's voracious demands.

She never resisted him. But out of his sight she would place her sickly infant down carefully on a bed of leaves or a nest of branches. If the coupling permitted it, she would look across that way, and even reach out to touch or stroke the child.

Eventually One-eye noticed this.

It enraged him. He was already lying on top of her. He pinched her chin in his right hand, making her face him, and he punched her hard on the lumps in her brow, making her scream. Then he grabbed her ankles and pushed them back towards her head, and entered her savagely.

When he was done he pushed her away and began to beat her, aiming precise blows at her belly and kidneys. When she curled in on herself he grabbed her arms and pulled her open, making her lie unprotected on her back, and rammed his fist over and over into her solar plexus.

The world dissolved into fragments, red as blood, white as bone.

When she came to she could barely move. Her belly and back were a mass of pain, and one eye was covered with a film of drying blood.

Silverneck had taken her baby. The older woman cradled him on her lap, and was even allowing him to suck on her cracked, dry nipples.

With a groan, Shadow let the world fall away again.

After a time, she was aware of a looming shape before her. Her child was sleeping uneasily at her breast. She cringed, trying to curl tighter.

But a gentle hand touched her shoulder, and pushed her gently back. It was Silverneck. She was carrying a pepper. Its stem had been pulled out, and it was full of water. Shadow drank greedily. But her lips were cracked and swollen, and she felt the water dribble down her chin.

It was dark before she found the strength to clamber a little way up into a tree, and construct a rough nest.

Reid Malenfant:

Malenfant was bent double. His arms were pinned behind his back. Something was jolting him, over and over. His head felt like it would explode. It was like the feeling you got after a few days on orbit, when your body fluid balance hadn't yet adjusted to microgravity, and blood pooled in your head.

But when he forced his eyes open – the light stabbed bright, making him squint – he saw, in glimpsed shards, a ground of rust-red dust, powerful bare legs pumping.

Not on orbit, it appears, Malenfant. He was being carried over somebody's shoulder, in a fireman's lift. But his head was upside down, and with every step his cheek crashed into the back of his carrier.

He threw up. It was a spasm of gut and throat; suddenly hot yellow-green fluid was spilling down the naked back before his eyes.

There was a loud hoot of protest. With a shrug he was thrown off the shoulder, as if he were as light as a feather, with a good two yards to fall to the ground.

The fall seemed long, slow-motion. He couldn't raise his bound arms to protect himself. He landed head-first.

When he came to again his head ached even worse than before. He was lying on his side. All he could see was red dust, and a pair of grimy buckskin boots. His legs were free. But his arms, still pinned behind his back, felt like they were half-wrenched out of their sockets.

A buckskin boot dug into his stomach to tip him over, none too gently. He finished up on his back, as helpless as a landed fish. It felt as if his neck was in his own warm vomit.

Faces loomed over him. One pushed closer. It was a bearded man, aged perhaps forty; his face was round, greasy, suspicious.

Malenfant tried to speak. 'Let me up,' he gasped.

The man's eyes narrowed. 'English? But no argot I ever heard. What are you, a Frenchie?' His accent was thick, the vowels twisted, almost incomprehensible.

Somebody said, 'He's sick. Leave him. We ain't here for this.'

Beyond the bearded man Malenfant saw McCann; he seemed composed, though his arms were bound. 'Sprigge. In the bowels of Christ I beseech you. *He is an Englishman.*'

The bearded man – Sprigge – glared at McCann. Then he turned back to Malenfant. 'Get him up.'

Ungentle hands dug into Malenfant's armpits and hauled him off the dirt. He managed to get his feet on the ground. But he couldn't keep his eyes targeted; they slid sideways in their sockets as if he were drunk, and when he was let go he fell back into the dirt.

His NASA boots were gone. His feet were bare, grimy and bleeding. They even took my socks, he thought. He wondered what had happened to his pack.

Sprigge stood over Malenfant again. 'Get up or I leave you for the Elves.'

Malenfant slumped forward. He managed to get up onto one knee, got one foot on the ground, and pushed himself up. This time he staggered, and his head still spun, but he stayed upright.

McCann said, 'You can't expect the man to walk.'

Sprigge nodded, and snapped a finger.

A huge Runner stepped up to Malenfant. He was naked, dust-encrusted – and his head was small, like a child's, though his face was weather-beaten and scarred. From the look of the dribble of vomit down his back, this had been Malenfant's reluctant mount.

The Runner kneeled in front of Malenfant, his hands making a stirrup. Malenfant stared stupidly.

McCann said, 'Use him, Malenfant.' Now Malenfant saw that McCann was sitting on the shoulders of another huge Runner, like a child riding on its father. The Runner's head was bowed, his eyes fixed on the dirt. McCann seemed relaxed, almost comfortable. 'Follow my lead, Malenfant. One must keep up the front.'

'. . . I.'

Julia walked up to Malenfant. Her head was bowed, and her wraps of skin had been ripped away, leaving her naked. But her hands were unbound.

Sprigge touched his belt, where a whip was coiled.

Julia kept her gaze directed at the dirt, not looking the humans in the face. She said, 'Carry Mal'fan'.'

Sprigge barked a laugh. 'So you use a Ham's quim, Sir Malenfant. Your punishment will sting if you let Praisegod Michael witness such iniquity.' But he stepped back.

Julia slid her arms under Malenfant's body and lifted him effortlessly, like a child.

The party formed up and began to move off over the dirt.

The party was made up of perhaps a dozen Runners. Most were naked, though some wore loincloths. Some of them bore heavy packs, or loads on their heads and shoulders. Two of them were dragging the carcass of an immense bull antelope on a crude travois. The rest of the Runners had passengers: buckskin-clothed men sitting on their shoulders, stubby whips in their hands. All the Runners walked silently, just waiting for instruction. Several of them had scars striped on their shoulders and bellies.

There was one other hominid: a Ham, dressed in clothes as comparatively well-stitched as those of the humans. He carried a whip; perhaps he was a supervisor, a boss.

Malenfant saw that Julia's breasts were scratched, as if by finger-nails, or teeth. 'Did they hurt you?'

She did not answer.

McCann's Runner came trotting alongside. 'She shouldn't speak to you, Malenfant,' McCann said urgently. 'It will be a whipping for her if she does, and perhaps for you. She knows how to behave with these types; you must learn, and fast. These brutes had a little gruesome fun with her, but yon Constable Sprigge stopped them. I sense there is a core of decency in that man, under the dirt and violence. Perhaps that will assist us as we deal with these Zealots . . .'

'Zealots,' Malenfant growled.

McCann said grimly, 'I did not expect to encounter them here. They are clearly expanding their area of operations – which is all the worse for us. Listen to me, Malenfant. Your romantic quest for Emma is going to have to wait. It's vital to keep up a front. All that keeps us from doing the carrying rather than being carried is that these fellows accept us as human beings. So you must act as if it is your privilege, no, your *right*, to use the muscles of these poor creatures as if they belonged to you. And don't forget, you're English.' He eyed Malenfant. 'A colonial type like you might take it as a great indignity to have to impersonate a Britisher. But I believe any of these ruffians would run you through if they suspected you were a French or a Spaniard or a Portugoose . . .'

Malenfant said bitterly, 'You know what? I miss America. In America you can travel more than a couple of miles without getting robbed, attacked, kidnapped or trussed up.'

'Chin up, sir. Chin up.'

Malenfant's thinking dissolved. Lulled by the stink of the dust, his weakness, and Julia's steady warmth, he dozed.

Somewhere thunder cracked, and when he looked up he saw more fat clouds scudding across the sky.

Half a day after the capture of Malenfant and the others, the party reached the fringes of the Zealot empire.

They crossed a plain scattered with broken rock fragments. The rim of a broad young crater loomed over the horizon; perhaps they were in the crater's debris field. In any event it was slow, difficult going, as the Runners had to pick their way past huge sharp-edged boulders.

They came to a place where a thin, sluggish stream ran, and green growing things clustered close to its banks. The land had been cleared. Malenfant saw how the rocks had been piled up into waist-high dry stone walls, mile after mile of them. The rocks must have been broken up before they were moved, a hell of a labour – but then labour was cheap here.

In a field close to the river, a team of Runners was drawing a wooden plough. The four of them were bound together by a thick leather harness, and wooden yokes lay over their shoulders. The Runners were followed by a Ham, a stocky man who carried a long whip.

When Sprigge's party came alongside, the Ham overseer stared at Julia. Then he turned back to his charges and lashed them, a single stroke that cut across all four backs. The Runners, their faces empty, did not look up from the dirt they tilled.

'Good God,' Malenfant said, disgusted.

'It would pay you not to blaspheme in this company,' McCann said evenly. 'And besides, is it any less cruel to use an ox or a horse for such a purpose?'

'Those draught animals aren't oxen, McCann. They are hominids.'

'Hominids, but not people, Malenfant,' McCann said sadly. 'If they have no conception of pain – if even their Ham boss does not – then what harm is done?'

'You can't believe that's true.'

McCann said stiffly, 'I would sooner believe it than join those poor Runner gentlemen behind their plough.'

They passed a small farmhouse, just a rough sod hut. In a yard of red mud, children were playing – they looked like human children, a boy and a girl. They gazed at the approaching party, then ran into the hut. A man emerged from the hut, stripped to the waist, bare-headed. He looked apprehensive.

From his Runner mount, Sprigge nodded to him. 'No tithes to collect today, George.'

'Aye, Master Sprigge.' The man George nodded back, cordially enough, but his eyes were wary, fixed on Sprigge as if he were a predator.

They moved on, following the river as it worked its way towards the Beltway forest. As the land became less arid, the cultivation spread away from the river bank. Soon Malenfant was surrounded by fields, toiling hominids, an occasional human. It might have been a scene from some vision of the old west, or maybe the European Middle Ages, if not for the humanoid forms of the beasts of burden here, the unmistakably Neandertal features of their supervisors, and the unremitting crimson glower of the land itself.

But this was a genuine colony, he thought, a growing community, for all its ugliness – unlike the dying, etiolated English camp.

Rain began to fall. The rough path by the river bank soon turned to mud, and the party trudged on in miserable silence. Malenfant tucked his head closer to Julia's chest. With remarkable kindness she leaned over him and sheltered him from the rain with her own bare back, and Malenfant could not find the strength to protest.

Again he dozed.

When he woke, he was dumped on his feet. They had reached the Zealot fortress, it seemed.

They were in a clearing, surrounded by dense wood; Malenfant hadn't even noticed they had come back to the forest. Ditches, ramparts, gates and drawbridges stretched all the way around the township. Sharpened stakes were stuck in the sides of the ramparts, so that the compound bristled, like some great hedgehog of wood and mud.

A big gate was opened. They were pushed inside.

The encampment was a place of rambling muddy paths and ugly, low-tech buildings placed haphazardly. There was one central building that looked more sturdily built, mud brick on a wooden frame, like a chapel. Aside from that, the huts were so rough they seemed to have grown out of the debris that littered the muddy ground. They were built of stripped saplings and wattles, and laid over with palm fronds. Everything showed signs of much use and recycling; here was half of what looked like a dugout canoe, for example, serving as a chicken-coop.

There were no straight lines anywhere, no squares or rectangles, no hard edges; everything was sloppy, all the lines blurred. It was as if the first arrivals here had just marked out trails where they wandered and put up their wattle-and-daub huts where they felt like. There was none of the regularity and discipline of the British compound: Malenfant sensed McCann's impatience at this disorderliness.

Malenfant's arms were untied. He could barely move them because of cramp, and he could feel where the cord had cut into his wrists.

With McCann, he was pushed into a dark, stinking sod hut. He couldn't see what had become of Julia. The hut was dark, the floor was just mud, uneven. A door of saplings bound together by liana twine blocked the door.

Malenfant limped to a dark corner and slumped there. The floor was greasy and black; when he lifted his hand a great slick sheen came away with it. The whole place stank like a toilet.

Termite passageways, like the stems of some dead plant, curled up the walls and disappeared into the wooden beams and the thatch. A gecko clambered across the ceiling, incurious.

He hadn't eaten or drunk anything since being hit over the head by the Zealots. He felt as if he had been systematically pummelled, all over his body, with a baseball bat. And here he was in some quasi-medieval prison block, lying in filth. The world he had come from – of NASA and Houston and Washington, of computers and phones and cars and planes – seemed utterly unreal, evanescent as the shining surface of a bubble, a dream.

What a mess, he thought.

McCann was waxing enthusiastic. 'I see the pattern, Malenfant. The Hams and Runners surely do not have the wit to be rebellious or to long for escape; unlike human slaves it is unlikely they can conceive of *freedom*. Besides, if you get them young enough, you can quite easily break their spirits, as with a young horse. If each man controls, say, ten of the Ham bosses, and then each Ham in turn controls ten Runners, you have a formidable army of workers. And at the top of it you have this fellow Praisegod Michael of whom Sprigge has spoken, who creams off the tithes. It is like a vast, spreading, self-sustaining –'

'Prison camp,' Malenfant said sourly.

'Oh, much more than that, Malenfant. Think how carefully the strata of this little society are defined. You have the humans, with of course their own ranks and order. Beneath them you have your Hams, who in turn lord it over the Runners. And since in this case each lower rank is clearly the intellectual inferior of that above, you have a social order that reflects the natural order. It is a hierarchy as stable as a cathedral.'

Malenfant growled, 'I thought you despised the Zealots. You wouldn't tell me a damn word about them.'

'I think I am beginning to see I have underestimated them, Malenfant. Oh, this is a place of repellent squalor, of blood and mud. It *is* cruel, Malenfant. I don't deny it. But those subject to the greatest cruelty, as far as I can see, are those least capable of perceiving it. And as a social arrangement it is intricate and marvellous. One must admire efficiency when one finds it, whatever one's moral qualms.'

He sounded brittle, almost feverish, Malenfant thought dully. This bizarre mood of his, this fan-worship of the Zealots, could probably evaporate as fast as it had come.

The hell with it. Malenfant closed his eyes.

But still, he saw Emma's face in his mind's eye, bright and clear, as if she stood before him. He probed a pocket on his sleeve. The spyglass lens still nestled there, hard and round under his fingers, comforting.

McCann went to a window – just a hole in the wall, unglazed. He called, 'We need water and food. And tell him, Sprigge! Tell your Praisegod Michael we are Englishmen! It will go worse for you if you fail!'

McCann shook him awake. 'We have an invitation to dinner, Malenfant! How jolly exciting.'

A sullen Zealot had brought them a wooden pail of water. They both inspected this suspiciously; they were ferociously thirsty, but in the dim light diffusing from the window, the water looked cloudy.

McCann shrugged. 'Needs must.' He plunged his hands into the water and scooped up mouthfuls, which he gulped down.

Malenfant followed suit. The water tasted sour, but it had no odour.

When they were done they used the rest of the water to wash themselves. Malenfant cleaned dried blood and grit out of wounds on his bare feet, wrists and neck.

McCann used the water to slick down his hair. He even produced a tie from one jacket pocket and knotted it around his neck. 'Impression is everything,' he said to Malenfant. 'Outer form. Get that right and the rest follows. Eh?'

The door was pushed open, its leather hinges creaking. Sprigge walked in, looking as dusty as when they had all walked in from the plains. 'You have your wish, gentlemen.' He raised his fist. 'But any defiance or dissimulation and you'll know my wrath.'

McCann and Malenfant nodded silently.

They were led out of the hut, into a broad compound. It was raining, and the evening was drawing in. The ground was just red dirt, hard-packed by the passage of human feet. But it was heavily rain-soaked, and Malenfant felt the mud seep between his naked toes.

People moved between the huts, carrying food and tools or leading children by the hand. They seemed to be humans, but they were small, skinny, stunted folk, dressed in filthy skin rags. There were no lanterns, and the only light inside the huts came from fire hearths.

McCann murmured to him like a tour guide. 'They do not approach us; the authority of this Praisegod Michael of theirs is binding. Look there. I think that hut yonder is a house of ill-fame.'

'A what? . . . Oh. A brothel.'

'Yes, but a brothel stocked with Runners – women and boys, so far as I can tell. There are contradictions here, Malenfant. We have a community run by this Praisegod fellow, seemingly on rigid religious lines. And yet here is a bordello operating openly.'

The rain grew heavier. The Zealot compound was turning to a muddy swamp. The buildings seemed to slump in defeat, as if sliding back down into the earth from which they had been dragged. And the people, humans, Runners and Hams alike were wan figures, all the same dun colour, images of misery.

McCann stamped through puddles contemptuously. 'These people don't know what they are doing,' he barked. 'We coped rather better. Culverts! Storm drains!' And with broad sweeps of his arms he sketched an ambitious drainage system.

They were brought to the compound's central structure, the solid-looking chapel. Well, maybe it really was a chapel; now Malenfant saw it had a narrow spire.

Sprigge led the two of them along a short, dark hallway. Grilles of tightly interwoven wooden laths were set in the floor. Malenfant glanced down. He thought he saw movement, eyes peering up at him. But the light was uncertain.

They arrived at a large, bright room. It had neat rectangular windows – unglazed, but covered with sheets of what looked like woven and scraped palm leaves, so that they admitted a cool yellow light. Lanterns burned on the walls, each just a stone bowl cupping oil within which a wick floated, burning smokily. At the head of the room was a stone fireplace, impressively constructed from heavy red blocks – perhaps ejecta from the crater field they had crossed. No fire burned beneath the blackened chimney stack, but there was a large, impressive crucifix set over the fireplace. At the other end of the room was a plain altar, set with goblets and plates, all of it carved from wood.

At the centre of the room was a small, unevenly made, polished wooden table. A man sat behind the table, eating steadily. There were no plates; the man ate bits of fish and meat off what looked like slabs of thick bread.

The man wore a black robe that swept to the ground, with a napkin thrown over his shoulder. A band of silver-grey hair surrounding a crown that looked shaved, like a tonsure. His narrow face was disfigured by warts.

This was, presumably, Praisegod Michael. He ignored Malenfant and McCann.

Behind Praisegod two Ham women stood, backed up against the wall. They were both dressed in modest, all-covering dresses of soft leather, and they kept their eyes on the floor.

Sprigge nudged McCann, and indicated they should sit on the floor before the table. McCann complied readily enough. Malenfant followed his lead. Sprigge stepped back, and took a station at the corner of the room.

As Praisegod Michael ate, everybody in the room waited in silence.

Malenfant couldn't take his eyes off the food.

There was a puree of what looked like chicken mixed in with rice and some kind of nuts. An animal like a young piglet, roasted, had been carved and set before Michael, and he picked at its white flesh. Other side dishes included some kind of beans cooked in what smelled like meat stock, and mushrooms in a kind of cream, and a green salad. There was even wine – or anyhow it looked like wine, served in a delicately carved wooden goblet.

At length Praisegod Michael slowed down. More than half the piglet was left on its serving plate. Michael belched, and mopped his lip with a scrap of cloth.

Then he looked up, directly into Malenfant's eyes. Malenfant was jolted by the intensity of his gaze.

One of the Ham women behind him stepped forward. Malenfant was startled to recognize Julia. With heavy grace she took the unfinished dishes from Michael, and set them on the floor before McCann and Malenfant.

Malenfant reached straight for the pork, but McCann touched his arm.

McCann closed his eyes. 'For this blessing, Lord, we thank You.'

Michael watched coldly.

Now McCann began to eat, using his fingers to tear at the pork. Malenfant followed suit.

Michael spoke. 'Your Ham girl is well-tempered,' he said to Malenfant. His voice was deep, commanding, but his accent was powerfully strange.

Malenfant said, 'She isn't *my* anything.'

McCann said quickly, 'She has an even nature, and is wise for a Ham.'

Michael's gaze swivelled to McCann. 'I know of you, or at least men who speak like you. Once one was brought here.'

McCann blanched. 'Russell. Is he –'

'He died for his sins.'

There was a long silence. McCann's eyes were closed, even as he chewed steadily on the meat. Then he said carefully, 'There are only a handful of us – a handful, and Hams and Runners. We have no women, no children. We are weak old men,' he said, looking directly at Michael. 'We are no threat to your – umm, your expansion.'

Michael got out of his chair. Tall, cadaverously thin, his arms clasped before his belly, he walked around the table and studied McCann and Malenfant. 'My soldiers will spare them.'

'They live in God,' McCann said fervently.

Michael nodded. 'Then let them die in God. But you talk of an *expansion*.'

McCann said hastily, 'I am sorry if –'

'Whenever anything in this world is exalted, or exalts itself, God will pull it down, for He alone will be exalted,' said Praisegod Michael. His speech was rapid, his delivery flat. He laid his hand on Julia's flat brow; she did not react. 'My language is not of kingdoms and kings, empires and emperors. No king I, but a Protector,' he said.

McCann was nodding vigorously. 'I see that. Yes, I see that. As men we are different – we come from different worlds – but differences between men are as nothing compared to the gulf between men and animals. There are few enough strong men scattered over this world, Praisegod Michael, to shoulder the responsibility.'

Michael regarded him. 'God hath poured this confused nation from vessel to vessel, until He poured it into my lap. Perhaps it is divine providence that brings you here.'

McCann smiled. 'Providence, by God's dispensation. Indeed.'

Praisegod Michael turned to Malenfant. 'And what of this one?

His eye is defiant, his accent strange. What is your religion, man? Popish? Atheistical?'

McCann said quickly, 'His faith is as strong as mine.'

Michael smiled thinly. 'Then perhaps he will have the courage to say it for himself.' He seemed to come to a decision. 'You are right. There are few enough decent men here. But can I trust you? . . . Tomorrow we hunt. Accompany me, and we will talk further.' He knelt before his altar, his eyes closed.

Sprigge motioned Malenfant and McCann to follow him out of the room.

Back in their crude hut, McCann seemed excited. 'He is English – that is clear enough – but I would say that his history must have split off from our own no later than our seventeenth century . . . Perhaps you number your dates differently. Well, it looks as if the Zealots have been here since then. But they seem to have made no significant progress, socially or mechanically, since those days . . .'

Malenfant said sourly, 'What difference does it make?'

'*We understood each other*, Malenfant. Don't you see? Myself and this Praisegod. His is a faith which has much in common with my own. He spoke of providences. Through providences, you see, God intervenes in the world, to make His will visible. And I have no doubt that Praisegod will count himself among the Elect – that is, those who are already destined to be saved – but he has surely been cast in a world of Reprobates, the already damned.' He smiled, and his eyes glinted in the dark. 'I understand him. I can do business with this man.'

Malenfant frowned. 'But his "business" seems to be to enslave those he regards as lesser than him.'

'Ah, but that's the delicious irony of it all, Malenfant – oh, but I forget, you slept and did not see – I spied a man coming out of the Runner bawdy-house, his trousers dangling around his knees. A more unspeakable wretch you never saw. But *I could make out clearly that he had a tail*. Malenfant, our grandiloquent Praisegod Michael, the saviour of the world, has a monkey's tail!'

After a minute, Malenfant began to laugh. McCann joined in. Once they started, they couldn't stop.

Joshua:

Joshua and Mary, breathing hard, stepped gingerly over crushed branches and uprooted shrubs. They reached the edge of the cliff and peered down. The sky seed still lay where it had fallen, when they had pushed it over the cliff: trapped well below the lip of the cliff, pinned by a ledge and a thick knot of shrubbery.

Joshua grinned. Every few days he had come clambering up the trail to this battered clearing, to see again what they had done to the sky seed.

The seed was safe here. The feeble muscles of the Zealots would never succeed in hauling this prize up from such a place – and the Nutcracker-folk, though good climbers, were surely too stupid even to envisage such a thing. Only the People of the Grey Earth, with their brains and powerful bodies, could retrieve the sky seed from where it rested, pinned against the cliff's grey breast –

Voices screamed, all around them.

They whirled, shocked.

There were only trees and bushes and leaves, some of them shaking violently, as if in a wind, though there was no wind.

From nowhere a spear flew. It lanced into Joshua's shoulder, neatly puncturing it through.

He was knocked back. He fell on the spear. It twisted, and there was savage pain.

And now something new descended over him, a thing of ropes and threads knotted together, that tangled up his legs and arms and head.

Leaves and twigs fell away, and suddenly there were people: men, all around them. They were Skinnies. They carried spears and knives that glinted. Still screaming, they threw themselves forward. It had all happened in a heartbeat, overwhelming, bewildering. The Zealots had just melted out of the trees: one instant they were not there, the next they were there, an overwhelming magic beyond Joshua's experience.

Their blows and kicks were feeble, but there were many of them, and they clung to Joshua's limbs while punching his stomach and chest and head. He heard Mary cry out, an angry, fearful roar.

'. . . Looks like Tobias was right. A fine old pair we trapped here!'

'Wrap up yon buck and give us a hand with the maid, will you? She's struggling like a bear . . .'

Joshua lay passively, defeated by shock as much as the spear, peering up at the indifferent sun. He saw that the men had got Mary on the ground, and had ripped open her skins.

'By the tears of the Lord –'

'Get her legs. Get her legs.'

'The buck is for the minister. This one's for us, eh, lads?'

'Face like a bear but the tits of an angel. She's going to take a bit of stilling, though . . .'

Joshua came to himself. With a bellow he wrenched himself over, rolling onto his belly. Zealots, yelling, went flying. For a moment he was free of their weight and their blows. But the spear ground into the dirt, opening his wound wider, and he cried out.

But Joshua's struggle had distracted Mary's attackers, and she had got one arm loose. With a fist more massive than any Skinny's, she pounded at the temple of one of her assailants. Joshua heard the crunch of bone; a Zealot went down.

'God's wounds. Peter – Peter!'

'Get her, lads! –'

Mary struggled to her feet, her ripped skins swinging, her small breasts glistening with blood. She had her back to the forest. The men, all save the fallen one, made a half-circle to face her, wielding their weapons. Their lust had been replaced by caution, Joshua saw, for even a half-mature Ham girl, if free, was more than a match for any one of the Skinnies.

But she could not defeat them all.

With a last, regretful glance at Joshua, she turned and crashed into the trees. Though she made an immense racket, she had soon disappeared, and Joshua knew that the Zealots could not follow her.

He let his head slump to the blood-soaked ground beneath his face.

A shadow crossed him. 'This is for Peter.'

A boot hurtled at his face.

Reid Malenfant:

The morning after their capture, Malenfant and McCann found their door was not barred, no guard posted.

They crept out into light still tinged grey with dawn.

Already the business of the day was starting. Runners and Hams were working silently to sweep the ground clear of yesterday's debris, and to fill the water casks that sat outside each hut. It was strange to see specimens of *Homo neandertalensis* and *Erectus* dressed in crudely sewn parodies of clothing, their heads and bodies strikingly misshapen in the uncertain dawn light, coming and going as they pursued their chores. It was like a mockery of a human township.

Away from the Zealots, neither Hams nor Runners made any attempt to use human language; they simply got through their work with steady dullness, united in blank misery.

There was a specialized group of Runners who were used solely to carry passengers. Some of them wore primitive harnesses. But these unfortunates were stooped, with over-developed shoulders and necks, and what looked like permanent curves to their backs. Their shoulders and thighs bore bright red weals.

Malenfant said, 'Look at those scars. These Zealot jockeys don't spare the whip.'

McCann grunted, impatient. 'Have you much experience in the husbandry of animals, Malenfant? None of them look terribly *old*, do they? – I would wager that under excessive loading their bodies break down rather rapidly once the flush of youth is over.

'But the whip is surely necessary. In Africa I knew a man who tried to train elephants. You may know that while your Indian elephant has been tamed by the locals for centuries, your African runs wild. My acquaintance struggled to master his elephants, even though he imported experienced mahouts from India; freedom runs in the blood of those African tuskers, and they are far more intelligent than, say, a horse.'

'Hence the whip.'

'Yes. For it is only by severe and strict punishment that such intelligent beasts can be controlled. Even then, of course, you can never be sure; even in India the tamest-looking elephant with a grudge against his mahout may wait years, decades – but he will take his one chance and gore or trample his tormentor, careless of his fate.

'Now your Runner, who is after all a man, if a different stripe of man, is surely more intelligent than an elephant. Hence, as you say, the whip. And perhaps other practices have been developed. See there – that grizzled, rather bent old chap is tied up to the boy.' The old man and the boy, sitting in the dirt, listless and naked, were attached by tight bonds around their ankles. 'If you want to break an animal you will sometimes put him in with an older beast. The tamed creature may prove an example in the work to be done, and so forth. But in addition the young perceives there is no hope, you see, and quits his rebelliousness sooner.'

Malenfant said, 'I don't understand why these Runners don't just up and get out of here.'

McCann pulled his walrus moustache. 'These boys have probably been in captivity since they were very young – either born here, or wrest from their dead mothers' arms in the wild. They know nothing else; they cannot imagine freedom. And these wretches could not run off if you turned them free tomorrow. See how they limp – the scars on the backs of their ankles? Hamstrung. Perhaps that explains their demeanour of defeat. They are creatures evolved, surely, for one thing above all else – running – and if they cannot run any more, they have no aspiration. Perhaps it is humane to excise the very possibility of escape; believe me, hope harms a creature far more than despair ever did . . .'

Praisegod Michael emerged from his chapel-like residence. His black robe flapped about his ankles, heavy, as he walked. He threw his arms wide, loudly sniffing the air. Then he fell to his knees, bowed his head, and began to pray.

Praisegod's hunting party formed up rapidly. There were to be five humans (or near-humans) – Praisegod, his man Sprigge and one other Zealot, and Malenfant and McCann – along with four Hams, and ten Runner bearers.

One of the Hams was just a child, about the size of a human ten-year-old. This boy seemed dressed in clothing of a somewhat finer cut than most of the Zealots. Praisegod kept him close by, sometimes resting his hand on the boy's flattened skull, or cupping him under his chinless jaw. The boy submitted to this, and ran small errands for Praisegod.

Five of the Runners were to carry equipment – home-made spears and crossbows. The rest were there to carry the humans.

Malenfant's mount was to be one of the older, more broken-down specimens he had observed that morning. The hominid stood before him, as tall as Malenfant despite his stoop, his very human eyes empty of expression.

Malenfant flatly refused to climb aboard his shoulders.

McCann leaned towards him. 'For God's sake, Malenfant,' he hissed.

Praisegod Michael watched this with a thin amusement. 'Do you imagine you spare this stooped one discomfort or indignity? There is no soul behind those deceptive eyes, sir, to experience such complicated passions. I trust your compassion will not pour away when your bare feet are bleeding and sore . . . But perhaps you are right; he is rather worn down.' He nodded to Sprigge.

Sprigge tapped the old Runner's elbow, and he obediently knelt on the ground. Sprigge stepped behind him and drew a knife from his belt – metal, very old, sharpened and polished until the blade was a thin, fragile remnant.

'Shit.' Malenfant lunged forward, but McCann grabbed his arm.

Distracted by the commotion, the Runner saw the knife. His battered face twisted in animal rage. He started to rise, perhaps for the first time in his life defying those who used him.

But Sprigge wrestled him to the ground and knelt on his back. He sliced the knife through the old Runner's throat. Blood spurted, a brighter red shining in the crimson dirt. Still the Runner fought; he didn't stop struggling until his head had been all but sawn off his body.

McCann released Malenfant. 'The rogue elephant and the mahout, Malenfant,' he whispered grimly. 'And if you defy, you will only make matters worse for the creatures here.'

'Thank you, sir,' Praisegod said to Malenfant, his look calculating, mocking. 'You perceived a lack which I have been remiss in correcting. Well, it is done, and the sun is already high. Come now.' And he slapped the face of his own mount, who trotted away to the west, away from the rising sun.

The others hastily mounted, and the hunting party proceeded at a steady jog after Praisegod, the Runners' bare feet thumping into the earth, the Hams following the graceful Runners as best they could with their awkward, bow-legged style.

*   *   *

They reached the fringe of the forest, and moved out onto the plain.

The forest floor hadn't been so bad for Malenfant's bare feet, save for bites, for which he'd no doubt suffer later. But after a half-mile of desert his feet were aching and bloody. And as the miles wore away he began to dig deep into his already shallow reserves of energy. Malenfant knew they had had no choice but to go along with Praisegod Michael's invitation to join his hunt, which was obviously some kind of bullshit character test. He tried to see it as an opportunity. But there was nowhere to run, nowhere to hide.

He found his thoughts dissolving, his purpose reducing merely to a determination to keep one foot moving in front of the others, to show no weakness.

The weather fell apart. A lid of boiling cloud settled over the sky, making the small world seem flat and enclosed, washing the colours out of everything. And then the rain came, a ferocious storm that stippled the crimson sand with miniature craters. Much of the water drained quickly into the dry soil, but soon rivulets were running over the ground, and the sand turned into clinging mud.

Praisegod called a halt. The humans dismounted. Malenfant rested, hands on his knees, breathing deep of the thin air.

Under the brisk supervision of the Hams, the Runners unloaded sheets of sewn-together leather. They quickly put together a kind of tepee.

The Zealots, with McCann and Malenfant, huddled in the tepee. Inside there was a stink of old leather and damp bodies and clothing. The other hominids were excluded – all save Praisegod's Ham boy, who snuggled close to the Zealot; Praisegod stroked his cheek with in-turned fingers. The other Hams had a few sections of skin that they held up over themselves, to keep the rain off their heads.

As for the Runners, they had no shelter at all. They huddled together under a rain so thick it turned the air grey, their knees tucked into their chests, naked, visibly shivering.

McCann saw Malenfant watching the Runners. 'You should not concern yourself,' he said. 'In the wild they have no conception of shelter. If it rains they get wet; if they catch a chill they die. Nothing in their present circumstances changes that.'

Praisegod had been reading passages in a book, a clumsy thing of scraped-leather pages, presumably a Bible or a prayer book. He leaned forward, as if trying to find a more comfortable position for the comical, stubby tail he must have curled up under his robe. 'I suspect you fear the rain, Malenfant.'

Malenfant frowned. 'Ah, bullshit. All this turbulent weather has got to be a result of that new Earth in the sky. It's a bigger world: you're going to get tides, 'quakes, atmospheric disruptions –'

'Your language is a jabber. Perhaps you believe the rain will wash away this puny world, and you along with it. Well, it will not; for if this island resisted the very Flood itself, a little local rain will not harm it now.'

'Ah.' McCann was smiling. Malenfant could tell what he was thinking. *This is what this guy believes. Don't say anything to contradict him.* McCann said, 'We are on an island, an island that survived the Flood. Yes, of course.' He glanced out at the huddled Runners. 'And that explains *them*.'

Praisegod said, 'They are less than men yet more than the animals. What can they be but *Homo diluvii testi* – witnesses of the Flood? This island was spared the rising waters; and so were its inhabitants, who must have crowded here with the ignorant instincts of any animal.'

'Then,' said McCann carefully, 'we are privileged to glimpse the antediluvian order of things.'

'Privileged or damned,' Sprigge muttered, staring at the Neandertal boy on Praisegod's lap. 'This place is an abomination.'

'Not an abomination,' snapped Praisegod. 'It is like a strange reflected Creation. Man was born to look up at the orders of beings above him, the angels, prophets, saints and apostles, who serve the Holy Trinity. Here, we look *down*, down on these creatures with men's hands and faces and even tongues, but creatures without mind or soul, who sprawl in the mud.'

They talked further, an incoherent conversation of disconnected fragments, peppered by misunderstanding, suffused by mistrust. But Malenfant slowly learned something of Praisegod Michael.

The Zealot township had been a godless place when Praisegod was a child, given to anarchy and lawlessness, weakened by the endless green lure of the forest. But – so Michael was told by his parents – God was involved in every detail of life. God watched the daily deeds of men and punished their sins, and the Elect – those who obeyed God's law – would be saved. Praisegod learned this in prayer and torment, in misery and distrust, at the hands of what sounded to Malenfant like abusive parents.

And then they abandoned him, just melted away into the bush, leaving the child to the tender mercies of the townspeople.

Life had been very hard for the young Praisegod, it seemed. But eventually he had rediscovered the religion inside himself. He drew strength from this inner core. And when the growing, toughening Praisegod had come to see that he himself was one of the Elect, his duty had become clear: to devote himself to God's fight and the establishment of His kingdom on this fragmentary world.

He had pursued that goal from then on with an ever-burning zeal and an unswerving fixity of purpose that had turned this gaunt, lisping, wart-ridden preacher into something like a man of true destiny.

But there was a cost, of course.

To the Zealots, it seemed to Malenfant, the other hominids, the pre-sapients, barely even existed. They had no language, no clothing, no religion, and therefore they had absolutely no rights under God or man. They were animals, no more than that, regardless of the curiosity of their gaze, the pain in their cries, their misery in enslavement: simply a resource for exploitation.

Malenfant leaned forward. 'I'm curious. What do you want, Praisegod Michael? What do you want to achieve among all these animals?'

Michael's eyes were bright. 'I seek only to emulate Ramose, who led his nation out of Egypt to the land of Canaan . . .' Malenfant soon realized that this 'Ramose' was a kind of analogue of Moses from his own timeline, like the John who had replaced Christ in McCann's history. 'I believe I have seen the providence of God, for surely it is by His dispensation I have been given my place here. And I have no choice but to follow that providence.'

McCann seemed to be growing agitated. 'But one must search for the truth of providences, Praisegod Michael. One must be wary of the exaltation of the self.'

Michael just laughed. 'You have not lived in this land long. You will learn that it is only *I* who stand between these mindless apes and chaos itself.' His hands, apparently without conscious volition, stroked the Neandertal boy's broad chest. He glanced out of the tepee's flap door; the rain had slackened. 'Come. Time enough for theology later. For now there is a hunt to be made, bellies to be filled.' And he led the way out of the tepee.

'The man is too much,' McCann said, glowering at Praisegod's back. 'He takes divinity on himself. He is close to blasphemy.

He likens himself to Bay – that is, his own twisted version of Bay.' Malenfant guessed that Bay was another of Moses' parallel-historical pseudonyms. 'Malenfant, the man is a self-aggrandizing monster. He must be stopped. Otherwise, what will come to pass, as Praisegod's blasphemous hordes swarm like locusts over this wretched Moon?'

Malenfant shrugged. For all McCann's talk of Praisegod's ambitions, he found it hard to take seriously anybody who lived in a mud hut. 'He's vicious. But he's a shithead. Anyhow I thought you were going to do business with him.'

McCann glared at him, angry, frustrated. And Malenfant saw that McCann's mood had switched, just as he had feared. It was as if a veneer had been stripped away.

Malenfant felt only dismay. He just wanted to get out of here; if McCann went off the rails, he had no idea how he was going to handle the situation.

Now there was a commotion up ahead. Sprigge had reached the huddle of Hams. Two of them were standing unsteadily, while the third sprawled in the mud. Sprigge began to beat the Hams vigorously.

'It is the wine,' Praisegod remarked. 'They steal it from us and hide it in their clothing. Though their bellies are large, their brains are small, and they cannot take it as men can.'

The Runners watched apathetically as the Hams were chastised.

The sky cleared rapidly. Through high thin clouds the sunlight returned. The red dust began to steam under their feet, making the air humid.

A little after noon, they reached the fringe of a belt of dense forest. They made a rough camp in the shade of the wood, spreading out their clothes and goods to dry. The Runners were tied up by their necks or ankles to tree trunks, but were able to forage for food among the roots of the trees.

McCann nodded. 'Efficient. It saves their carrying their own provision. And while their fingers are nimble with food, their minds are too empty to puzzle out knots.'

Sprigge was to lead a hunting party into the forest. He would take four Runners, and – as a punishment – all three Hams, who seemed to have crashed into catastrophic hangovers. Both McCann and Malenfant were invited to join them; McCann agreed to go, but Malenfant refused.

Praisegod settled down on a sheet of leather. The other Zealot, a squat, silent man, dug foodstuffs from out of the Runners' packs and laid them out. Praisegod nibbled on nuts, fruit and dried meat; he pressed titbits into the mouth of his Ham boy, fingering the child's lips each time.

Malenfant sat in the dirt, waiting for a turn at the food. The silent Zealot sat alone some distance away, chewing on something that looked like beef jerky; he watched Malenfant warily.

Praisegod said, 'So you declined to join the hunt, Sir Malenfant.' He smiled coldly. 'You are not a hunter, then – not a woodsman or a man of the heath either, I would say. What, then? A scholar?'

'A sailor, I guess.'

'A sailor.' Praisegod chewed thoughtfully. 'In my father's day some effort was made to escape this antediluvian island. Men took to the desert, which stretches west of this place. And they built boats and took to the sea, which stretches away to the east. Most did not come back, from either longitude. Those who did reported only emptiness – deserts of sand or water, the land populated by lowly forms. Of course you and your friend have yet to confess what marvellous ship, or providential accident, brought *you* here.'

'So that you can use it to get out of here,' Malenfant said cautiously. 'Is that what you want?'

Praisegod said, 'I do not long for escape. I know what *you* want, Reid Malenfant, for I have discussed your state of mind with your wiser companion. You seek your wife. You have wagered your life, in fact, on finding her. It is a goal with some nobility, but a goal of the body, not the soul.'

Malenfant smiled coldly. 'It's all I have.'

The hunting party returned.

Two of the Runners carried limp, hairy bodies, slung over their shoulders. They looked to Malenfant like the chimp-like Elf-folk. One was an adult, but the other was an infant, just a scrap of brown-black fur. The other two Runners bore a net slung on a horizontal pole. A third Elf squirmed within the net, frightened, angry, jabbering, a bundle of muscle and fur and long, human-like limbs. Malenfant could see heavy, milk-laden breasts.

Praisegod got up to greet the party, an expression of anticipation on his cadaverous face. His Ham boy clung to Praisegod's robe and stayed behind him, evidently frightened of the Elf's jabber. Under Sprigge's sharp commands, two of the Runners and the Hams set to constructing a large fire, with a spit set over it.

McCann approached Malenfant, his hands scratched by branches and brambles, his face red with exertion. His mood seemed to have swung again. 'Quite an adventure, Malenfant! – you should have seen it. The Runners are remarkable. They crept like shadows through that forest, closing on those helpless pongids like Death himself. They caught these three, and though the Elves fought, our fellows would have despatched them all in seconds if not for Sprigge's command . . .'

The Hams had wrestled the live Elf to the ground, and were cautiously lifting away the net. The Elf squirmed and spat – and Malenfant thought she looked longingly at the corpse of the infant, piled carelessly on top of the adult's body. Perhaps she was the child's mother.

Praisegod walked around the little campsite until he had found a fist-sized rock. He turned to Malenfant, holding out the rock. 'Sir, you omitted the hunt. Will you share in the kill?'

Malenfant folded his arms.

'No?' Praisegod motioned to Sprigge.

Now, at a sharp command from Sprigge, a Runner approached, bearing a fire-hardened spear. With a single powerful gesture he skewered the Elf, ramming the pole into her body through her anus, pushing until its tip emerged bloody from her mouth.

This time it was Malenfant who had to restrain McCann.

The Elf was still alive when the Hams lifted the pole onto the spit frames – Malenfant heard her body rip as it slumped around its impaling pole – and, he thought, she was still alive, if barely, when a burly Runner went to work on her skull, curling back the flesh and cracking the skull as if it was the shell of a boiled egg.

Praisegod studied Malenfant. 'Perhaps it would have been merciful to kill it first. Or perhaps not; this creature cannot comprehend its fate in any case. It is the brains, you see; freshness is all for that particular delicacy.'

McCann broke away from Malenfant. He strode towards Praisegod Michael, his fists bunched, his face purple. 'Now I know what you are, Praisegod. No Bay, no Ramose! *Him the Almighty Power / Hurl'd headlong flaming from th' Ethereal Sky / With hideous ruin and combustion down / To bottomless perdition.* You are no man of God. This is Hell, and you are its Satan!'

Sprigge slammed his fist into the back of McCann's head, and the Englishman went sprawling.

Praisegod Michael seemed unperturbed. 'Blasphemy and anarchy, sir. Flogging, branding and tongue-boring will be your fate. That is God's law, as I have interpreted it.'

McCann tried to rise. But Sprigge kicked his backside, knocking him flat again. Two of the Runners ripped McCann's jacket from his back, exposing an expanse of pasty skin, and Sprigge loosened his whip.

Malenfant watched this, his own fists bunched.

Don't do it, Malenfant. This isn't your argument; it's not even your damn world. Think of Emma. She is all that matters.

But as Sprigge raised his arm for the first lash, Malenfant hit him in the mouth, hard enough to knock him flat.

He didn't remember much after that.

Shadow:

For days after her latest beating at One-eye's hands, Shadow had stayed in her nest. There was a little fruit here, and dew to be sucked from the leaves. She found something like contentment, simply to be left in peace.

But the child developed rashes on his belly and inner thighs, and Shadow herself lost a lot of hair around her groin. Her hair, and the child's, were matted with urine and faeces. In her illness she had failed to clean the child, or herself when the child fouled her.

She clambered down from the tree and set the child on the ground. When Shadow propped him up the child was actually able to sit up by himself – wobbling, his legs tangled, that great strange head bobbing like a heavy fruit, but sitting up nevertheless. She bathed him gently, with cool clean water from a stream. The coolness made the rash subside. The child's infection was subsiding too, and his nose was almost free of snot.

The child clapped his little hands together, looked at them as if he had never seen them before, and gazed up at his mother with wide eyes.

Shadow embraced him, suddenly overwhelmed by her feelings, warm and deep red and powerful.

And a great mass caromed into her back, knocking her flat.

Her child was screaming. She forced herself to her knees and turned her head.

One-eye had the infant. He was sitting on the ground, holding the baby by his waist. The child's heavy head lolled to and fro. One-eye was flanked by two younger men, who watched him intently. One-eye flicked the side of the child's skull with a bloody finger, making the head roll further.

Shadow got to her feet. Her back was a mass of bruises. She walked forward unsteadily, and with every step pain lanced. She stood before One-eye and held her hands out for her child.

One-eye clutched the child closer to his chest, not roughly, and the child scrabbled at his fur, seeking to cling on. The other men watched Shadow with a cold calculation.

Shadow stood there, bewildered, hot, exhausted, aching. She didn't know what One-eye wanted. She sat on the ground and lay back, opening her legs for him.

One-eye grinned. He held the child before him. And he bit into the front of its head. The child shuddered once, then was limp.

Shadow's world dissolved into crimson rage. She was aware of the child's body being hurled into the air, blood still streaming from the wound in his head, as limp as a chewed leaf. She lunged at One-eye, screaming in his face, clawing and biting. One-eye was knocked flat on the ground, and he raised his hands before his bloody face to ward off her blows.

Then the other men got hold of her shoulders and dragged her away. She kicked and fought, but she was weakened by her long deprivation, her beatings and her illness; she was no match for two burly men. At last they took her by an arm and a leg. They swung her in the air and hurled her against a broad tree trunk.

The men were still there, One-eye and the others, sitting in a tight circle on the ground. They were working at something. She heard the rip of flesh, smelled the stink of blood. She tried to rise, but could not, and she fell back into darkness.

The next time she woke she was alone. The light was gone, and only pale yellow Earthlight, filtered through the forest canopy, littered the ground.

She crawled to where the men had been sitting.

She picked up one small arm. A strip of gristle at the shoulder showed where it had been twisted from the torso. The hand was still in place, perfectly formed, clenched into a tiny fist.

*   *   *

She was high in a tree, in a roughly prepared nest. She didn't remember getting there. It was day, the sun high and hot.

She remembered her baby. She remembered the tiny hand.

By the time she clambered down from the tree, her determination was as pure as fast-running water.

Emma Stoney:

Emma trudged wearily over the soft sand of the ocean shore. The ocean itself was a sheet of steel, visibly curving at the horizon, and big low-gravity waves washed across it languidly.

This strip of yellow-white beach lay between the ocean and a stretch of low dunes. Further inland she saw a grassy plain, a blanket of green that rippled as the wind touched it, studded here and there by knots of trees. A herd of grazing animals moved slowly across the plain, their collective motion flowing, almost liquid; they looked like huge wild horses. The stretch of savannah ended in a cliff of some dark volcanic rock, and a dense forest spilled over the lip of the cliff, a thick green-black. It was a scene of life, of geological and biological harmony, characterized by the scale and slow pace of this world. In any other context it might have been beautiful.

But Emma walked warily, the rags of her flight suit flapping around her, her loose pack strapped to her back with bits of vegetable rope, a wooden spear in one hand and a basalt axe in the other. Beautiful or not, this was a world full of dangerous predators – not least, the humans.

And then she saw a flash of blue fabric, high on the cliff.

She walked up the beach towards the cliff, trying to ignore the hammering of her heart.

Every day her mood swung between elation and feverish hope, to bitterness that bordered on despair. One day at a time, Emma. Think like a Ham. Take it one day at a time.

But now she could see the lander itself. She broke into a run, staring, wishing her eyes had a zoom feature.

It was unmistakably NASA technology, like a stubby scale-model Space Shuttle, with black and white protective tiles. It was surrounded by shreds of its blue parafoil. But it was stuck in a clump of trees, halfway down the cliff; it looked like some fat moth clinging to the rock.

'Nice landing, Malenfant,' she murmured.

Disturbingly, she saw no sign that anybody had done anything constructive up there. There were no ropes leading up or down the cliff, no stars and stripes waving, no SOS sign carved into the foliage.

Maybe the crew hadn't survived the crash.

She put that thought aside. They could have gotten out before the lander had plummeted over the cliff, even ejected on the way down. There were many possibilities. At the very least, there should be stuff she could use – tools, a first aid kit, maybe even a radio.

Messages from home.

What was for sure was that she was going to have to get up that cliff to find out. And she wasn't going to make it up there alone.

There was an encampment of Hams, a squat hut of skin weighted down with stone, almost directly under the blue flash. She could see them moving around before the hut, slabs of muscle wrapped in crudely cut skins.

That was how she was going to get up that damn cliff.

She forced herself to slow. One step at a time, Emma; you know the protocol. It was going to be hard to be patient, to engage a new group of Hams once again. But that was what she was going to have to do.

She dropped her pack at the edge of the sea, and splashed her face with salt water. Then she walked up and down the beach, picking out bits of scattered driftwood. She found a long, straight branch, and selected a handful of thorny sticks. She took her favoured hand-axe and, with a skill born of long hours of practice and many cut fingers, she made notches in one end of the stick, wide enough to fit the thorny twigs. Then she took a bit of rawhide string from her pack, and wrapped it around the stick, lashing the barbs in place.

Thus, one harpoon.

She slipped off her boots and socks and coverall and waded into the shallows, harpoon raised.

Fishing had become her speciality. It didn't seem to have occurred to any of the Ham communities here to figure out how to catch fish, either in the ocean or in freshwater streams. Fish meat, exotic but appealing, made a good bribe.

There was a ripple at her feet, a roughly diamond shape that emerged briefly from the sand. She stabbed down hard, feeling the crunch of breaking wood.

She found she had speared a skate, a big brown fleshy square of a fish, maybe two feet across. Skate buried themselves in the mud, coming up at night to hunt shellfish. Her catch was wriggling violently, and it was all she could do to hold on to the harpoon. With a grunting effort she heaved the skate over her head and out onto the sand, where it flopped, slowly dying. One bit of lingering squeamishness was a reluctance to kill anything; acknowledging the hypocrisy, she let her victims die instead.

She splashed out of the water. Briskly she inspected her harpoon, considering whether it was worth keeping; she had learned to conserve her energy and time, never throwing away anything that might be used again. But the barbs were broken. She stripped off the hide string and stuffed it back into her pack, and let the bits of the harpoon fall, abandoning this thing she had made that would have been beyond her imagining a few months ago, forgetting it as carelessly as any every-day-a-new-day Ham craftsman.

With her hand-axe she skinned and gutted the fish. You had to avoid the guts, and the skin could be coated by toxic mucus or dangerous spines: tricks she remembered from her childhood camping-in-the-woods days.

Then she pulled on her coverall and boots, picked up the skate meat and her pack, and walked steadily up the beach towards the Ham encampment.

These Hams accepted her silent presence in the corner of their hut, as readily as every other group she had encountered. They predictably turned away from her first offer of skate meat. But she continued to bring home gifts from the sea, until they had, one by one, experimentally, begun to taste the pale, sharp flesh.

So she settled into her corner of the communal hut, wrapping herself each night in grimy bits of parachute canvas, watching the Hams, waiting for some opportunity to find a way up the cliff to the lander.

She learned their names – Abel and Ruth and Saul and Mary – odd quasi-Biblical names, presumably bequeathed to them, like their fractured English, by some ancient contact with humans, Zealots or other 'Skinny-folk'. She tried to follow their complex social interactions, much of it centring on speculative gossip about the vigorous child-woman Mary.

They were typical Hams. Come to that, *all* Hams were typical Hams.

Their English was broken – mispronounced, with missing or softened 'G' and 'K' and 'th' sounds and vowels that blurred to sameness. The language had tenses – past, future – and there were even conditionals, used for instance by gossiping women as they speculated what would follow if Mary gave herself to Saul, or if she fell for Abraham's clumsy wooing first. But their language was elemental, with a simple vocabulary focusing on each other, their bodies, the hut.

As for Mary herself, she was clearly at the centre of a storm of hormonal change, relishing and fearing all the attention she got at the same time. But she never teased, Emma observed, never led any of the men on. Deceit seemed utterly unknown to these people. They were clever in many ways, but whatever they used those big brains for it wasn't for lying to each other, as humans did.

All this dubious anthropological speculation served to occupy her mind. But it was all spectacularly useless when it came to bringing her closer to her central goal of reaching the big black and white moth suspended on the cliff over their heads, in which none of the Hams showed the slightest interest.

Manekatopokanemahedo:

Manekato pushed into the forest. The foliage was dense, dark green, damp, cold, and it seemed to clutch at her face and limbs. The shadows stretched deep all around her, concealing subtle, elusive forms, as if wild creatures were Mapping themselves into and out of existence all around her.

Briefly she considered going back to the compound and seeking a new symmorph – perhaps with better dark-adapting vision. But as she worked deeper into the wood her body moved increasingly easily, her feet and hands clutching at branches and roots, and a clear sense of direction worked with her powerful hearing to guide each footfall. She dismissed her fears; she even felt a certain deep exhilaration. We came from the forest, she thought, and it is to the forest that I now return.

She was seeking Without-Name, who had left the encampment of exiles.

Even before her final departure Without-Name had taken to spending increasingly long times away from the compound. After her challenge by Nemoto over the captured Zealot, she had not brought back further 'specimens', but at times Manekato thought she had glimpsed blood on her dirt-matted fur, and even on her lips.

To her surprise the little hominid Nemoto had expressed sympathy with Without-Name. '*Without-Name is out of control. But she is right. You are too slow, too cerebral, Mane. Perhaps your minds have grown over-ornate, and are strangled by their own complexity. It is time to confront the Old Ones, not to theorize over them . . .*'

It had been deeply shocking for Manekato to hear such critical sentiments expressed by a mere lower hominid.

Still, Without-Name had become an increasing distraction, a wild blood-stained rogue planet crashing through the orderly solar system of purpose and knowledge acquisition which Manekato had sought to establish. Babo and others had expressed relief when Without-Name had finally failed to return from one of her ambiguous jaunts. But Manekato had sensed that Without-Name would cause them all severe and unwelcome problems yet.

Finally Manekato had been disturbed by a cacophony of cries, coming from deep in the nearby belt of forest. Something there had died, in great pain and anguish; and Manekato had had a powerful intuition that it was time for her to seek out Without-Name and meet her on her own terms.

And so here she was, just another hominid picking her way through the forest.

She emerged from the bank of trees. Beyond a stretch of rock-strewn ground, a low cliff rose: broken and eroded, perhaps lime-stone, pocked with hollows and low caves, overgrown with moss and struggling trees. Somewhere water trickled.

The sky was clouded over. The place was claustrophobic, enclosing. She could smell blood, and dread gathered in her heart.

A hominid walked out of one of the caves. To judge by the sewn skins he wore, he was a Zealot, like the specimen Without-Name had brought back to the camp. He carried a crossbow, and his tunic and leggings were splashed with dirt and blood. He saw Manekato, standing alone at the edge of the forest. His eyes widened. He dropped his bow and ran back into the cave. '*Daemons! Strange Daemons!*'

Manekato gathered her courage. She stepped forward, crossing the rock-strewn floor.

She paused in the cave's entrance, giving her eyes time to adapt to this deeper dark. The cave's roof was a layer of rock just above her head. It was worn smooth, as if by the touching of many fingers; perhaps this place had been inhabited for many generations. The cave stank of hominid, of crudely prepared food, of stale urine and faeces and sweat – and of blood.

A shadow moved before her. As it approached the light, it coalesced into the form of Without-Name. Her fur was splashed with blood, and a gouge had been cut into her arm.

'I suppose I have been expecting you,' she growled. 'Are you aware what a target you provide, silhouetted against the light? We have not fought a war for a million years, Manekato; we have lost our instincts for survival.'

'What have you done, Renemenagota?' Manekato reached out and touched the wound in the other's arm. It was a deep slice over the bicep, still leaking blood – it had not even been cleaned. 'I see your victims did not submit quietly.'

Without-Name barked laughter. 'It was glorious. Come.'

She turned and led the way deeper into the cave, and Manekato followed reluctantly.

At the back of the cave a lamp of what looked like burning animal fat flickered in a hollow on one wall; the rock above was streaked with black grease. By its light Manekato saw she was walking over scorched patches of dirt – hearths, perhaps, all cold and disused. Bits of stone and bone and wood were scattered everywhere. At the rear of the cave, animal skins had been stretched over rough frames of wood.

There were hominids here. They were Zealots, dressed in their characteristic garb of crudely sewn skin. When Manekato knuckle-walked towards them they yelled and grabbed their weapons.

Without-Name held up her hands. '*She is weak. She will not harm you.*'

The Zealots hurried out of her way, jabbering their alarm to each other.

Beyond the Zealots there was a mound of slumped forms.

They were hominids, all dead. They were the powerful squat creatures Nemoto called Hams. They had been slaughtered by crossbow bolts and spear thrusts. They had not died easily: ripped throats and gouged eyes and severed limbs testified to that, as did the injuries nursed by the Zealots. Blood soaked through the grisly heap, and spilled guts glistened on the floor beneath.

Without-Name's eyes glittered. 'You cannot engage these fellows hand-to-hand; the power of these stocky bodies is simply too great. But they work strictly short range. And so they fell to our bows and throwing spears as they tried to close with us, one after the other. Once they were down it was a case of moving in to finish them off. But they fought on even with their bellies torn open, their throats cut. Well, this was their home for uncounted generations – you can see that – they were fighting as we would for our Farms . . .'

Manekato discerned a smaller bundle, laid on top of the heap of corpses. It was an infant, its age impossible to tell, one leg bent back at an impossible angle. 'Did this little one give you a good spectacle, Renemenagota?'

Without-Name shrugged. 'The Zealots took most of the smaller infants back to their stockade. You can't tame an adult Ham, you see; you have to get them young to break them. This one wouldn't leave its mother's side. The efforts to remove it resulted in a snapped leg.' She grinned, her teeth showing bright in the gloom. 'Praisegod Michael was here. Their leader, you see; the leader of the Zealots. He uttered words over the corpses, blessing them, commending their souls to the afterlife he believes awaits us – or rather awaits *his* sort of hominid; he isn't so sure about the rest of us. Michael said his prayers over this little creature and then cut its throat. A delicious contradiction, don't you think?

'You should see the ambition that burns in Michael's eyes! He dreams of cleansing his world of such *creatures of the Devil* as this – what an ambition! – but he has lacked the understanding to make it so. He was wary of me when I approached him – no, contemptuous, because for him I am less than human. But I forced him to listen to me. I made him see that by taking his captives and training them properly, he increases his resources, you see, which he can deploy for further conquest; once initiated, it is a simple exponential growth.'

'You spoke to this monster – you are *working* with him?' Manekato said tightly, 'Whoever this *Praisegod* is, his reasons for wishing to destroy the Hams and the others have surely more to do with the flaws in his own heart than any ideological justification.'

Without-Name grabbed her arm and held it tight; Manekato felt moisture, blood and sweat, soaking into her fur. 'Of course Praisegod Michael is mad. But it is a glorious madness.'

Manekato prised her arm away from Without-Name's grip. Regretfully she said, 'Glorious or not, I have to stop you.'

Without-Name laughed. 'You do not have the imagination or the courage for that, Manekato.'

The Zealots were returning to the pile of Ham corpses. They were cutting away ears and hands, perhaps as trophies. But their movements were characteristically sluggish, like pale worms moving in the dark.

Joshua:

Joshua lay on the filth-crusted floor of his cell.

He was left alone for days. It was worse than any beating. There was nobody to look at him.

The People of the Grey Earth were never alone by choice. They spent their entire lives in their tight-knit communities, surrounded day and night by the same faces, change coming only through the slow tide of birth and death. Some women spent their entire lives within a hundred paces of where they were born. Even parties of hunters who ranged farther in search of big game would not mix with other groups of hominids, even other Hams; strangers were like faces in a dream, remote, not real.

He tried to picture the hut, the people coming and going about their business. He tried to recall the faces of Abel and Saul and Mary and Ruth and the others. The life of the people was going on, even though he was not there to be looked at – just as it had continued after the death of Jacob, the endless round of days and nights, of eating and sleeping and fornicating, of birth and love and death.

Jacob was dead. Was Joshua dead?

Away from others, Joshua was not even fully conscious. As the light came and went, he felt himself crumble. He was the walls, the filthy floor, the patch of daylight in the roof.

. . . And yet he was not alone, for there were people in the walls.

Faint marks had been scratched there, perhaps by fingernails, or with bits of stone. Some of them were so ancient they were crusted with dirt, and could be detected only by the touch of his fingertips. Perhaps they were made by Skinny or Nutcracker-man or Elf or Runner. But not by Ham, for no Ham made marks like these.

Scratches on the wall. Patterns that pulled at his consciousness. Boxes and circles and lines that longed to speak to him.

* * *

He was in a cave. But it was not a cave, for its walls were made of rocks piled one on top of the other. Sometimes the people would build walls, lines of rubble loosely piled, to help keep out the small animals that foraged at night. Joshua knew what a wall was. But *these* walls went up, high above Joshua's head, too high for him to reach.

And there was a roof made of rocks too, suspended over his head. On first waking here, he had cringed, thinking a sky full of rocks was descending on him. But the roof did not fall. He learned to uncurl, even to stand – though each time he woke from sleep he forgot about the roof, and whimpered in terror and curled in a corner of the cell.

The only light here came from a hole in the roof. He saw the days come and go through that hole, night succeeding day. He would lie on his back staring at the little circle of light. But when it rained, the water would pour through the hole, and he would huddle in a corner, shivering.

Sometimes a face would appear in the hole, the face of a Skinny. Stuff would be thrown down at him. Sometimes it would be food that he would scrabble to collect from the floor. The food was poor, scraps of cut-up vegetable or fruit peel or bits of gristle, some of it already chewed, sour with the saliva of Skinnies. But he devoured it all, for he was constantly hungry.

Sometimes they would hurl down water at him, usually brackish and stinking, enough to drench him. It would drain away out of a hole in the centre of the blackened, worn floor, taking much of his own shit and piss with it. When the water came he would stand with his mouth and hands open, catching as much as he could. And when it had finished he would scrape at the filth-blackened floor with his fingers, collecting as much of the water as he could, even lick the floor with his tongue.

But sometimes all the Skinnies would throw down was their own thin shit, or they would piss in the hole, trying to hit him as he scurried from side to side.

His memories of how he had come here were blurred.

He remembered the clearing. After Mary had escaped he had been picked up by many Skinnies, all grunting with the effort. With every jolt his shoulder had blazed with pain. They had thrown him onto a platform made of strips of cut-up wood. And then the platform had been dragged away, along broad trails burned into the woods.

He remembered entering the stockade. It was a great wall of sharpened tree trunks driven into the ground, many times higher than Joshua could have reached. Inside there were huts of sod and wood, dark hovels whose stink had struck him as he was dragged past. There were many animals, goats and rabbits and ducks. There were many, many Skinnies, with grimy skin and brown teeth.

And there were Hams. They dragged at ropes and pushed bits of wood and dug at the ground. Joshua had hooted to the Hams, seeking help. Though the Hams were few, they could surely overpower these Skinny folk easily. But they had not responded, not even looked up, and he had been silenced by a slamming blow to his mouth.

They had removed his skins, and he was naked. And he had been thrown into this darkened cell.

The punishment had started immediately.

There had been Skinnies around him. Some of them were grinning. One of them carried a stick whose tip glowed bright red. Joshua stared at the glowing stick; it was one of the most beautiful colours he had ever seen. For one brief instant he left his aching body, and was the fiery glow.

But then the Skinnies shoved him on his back, trapping his limbs. The man with the glowing stick held it before Joshua's face – he could feel heat, like a fire – the man rammed it into the wound in his shoulder.

Only fragments after that, dark red fragments soaked with pain. Fragments, fading into dark.

But Joshua welcomed the presence of those who beat him. For at least, then, he was not alone.

One day he saw faces in the scratches on the wall. Faces that peered out at him, the faces of Skinnies.

No, not faces: one face, over and over.

The face of a man, thin, bearded, a circle over his head. The man looked at him, but did not look at him. Sometimes Joshua yelled at him, punched the face. But the wall would return, scraping his knuckles, and the man, not replying, would disappear into his web of scratches.

Joshua was dead. He was in a hole in the ground, like Jacob. But there were no worms here. There were only the faces, looking at him, not looking at him.

He screamed. He cowered in the corner, as he did when his captors pissed on him.

That was how the Skinnies found him one day, when they burst into his cell with their clubs and rocks and whips. They mocked him, kicking at his back and kidneys, and they pulled him out of the corner and stretched him.

A leering face hovered over him. 'We'll break you yet, boy, while there's still some work left in that hulking body of yours.' He arched his back, trying to see the man in the wall.

There was laughter. 'He's looking for Jesus.'

Running footsteps. A boot launched at his face. He felt a tooth smash at the back of his mouth.

'Help!' he cried. 'Help me, Chee-sus!'

The gaolers staggered back, open-mouthed, staring.

A day and a night. His tooth was a pit of pain.

Skinnies were in the cell. Joshua scuttled to his corner, expecting the usual blows.

But a net was thrown over him. He did not resist. His hands and arms and feet and legs were tightly bound, and then his legs folded behind his back and tied up to his waist.

Wrapped in the net, he was dragged out of his cell.

Outside was a long, narrow cavern. There was no daylight, but fires burned in pits on the wall. He saw only the floor and walls, the lumping shadows of his gaolers as they dragged him, letting his bruised limbs and head rattle on the floor.

They paused, and there was a clanking, clattering noise. Joshua lifted his head dully.

He was facing an open cell. A man sat in the cell, a Skinny. But this was a Skinny like none Joshua had ever seen. He had no hair on the top of his head, none at all, although stubble clustered on his cheek. And his clothing, though filthy, blood-stained and torn, was not like the skin the Zealots wore. It was blue: a blue membrane, like the wings of the sky seed.

Joshua, electrified, gasped with recognition.

The man was looking at him. 'My name is Reid Malenfant,' he said gently. 'If you get out of here, remember that. Malenfant.'

Joshua worked his mouth; it was crusted with blood and his lips were cracked. 'Mal'fan'.'

Malenfant nodded. 'Good luck to you, friend.'

And then the door was slammed.

Shadow:

She stayed away from the others. She slept in nests at the periphery of the crater-wall forest, and fed from trees and shrubs far from the movements of the rest of the group.

She searched for cobbles in streams and on the exposed, eroded crater walls.

She had not grown old enough to acquire more than the most basic tool-making skills. So it took her many tries, chipping at cobbles with stones and bits of bone, before she had manufactured something that felt right. It was a lens-shaped cobble, with one crudely sharpened edge, that fit neatly in her hand.

Through these days her determination burned, clear and unwavering.

Burned until she was ready.

Joshua:

Joshua was in a new place. The walls were white, like snow. The floor shone, smooth as a bamboo trunk.

Joshua stood naked at the cell's centre. Heavy ropes bound his hands before him and his feet, and the ropes were fixed to a great bar dug out of the rock floor beneath him. There were big holes in the walls covered by palm fronds, and through them Joshua could see daylight. He sniffed deeply, but his cavernous nostrils were clogged with snot and blood.

There were people in the walls.

The marks on these walls were not mere scratches. They were vivid images in bright blood-red and night-black, and in them Joshua saw the thin, bearded man. The man was much clearer here than in the deep cell – so clear he never went away – and there were many of him, shining brightly, even one version of him fixed to a tree trunk and bleeding.

Joshua cowered.

'Well might you avert your eyes from the Lord's countenance.'

Joshua turned. A man had spoken. A Skinny. He was taller than

Joshua, his hair grey, and his black clothing swept to the ground. His black robes were skin, finely worked, black like charcoal from a hearth.

Joshua cringed. But no blow came. There was only a hand on his forehead, light, almost curious, exploring his brow ridges.

'Well might you hide your face for shame of what you are. And yet you called out for the Lord's help – so the brutes assigned to break you assured me ... Stand up, boy.' Joshua received a hard toe cap to the side of his leg. 'Up, Ham.'

Reluctantly Joshua stood.

The man had a sharp nose, and warts on his face, and eyes such a pale blue they made Joshua think of the sky. He walked around Joshua, and touched his chest and back. His hands were very soft. 'I did ask for you to be cleaned up,' he said absently. 'Well. You may call me Praisegod Michael. Do you understand? I am Praisegod Michael. *Praisegod.*'

'Prai'go'.'

'Praisegod Michael, yes.' Praisegod peered into his eyes. 'What brows, what a countenance ... And you, do you give yourself a name?' When Joshua didn't reply, Praisegod pointed to his own chest. 'Praisegod Michael.' And he pointed to Joshua.

Joshua spoke his name. When he moved his mouth his smashed tooth hurt; he could feel pulp leak into his mouth.

Praisegod laughed. '*Joshua.* My fathers named your fathers, when they found themselves sharing this Purgatorial place with you ... And now you pass on the names one to the other, down through the generations, like heirlooms in the hands of apes. Very well, Joshua. And *what* are you?'

The man's thin face, with its flat brow and high, bulging forehead, terrified Joshua. He had no idea what Praisegod wanted.

Praisegod produced a short, thick whip. With practised motions he lashed at Joshua's shoulder. The pain was great, for that was the site of Joshua's spear wound. But the skin was not broken.

'If you do not answer, you will be treated so,' Praisegod said evenly. 'But let me answer for you. You have a man's name, but you are not a man. *You are a Ham.* That is another name my father gave yours, and it is appropriate. Do you know who Ham was?'

A failure to reply brought a fresh lash of the whip.

'Ham, father of Canaan, son of Noah. He failed to respect his father. *Cursed be Canaan; a servant of servants shall he be unto his brethren.* Genesis 9,25. A servant of servants, yes; that is your place, boy. But then you know nothing of Noah, do you? You are an animal – a magnificent one, perhaps, and yet an animal even so. From your misshapen head to your splayed feet you signify antediluvian stock – if not pre-Adamite, indeed.' Praisegod seemed to be growing angry. Joshua watched him dully. 'The world was cleansed of your kind by the waters of the Flood. But you survive beyond your time in this dismal pit. And now you call on the Lord Himself –'

Another lash to the shoulders, and Joshua flinched. Then a blow to the back of the legs forced Joshua to his knees.

Praisegod Michael grabbed Joshua by his hair, making him raise his head. 'Look on His merciful face. What can *you* know of His benison? Do you know what my fathers suffered to bring the Word to this world? When they fell here, they had nothing: nothing but the clothes they wore. *They were set upon by beasts like yourself*; they starved; they fell prey to diseases. And yet they survived, and built this community, all by the strength of their hands, and their faith.

'And in all this they remembered the Word. They had no Book with them, not a single copy. But they remembered. They would sit around their fires and recite the verses, one after another, seeking to recall it for their children, for they knew they had no way home.

'And *that* is how the Word of the Lord came to this pit. And now you, an animal of the field, with your thunderbolts of stone, you presume to call on Him for help? . . .'

Joshua folded over himself, letting the whip fall. He felt his flesh break, and the whip dug deeper into the wounds it had made.

Shadow:

The fungal growth now framed her vision, black as night.

When she heard the roosting calls of the people, she slid through the trees. The people nested, silhouetted high against a cloud-laced earth-blue sky. She recognized One-eye by the grunting snores he made, the stink of a body she had come to know too well.

She slipped up the trunk of the tree, her long hands and feet gripping. With scarcely a rustle, she clung to branches above One-eye's rough nest.

He lay on his back, hands wide, legs splayed, one foot dangling over the edge of his nest. His mouth was open, and a thin stream of drool slid down his chin. He had an erection, dark in the Earthlight.

She clung to the branches with her feet and legs, and hung upside down over him. She took his penis in her mouth and sucked it gently, rubbing the shaft with her lips. In his sleep, he moaned.

Then she bit down, as savagely as she could.

He screamed and thrashed. She could hear answering hoots from surrounding nests.

She flung herself down on him. His eyes were wide and staring, and she thought she could smell blood on his breath. He was stronger than she was, but he was already in intense agony, and she had the advantage of surprise. He pushed feebly at her face with one hand. She grabbed the hand, pulled a finger into her mouth, and nipped off a joint with a single savage bite. He howled again, and she spat the bloody joint into his open mouth, making him gag.

Then she raised her shaped cobble and slammed it against the side of his head.

Joshua:

A day and a night, here in this white place, without food or water.

Men scrubbed him roughly. They mopped away the blood and shit from the floor.

Praisegod was prone to swings of mood, which Joshua neither understood nor could predict. Sometimes there was coldness, cruelty, beatings. But sometimes Praisegod would gaze at him with bright eyes, and run his hands over his battered body, as a mother might stroke a child. Joshua quickly learned to dread such moments, for they always finished in the most savage beatings of all.

And yet he longed for Praisegod Michael to stay, rather than leave him alone.

He lay on his side, staring at the marks on the walls – not the face of *Chee-sus*, but strange angular lines, the loops and whorls. Bewildered by pain and exhaustion, he stared and stared, trying to lose himself in the lines, trying to see the faces there.

'What is it you see, boy? Can you read? Can you read the Lord's words? Do you hear what they tell you?' Showing his sporadic, chilling tenderness, Praisegod Michael was kneeling on the floor, with Joshua's head on his lap.

His mouth dry, his tongue thick, Joshua whispered, 'People.'

'People?' Praisegod Michael stared at the marks. '*These* are words, and *these* are pictures. The words speak to us . . . Ah, *but they do not*, do they? Marks on the wall do not speak. They are *symbols*, of the sounds we make when we speak, which are themselves symbols of the thoughts we concoct . . . Is that what you mean?' His hands explored Joshua's body with a rough eagerness. 'What lies inside that cavernous head of yours? The words you utter are themselves symbolic – but your kind have no books, no art. Is that why you cannot understand? Would you like me to tell you what those letters say to me?' He pointed at the wall. '*After this I looked, and there before me was a door standing open in Heaven.* Revelation 4,1.'

'Heav'n,' Joshua mumbled.

'The sky, child, where we will pass when we die.'

Joshua twisted his head to see Praisegod's face. 'Dead.'

'No.' Praisegod was almost crooning, and he rocked Joshua back and forth. 'No, you poor innocent. You are alive. And when you die, you will be alive again in Christ – if His mercy extends to your kind . . .'

'Dead,' said Joshua. 'Dead. Gone. Like Jacob.'

'Dead but not gone! The corpse in the ground is the seed that is planted in the earth. So we will all bloom in the spring of the Lord. *And I saw the dead, great and small, standing before the throne, and books were opened.* But I am talking in symbols again, ain't I? A man is not a seed. But a man is *like a seed.*'

Suddenly he pushed Joshua away. The Ham's head clattered on the floor, jarring his aching tooth.

'You can know nothing of what I speak, for your head is empty of symbols . . . Ah, but what if my religion is nothing but symbols – is that what you are thinking? – the symbol of the seed, the Mother and Child – a dream concocted by words rattling in my empty head?' Now Joshua felt kicks, hard, frantic, aimed at his back and buttocks. 'O you witness to the Flood, O you underman! See how you have planted doubts in my mind! How clever you are, how cunning! You and that Daemon of the forest, Renemenagota, she of the ape build and mocking, wise eyes . . . The Daemons make me promises. They can take my vision and make it real, make this antediluvian island a godly place. So they say. So *she* says. Ah, but in her dark eyes I sense mockery, Joshua! Do you know her? *Did she send you?* . . . How you madden me! Are you agents of Satan, sent to confuse me with your whispers of God's work? . . .'

But now Praisegod leaned over Joshua again and grabbed his face. Joshua saw how his eyes were red and brimming with tears, his face swollen as if by weeping. '*Can sin exist here?* The brutes who serve me have their Runner women, their whores with the bodies of angels and the heads of apes. I, I am not of that kind ... But now, here! Here!' He grabbed Joshua's bound hands and pushed them into his crotch; Joshua could feel a skinny erection. 'You are destroying me!'

And the beatings went on.

Joshua lay on the floor, his own blood sticky under his face. Pieces moved around in his head, just as they had before: when he saw the sky seed fall from the sky, when he put together the cobble from the bits of shattered stone.

The kind Skinny's face peered through a cloud of pain and black-edged exhaustion.

He whispered, ''Fore me was door standin' open Heaven.'

Praisegod Michael was here. Panting, he gazed into Joshua's eyes. 'What did you say?'

But Joshua was, for now, immersed in his own head, where the pieces were orbiting one another, the flakes sticking to the core of the cobble one by one. The Grey Earth. The seed that fell from the air. The door in the sky.

Joshua was, in his way, a genius. Certainly none of his kind had experienced such a revelation before.

'Heav'n,' he said at last.

Praisegod Michael pushed his ear close to his mouth to hear.

'Heav'n is th' Grey Earth. Th' seed. Th' seed takes th' people. Th' people pass through th' door. Door to heaven. To Grey Earth.'

'By God's eyes.' Praisegod Michael stumbled back. 'Is it possible you *believe*?'

Joshua tried to raise his head. 'Believe,' he said, for he did, suddenly, deeply and truly. 'Th' door in th' sky. Th' Grey Earth.'

Praisegod Michael stalked around the cell, muttering. 'I have never heard an ape-thing like yourself utter such words. Is it possible you have *faith*? And if so, must you therefore have a *soul*?' Again he stroked the heavy ridges over Joshua's eyes, and he pressed his gaunt body close to the Ham's. 'You intrigue me. You madden me. I love you. I despise you.' He leaned closer to the Ham, and kissed him full on the lips. Joshua tasted sourness, a rank staleness.

'*Graah –*' Praisegod rolled away, lying sprawled on the floor, and vomited, so that thin bile spread across the shining floor.

Then he stood, trembling, striving for composure. 'I would kill you. But if you have the soul of a *man* – I will not risk damnation for you – if you have not damned me already!' He smiled, suddenly cold, still. 'I will send you out. You will spread the Word to your kind. You will be a Saul of the apes.' He raised his pale eyes to the light from the window. 'A mission, yes, with you as my acolyte – *you*, a pre-Adamite man-ape.'

Joshua stared at him, understanding nothing, thinking of a door in the sky.

But now Praisegod stood over him again, and again he spoke tenderly. 'I will help you.' He reached into his clothing and produced a knife. It was not of stone; it glittered like ice, though Joshua could see how worn and scuffed it was. 'No beast should speak the Word of God. Here.' He put his fingers inside Joshua's mouth. The fingers tasted of burning. He pushed down, until Joshua's mighty jaw dropped.

Then, without warning, he grabbed Joshua's tongue and dragged it out of his mouth. Joshua felt the slash, a stab of pain.

Blood sprayed over Praisegod Michael.

Shadow:

The next morning the women surrounded Silverneck, as usual. With their infants clambering over them, they munched on figs.

With a crash, One-eye fell from his tree. His hands and feet left a smear of blood where they touched bark or leaves, for several of his fingers and toes had been nipped off. White bone showed in a huge deep wound on the side of his head. And his penis was almost severed, dangling by a thread of skin. His fur was matted by blood and piss and panic shit.

The women stared.

He looked about vaguely, as if blinded, and he mewled like an infant. Then he stumbled away, alone, into the deeper forest.

Shadow walked out of the tree cover.

Silverneck moved aside for her. One of the younger women growled, but Shadow punched her in the side of the head, so hard she was knocked sideways. Shadow sat with the group, and clawed figs into her mouth. But nobody looked at her, nobody groomed her, and even the children avoided her.

That night, when the roosting calls went out, One-eye did not return.

Reid Malenfant:

Malenfant was kept chained up in a dark, filthy cell. It was just a brick-lined pit, its damp mud floor lined with packed-down filth. The only light came from a grilled window high in the ceiling. The door was heavy with a massive wooden bolt on the outside.

He reached out to touch the walls. The bricks were rotten. Maybe he could dig out handholds and climb up to that window.

And then what? What then, after you climb out into the middle of Praisegod's courtyard? . . .

You are not dealing with rational people, Malenfant.

It was true Praisegod had built a place of relative order here. But this was an island of rigidity in a world of fluidity and madness, a world where mind itself was at a premium, a world where the very stars regularly swam around the sky, for all Praisegod's zeal and discipline – just as, Malenfant suspected, Praisegod's own inner core of horror constantly threatened to break through his surface of control.

There was nothing he could do, nothing to occupy his mind.

Sometimes the most courageous thing was doing nothing. *Do-nothing heroics*: was that a phrase from Conrad? If there was really, truly no way you could change your situation, the last thing you wanted to do was to pour so much energy into fighting your fear that you burned yourself up before the chance came for a break.

As he sat in the dark and the filth, utterly alone, Malenfant wondered how long his own do-nothing heroics would sustain him.

At last he was brought before Praisegod Michael.

At Praisegod's chapel-residence Malenfant was kept waiting, standing before Praisegod's empty desk bound hand and foot, for maybe an hour.

Finally Praisegod walked in, slowly, contemplative, his Ham boy at his side. Praisegod didn't look at Malenfant. He sat at his desk, and a Ham girl brought in a tray of chopped fish set on slabs of hard, dark bread, with a bowl of what looked like mustard and a wooden goblet of wine. Praisegod ate a little of the fish, dipping it in the mustard, and then he passed the rest to the Ham boy, who sat on the floor and ate ravenously.

Praisegod's manner seemed distracted to Malenfant, almost confused. He said rapidly, 'I have been forced to punish Sir McCann. You see why – you witnessed his blasphemous disrespect. His soul is hard, set in a mould of iniquity. But you – you are different. You seek the woman you love; you are moved by a chivalrous zeal. In you I see a soul that could be turned to higher goals.'

'Don't count on it,' Malenfant said.

Praisegod's eyes narrowed. 'You should not presume on God's grace.'

'This place has nothing to do with God,' Malenfant said evenly, staring hard at Praisegod. 'You play with human lives, but you don't even see that much, do you? Praisegod, this place – this Moon – is an artefact. Not made by God. *Humans*. Men, Praisegod. Men as different from you or me as we are different from the Elves, maybe, but men nevertheless. They are moving this whole damn Moon from one reality strand to the next, from Earth to Earth. And everything you see here, the mixing up of uncounted possibilities, is because of that moving. Because of *people*. Do you get it? God has nothing to do with it.'

Praisegod closed his eyes. 'This is a time of confusion. Of change . . . I think you may yet serve my purpose, and therefore God's. But I must shape you, like clay on the wheel. But there is much bile in you that must be driven out.' He nodded to Sprigge. 'A hundred stripes to start with.'

Malenfant was dragged out of the room. 'You're a savage, Praisegod. And you run a jerkwater dump. If this is some holy crusade, why do you allow your men to run a forced brothel?'

But Praisegod wasn't listening. He had turned to his Ham boy, and stroked his misshapen head.

Malenfant was taken to a room further down the dismal corridor.

He found himself stretched out over an open wooden frame, set at forty-five degrees above the horizontal. His feet were bound to the base of the frame. Sprigge wrapped rope around his wrists and pulled Malenfant's arms above his head until his joints ached.

Sprigge looked Malenfant in the eye. 'I have to make it hard,' he said. 'It'll be the worse for me if I spare you.'

'Just do your job,' Malenfant said sourly.

'I know Praisegod well enough. That fat Englishman just riled him. He thinks you might be useful to him. But you must play a canny game. If you go badly with him, he'll ill use you, Malenfant. I've seen that before too. He has a lot of devices more clever than my old whip, I'll tell you. He has gadgets that crush your thumbs or fingers until they are as flat as a gutted fish. Or he will put a leg-clamp on you, a thing he'll use on recalcitrant Runner folk, and every day we have to turn it a little tighter, until the bones are crushed and the very marrow is leaking into your boots.'

Malenfant tried to lift his head. 'I don't have any boots.'

'Boots will be provided.'

A joke? He could dimly make out Sprigge's face, and it bore an expression of something like compassion – compassion, under a layer of dirt and weathered scars and tangled beard, the mask of a hard life. 'Why do you follow him, Sprigge? He's a madman.'

Sprigge tested the bonds and stepped back. 'Sometimes the lads go off into the bush. They think life is easier there, that they can have their pick of the bush women, not like the bleeding whores they keep here. Well, the bush folk kill them, if the animals or the bugs don't first. As simple as that. Without Praisegod we'd all be prey, see. He organizes us, Sir Malenfant. We're housed and we're fed and nobody harms us. And now that he's taken up with the Daemons – well, he has big ideas. You have to admire a man for that.'

Malenfant thought, What the hell is a Daemon? He felt his jacket being pulled off his back. The air was damp and cold.

'Now, a hundred stripes is a feeler, Sir Malenfant. I know how you'll bear it. But you'll live; remember that.' He stepped away, into the dark.

Malenfant heard running footsteps.

And then he heard the lash of the whip, an instant before the pain shot through his nervous system. It was like a burn, a sudden, savage burn. He felt blood trickling over his sides and falling to the floor, and he understood why the frame under him had to be open.

More of Sprigge's 'stripes' rained down, and the pain cascaded. There seemed to be no cut-off in Malenfant's head, each stroke seemingly doubling the agony that went before, a strange calculus of suffering.

He didn't try to keep from crying out.

Maybe he lost consciousness before the hundred were done.

At last he was hit by a rush of water – it felt ice-cold – and then more pain reached him, sinking into every gash on his back, like cold fire.

Sprigge appeared before him. 'The salty back,' he said, cutting Malenfant's wrists free. 'It'll help you heal.'

Malenfant fell to the floor, which stank of his own blood, like the iron scent of the crimson dust of this rusted Red Moon.

A heavy form moved around him in the dark. He cowered, expecting more punishment.

But there was a hand on his brow, water at his lips. He could smell the dense scent of a Ham – perhaps it was Julia. The Ham helped him lie flat on his belly, with his ripped jacket under his face. His back was bathed – the wounds stung with every drop – and then something soft and light was laid over his back, leaves that rustled.

The square window in the ceiling above showed diffuse grey-blue. It was evening, or very early morning.

He was left alone after that, and he slept, falling into a deeper slumber.

When he woke again that square of sky was bright blue. By its light he saw that the leaves on his back were from a banana tree. His pain seemed soothed.

'. . . Malenfant. Malenfant, are you there?'

The voice was just a whisper, coming from the direction of the door.

Malenfant got his hands under his chest, pushed himself up to a crawling position. He felt the leaves fall away from his back. His bare chest was sticky with his own dried blood, and with every move he felt scabs crack, wounds ache.

He crawled to the wall by the door, kneeling there in the mud and blood.

'McCann?'

'Malenfant! By God it's good to hear the voice of a civilized man. Have they hurt you?'

Malenfant grimaced. 'A "feeler", Sprigge called it.'

'It could get worse, Malenfant.'

'I know that.'

McCann's voice sounded odd – thick, indistinct, as if he were talking around something in his mouth. *Flogging, branding, tongue-boring*, Malenfant recalled. The penalty for blasphemy.

'What have they done to you, Hugh?'

'My punishment was enthusiastically delivered,' McCann lisped.

'One must admire their godly zeal . . . And the beatings are not the half of it. Malenfant, he has me labouring in the fields: pulling ploughs, along with the Runner slaves. It is not the physical trial – I can barely add an ounce to the mighty power of my Runner companions – but the indignity, you see. Praisegod has made me one with the sub-men, and his brutish serfs mock me as I toil.'

'You can stand a little mockery.'

'Would that were true! Praisegod understands how to hurt beyond the crude infliction of blows and cuts and burns; and the shame of this casting-down has hurt me grievously – and *he* knows it. But his punishment will not last long, Malenfant. I am not so young nor as fit as I was; soon, I think, I will evade Praisegod's monstrous clutches once and for all . . . But it need not be so for you. Malenfant, I think Praisegod has some sympathy for you – or purpose, at least. Tell him whatever it is you think he wants to hear. That way you will be spared his wrath.'

Malenfant said softly, 'You were the one who said you could do business with him.'

'Do as I say, not as I do,' McCann hissed. 'It is my faith, Malenfant, my faith. Praisegod arouses in me a righteous rage which I cannot contain, whatever the cost to myself. But he is an intelligent man, a cunning man. I suspect his grasp of his ugly crew here was slipping. I have heard the men mutter. They tell fortunes, you know, with cowry shells – much handled, shining like old ivory . . . Superstition! A fatal flaw for a regime whose legitimacy comes entirely from religion. He was on his uppers, Malenfant, until quite recently. But now his inchoate ambitions have found a new clarity, a *plausibility*. He has found new allies: these Daemons, whoever or whatever they are. He has suddenly become a much more credible, and dangerous, figure . . . If I had half a brain I would stay in his fold.

'But you are different, Malenfant. Without faith – a paradoxically enviable condition! – you have no moral foundation to inhibit you; you must lie and cheat and steal; you must kowtow to Praisegod; you must do everything you can, everything you *must*, to survive.'

'I'll try,' Malenfant gasped.

'Will you, my friend? Will you truly? There is a darkness in you, Malenfant. I saw it from the beginning. You may choose, without knowing it, to use Praisegod as the final instrument of your own destruction.'

'What the hell are you talking about?'

'You must look into your heart, Malenfant. Think about the logic of your life . . . The day advances. Soon I will be called to my work in the fields, and I must sleep if I can.'

'Take care of yourself, Hugh.'

'Yes . . . God be with you, my friend.'

That night Malenfant called McCann's name. The only reply was a kind of gasping, inarticulate, and a moist slithering.

The night after that Malenfant called for McCann, over and over, but there was no reply.

Emma Stoney:

She had first become aware of Joshua as an absence. There was a spare place at the hearths of Ruth and others, portions of meat left set aside by the hunters. It was a pattern she had noticed before when somebody had recently died; the Hams clearly remembered their dead, and they made these subtle tributes of absence – halfway to a ritual, she supposed.

Then, one day, Joshua came back.

Within a couple of days it was clear Joshua was not like the other Hams.

He was perhaps twenty-five years old, as much as she was any judge of the ages of these people. His body bore the marks of savage beatings, and his tongue seemed to be damaged, making his speech even more impenetrable than the rest.

No Hams lived alone. But Joshua lived alone, in his cave beyond the communal space around the hut. Hams did not go naked – but Joshua did, wearing not so much as a scrap of skin to cover his filth-encrusted genitals. Hams cut their hair and, crudely, shaved their beards with stone knives. Joshua did not, and his hair was a mane of black streaked with grey, his beard long but rather comically wispy under that huge jaw. Hams joined in the activities of the community, making tools, gathering and preparing food, repairing clothes and the hut. Joshua did none of this.

Hams did not make markings, or symbols of any kind – in fact they showed loathing of such things. Joshua covered the walls of his cave with markings made by stone scrapers and bits of bone. They might have been faces; he sketched rough ovals and rectangles, criss-crossed by interior lines – noses, mouths? – over and over. The marks were crude scratches, as if made by a small child – but still, they were more than she had ever observed any other Ham to make.

The other Hams tolerated him. In fact, since he did no gathering or hunting, by providing him with food they were keeping him alive, as she had seen other groups sustain badly injured, sickly or elderly individuals. Perhaps they thought he was ill, beyond his body's slowly healing wounds.

Certainly, by the standards of his kind, he was surely insane. Studying this Ham hermit from afar, Emma concluded that whatever his story, she had best avoid him.

But when Joshua spotted her, the matter was taken out of her hands.

She was walking up the beach from the sea. Her catch of fish had been good that day, and she had used a scrap of blue 'chute cloth from her pack to carry it all.

Joshua was sitting outside his cave, muttering to himself. When he saw her blue cloth, he got to his feet, hooted loudly, and came running.

Other Hams, close to the hut, watched dully.

Joshua capered before her, muttering, his accent thicker than any she had heard before. He was gaunt, and his back was still red with half-healed welts. But he might have been three times her weight.

Emma reached for the stone knife she kept tucked in her belt. 'Keep back, now.'

He grabbed the blue cloth, spilling the fish on the sand. He sniffed the cloth with his giant, snot-crusted nostrils, and wiped it over his face. 'This,' he shouted. '*This!*'

She frowned. 'What is it? What are you trying to tell me?'

'Th' door in the sky,' he said. 'Th' door in Heaven. Th' wings of th' seed.' His voice was horribly indistinct – and when he opened his mouth to yell these things at her, she saw a great notch had been cut out of his tongue.

She should get out of here, flee to the sanctuary of the hut, get away from his deranged grasp. But she stayed. For no other Ham had used phrases like 'the door in the sky'.

She asked cautiously, 'What door?'

'Th' sky seed. Th' Grey Earth. Th' seed fell th' sky.'

She understood it in a flash. She whirled and pointed to the lander, stranded on the cliff face. 'Is that what you're talking about? The lander – the thing that fell from the sky?' She grabbed back the bit of cloth. 'Under a parachute. A blue 'chute, wings, like this.'

For answer he bellowed, 'Sky seed!' And he turned away and ran full tilt towards the foot of the cliff, beneath the lander.

Emma watched him go, her heart thumping.

She could stay here her whole life and never persuade the Hams to help her get to the lander. Maybe it took an insane Ham even to conceive of such a project. A Ham like Joshua.

Now or never, Emma.

She grabbed her pack and ran after Joshua.

There was a trail, of sorts, that led from the beach to the top of the cliff. At least Joshua showed her the way; she couldn't have managed at all otherwise. But it was a trail for Hams – or maybe goats – certainly not for humans. The scrambling and climbing was a major challenge for Emma, never super-fit, never any kind of climber. Nevertheless, by sheer force of will, she kept up.

At the top of the cliff she fell back, exhausted, her heart pumping and her lungs scratching for air. It was like her first few days after the portal, when she had struggled to acclimatize to this strange mountain-top world.

Joshua immediately plunged into the cliff-top forest. Emma forced herself to her feet and followed.

Joshua crashed through the dense forest by main force, pushing aside branches, saplings and even some mature trees. He seemed careless of the noise he made and the trail he left behind – again unlike most Hams, who took care to pass silently through the dangerous twilight of the forest.

At last they pushed into a clearing. Here the trees had been battered flat, she saw, and bits of blue cloth clung to scattered branches. Her heart thumped harder. Joshua ran across the clearing to the far side, where a last line of trees had been broken down, exposing blue-grey sky. She followed him.

She found herself at the lip of the cliff, looking down on a trail of scraped rock and bits of cloth and 'chute cord. And there, really not so far beneath the lip of the cliff, like a fat bug trapped in some huge spider-web, lay the lander.

Joshua squatted on his haunches and pointed down at the lander. 'Sky seed,' he said excitedly. 'Sky seed!'

She gazed hungrily down at the lander: crumpled, battered, stained and weathered, but intact. She saw no sign that anybody had climbed out of it since its plummet down the cliff.

From here the lander looked very small. Specifically, she couldn't see any sign of an engine pack, no way the thing could get itself off the ground and back to Earth.

She sat back, forcing herself to think. Sitting here with a Neandertal the internal politics of America seemed a remote abstraction – but still she couldn't believe that the US government would sanction any kind of one-way mission, even for someone as persuasive as Reid Malenfant. But that meant – she thought, her brain working feverishly – that the engine had to be somewhere else.

She grabbed Joshua's arms, and immediately regretted it; his skin was covered in filth and scabs. He flinched back from her touch, as if she intended to hurt him. She let go, and held her empty hands up before him. 'I'm sorry . . . Listen to me. *There must be another lander*. I mean, another sky seed. A second one.' But Hams did not count. She held her hands up to mime two landers coming down from the west, one after the other. But Hams did not use symbols.

She pointed, bluntly. 'Sky seed. Down there. Sky seed.' She pointed into the forest, at random. 'Over there.'

He frowned. He pointed west, deeper into the forest. 'Ov' there.'

She took a deep breath. *I knew it.*

But now Joshua was jabbering, pointing at the lander and the sky. 'Sky seed. Praisegod. *There 'fore me was door standin' open Heav'n*. Sky seed in Heav'n. People of th' Grey Earth. People of Heav'n.' And on and on, a long, complex, baffling diatribe.

She peered into his ridged eye sockets, struggling to understand what was going through that mind – so alien from hers, and damaged too.

Bit by bit she got it.

Joshua had seen the lander come down from the sky. He had seen the second lander too. She knew that Hams believed their people came from a place in the sky, which they called the Grey Earth. Joshua, alternately, called it Heaven. As best she could make out he wanted to use the lander to take his people home, to Grey Earth, to Heaven.

'Was it the Zealots who taught you about Heaven? Did the Zealots hurt you? Did this Praisegod hurt you?'

'Prai'go' Michael,' he mumbled. 'Mal'fan'.'

Suddenly she couldn't breathe. She grabbed his shoulders, mindless of the filth, resisting his flinching. '*What did you say?*'

'Mal'fan'. Zealots. Mal'fan'.'

The Zealots had Malenfant. *Malenfant was here.*

She sat back on her haunches, breathing in gasps. 'Do you know where Malenfant is being held? – no, you can't tell me that. But you could show me.' She studied Joshua, who gazed back at her. 'Listen to me. There is something you want. There is something I want. This is what we will do. You take me to Malenfant . . . If you do this, I will give you the lander. It will take you home, to Heaven, to the Grey Earth.'

It took a long time to make him understand all of this. It might have been the first time in the history of these Hams, she thought, that anybody had tried to strike a bargain.

And, as she had absolutely no intention of using the lander for anything else but getting herself and Malenfant out of here, it might have been the first time anybody had told a Ham a lie.

Reid Malenfant:

Uncounted days after his whipping, Malenfant was again dragged before Praisegod Michael.

Malenfant stood as straight as he could, his arms tied behind his back, a new skin jacket over his upper body. He seethed with resentment at his own pain and humiliation, anger at what he suspected had become of McCann, and a kind of self-righteous disgust at Praisegod.

Get a hold of yourself, Malenfant. Do business, remember.

'What now, Praisegod? Another beating?'

Praisegod walked around Malenfant. Malenfant saw how his right leg spasmed, as if he wished to flee; he seemed unusually agitated. Praisegod Michael was a man of depths, all of them murky.

Praisegod's Ham boy sat on the edge of the desk, staring at Malenfant.

'I do not wish to punish you, Sir Malenfant. I can tell you have twice the mentation of Sprigge, here. I would rather obtain your support.'

'You know nothing about me.'

Praisegod said, 'Where we came from does not matter, Malenfant. For we cannot escape this place; men have spent their lives to prove that. And as your friend McCann understood, what unites men, in this world of animals, is greater than that which separates us. All that matters is that we are here, now, and we must make the best of it. Though it has the face of a work of Satan, this island is a world made by God – of course it is; to argue otherwise would be to support the heresy of Manichaeus. Therefore it is perfectible, and therefore there is good work to be done here by righteous men . . . There is much to be done here.'

Malenfant eyed him. Praisegod was a shithead, yes. He wasn't about to conquer the Red Moon. But a shithead like this could cause a lot of suffering to a lot of people, and near-people. 'Perfectible? Right. I know your kind. You intend to build an empire, Praisegod. A *perfect* empire, soaked in blood.'

'What is blood?' Praisegod said easily. 'If men stand against us, they will be as stubble before our swords. And as for the rest, to spill the blood of an animal is not a sin, Malenfant. Indeed, given that these soulless apes show a mockery of man's features, I am convinced that to cleanse the worlds of their obscene forms is a duty.'

'So you will use the Hams and the Runners as a resource to build your empire on this Moon. And when the hominids' usefulness has passed, you will exterminate them.'

Praisegod's predator's eyes gleamed. 'It is time for your answer, Malenfant.'

Malenfant closed his eyes.

Stay alive, Malenfant. That's all that matters. The creatures on this Red Moon mean nothing to you. A little while ago you didn't even know they existed. (But some of them have helped me, even saved my life . . .) And they are not even human. (But they are differently human . . .) This Praisegod may be difficult, but he is powerful. If you can work with him he may even help you achieve your goal – which is, was and always will be to find Emma. (But he's a psychopathic monster . . .)

He imagined he heard Emma's mocking voice.

You can't do it, can you? You never were too good at politics, were you, Malenfant? – even in NASA – any place where the ancient primate strategies of knowing when to fight and when to groom, when to dominate and when to submit, were essential. Ah, but this is about more than politics, isn't it, Malenfant? Are you growing a conscience? You, who lied his way to Washington and back to get his BDB off the ground, who used up people and spat them out on the way to achieving what you wanted? Now you stand here on this jungle Moon and you can't swallow a few preachy platitudes to save your own worthless hide? . . .

Or, he thought, maybe McCann was right about me. So was my mother-in-law, come to that. Maybe all I ever wanted to do was crash and burn.

Praisegod's foot was tapping out its nervous drumbeat. The Ham boy, seeming to sense the tension between the two men, slid off the desk and crawled behind Praisegod's chair.

Malenfant took a breath. He said, 'Why are you really so dead set against the hominids?' He glanced at the Neandertal boy; one eye and a thatch of ragged dark hair protruded from behind the chair leg. 'Does this boy warm your bed, Praisegod Michael? Is that why you have to destroy him?'

Malenfant saw white all the way around Praisegod's pupils, and a dribble of blood and snot was leaking from his nose. The man stood before Malenfant, close enough to smell the fishy stink of his breath. He whispered, 'This time the whips will fillet the flesh off you, until the men will be flogging your neck and the soles of your feet. And I, I will prevail, in the light of His countenance.'

Malenfant had time for an instant of satisfaction. *Got through to you, you bastard.* Then he was clubbed to his knees.

Emma Stoney:

She spent days in the cliff-top forest, spying, scouting.

This patch of forest was damp and thin. There were extensive clearings where old trees had fallen to the ground in chaotic tangles of branches. Paths wound among the trees, marked out through rotting leaves, fungus-ridden trunks, brambles and crushed saplings. Many of these paths were made no doubt by animals, or perhaps hominids, the Nutcracker-folk or the Elf-folk. But some of them were, unmistakably, the work of humans; straight, sometimes rutted by wheels.

And the human paths converged on a township, a brooding, massive structure at the heart of the forest. It was the fortress of the Zealots.

The great gate of the compound would open a couple of times a day to let out or admit parties, apparently for hunting and provisioning. The open gates, swinging on massive hinges of rope, revealed a shabby cluster of huts and fire-pits within. The Zealot foragers, always men, always dressed in drab green-stained skins, were armed with pikes and bows and arrows. They stayed alert as they made their way along the paths they had worn between the trees.

The returning parties would call out informal *halloos* to let those inside know they wanted in. Nobody seemed to feel the need for passwords or other identifiers. But the gate openings were brief, and the forest beyond was always carefully watched by armed men. The foragers would return with sacks full of the forest's fruits, or with bats or animals, commonly small hogs, or even grain and root vegetables brought in from the hinterland that must stretch beyond the forest.

But they would also bring home Elves, even the occasional Nut-cracker, suspended limply from poles, heads lolling. The Zealots had no taboo, it seemed, over consuming the flesh of their apparent near-relatives – which she heard them call, in their thick, strangulated accent, *bush meat*. The hunters seemed to prize the hands and ears of infant Elves, which they would hack off and wear around their necks as gruesome trophies.

Also, less frequently, they brought home captured Runners. The Runners were always returned alive. The men and boys were evidently beaten into submission, their backs bearing the scars of whips and their faces misshapen from blows; they trudged through the forests with ropes around their necks and wrists, and with their long legs hobbled so they had to shuffle. She supposed the male Runners were brought back to the stockade as slave labour. Their strong, supple bodies and clever hands well qualified them for the role.

Perhaps some of the captured women and girls were used that way too, but Emma suspected they had a darker fate in store. They were returned to the township with bite marks and scratches on their breasts and blood running down their legs. Some of the boys seemed to have been similarly abused. Evidently the hunters took the breaking-in of a new captive as a perk of the job. Emma had no way of knowing how many of these victims had fought too hard, and ended their lives in the forest in uncomprehending misery beneath the grunting bodies of the Zealots.

She was relieved her instinct had always been to keep out of sight of these people. She didn't quite know what reaction they would have to finding a human woman alone in the forest, but she didn't feel inclined to take a chance on their charity.

At last her spying paid off. She overheard a group of hunters, as they lazed in the shade of a fig tree, feeding themselves on its plump fruit and talking loosely. Their gossip was of a major expedition – it almost sounded military – to take on a new group the Zealots called the *Daemons*. The Zealots sounded alternately apprehensive and excited about the coming conflict; there was much speculation about the quality of the women among the Daemons.

Emma knew nothing about these Daemons, and couldn't care less. But if a large number of the township's able bodies was going to be taken away, she sensed a window of opportunity.

She sat in the cave before Joshua, holding his massive head with both her hands on his filthy cheeks, making him face her. 'Hunting Praisegod Michael. Tomorrow. Hunting Praisegod. Do you understand?'

'Hunt Prai'go',' he said at last, thickly, his damaged tongue protruding. 'Tomorr'.'

'Yes. Tomorrow. Wait until tomorrow. All right?'

He gazed back at her, his eyes containing an eerie sharpness that none of his people seemed to share. Perhaps there was madness there – but even so, it was a much more human gaze than any she had encountered since losing Sally and Maxie. But there was absolutely no guile in those eyes, none at all, and no element of calculation or planning.

She released him.

He picked up a rock he had been knapping, and resumed working on it, steady, patient. She sat down in the corner of the cave, her legs drawn up to her chest, arms wrapped around her knees, watching him. The blue-grey glow of the sky, leaching of light, reflected in his eyes as he worked; often, like most Ham knappers, he didn't even look at the stone he was working.

Tomorrow, this child-man would have to take part in a concerted assault.

Not for the first time Emma wondered what the hell she was doing here. *How have I come so far? I'm an accountant, for God's sake* . . .

She had spent the days waiting for the Zealots' expedition trying to raise a fighting force from among the Hams. But she had quickly learned that it was impossible to turn these huge, powerful, oddly gentle creatures into anything resembling soldiers – not in a short time, probably not if she kept at it for ever. She had hit at last on the notion of making the assault a hunt, the one activity where the Hams did appear to show something resembling guile.

But even now she didn't know how many of them she could count on. She, and Joshua, had managed to enthuse a few of the younger men to join the battle. But when she approached them the next day even the most ardent would-be warriors would have forgotten all about the project.

Another problem was that the Hams' *only* notion of actual combat was hand-to-hand: just yesterday she had seen three of the men wrestle an overgrown buck antelope to the ground with their bare hands. It was a strategy that had worked for them so far, evidently, or the cold hand of natural selection would long ago have eliminated them – even if they paid the price in severe injuries and shortened lifespans. But it wasn't a strategy that would work well in a war, even against the disorganized and weakened rabble she hoped the Zealots would prove to be.

In the end, she realized, the Hams would fight (or not) according to their instinct and impulse, and they would fight the way they always had, come what may. She would just have to accept that, and deal with the consequences.

Joshua turned the rock over in his hands, running his scarred fingertips over the planes he had exposed, gazing intently at it. Unlike her, he wasn't fretting about tomorrow. She sensed a stillness about his mind, as if it were a clear pool, clear right to the bottom, and in its depths all she could see was the rock. It was as if Joshua and the rock blurred together, becoming a single entity, as if his self-awareness were dimming, as if he were more aware of the microstructure of the rock even than of himself.

With her head echoing as ever with hopes and fears and schemes, Emma couldn't begin to imagine how that might feel. But she knew she envied him. Since starting to live with the Hams she had often wished she could simply switch off the clamour in her head, the way they seemed to.

Now Joshua lifted his worn bone hammer – the only possession he cherished – and, with the precision of a surgeon, tapped the rock. A flake fell away. It was a scraper, she saw, an almost perfect oval.

He lifted his head and grinned at her, his scarred tongue protruding.

The Zealots' attacking army had drawn up in rough order outside the stockade, armed with their crossbows and knives and pikes.

There looked to be fifty men and boys, and they had been followed by about as many Runner bearers, all of them limping, their arms full of bundles of weapons and provisions.

Emma watched the soldiers prepare, curious. The pikemen, in addition to their immensely long pikes, had leather armour: breast-plates and backplates, what they called gorgets to protect their throats, and helmets that they called pots. They carried provisions in leather packs they called snapsacks. There was even a cavalry, of sorts; but the soldiers rode the shoulders of men, of Runners. They were marshalled by an insane-looking cleric type, in a long robe of charcoal-blackened skin – and by a hominid, a vast, hulking gorilla-like creature with rapid, jerky movements and swivelling ears. Was it a Daemon? At least eight feet tall, it looked smart, purposeful; Emma hadn't seen its like before.

Not your problem, Emma.

The army, its preparations nearly done, sang hymns and psalms. Then a man they called Constable Sprigge stood on a rock before them, and began to pray. 'Lord, you know how busy I must be this day. If I forget Thee, do not Thou forget me . . .' Emma found the wry soldiers' prayer oddly moving.

And with that the army marched off through the forest. The Zealot fortress was as weakened as it would ever be.

She crouched by the stockade gate, her heart beating like a hammer drill, clutching the shortest, sharpest thrusting spear she could find. She surveyed her own motley army. In the end, only the big man, Abel – Joshua's brother – and the oddly adventurous girl Mary had elected to join her and Joshua on this expedition. Three Hams counted physically for a lot more than twice as many Zealots. And she was planning nothing more than a smash-and-grab raid, a commando operation, a mission with a single goal. But still, there were only four of them – three child-people and herself, and she was certainly no soldier.

She was frightened for the Hams, already guilty for the harm they would surely suffer today – and, of course, profoundly frightened for herself, middle-aged accountant turned soldier. But this was the only way she could see to get to Malenfant. And getting to him was the only way she was ever going to get out of this dismal, bizarre place – if he really was here, if he was still alive, if she hadn't somehow misunderstood Joshua, fooled by his damaged tongue and her own aching heart. And so she put aside her fears and doubts and guilt, for there was no choice.

She kept her Hams quiet until she was sure the ragged Zealot army was out of hearing.

Manekatopokanemahedo:

The compound was calm, quiet, orderly. Workers trundled to and fro over the bright yellow floor of Adjusted Space, pursuing their unending chores.

But not a person moved. They stood or sat or lay in a variety of poses, like statues, or corpses, arrayed beneath the huge turning Map of the world. The core activity here was internal, as each person contemplated the vast conundrum of the Red Moon.

After two million years of continuous civilization, nobody rushed.

But to Manekato, after her vivid experiences in the forest, it was like being in a mausoleum. She found a place of shade and threw herself to the ground. A Worker came over and offered her therapeutic grooming, but Manekato waved it away.

Nemoto came to her. She carried her block of paper, much scribbled-on. She sat on the floor, cross-legged, and regarded Manekato gravely. '*Renemenagota of Rano represents a great danger.*'

Manekato snapped her teeth angrily. '*What do you know of the hearts of people? You are not even a person. You are like a Worker . . .*'

But Nemoto showed no distress. '*Person or not, I may perceive certain truths more clearly than you. I see, for instance, that you are troubled on a deep level. You are human, but you are still animal too, Manekato. And your animal side is repelled by the cold efficiency of this place you have built, and is drawn to the dark mysteries of the forest. Perhaps my lesser kind have a better understanding of the shadows of our hearts.*' But there was defiance in her pronunciation of that word *lesser*.

Manekato felt shamed. Hadn't she just taken out her own distress and confusion on a weaker creature – this Nemoto – just as Without-Name had punished the hominids she had captured? She propped herself up on her elbows. '*What is it you want?*'

'*I have a hypothesis,*' said the little hominid.

Manekato sighed. More of Nemoto's theories: partial, immature, expressed badly and at the pace of a creeping glacier – and yet suffused by an earnest need to be understood, listened to, approved. She nodded, a gesture she had learned from Nemoto herself.

Nemoto began to spread pages of her paper block over the floor. The paper bore columns labelled *Earth*, *Banded Earth*, *Grey Earth (Hams)*, and so on, though some columns were headed by nothing but query marks. And the paper was covered with a tangle of lines and arrows that linked the columns one to the other.

'*I have elaborated my views,*' Nemoto said. '*I have come to believe that this Red Moon has played a key role in human evolution. Consider. How do new species arise, of hominids or any organism? Isolation is the key. If mutations arise in a large and freely mixing population, any new characteristic is diluted and will disappear within a few generations. But when a segment of the population becomes isolated from the rest, dilution through interbreeding is prevented. Then, when a new characteristic appears within the group – and provided it is beneficial to the survival of the group and the individuals within it – it will be reinforced. Thus the isolated group may, quite rapidly, diverge from the base population.*

'*And when those barriers to isolation are removed, the new species finds itself in competition with its predecessors. If it is better adapted to the prevailing conditions, it will survive by out-competing the parent stock. If not, it declines.*

'*When our scientists believed there was only one Earth, they suspected the evolution of humanity had been the consequence of a number of speciation steps. The ape-like bipedal Australopithecines gave rise to tool users, who in turn produced erect hairless creatures capable of walking on the open plain, who in turn gave rise to various species of* Homo sapiens *– the family that includes myself. It is believed that at some points in history there were many hominid species, all derived from the base Australopithecine stock, living together on the Earth. But my kind –* Homo sapiens sapiens *– proved the fittest of them all. By out-competition, the variant species were removed.*

'*Presumably, each speciation episode was instigated by the isolation of a group of the parent stock. We had generally assumed that the key isolating events were caused by climate changes: rising or falling sea levels, the birth or death of forests, the coming and going of glaciation. It was a plausible picture. Before we knew of the Red Moon.*'

'*And now your radical hypothesis –*'

Nemoto tapped her papers. '*What if the vagaries of the Red Moon* were involved in all this? Look here. This central column sketches the history of the Earth.'

'Your *Earth*.'

Nemoto smiled, her small naked face pinched. '*Assume that the base Australopithecine stock evolved on Earth. Imagine that the Red Moon with its blue Wheel portals scooped up handfuls of undifferentiated Australopithecines and, perhaps some generations later, deposited them on a variety of subtly different Earths.*'

'*It is hard to imagine a more complete isolation.*'

'*Yes. And the environments in which they were placed might have had no resemblance to those from which they were taken. In that case our Australopithecines would have had to adapt or die. Perhaps one group was stranded on a world of savannah and open desert –*'

'*Ah. You are suggesting that the hairless, long-legged Runners might have evolved on such a world.*'

'*Homo erectus – yes. Other worlds produced different results. And later, the Red Moon returned and swept up samples of those new populations, and handed them on to other Earths – or perhaps returned them where they had come from, to compete with the parent stock, successfully or otherwise.*

'*My species shares a comparatively recent common ancestor with creatures like the Hams – which are of the type we call Neandertals, I think. Perhaps a group of that ancestral stock was taken to the world the Hams call the Grey World, where they evolved the robust form we see now. And, later, a sample of Hams was returned to the Earth. Later still, groups of* Homo sapiens sapiens *– that is, my kind – were swept here from the Earths of the groups called the English and the Zealots, and no doubt others.*' She gazed at her diagrams. '*Perhaps even my own kind evolved on some other Earth, and were brought back by the Moon in some ancient accident.*'

Manekato picked her nose thoughtfully. '*Very well. And my Earth – which you have labelled "Banded Earth"?*'

Somewhat hesitantly, Nemoto said, '*It seems that your Earth may have been seeded by Australopithecine stock from my Earth. You seem to have much in common, morphologically, with the robust variant of Australopithecines to be seen in the forests here, called Nutcrackers.*'

Manekato lay back and sighed, her mind racing pleasurably. '*You fear you have offended me by delegating my world to a mere off-shoot. You have not. And your scheme is consistent with the somewhat mysterious appearance of my forebears on Earth – my Earth.'* She glanced at Nemoto's sketches. *'It is a promising suggestion. This strange Moon might prove to be the crucible of our evolution: certainly it is unlikely that hominid forms could not have evolved independently on so many diverse Earths. But such is the depth of time involved, and such is the complexity of the mixing achieved by our wandering Moon, the full picture is surely more complicated than your sketch – and it is hard to believe that your Earth just happens to be the primary home of the lineage . . . And how is it that so many of these other Earths share, not just hominid cousins, but a shared history, even shared languages? Your own divergence from the Zealot type must be quite ancient – their peculiar tails attest to that – and yet your history evidently shares much in common with them.'*

Nemoto frowned, her small face comically serious. *'That is a difficulty. Perhaps there is such a thing as historical convergence. Or perhaps the wandering of the Moon has induced mixing even in historical times. Cultural, linguistic transmission –'*

It was a simplistic suggestion, but Manekato did not want to discourage her. *'Perhaps. But the truth may be more subtle. Perhaps the manifold of universes is larger than you suppose. If it were arbitrarily large, then there would be an arbitrarily close match to any given universe.'*

Nemoto puzzled through that. *'Just as I would find my identical twin, in a large enough population of people.'*

'That's the idea. The closer the match you seek, the more unlikely it would be, and the larger the population of, umm, candidate twins you would need to search.'

'But the degree of convergence between, say, the Zealot universe and my own – language, culture, even historical figures – is so unlikely that the manifold of possibilities would have to be very large indeed.'

'Infinite,' said Mane gently. *'We must consider the possibility that the manifold of universes through which we wander is in fact infinite.'*

Nemoto considered that for a while. Then she said, *'But no matter how large the manifold, I still have to understand* why *this apparatus of a reality-wandering Moon should have been devised in the first place – and who by.'*

Manekato studied Nemoto, wishing she could read the hominid's small face better. *'Why show me your schema now?'*

'*Because*,' Nemoto said, '*I believe all of this, this grand evolutionary saga, is now under threat.*'

Manekato frowned. '*Because of the failure of the world engines?*'

'*No*,' Nemoto said. '*Because of you. And Renemenagota of Rano.*'

A shadow fell over Manekato's face. 'Your ape may be right, Mane. You should listen to it.'

It was Without-Name. She stepped forward, carelessly scattering Nemoto's spidery diagrams.

Emma Stoney:

Emma lifted her head. '*Hall-oo! Hall-oo!*' Her call, though pitched higher than that of the men who mostly ventured outside the stockade, was, she was sure, a pretty accurate imitation of the soft cries of returning hunters.

Within a couple of minutes she heard an answering grunt, and the rattle of heavy wooden bolts being slid back.

All or nothing, she thought. Malenfant – or death.

When the heavy gate started to creak open, she yelled and threw herself at it. Her flimsy mass made no difference. But the Hams immediately copied her, making a sound like a car ramming a tree. The splintering gate was smashed back, and she heard a howl of pain.

The Hams surged forward. There were people in the compound, women and children. As three immense Hams came roaring in amongst them, they ran screaming.

Emma glanced around quickly. She saw a litter of crude adobe huts, that one substantial chapel-like building at the centre, a floor of dust stamped flat by feet and stained with dung and waste. She smelled shit, stale piss.

Now the door to one of the buildings flew open. Men boiled out, pulling on clothing. Inside the building's smoky darkness Emma glimpsed naked Runner women, some of them wearing mockeries of dresses, others on beds and tables, on their backs or their bellies, legs splayed, scarred ankles strapped down.

Grabbing pikes and clubs and bows, the men ran at Abel, howling. With a cry of pleasure Abel joined with them. He brushed aside their clubs as if they were twigs wielded by children. He got two of the Zealots by the neck, lifted them clean off the ground, and slammed their heads together, making a sound like eggs cracking.

But now the bowmen had raised their weapons and let fly. Emma, despising herself, huddled behind Abel's broad back. She heard the grisly impact of arrows in Abel's chest. He fell to his knees, and blood spewed from his mouth.

The archers were struggling to reload. Mary hurled herself at them, fists flailing.

Emma grabbed Joshua's arm. 'Malenfant! Quickly, Joshua. Malenfant – where?'

For answer he ran towards the chapel-like central building. Emma touched Abel's back apologetically, and ran after Joshua towards the chapel. She seethed with rage and adrenaline and fear. This had better be worth the price we're paying, Malenfant.

Manekatopokanemahedo:

Manekato stood quickly. Nemoto hurried behind her, sheltering behind her bulk. Babo came running to join them, his legs and arms levering him rapidly over the floor of Adjusted Space. Other people gathered in a loose circle around this central confrontation, watching nervously. Workers scuttled back and forth, seeking tasks, trying to discern the needs of the people, ignored.

For the first time it struck Manekato just how physically big Without-Name was – towering over a lesser hominid like Nemoto, but larger than Manekato too, larger than any of the other people on this expedition. Physical size did not matter at home, on civilized Earth. But on this savage Moon, strength and brute cunning were key survival factors; and Without-Name seemed to relish her unrestrained power.

And now Manekato noticed a new hominid following in Without-Name's wake. It was a male, taller than Nemoto, rake-thin, and he was dressed in a tight robe of animal skin stained black, perhaps by charcoal. He drew a Ham boy after him. The boy was dressed in elaborate clothing, and he had a collar around his neck, connected to a lead in the tall hominid's hand.

Babo said tightly, 'And is this your Praisegod Michael, Renemenagota of Rano?'

Without-Name raised one hand.

Crossbow bolts thudded into Babo's belly and chest and upper arms. He cried out softly, dull surprise on his face. He crumpled forward and fell on the bolts, making them twist, and his cries deepened. A Worker rushed to tend Babo's wounds, but Without-Name kicked it away.

Manekato, stunned, saw that the circular platform was surrounded by hominids – Zealots, in their sewn skins. Some of them, bizarrely, were riding on the shoulders of Running-folk. They seemed afraid, but they held up their crossbows and spears with defiance.

Praisegod Michael passed his hands over Babo's shuddering form, making a cross in the air. *'Behold, Esau my brother is a hairy man, and I am a smooth man . . .'*

Manekato found words. 'Renemenagota – what are you doing?'

'Providing you with a purpose.'

'Your army of hominids would be no match for the power we could deploy,' Manekato whispered.

'Of course not – *if* you choose to deploy it,' Without-Name said mockingly. 'But you won't, will you? Meanwhile these hominids believe they are soldiers of God. They have only their simple hand-made weapons, but their heads are on fire. And so their crossbow bolts will best all your learning and technology. And under my guidance, they will sweep the world.'

Now Nemoto stepped out from behind Manekato. Without-Name eyed the little hominid with undisguised loathing.

But Praisegod Michael faced her, apparently unsurprised to find her here. *'You are the one called Nemoto. Malenfant told me I would find you here.'*

'I know your kind,' Nemoto said. She turned to Manekato. *'You must stop this, here and now. You have not seen such things before, Manekato. With Renemenagota's organizational skill, Michael and his fellows will march on, overwhelming others with their savagery and determination, armed with an unwavering faith that will lead them to their deaths if necessary. Those they do not destroy will be forcibly converted to the creed. By the second generation the conquered will regard themselves as soldiers of the conquering army. We are limited creatures, Manekato, and we do not have the strength of mind to fight off a contagion of seductive but lethal ideas. You must stop this for the slaughter that will follow if you don't.'*

Babo twisted on the ground, his hands clamped to his stomach, his face a rictus of pain. 'Yes,' he hissed. 'Exponential growth,

Mane. They will conquer, acquire resources to fuel further expansion, thus acquiring still more, and all driven by a dazzling virus of the mind.'

Manekato said, 'It is – unbelievable.'

Nemoto faced her. *'Manekato, you must save us from ourselves – and save this machine-world from the deadly manipulation of Renemenagota.'*

Without-Name stood before her, her immense biceps bunched, gazing into her eyes, so close Manekato could smell blood on her breath. 'Perhaps this ape-thing is right, Manekato. Will you take its advice? – Ah, but then you would have to become like me, wouldn't you, and how you dread that! You must destroy me – but you cannot, can you, Mane?'

Babo, on the floor, groaned and raised one bloody arm. 'But I can, Renemenagota of Rano.'

A sudden wind, hot and dense, billowed before Manekato's face.

People staggered back, crying out. Nemoto took hold of Babo's arm, anchoring herself against the gusts.

A tube of whirling air formed over the platform. It was the end of a winding column that stretched down from the sky, silvery-grey, suddenly tightly defined. It was a controlled whirlwind, like that which had stormed around the Market for two hundred thousand years.

And in the heart of the column of tortured air was Renemenagota. She raised her fists, briefly bipedal like those whom she had sought to lead. But she could land no blows on the twisting air, and it paid no heed to her screamed defiance.

In a brief blur of brown and black, she was gone.

The whirlwind shrivelled, shrinking back up into the lid of cloud that had covered the sky. A cloud of crimson dust came drifting down on the platform.

Mane, stunned, bewildered, looked around. Nemoto still clung to the fallen Babo. Of the ring of armed Zealots there was no sign.

Praisegod had been bowled over. He lay on his back on the platform, his black clothing scattered around him. His eyes flickered, cunning, calculating, the eyes of a trapped animal seeking a way out.

But his pet Ham boy stood over him.

Praisegod lifted his hand to the boy, asking for help, forcing a smile.

The boy bunched his fist and rammed it into Praisegod's chest, through clothing, skin, an arch of ribs.

Praisegod shuddered and flopped like a landed fish. The Ham's squat face was expressionless as he rummaged in that bloody cavern. Then the Ham boy grimaced, and the muscles of his arms contracted.

Praisegod's head arched back, and his voice was a rasp. '*Why have you forsaken me? . . .*'

Then, his heart crushed, he was still.

Emma Stoney:

There was a lot of shouting going on. Mary was running around the compound, busily engaging her foe. Though Abel had fallen, Mary was moving too quickly for the archers to get an accurate sight on her, and every time she got close enough she was slamming heads, breaking arms and generally kicking ass with a joyous vigour.

The chapel, built of mud brick around a sturdy wooden frame, was as substantial as it looked. Emma ducked into the building and slammed the door, and ran a heavy wooden bolt into a notch.

Within seconds fists were hammering on the door.

'Quickly,' she said to Joshua. 'Malenfant. Where?'

But Joshua did not reply, and when she turned, she saw that he was facing a crucifix, gazing at the gentle, anguished face of a Messiah. Joshua cringed, but was unable to look away.

The yelling at the door was growing intense, and the first hints of organized battering were detectable. Emma couldn't wait any longer. She cast around the little chapel, shoving aside furniture and a small, ornately carved wooden altar.

And she found a hatchway.

The hatch opened on a small, dark shaft, fitted with stubby wooden rungs. Emma clambered down hastily, to find herself in a short corridor. A single wicker torch burned fitfully in a holder. She grabbed it and hurried along the corridor.

The corridor led to two wooden doors. One door was swinging open, and Emma recoiled. The cell within was just a pit, with a filth-crusted floor and blackened, scratched walls; it stank of blood and vomit and urine.

The other door was shut. Emma hammered on it. 'Malenfant! Are you there?' The wood was so filthy her hands came away smeared with deep black.

No reply.

Struggling to hold up the torch, she made out a thick bolt, just wood, a smaller copy of the one on the compound gate. She hesitated for a heartbeat, her hand on the bolt.

She reminded herself that she actually had no idea what lay on the other side of this door. But you've come this far, Emma.

She pulled back the bolt, dragged open the door. She held the torch in front of her protectively.

There were two people here. One was sitting on the floor, hands crossed over her chest for protection – her, for it was a woman, in a long dress that looked finely made. But despite the dress and the tied-back hair, that protruding face and the ridged eyes marked her out as a Ham.

The other was a man. He was wearing a blue coverall, and he was curled up in the dirt, folded on himself.

Emma hurried to him. Gently she lifted aside his arm, to reveal his face. 'Do you know me? Do you know where you are? Oh, Malenfant . . .'

He opened his eyes, and his face worked. 'Welcome to hell,' he whispered.

The Ham woman slipped her arms under Malenfant and cradled him, with remarkable tenderness. She said her name was Julia; her English, though slurred by the deficiencies of the Ham palate, was well-modulated and clear.

With Malenfant limp but seemingly light as a baby in Julia's arms, they clambered out of the pit and back into the chapel.

Still the Zealots battered at the door. Joshua remained in his ape-like crouch, his head buried in his big arms. He was whimpering, as if horrified by what he had done.

Gently Emma pulled his arm away from his face. His cheeks were smeared with tears. 'No time,' she said. 'Mary. Skinnies hurt Mary. Joshua help.'

It took an agonizing minute of repetition, with the hammering on the door turning into a splintering, before he responded.

He got to his feet with a roar. He ran to the door, dragged it open, and with a sweep of his massive arm he knocked aside the scrambling crowd of Zealot men. He forced his way outside, calling for Mary.

Julia followed, carrying Malenfant. Emma stayed close by her side, cradling Malenfant's lolling head.

4

WORLD ENGINE

Reid Malenfant:

'You always were a heathen bastard, Malenfant. No wonder Praisegod had it in for you. I remember the trouble we had when we chose a church. Even though it was a time when overt religiosity was a career asset if you wanted to be part of the public face of NASA.'

'I did like that chapel at Ellington. Kind of austere, for a Catholic chapel. Not too many bleeding guys on the wall. And I liked the priest. Monica Chaum, you could go bowling with.'

'Well, I liked the chapel too, Malenfant. I found it comforting. A place to get away from the squawk boxes and the rest, when you were in orbit.'

'*On* orbit. You never told me that.'

'There are lots of things you don't know about me, Malenfant. I remember one Christmas Eve when you were up there, doing whatever you did. *Christmas Eve*, and I was alone. I was sick of it all, Malenfant. I wanted to go to church, but I didn't want people gawping. So I asked Monica if she would open up the church for me. Well, she dug out the organist, and she went through the church lighting all the candles, just as they would be lit for the Midnight Mass that night, and the organist played the programme planned for the service. When I walked in and saw it was all there just for me – well, it was one of the most beautiful sights I ever saw.'

'I remember that Christmas. I asked Monica to get you a gift. It was a dress. I picked it out.'

'Oh, Malenfant. It was at least five sizes too big. Monica had to apologize; *she* knew. No wonder you can't figure out the Fermi Paradox, Malenfant, if you don't know your own wife's dress size . . . I never liked being alone, you know.'

'Nobody does. I guess that's why we're here, why we swung down from the damn trees. Every one of us is looking for somebody . . .'

'Stop it. Even now, you'd rather talk about issues, about human

365

destiny and the rest of the garbage, anything but us. Anything but *me*. When you're gone I'll be alone here, Malenfant – truly alone, more alone than any person I can think of – to all intents and purposes the only one of my kind, on the whole Moon, in this whole *universe* . . . It's unimaginable. I'm an accountant, Malenfant. It's not supposed to be like this. Not for me. And it's all your fault. Do you want to know what I'm afraid of – really afraid of?'

'Tell me.'

'Chronic reactive depression. You ever heard of that? I looked it up once. You can die of loneliness, Malenfant. Four months, that's all it takes. You don't have to be a failure. Just – outcast.'

'I'm sorry.'

'Bullshit.'

Shadow:

There was little food to be had on the plain. The Elf-folk had carried some food from their crater-wall forest, figs and bananas and apples. But now the sun was setting, the footsteps made by the people in the bare patches of dust were little pools of shadow, and most of the food was gone. Plaintively, as they trooped after Shadow across the dusty grass, many of them looked back to the forest they had left.

They came to the site of an old kill. The bones were so scattered and worn by the teeth of successive predators and scavengers that it was impossible to tell what animal it might once have been.

Nevertheless Shadow stopped here. She sat amid the bones and, with a grunt, passed water into the dirt. The fungal growth on her face was a thick mask over her brow and cheeks and nose, making her look alien, ferocious, and some of the more livid scars on her body seemed to glow as bright red as the dust at her feet.

The others followed her lead: first Stripe, the strongest of the men, then Silverneck and the women who followed her. Infants clambered down to the dusty ground and plucked yellow grass blades, stuffing them into their mouths with rust-red fingers.

The adults huddled together uneasily. On this vast table-top of a landscape the Elf-folk were a dark knot, easily visible, horribly vulnerable. Nevertheless Shadow seemed content to stay here, and so stay they must.

None of the people sat close to Shadow.

Some of them made small offerings to her: a fig, an apple they had carried in their hands. Soon a small pile of food built up. Without acknowledging the people, Shadow reached down and took pieces of the food.

The sun sank further, its edge dipping below rounded hills. A nervy young man, Shiver, emitted a hesitant, hooting roosting call. But there were no trees here to make nests, and the gentle, eerie sound only made the people huddle still closer.

Silverneck sat on the fringe of the group. She picked up a bone from the litter around her. It was a section of a skull. The face was almost intact: she pushed her fingers into eye sockets, nostrils. This might have been a person, an Elf, a Ham, a Nutcracker, a Runner. She ran her finger along it, picking out scrapes and notches, made by teeth or, perhaps, tools. She was almost naked of fur now, so frantically had she been groomed by the other women in these days of turmoil and doubt. Her remaining hairs clung in patches to her blue-black skin and stuck out from her body; the low reddening sunlight made her hair glow, as if she was surrounded by a soft cloud.

Shiver was sitting close to a woman, Palm, barely out of her adolescence. She in turn was resting against her mother's stolid back. Shiver was eating an apple, slowly, his eyes fixed on Palm. His erection was obvious. Shiver started flicking bits of the apple at Palm; the half-chewed fragments landed at her feet, or on her lap.

Without looking at Shiver, Palm picked up the morsels and popped them in her mouth. Gradually, in silence, all but imperceptibly, Shiver moved closer to the girl, his erection dangling before him.

With a sigh, Palm folded back from her mother and lay on the ground, legs separated, her arms stretched above her head. Shiver slid over her and entered her, all in one liquid, silent movement. With a few thrusts he reached orgasm, and withdrew smoothly. Seconds later he and Palm were sitting side by side as if nothing had happened.

Stripe, the boss man, absently grooming Silverneck, had noticed none of this challenge to his status.

Shadow had watched it all. But she cared nothing for such reproductive play. Shadow's dominance had nothing to do with the community's traditional bonds, sex and children.

After the death of One-eye she had soon become the strongest of the women. And the men – even mighty Stripe – had learned to submit to her power. Though many of them outsized her, her naked, unbridled aggression gave her an edge in most contests. Many of the men and boys cradled hands and feet missing fingers or toes, nipped away by Shadow as an indelible mark of their defeat.

And now she had led them all far from home, far from the trees and shrubs and streams and clearings they knew, across this crimson plain – for a purpose only Shadow, in the deepest recesses of her mind, understood.

A small boy approached Shadow. He had his eyes fixed on the pile of fruit before her. His mother, Hairless, growled warningly, but he feigned not to hear. The boy grabbed his infant sister, and, pulling a twisted, funny face, began to wrestle with her. She joined in, chortling. Soon he was on top of her, making playful pelvic thrusts, and then she rolled on top of him. But every roll took them closer to Shadow's food pile.

As soon as the boy was close enough, his hand whipped out to grab a fig. He tucked it in his mouth, immediately abandoning his play, and walked back towards his mother.

One of the women laughed at his clever deceit.

A sharpened cobble hissed through the air. It caught the boy at the top of his spine, laying open the flesh. He howled and went down. Hairless hurried forward and grabbed him. He curled up in her lap, screaming with pain, as she tended the wound.

Stripe picked up the bloody cobble, wiped it on the grass, and passed it back to Shadow.

The group sat in silence, save for the screams of the boy, which took a long time to subside.

The sun slid beneath the horizon. Light bled from the sky.

The people huddled in a close circle. The adults had their backs to the dark, with the children and infants at the centre of the circle. Without fire, without weapons that could strike at a distance save a handful of stones, these hominids were defenceless against the creatures that prowled the savannah night.

Nobody but the infants would sleep tonight. But they feared Shadow more than they feared the dark.

When the dawn came, they found that the boy who had stolen Shadow's fig had gone. As the group moved on, Hairless, his mother, was inconsolable. She had to be half-carried by her sisters and mother, until the memory had started to fade.

At last they reached the cover of trees. This was a forest that lapped at the foot of a tall mountain range; bare rock shone high above.

With relief, they slipped into the trees' shadows. Some submitted to ancient green impulses and clambered high into the trees to make nests, even though the day was not yet half over.

But Shiver, clambering high, found a nest already made. He broke it apart, hooting loudly, his fur standing on end.

Then others joined in the noise, for they began to find discarded fruit peel, and even an abandoned termite-fishing stick. They sniffed and licked these remnants; they were fresh. Others had been here, and recently.

And then, as they spread deeper through the new forest, seeking shoots and fruit-bearing shrubs and trees, a child yelled. The adults came crashing through the undergrowth to see, their hair bristling.

A small girl was standing at the edge of a clearing where a great tree had fallen; its carcass lay on the ground, surrounded by crushed bushes. The girl was facing a child a little older than she was. It was another girl, standing unsteadily, gazing back nervously.

It was in fact Tumble, Shadow's small sister. But Shadow did not recognize her. And Tumble, even if she had remembered Shadow, would not have known this scarred creature with her grotesque fungal mask.

Shadow had come home: transformed, unrecognizable, infused with a new and deadly purpose.

It was no coincidence that the encounter had taken place so quickly. As the forest remnants had continued to shrink back, the Nutcracker-men, living in the green heart of the forest, had managed to hold their territory against the incursions of hungry Elf-folk. So the Elves had been restricted to the shrinking forest fringe, patrolling ever closer to its border with the mountains or the plain.

The little girl stepped forward, and tentatively touched Tumble's face. Tumble nipped her finger playfully. In a moment they were rolling in the dry leaves, wrestling. When the little girl reached for Tumble's genitals, Tumble shrank back, but then she submitted, curiously, to the gentle touch. Then they chased each other over the fallen tree trunk, and started to play together with the fallen leaves. They pushed them into great piles, and rolled in the leaves, throwing handfuls over their heads and rubbing them against their faces.

Now, on the far side of the little clearing, silent shadows flitted through the trees. They were adults, some carrying infants. Led by Stripe and Silverneck, the people stepped forward into the clearing. A loose circle of watchful adults surrounded the playing children.

Only Shadow stayed in the dark green shade.

Silverneck walked forward. She was met by a large, calm woman. She was Termite, Shadow's mother. Cautiously, eyes locked, the women began to groom, plucking at each other's hair. More children joined in the play on the forest floor.

The men were more tentative. They eyed each other warily and made subdued displays, showing bristling hair and waving erections.

Suddenly Shiver ran forward towards the other men. He yelled, stamped and slapped at the ground and drummed with his flat hands on a tree trunk, uttering loud, fierce calls. Then he retreated quickly to the safety of his own group.

He was imitated by a burly man from the other group. This was Little Boss. His display of strength was vivid. He hurled rocks on the ground, making them shatter, and pulled branches this way and that. Never as dominant since the death of his mentor, Big Boss, he was still a massive, powerful presence. The invading men retreated subtly, raising their fists and hooting. But Little Boss too drew back to his friends.

So it went on, with the children playing, the women grooming or making tentative sexual contact, and a display of noisy aggression by the men. But not a single punch or kick was landed, or stone thrown in earnest.

Now one small, muscular man broke out of the group and approached the woman Hairless. He was Squat, another of Shadow's original group. He seemed fascinated by Hairless's baldness, and he stroked her bare blue-black skin. She responded, cupping his scrotum in her hand.

Within a few minutes they had coupled, belly to belly.

After that the groups separated, the men issuing a few last threats to each other, the women apologetically abandoning their grooming. Mothers had to pry their children away from their fascinating new playmates.

Shadow watched all this. And when her old family group dispersed into the trees, she followed.

Manekatopokanemahedo:

The delegation of angry and fearful citizens was led by a stocky, sullen woman called Hahatomane, of the Nema Lineage.

They met at the centre of the platform of Adjusted Space. Manekato waited patiently, resting easily on her knuckles, with Babo and Nemoto to either side of her. Hahatomane stood facing her, with her followers in a rough triangle behind her, and attended by Workers that crawled or hovered.

'What is it you want to talk about, Hahatomane of Nema?'

'That should be obvious,' Hahatomane said. She glanced into the sky, where the rising Earth was a fat banded ball, almost full. 'Renemenagota of Rano is already dead. Many others of us have suffered unspeakable deprivations. This is a foolish quest, devised by foolish Astrologers, which will not help germinate a single seed. We have done what we can. We should leave Workers here to complete the rest, and return to Earth before more of us lose our lives or our sanity.'

Babo stepped forward. Though the medical Workers had striven to heal his injuries, the Zealots' crossbow bolts had been laced with an exotic poison of vegetable oils and fish extracts, and he suffered internal agonies that caused a heavy limp. 'But you have no place on Earth, Hahatomane. Your Farm is destroyed by the tides and 'quakes, and the Nema Lineage is extinguished.'

Hahatomane kept her gaze locked on his sister. 'You do us a dishonour by keeping a man and your ugly *hominid* by your side, Manekato of Poka,' she said. 'I do not hear the words of this one.'

'Then you should,' Manekato said quietly. 'For we are all hominids. We are all people, in fact, of one flavour or another.'

Hahatomane bared her teeth, an unconscious but primal gesture. 'We do not recognize you as any form of leader, Manekato.'

'Fine. If you wish to leave, do so.'

'And you —'

'I intend to stay on this Moon until I have unravelled the mystery of its design.'

Hahatomane growled. 'Then none of us can leave.'

Everybody understood that this was true. If this expedition were a success its members would be honoured, even allowed to carve out new Farms. But if Hahatomane were to split the group, those who abandoned the project could expect nothing but contempt. This was the true source of Manekato's power, and Hahatomane knew it.

Hahatomane's shoulders hunched, as if she longed to launch herself at Manekato's throat – and perhaps it would be healthier if she did, Mane thought. Hahatomane said, 'You drag us all into your folly, Manekato of Poka. I for one will be happy to witness your inevitable disillusion.'

'No doubt on that day you will remind me of this conversation,' Manekato said.

Hahatomane snorted her frustration and turned away. Her followers scattered, bemused and disappointed, and Workers scuttled after them, bleating plaintively.

Manekato sat on the yellow floor. Now that the confrontation was over she felt the strength drain out of her. Babo absently groomed her, picking non-existent insects from the heavy fur on her back. Nemoto sat cross-legged. She had a large bunch of young, bright yellow bananas, and she passed the fruit to Manekato and Babo.

'You did well,' Babo said; then, glancing at Nemoto, he repeated the remark in her tongue, slowing his speech to suit her sluggish oxygen-starved pace of thinking.

Manekato grunted, and spoke in Nemoto's language. '*But I would rather not endure such encounters. We faced off like two groups of Elf-creatures, in their matches of shouting and wrestling. Hahatomane's group even surrounded themselves with Workers to make themselves look larger and stronger, just as male Elves will make their hair bristle in their aggressive displays.*'

Nemoto laughed softly. '*We are all hominids here, all primates.*'

Babo said, '*But it is cruel to be reminded of it so bluntly. Perhaps there is something in the bloody air of this place which has infected us.*'

'*That is foolish and unscientific,*' Manekato said. '*Even Earth is no paradise of disembodied intelligence and pure reason.*' She glanced at the banded planet that shone brightly in the sky. '*Think about it. Why have we clung to our scraps of land for so many thousands of generations?*'

Babo looked offended. '*To cultivate every atom, the final goal* of Farming, is to pay the deepest homage to the world which bore us –'

'That's just rationalization, brother. We cling to our land because it is an imperative that comes to us from the deepest past, from the time before we had minds. We cling to our land for the same reasons that Nutcrackers cling to their tree nests – because that is what we do; it is in our genes, our blood. And what of the exclusion we suffered when we lost our Farms? Why must it be so? What is that but savage cruelty – what is that but sublimated aggression, even murder? No, brother. This Moon has not polluted our souls; we brought the blood and the lust with us.'

'You should not be so harsh on yourselves,' Nemoto said.

Even now Manekato felt a frisson of annoyance that this small-brained hominid was trying to comfort her.

But Babo said, 'She's right. Isn't it possible to celebrate what we have achieved, despite our limitations? Can we not see how we have risen above our biological constraints?'

Manekato said, 'That is true of your kind, Nemoto. You spoke of the contagions of madness that sweep your people. And yet those grand obsessions have driven your kind to a certain greatness: a deep scientific description of the universe, an exploration of your world and others, even a type of art . . . Achievements that press against the boundaries of your capabilities. We, by comparison, have done little to transcend our biology – have done little for the past two million years, in fact, but squat on our Farms. Two million years of complacency.'

'Again that is harsh,' Nemoto said. 'Two million years of peace, given the savagery in your breast, is not a small achievement. We must all strive to embrace the context provided by this place – perhaps that is one of its purposes.'

'Yes,' said Babo. 'There are many ways to be a hominid. The Red Moon is teaching us that.'

'And,' said Nemoto, 'we must anticipate meeting the Old Ones, who may be superior to us all. Then we will see how long a shadow we cast in their mighty light.'

Babo said, 'But are you content with such abstractions, Nemoto? Don't you long for home too?'

Nemoto shrugged. 'My home is gone. One day there were eight billion people in the sky; the next they had all vanished. The shock continues to work through my psychology. I don't welcome exploring the scar.'

The three of them sat in their small ring, soberly eating the sweet young bananas, while Workers politely scuttled to and fro, removing the discarded skins.

Reid Malenfant:

Much of the time he slept, drifting through uneasy, green-tinged dreams of the kind that had plagued him since the day he had come to this unnatural Moon. And then the dreams would merge into a fragmented wakefulness, fringed by blood and pain, with such soft transitions he couldn't have said where dream finished and reality began.

He was lying on his side – he could tell that much – with his arms and legs splayed out in front of him, like a GI Joe fallen off the shelf. He didn't even know where he was. He was surrounded by wood and earth. Some shelter, he supposed, something constructed by hands and eyes and brains, human or otherwise.

It was all very remote, as if he were looking down a long tunnel lined with brown and green and blood-red.

He supposed he was dying. Well, there wasn't a damn thing he could do about it, and he had no desire to fight it.

But if he could feel little with his busted-up body – taste nothing of the glop that was ladled into his mouth, barely sense the warm palm oil that was rubbed into his limbs – there was one thing he could still feel, one anguished pinpoint that pushed into him whenever he made out Emma's face.

Regret.

'Regret what, Malenfant?'

'Regret I'm going to die not knowing *why*.'

'You're dying because some psychopathic religious nut had you beaten to death. That's why.'

'But *why the Red Moon*? Why the Fermi Paradox –'

'Malenfant, for Christ's sake, is this the time or the place for –'

'Emma, give me a break. This is my death-bed. What other time and place is there? That damn Paradox baffled me my whole life. I thought the showing-up of this Red Moon, for sure the strangest event in human history since Joshua made the sun stand still in the sky, had to have something to do with that flaw in the universe. I guess I *hoped* it did. But . . .'

'But what?'

'It didn't work out that way. Emma, it just got more mysterious. Nemoto saw that immediately. Not only did we suddenly find that we inhabit just one of a whole bunch of universes, there are no signs of extraterrestrial intelligence in the other universes either. Not a trace. It's Fermi writ large – as if there is something wrong not just with this universe, but all our cosmic neighbours . . .'

'Malenfant, none of this matters. Not any more.'

'But it does. Emma, find the advanced guys. The ones with the light shows in the sky. That's what you've got to do. Ask *them* what the hell is going on here. Maybe they caused it. All this, the multiple realities, the wandering Moon. Maybe they even *caused* Fermi, in some way. That's what you must do, after . . .'

'After you're gone? Poor Malenfant. I know what's really bothering you. It's not that the question is unanswered. It's the idea that you won't be around when the answer comes. You always did think you were the centre of everything, Malenfant. You can't stand to think that the universe will go on without you.'

'Doesn't everybody feel that way?'

'Actually, no, not everybody, Malenfant. And you know what? The universe *will* go on. You don't have to save it. It doesn't need you to keep space expanding or the stars shining. We'll keep on finding out new stuff, visiting new places, finding new answers, even when you aren't around to make it happen.'

'Some bedside manner, babe.'

'Come on, Malenfant. We are what we are, you and I. I can't imagine us changing now.'

'I guess.'

Shadow:

She slid through the forest, stepping on roots and rocks to avoid dead leaves and undergrowth, silent save for the brush of her fur on the leaves. Her hair was fully erect, and her fungal mask seemed to glow with purpose and power.

There were three men with her. They were tense, fearful.

Shadow turned back to the men and grinned fiercely, knowing

how her teeth shone white under the hairless protuberance over her brow and cheeks. They grinned back, and they punched and slapped each other, seeking courage. The smallest and youngest, Shiver, absently sucked the forefinger of his right hand; it was a stump, the first two joints nipped off by Shadow.

Shadow moved forward once more, and the men followed.

She froze. She had heard the soft whimper of an infant – and there, again.

She roared and charged forward, crushing through low shrubbery.

A woman and child were in the low branches of a tree. They had been eating fruit; the forest floor beneath the tree was littered with bits of yellow skin. The woman was called Smile. She was in fact a sister of Termite's, an aunt of Shadow. Shadow did not know this – nor would it have made any difference if she had known.

Smile tumbled out of her tree. She landed with a roll on the forest floor, got to her feet and turned to flee. But her child, less than three years old, was still in the tree. He clung to a branch, screaming. So Smile ran back, scrambled up the tree, collected the child, and dropped back to the ground. But she had lost her advantage; now the attackers were on her.

Shadow grabbed her by the shoulders and pulled her to the ground. Shiver joined in, kicking and stamping. Stripe grabbed the infant from his mother's arms. He held the child by his feet and flailed him this way and that, slamming him against a tree trunk. The child was soon limp, and Stripe hurled him away, sending the little body spinning into a clump of undergrowth.

With grim determination, Smile fought against the odds. She twisted and bit Shiver hard on the shoulder. He howled. She managed to ram his body into Shadow and the others, momentarily reducing them to a tangle of flailing limbs.

That was enough of a break for Smile to get away. She scrambled into a fig tree. Stripe followed her. But Smile clambered around the branches, evading him, screaming. Now Shadow climbed up the tree, more stiffly than Stripe, for her lifetime of injuries and beatings had left their mark.

But as she approached, Smile made an almighty leap. She crashed into the branches of another tree, and tumbled to the ground. In an instant she was on her feet. She ran to the foliage where her child had fallen, picked up the limp body, and ran into the deeper woods.

Shiver pursued, but she was soon out of his reach. He ran back and forth across the bloodied forest floor, howling and throwing rocks and kicking at the trees, ridding himself of his desperate aggression.

Shadow fell on Stripe. She jabbered at him, and hailed blows on his head and shoulders. He huddled over, long arms protecting his head and chest.

For now Smile had been spared. But it was only the beginning.

Shadow's next target was Little Boss. She took six men with her, armed with sticks and rocks, and patrolled the forest until she found him.

Little Boss was alone, drinking from a small stream. Beside him was a pile of cobbles, suitable for making sharp new tools. When he heard Shadow's party approach, he stood straight, hair immediately erect, and snarled defiance. By this time, the newcomers' murderous aggression was well known among Little Boss's group. But when he saw how many men had come with Shadow, Little Boss turned to run.

He was built for power, not speed.

Shiver was the first to catch him, seizing his legs and throwing him to the ground. Shadow pinned him down, sitting on his head and holding his shoulders. The other men fell on Little Boss, attacking with a savagery only impeded by the fact that they got in each other's way.

At last Shadow and the men backed off. Charged with energy, fists clenched, mouths and stone tools stained by blood, the men ran to and fro, howling and pounding their weapons against tree trunks and rocks.

Little Boss remained motionless for a time. Then, uttering faint screams, he sat up. He had great gashes on his face, legs and back. He could not move one leg. The ground where he had lain was stained by blood and panic shit. He looked back at his assailants, who were capering and howling their rage. He opened his mouth, as if to cry defiance. But a great bubble of bloody mucus formed there, and his voice was a strangle. When the bubble broke, Little Boss fell back, rigid as a falling tree.

Shadow fell on the body immediately. She pulled it by its ankles out into the clearing, sat on its chest, and immediately began to slice away its flesh with a new stone cobble.

With degrees of reluctance or enthusiasm, the others joined her. Soon they were all feeding.

The miniature war was brief but savage.

Shadow's only tactic was to isolate her targets and destroy them. But it was a tactic beyond the grasp of her opponents, and it worked over and over. The women, especially if burdened by infants, were easy prey. The men were picked off one by one, always by overwhelming force.

And as Shadow's group fed day after day on fresh meat, they grew stronger, and hungrier.

It finished as Shadow watched her acolytes fall on the body of her mother. In her last moments, before they opened her chest, Termite reached out a bloody hand to Shadow, who stayed unmoved.

And then Shadow went alone into the forest to hunt down the last free man, her brother, Claw. When Shadow returned to her warmongering group, the object she clutched in her hand was his heart.

But when the opponents were annihilated, the group, filled with a rage for blood and murder, anxious for more meat, began to fall on each other.

Reid Malenfant:

He remembered how his father, on learning of his inoperable tumour, had suddenly rediscovered the Episcopalian faith of his youth. Somehow that had hurt Malenfant – as if his father, in these last months, had chosen to draw away from him. But he hadn't been about to deny his dad the comfort he sought.

It had always seemed to him that religion was a kind of bargain. You gave over your whole life, a portion of your income and half your intellect, in return for a freedom from the fear of death. Maybe it wasn't such a bad bargain at that.

But look at the Hams: Julia and the rest, these Moon-bound Neandertals, as rational and smart as any human being, just as aware of the human tragedy of death and pain and loss – and yet, it seemed, quite without the consolation of religion. But they seemed able to cope with the dreadful truth of life without hiding from it.

Well, maybe they were tougher than humans.

And what about you, Malenfant, now the black meteor is approaching at last? Don't you need comfort – forgiveness – the prospect of continued existence beyond the grave of crimson dust that will soon welcome your bones?

Too late for me now, he thought. But it doesn't seem to trouble me. Maybe I'm more like a damn Neandertal than a human.

Or maybe Emma was right: that nothing mattered so much to him about where he was going, compared to what he was escaping from.

Julia was here, her concerned, Moon-like face swimming in the gloom before his eyes. He wondered absently if it was night or day.

After a time, Emma was here. She frowned, wiped at his mouth with a scrap of leaf, and tried to give him water.

'Things to tell you.'

'You need to save your strength for drinking. Eating. All that good stuff.'

'No time.'

'If you're going to start lecturing me about Fermi again –'

'I did my best, Emma.'

'I know you did.'

'I came all the way to this damn Moon to find you. I went to the White House. I built a rocket ship.'

'That always was the kind of stuff you were good at, Malenfant.'

'Looking out for you?'

'No,' she said sadly. 'The grand gesture.'

'I found you. But I can't do anything for you.'

She looked at him, her eyes blank, oddly narrowed. 'But was that ever the idea?'

'What else?'

'You're a complicated man, Reid Malenfant. Your motives aren't simple.'

'Your mother thinks I've been trying to kill you for years.'

'Oh, it's not that, Malenfant. It's not me you're trying to destroy. *It's you*. It's just that I'm sometimes in the way . . .'

He frowned, deeply disturbed, remembering fragments of conversations with McCann, Nemoto. 'What are you talking about?'

'What about Praisegod Michael?'

'He was a psychopath. I had to –'

'You had to *what*? Malenfant, it wasn't your fight. What does

Praisegod Michael matter to you, or me? If you really had been devoted to the cause of getting to me, you'd have said anything he wanted to hear, to keep your skin intact. But not you. You walked into his guns, Malenfant. Deliberately. And you must have known you couldn't win. On some level you *wanted* him to do this to you.'

'I was looking for you,' he said stubbornly. 'That's why I came to the Moon.'

'I'm sorry, Malenfant. I see what I see.'

He licked his lips with a tongue that felt like a piece of wood.

'Tell me this,' she said now. 'When we were in that damn T-38 over Africa, when the Wheel appeared in the sky –'

'Yeah.'

'*You could have turned away.*'

He closed his eyes. He thought back to those moments, the glittering sky-bright seconds of the crash, when he and Emma had been suspended in the deep African light, before the enigmatic alien artefact.

. . . Yes. He remembered how the aerosurfaces had bit, just for a second. He had felt the stick respond. He knew he could turn the nose of the plane away from the Wheel. It was a chance. He didn't take it.

'Yes,' he rasped. 'And then –'

And then there had been that instant of *exuberance* – the sense of relief, of freedom, as the T-38 hurtled at the Wheel, as he felt the little jet slide out of his control, as the great blue circle had rushed towards him, and he had reached the point where he could do no more.

'How did you know? The slaved instruments –'

'I didn't need to watch instruments, Malenfant. I know you. It's just – the way you are, the kind of person you are. You could no more help it than you could stop breathing, or keep from farting in your sleep.'

'I do that?'

'I never knew when would be a good time to tell you.'

'You picked a doozy.'

'Poor Malenfant. The universe never has made much sense to you, has it? – not from the grandness of the Fermi Paradox, not yourself, on down to your relationship with your first grade teacher.'

'She really was an asshole.'

'I've always known all about you, what you are, what you could not help but become. Right from the beginning, I've known. And I went along with you anyway. What does that say about me? . . . Maybe we're alike, you and I.' She reached up and passed her hands over his eyes. 'Sleep now.'

But sleep eluded him, though regret lingered.

'Listen, Malenfant. I've decided. You're right. I'm going to go on, to track down the Daemons – *Homo superior*, whatever they are. Every time this damn Moon shifts, people suffer and die, right here on the Moon, and on all the Earths. What gives those guys the right to screw up so many lives – so many billions of lives?'

'And you intend to stop them.'

'Malenfant, I don't know what I intend. I haven't had a plan since the day I fell through that blue Wheel and found myself here, covered in shit. I'll do what you always did. I'll improvise.'

'Take care.'

'Because you won't be around to look out for me? Malenfant, if it escaped your notice, *I* rescued *you*. All *you* did was lose your spacecraft, your sole companion and all your gear, and get yourself thrown in jail. Twice.'

'Anger can make you feel good.'

'. . . Yes. Maybe that's what I need. An enemy. Somebody to be mad at. Other than you, that is.'

'Why here?'

'What?'

'Why is it finishing like this, here, now, so far from home?'

'You always did ask big questions, Malenfant. Big, unanswerable questions. Why are there no aliens? Why is there something, rather than nothing? . . .'

'I mean it. Why did I have to run into a petty thug like Praisegod? Why couldn't it have been more –'

'More meaningful? But it is meaningful, Malenfant. There's a logic. And it has nothing to do with the Red Moon or the Fermi Paradox, or any of that. It's *you*, Malenfant. It's *us*. Your whole life has a logic leading up to this place and time. It just had to be this way.'

'The universe is irrelevant. That's what you're saying.'

'I guess so . . . But there are other universes. We know that now. We've seen them. Are there other destinies for us, Malenfant? . . . *Malenfant!*'

The tunnel was long now, and filling with an oily darkness. Her face was like a distant beacon, a point of light like a star in a telescope, and he struggled to see her. There was a dim awareness of hands working his body, hands pounding at his chest, heavy hands, not human.

The light went out, the last light.

Soft lips brushed his brow, gentle as a butterfly's wings, yet the most vivid event in all the collapsing universe.

Enough, he thought, gratefully, fearfully.

Manekatopokanemahedo:

It was time for the Mapping to the crater that promised to reveal the secrets of the world engine.

The people stood in a rough circle at the centre of the platform. The yellow floor was bare again, the temporary structures it had borne unravelled, spacetime allowed to heal. The great turning Map of the Red Moon had been folded away also, having served its purpose. There was nothing left but the platform, and its cargo of people.

Beyond there was only the unmanaged forest, where, perhaps, curious eyes gazed out at the creatures they had learned to call Daemons.

Manekato sought out Nemoto. The little hominid stood alone, ignored by the rest. She wore her much-repaired blue coverall, and over her shoulder she bore the bag of parachute fabric that contained her few artefacts.

Manekato knew that it would serve no purpose to tell Nemoto that possessions were meaningless, for anything desired could be reproduced at will, over and over, Mapped out of the raw stuff of the universe itself. In this, oddly, Manekato's kind had much in common with the more primitive hominids here. The Hams and Runners would manufacture tools for a single use and then discard them, without sentiment or longing. Perhaps Manekato shared with them some deep sense of the unstinting bounty of the universe – there would always be another rock to make a hand-axe – an intuition that Nemoto, caught between the two, coming from a culture of acquisition and limits, could never share.

Manekato sighed, aware of the drift of her thinking. As always, just as Without-Name had complained, too many philosophical ruminations! – Enough, Mane. It is time to act.

She took Nemoto's hand; it lay against her own, tiny and white and fragile. '*Are you ready?*'

Nemoto forced a smile. '*I have been fired across space by a barely controlled explosion devised by primitives. By comparison you are masters of space and time. I should feel confident in your hands.*'

'*But you don't.*'

'*But I don't.*'

Manekato said gently, '*A Mapping is only a matter of logic. You are a creature of logic, Nemoto; I admire that in you. And in the working-out of logic there is nothing to fear.*'

'*Yes,*' Nemoto said softly. But her hand tightened in Manekato's.

In due course, the Mapping was expressed.

Hand in hand, the people and their Workers – and one frightened *Homo sapiens* – drifted upwards from the platform. The great shield of Adjusted Space folded away beneath them, leaving a disc of light-starved, barren, crushed land. But Manekato knew that the denuded patch would soon be colonized by the vigorous life forms here, and she felt no guilt.

Then the Mapping's deep logic worked into her bones, and she was smeared over the sky.

She hung among the stars, suspended in a primal triumvirate of bodies: Earth, sun and Moon, the only bodies in all the universe that showed as more than a point of light to a naked human eye. But this was not Nemoto's Earth, or her sun; and it was nobody's Moon. How strange, she thought.

She had no body, and yet she was aware of Nemoto's hand in her own.

'*Nemoto?*'

'*. . . How can I hear you?*'

'*It doesn't matter. Can you see the Red Moon?*'

'*I see it all at once! – but that is impossible. Oh, Mane . . .*'

'*Try not to understand. Let the logic guide you.*'

'*But it is a world. It is magnificent,*' Nemoto said. '*It seems absurd, grandiose, to suppose that this is a mere cog in some vast machine.*'

It took Manekato a moment to secure the translation of 'cog'. '*Look at the stars, Nemoto.*'

'*I can't see them. The sun dazzles me.*'

'*You can see them if you choose,*' Manekato said gently.

'. . . *Yes*,' Nemoto said at length. '*Yes, I see them. How wonderful.*'

'*Are they the same stars as shine on your Earth?*'

'*I think so. And they are just as silent. Are we alone in all the human universes, Manekato?*'

'*Perhaps.*' She glared at the unchanging stars. '*But if we are alone, the stars have no purpose save what they can offer humanity. My people have sat in their Farms for two million years,*' Manekato said, '*a vast desert of time we could have spent cultivating the sky. Long enough, Nemoto. When this is over – Ah. I think –*'

And then the Mapping was done.

The platform coalesced, as spacetime adjusted itself for the convenience of the expedition. People moved here and there, speaking softly, trailed by Workers. Few of them showed much interest in their new environs; already the first shelters were coalescing, sprouting from the platform like great flat fungi.

Once again Manekato found herself injected into a new part of the Red Moon.

This place was bright, more open than the forest location. And she could smell ocean salt in the air. To the east, the way the gentle, salt-laden breeze came, the land rose, becoming greener, until it reached a crest that was crowned by a line of trees. As she studied the ridge of rock, she saw how it curved away from her. It was the rim of a crater. To the west was a broad plain of rock and crimson dust, all but barren. In the far distance, beyond a rippling curtain of heat haze, hominids ran across the plain. They moved silently and without scent, like ghosts.

Nemoto had slumped to the ground. She peered into her bag, rummaging through its contents, as if unable to believe that a Mapping could be completed without losing some key piece of her battered and improvised equipment.

Babo came to Manekato. 'Interesting. She behaves like an infant after her first Mapping. But then we arrive in the world *knowing* that reality has certain properties. Deep in our hind brains, the parts we share with these sub-human hominids and even more ancient lines, we store the deep intuition that a thing is either *here* or *there*, that it either exists or it does not – it cannot spontaneously leap between the two states. And Mapping violates all that. Perhaps we should admire Nemoto for keeping her sanity.'

'Yes.' Manekato rubbed his head fondly. 'For now our companions are all too busy rebuilding their houses to have much to complain about. Shall we investigate what we have come so far to see?'

He raised his hand, preparing to execute another short-range Mapping.

She grabbed his arm. 'No. Renemenagota was a monster. But I have come to believe that some of her intuition was sound.' Deliberately she walked forward, knuckles and feet working confidently, until she had stepped off the platform and onto the raw native ground. She scraped at the dirt, and clouds of crimson dust drifted into the air. Soon her feet and lower legs were stained a pale pink.

Babo grinned, showing white teeth. 'You're right, Mane. We are creatures designed for walking. Let us walk.' He jumped off the platform, landing with hands and feet flat, evoking more billows of dust.

Side by side they loped away from the compound, and began to scale the wall of the crater.

Shadow:

The Nutcracker-woman was eating her way through a pile of figs. A child played at her feet, rolling and scrabbling in dead leaves. The woman was about the same height as one of the Elf-folk, and she was covered in similar black-brown hair. But her belly seemed swollen compared to an Elf's – it housed a large stomach capable of fermenting her low-quality feed – and her head was a sculpture of bone, with a great crested ridge over the top of her skull, and immense cheekbones to which powerful muscles were anchored.

A rock hurtled out of the surrounding foliage. It slammed into the trunk of the fig with a rich hollow noise, then fell to the earth.

The Nutcracker-woman screeched and scrambled back. She stared at the fallen stone. At last, cautiously, she poked it with one finger, as if it were a living thing, a bat that had stunned itself on the tree. But the stone lay still, unresponsive.

And now a stick came spinning from another part of the foliage.

The Nutcracker-woman got to her feet, gathered up her infant, and looked about suspiciously, sniffing the air with her broad, dirty nostrils. She took a step away from the fig tree.

Shadow struck.

Manekatopokanemahedo:

The ground rose steadily.

Manekato could feel a layer of hard, compact rock beneath a thin skim of dust. Green things grew here, grass and shrubs and even a few low trees, but they struggled to find purchase. It was dry; there was no sign of the springs that sometimes could be observed bubbling from the shattered walls of craters. And, though the rise of the slope was steady, it was not becoming noticeably steeper.

The morphology of this formation was like no other impact crater or volcanic caldera she had encountered. The rim of a crater this size should be more sharply defined: a circular ridge, perhaps eroded into hillocks, with a splash plain of rubble and ejecta beyond. There was none of that here; the 'crater' was just an upraised blister erupting from an empty plain.

She glanced at Babo. She saw his mouth was working as he studied the rock, the vegetation, the dust, thinking, analysing.

Babo saw her looking, and grinned. 'I know what you're thinking,' he said. '*Artificial.* But then, we know this Red Moon is a thing of artifice, and we suspect this crater may be the key to its secrets. Why should we expect anything but artifice here, of all places?'

The climb had already been long, and Manekato halted and rested her weight on her clenched knuckles. Babo raised a handful of crimson dust and let it drift off in the air; she could smell its rich iron tang, and some of it stuck to the sweat-soaked palm of his hand.

She glanced to the west, over the landscape from which they had climbed. The Adjusted Space platform nestled at the foot of this slope, a bright splash, oddly ugly. Beyond it a plain of crimson dust stretched away, its colour remarkably bright, marked by the pale green of vegetation clumps. The horizon of this small world curved noticeably, a smeared band of muddy grey. The sky was a dome littered by high clouds, and to the west she saw the dingy stain of volcanic dust streaking the air.

It was not a spectacular view, but something in its sweep tugged at her imagination. If she were anywhere on her Earth she would see the work of people, and it had never before struck her quite how claustrophobic that could be. *This* was an empty, unmade land.

Babo pointed. 'Look. Down there.'

She saw that near the foot of the crater wall a group of hominids were working their way through the sparse coating of vegetation towards a fig tree. She thought they were Elves, the small, gracile creatures Nemoto called *Australopithecines*. They moved with stealth, and they approached the tree from several directions, surrounding it.

'I think they are hunting something,' Babo said. '. . . Ah. Look, there. Under the tree. It is another hominid.'

Manekato saw it now: a burly black-furred form, with a bony, crested skull and distended belly, this was the alternate variant of Australopithecines called a Nutcracker. This hominid had swollen, milk-laden breasts: a female. An infant huddled close to this mother.

The Elves crept closer.

Manekato murmured, 'Must this world see more sentience dissipated needlessly?'

'It is not our affair, Mane,' Babo said gently. 'They are only animals.'

'No,' she said softly.

Shadow:

The Elf-folk charged into the clearing.

The Nutcracker-woman squealed, dropped her child, and scrambled up the fig tree for safety. The child tried to climb after her, but her hands and feet were small and poor at grasping, and she fell back again.

Shadow was the first to grab the infant.

Shiver had the temerity to attempt to snatch a limb of the infant for himself; they might have torn it apart between them. But Shadow pulled the infant to her chest, in a parody of parental protectiveness, and bared her teeth at Shiver.

The Nutcracker-folk mother dropped out of her tree, screaming her rage, mouth open to show rows of flat teeth. Nutcracker-folk were powerfully built, and were formidable opponents at close quarters. She charged at Shadow.

But Stripe lunged forward. His big bulk, flying through the air, knocked her flat. But the Nutcracker-woman wrapped her big arms around Stripe's torso and began to squeeze. Bones cracked, and he howled.

Now more of the men threw themselves at the Nutcracker-woman. Shadow saw that some of them had erections. This was the first time they had hunted one of the Nutcracker-folk. The men had grown accustomed to using the Elf-women of the forest before killing them. Perhaps this Nutcracker-woman, when subdued, would provide similar pleasure.

Shadow took the Nutcracker infant by her scrawny neck and held her up. Her short legs dangled, and huge eyes in a small pink face gazed at Shadow. But she could never be mistaken for the child of an Elf; the exotic bony ridges of her skull saw to that.

Shadow opened her mouth, and placed the child's forehead between her lips.

Manekatopokanemahedo:

As the Nutcracker mother fought for her life, as the wild-looking Elf-woman, battered and scarred, lifted the helpless infant by its neck, Manekato raised her head and roared in anguish.

Shadow:

. . . And there was a flash of bright white light, and searing pain filled her head.

When Shadow could see again, the men were lying on the ground, some clutching their eyes, as dazzled and shocked as she was.

Of the Nutcracker mother and child there was no sign.

The men sat up. Stripe looked at Shadow. There was no prey, no meat. Stripe bared his teeth and growled at her.

Manekatopokanemahedo:

Babo touched Manekato's shoulder. 'You should not have done that,' he said regretfully.

'The Nutcracker-woman *knew*, Babo. She knew the pain she would endure if she lost her infant. Perhaps the child itself knew.'

'Mane –'

'No more,' she said. 'No more suffering, of creatures who understand that they suffer. Let that be the future of this place.'

One by one the scattered Elves were clambering to their feet. Still rubbing their eyes, they stumbled back towards the plain – all but one, the woman who had captured the infant. She stood as tall as she could on the rocky slope, gazing up in suspicion. Manekato and Babo were well sheltered by the trees here, and the creature could surely suspect no causal connection between Manekato and her own defeat anyhow. But nevertheless the Elf howled, baring broken teeth to show pink gums, and she hurled a rock as far as she could up the slope.

Then she turned and loped away, limping, her muscles working savagely even as she walked.

Manekato shuddered, wondering what, in this creature's short and broken life, could have caused such anguish and anger.

Babo sat on his haunches. 'An Air Wall,' Babo said. 'We will erect an Air Wall to exclude unwelcome hominids, and other intruders. We will move the platform inside the cordon.'

'Yes . . .'

'No more blood and pain, Mane.'

They turned, and began to clamber further up the crater wall.

It was not long before they had reached the summit of the crater rim wall – and found themselves facing a broad plateau. A thin breeze blew, enough to cool Manekato's face, and to ruffle her fur. The rock here was crimson-red, like a basalt or perhaps a very compact and ancient sandstone. It was bare of vegetation and very smooth, as if machined, and covered by a hard glaze that glistened in the sun's weak light. There was little dust here, only a few pieces of scattered rock debris.

It was as if the crater had been filled in. 'I don't remember this from the Mapped image,' Babo said, disturbed.

Manekato dug her fingers into the fur on his neck. 'Evidently we have limits.'

'But it means we don't know what we will find, from now on.'

'Isn't that a good thing? Isn't that why we came? Come, brother, let us walk, and let us remember our humility.'

They walked forward, for perhaps a mile. And then they came to a circular pit, geometrically perfect. It was only yards across. Light leaked out of it, trapped by dust motes, a shaft that reached dimly to the sky.

Manekato's imagination quailed. She reached for Babo's hand, reluctantly reminded of how she had guided Nemoto through the strangeness of the Mapping.

Babo grinned at his sister. 'This is strange and frightening – perhaps it is our turn to be humbled now – but I am sure we will find nothing that will not yield to the orderly application of science.'

'Your faith is touching,' she said dryly.

He laughed.

'But it is not time to approach it yet,' she said.

'No. We must study it.'

'Not just that.' They regarded each other, sharing a deep instinctive wisdom. 'This is not for us alone, but for all hominids.'

'Yes,' he said. 'But how long must we wait?'

'I think we will know . . .'

There was a blue flash, painfully bright, that seemed to fill Mane's head; it reminded her uncomfortably of the punishment she had imposed on the Elf-folk.

She raised her head. '. . . Ah. Look, Babo.'

In the sky swam a new world. It looked like a vast ball of steel. Its atmosphere seemed clear, save for streaks and whorls of cloud. But beneath the cloud there was no land: not a scrap of it, no continents or islands, nothing but an ocean that gleamed grey, stretching unbroken from pole to pole. There weren't even any polar caps to speak of: just crude, broken scatterings of pack ice, clinging to this big world's axes. The only feature away from the poles was a glowing ring of blood-red, a vast undersea volcano, perhaps. And here and there she saw more soot-black streaks of dust or smoke, disfiguring the world ocean; drowned or not, this was a geologically active world.

It was a startling, terrifying sight – Manekato's hind brain knew from five million years of observation that things in the sky weren't supposed to change suddenly, arbitrarily – and she tried not to cower.

'It is a new Earth,' Babo said thinly. 'So we have completed a transition, riding this rogue Red Moon. How interesting.'

'Yes.' She clutched her brother's hands. Despite his cool words, he was trembling. 'And now we are truly of this world, Babo.'

It was true. For Banded Earth, Manekato's Earth, had gone.

Emma Stoney:

With Joshua, Mary and Julia, Emma walked south, towards the place where – as the Hams put it – the wind touched the ground.

Emma was pretty much toughened up by now. So long as she avoided leg ulcers, or getting tangled up in lianas or bramble, and the snakes and the multitude of insects that seemed to target any bare flesh like heat-seeking missiles, she was able to maintain a steady plod, covering miles and miles each day, across desert or semi-scrub or savannah or even through denser forest.

The Hams had more trouble. Their sheer strength vastly exceeded her own, but long-distance walking was alien to their physiques. They looked awkward as they barrelled along, and after a couple of days she could see how they suffered aches in the hips and knees of their bow legs, and the low arches of their great flat feet. Also, she suspected, such sedentary creatures as these must suffer a deeper disturbance as they dragged themselves across the landscape, far from any settled community. But, though they moaned wordlessly and rubbed at the offending parts of their anatomies, they never complained, not to her or each other.

The days were long and hot, and the nights, spent under the crudest of lean-tos, cold and cruelly uncomfortable. The Hams seemed capable of sleeping wherever they lay down, their great muscled bodies tensed and hard even in their sleep, like marble sculptures. But Emma had to work hard to get settled, with bits of parachute silk wrapped around her, and socks and vests bundled into a ball under her head.

Much of this stuff was Malenfant's.

She had forced herself to take everything from him that might prove useful, even the little lens that had found its way from her hands to his. It wasn't sentiment – sentiment would have driven her to bury the stuff with him – but a question of seeking advantages that might prolong her own survival. Not that there was much left, even though Malenfant had come to this Red Moon as part of a purposeful expedition, unlike her own helpless tumble through the Wheel. Idiot, Malenfant.

Anyhow, each night she immersed her face in the ragged bits of Malenfant's clothing, seeking the last traces of his scent.

Day after day, they walked. The Hams never wavered in their course, each clumsy step directed by a wordless navigation.

It occurred to Emma to wonder how people who moved house less often than empires rose and fell on Earth were able to find their way across such challenging distances. She tried to discuss this with Julia. But Julia was unforthcoming. She shrugged her mighty shoulders. 'Lon' time. People come, people go. This way, tha'. See?'

No, Emma didn't see. But maybe it was something to do with their long Neandertal timescales – far longer than any human.

The Hams, squatting in their caves and huts, made nothing like the seasonal or annual congregations associated with human communities. But there had to be occasional contacts even so, for example when outlying hunting parties crossed each other's paths, or maybe when a group was forced to move by some natural disaster, a cave flood or a land slip.

And such was the static nature of the Ham world that even very occasional contacts – not even once a generation – would suffice to keep you up to date. Once you knew that Uncle Fred and Aunt Wilma lived in those limestone caves two days' hike west of here, you could be absolutely sure that they would always be there. And so, over generations, bit by bit, from one small clue after another, the Hams and their forefathers built up a kind of map of the world around them. The Ham world was a place of geological solidity, the locations of their communities as anchored as the positions of mountains and rocks and streams, shifting only with the slow adjustments of climate.

It was an oddly comforting world-view, filled with a certain calm and order: where nothing ever changed much, but where each person had her own place in the sun, along with every rock and stream. But it wasn't a human world-view. *People rooted like trees* . . . Though she struggled to understand, it was beyond her imagination.

And of course she might be quite wrong. Maybe the Hams worked on infra-sound like the elephants, or on telepathy, or astral projection. She didn't know, and as Julia was unable to answer questions

Emma was barely able to frame, she guessed she never was going to know.

And anyhow, after the first few days' walk, the direction they were all travelling became obvious even to her. Far to the south a column of darkness reached up to the sky: not quite straight, with a sinuous, almost graceful curve. It was a permanent storm, tamed, presumably, by some advanced technology she couldn't even guess at.

It was, of course, the fortress of *Homo superior*, whoever and whatever they were.

The Hams plodded on, apparently unaffected by this vision. But when the twister's howling began to be audible, banishing the deep silences of the night, Emma found it hard to keep up her courage.

The weeping came to her in the night.

Or in the morning when she woke, sometimes from dreams in which she fled to an alternate universe where she still had him with her.

Or, unexpectedly, during the day as they walked or rested, as something – the slither of a reptile, the chirp of an insect, the way the sunlight fell on a leaf – reminded her unaccountably of him.

She knew was grieving. She had seen it in others; she knew the symptoms. It wasn't so much that she was managing to function despite her grief; rather, she thought, this unlikely project to go challenge *Homo superior* was something to occupy the surface of her mind, while the darker currents mixed and merged beneath. Therapy, self-prescribed.

The Hams seemed to understand grief. So they should, she thought bleakly; their lives were harder than any human's she had known, brief lives immersed in loss and pain. But they did not try to soothe her or, God forbid, cheer her up.

There is no consolation, they seemed to be telling her. The Hams had no illusion of afterlife or redemption or hope. It was as if they were vastly mature, ancient, calm, compared to self-deluding mayfly humans, and they seemed to give her something of their great stolid strength.

And so she endured, day by day, step by step, approaching the base of that snake of twisting air.

* * *

It didn't surprise Emma at all when the Hams, with the accuracy of expert map-readers, walked out of the desert and straight into an inhabited community.

It was a system of caves, carved in what looked like limestone, in the eroded rim wall of what appeared to be a broad crater. The upper slopes were coated thinly by tough grass or heather, but the sheltered lower valleys were wooded. And the crater was at the very bottom of that huge captive twister, which howled continually, as if seeking to be free.

As she approached she made out the bulky forms of Hams, wrapped in their typical skin sheets, coming and going from scattered cave mouths that spread high up the hillsides.

Emma could see the advantages of the site. The cave mouths were mostly north-facing, which would maximize the sunlight they captured and shelter them from the prevailing winds. She suspected the elevated position of the caves was a plus too. Maybe the migration paths of herd animals came this way. Hams preferred not to have to go too far to find their food; sitting in their caves, gazing out over the broken landscape around the crater, all they would have to do was wait for their food supply to come their way.

. . . But that wind snake curled into the air above their heads, strange, inexplicable, filling the air with its noise – even if it didn't disturb so much as a dust grain. You'd think it would bother the Hams. She saw no sign that it did.

Emma and her companions walked to the foot of the crater wall, and began to clamber up. The adults glanced down at their approach, but turned away, incurious.

The first person who showed any interest in them was a child: stark naked, a greasy bundle of muscle and fat no more than three years old, with one finger lodged in his cavernous nostril. This little boy stared relentlessly at Emma and followed her, but at a safe distance of a yard or so; if she tried to get closer he backed away rapidly until his buffer of safety was restored. Ham children were much more like human children than their adult counterparts. But Ham kids grew fast; soon they lost the open wonder of youth, and settled into the comfortable, stultifying conservatism of adulthood.

She stepped into the mouth of the largest cave. The noise of the whirlwind was diminished. The sun was bright behind them, and Emma, dazzled, peered into the gloom.

The walls were softened and eroded, as if streaked with butter. There was a powerful stink of meat, coming from haunches and skins stacked at the back of the cave. The place was not designed for the convenience of people, she saw; the roof was so low in places that the Hams had to duck to pass, and crude lumps of rock stuck out awkwardly from the walls and floor. She recognized the usual pattern of Ham occupation: a floor strewn thick with trampled-down debris, an irregular patchwork of hearths. The roof was coated with soot from innumerable fires, and the walls at head height and below were worn away and blackened by the touch of bodies, generation on generation of them. This place had been lived in a *long* time.

Emma found a piece of wall that seemed unoccupied. She dumped her pack and sat down in the dirt.

A woman approached the travellers. Bent, her hair streaked with white, a tracery of scars covering her bare arms, she looked around eighty, but was probably no older than thirty-five or forty. She began to jabber in a guttural language Emma did not understand, with no discernible traces of English or any other human language. Julia seemed uncertain how to reply, but Mary and Joshua answered confidently. Neither party seemed ill at ease or even surprised to see the other.

Julia came to Emma.

Emma said, 'So can we stay?'

Julia nodded, a *Homo sap* gesture Emma knew she affected for her benefit. 'Stay.'

With relief Emma leaned back against the creamy, cool wall of the cave. She opened her pack and dug out her parachute silk blanket and a bundle of underwear to use as a pillow. The ground here, just crimson dust, much trodden and no doubt stuffed with the bones of Ham grandmothers, was soft by comparison with what she had become used to; soon she felt herself sliding towards sleep.

But she could hear the howl of that tame whirlwind, relentless, unnatural, profoundly disturbing.

She spent a full day doing nothing but letting her body recover, her head become used to the sights and sounds and smells of this new place.

Right outside the cave entrance, a stream of clear water worked its way through rocky crevices towards the impact-broken plain below. Its course was heavily eroded, so that it cascaded between lichen-crusted, round-bottomed pools. The people used the pools for washing and preparing food, though they drank from the higher, cleaner streams.

Emma waited until she wasn't in anybody's way. Then she drank her fill of the stream, and washed out her underwear, and spread it out to dry over the sunlit rocks.

As she tended her blistered feet and ulcerated legs, and made small repairs to her boots and underwear, she watched the hominids around her.

Her Ham companions seemed to settle in quickly, according to their nature. Mary, strong and powerful, spent happy hours wrestling with the younger men, besting them more often than not. By the end of the day she was hardening spear points in a hearth, apparently preparing for a hunt.

Julia seemed to make friends with a group of women and children who spent much of their time clustered around one hearth – she blended in so well, in fact, that Emma soon had trouble distinguishing her from her companions, as if she had been here all her life.

Joshua, a loner in his own community, was a loner here. He settled into a small, solitary cave, and Emma saw little of him. But the Hams here seemed to tolerate his eccentricities, as had his own people.

As for Emma, she was largely ignored, much as she been with her other communities of Hams. Unable to shake off a feeling of sufferance – after all, how would a Neandertal stray be treated if she wandered into a human community? – she did her best to keep out of everybody's way.

There was one old man who seemed to take a liking to her, however – *old*, meaning maybe ten years younger than she was. He was badly disfigured by a swathe of scar tissue that lapped up from where his right ear should have been to the crown of his head. She didn't have a word in common with this guy, and she couldn't ask him about his injury. But this wounded, smiling man seemed vaguely curious about her: curious enough, anyhow, to offer her meat. The meat was a prime cut, apparently from the shoulder of some animal – an antelope, maybe, but it could have been a rhino for all she knew. It was a groaning bloody slab two fingers thick and twice the size of a dinner plate. Her benefactor watched with absent interest as she rigged up a frame of sticks to cook it over the nearest fire.

It seemed he had no English name. She took to thinking of him as Scarhead.

The meat was frankly delicious, though she longed for green vegetables, gravy and a mellow Bordeaux to go with it.

The Hams worked hard, of course. But it struck her how *happy* they all seemed – or if not that, content. Evidently the game was bountiful here, the living easy; all these guys had to do was sit around and wait for the meat to come wandering past, season after season. They even had fresh running water, day and night, right outside the cave. She remembered fantasies as a child of finding Candy-land, where all the trees were chocolate and the streams lemonade, where you didn't have to work for anything, where you could take as much as you liked, just by reaching out. Was the way these people lived so different from that?

But what would humans do, she mused, if they stumbled on a situation like this?

Well, they wouldn't be satisfied with the generosity of Candy-land. They'd breed until the caves were overflowing. The hunters would start ranging farther until all the animals in the area were eaten or driven away. Then agriculture would start, with everybody forced to bend their bodies to back-breaking toil, day after day. As the population exploded the forests would be cut back, the animals decimated.

Then would come the famines and the wars.

So much for Candy-land. Maybe these Hams weren't just as smart as humans, she mused; maybe they were actually smarter.

On the third day she walked out of the caves, alone, and set off up the eroded hillside.

The rocks were broken and worn, and cut deeply by gullies, in some of which water still flowed. She found that the easiest way to make progress was to lower herself into one of the gullies and clamber up its smooth, sloping sides, taking care not to slip on moss or lichen, until the channel petered out and she had to transfer to another.

Though she was soon panting hard and sweating into her coverall, she could feel her heart and lungs pump, the muscles of her newly powerful legs tingling. You're in the best shape you've been in for years, girl.

The noise of the tame whirlwind howled ever louder. She resolutely ignored it.

Just below the summit she sat on a patch of bare rock, gathering her breath, getting the hassles of the climb out of her head. The eroded hillside, deeply punctured by its limestone gullies and caves, swept away beneath her. The sun was still low; it was maybe ten in the morning local time.

She stood and turned away from the plain. She walked up the last few paces to the crater's summit plateau, and faced the wind.

It was a wall of churning air: a cylinder, laden with dust, that must have been a couple of miles wide. It looked flat on her puny human scale, like the wall of a vast building. But it snaked into the sky, diminishing as her gaze followed it, and at its highest extremity it curled in the air, thread-like. The whole thing was streaked horizontally, like the clouds of Jupiter, by billows of crimson dust. The flow of the air seemed smooth, though here and there she saw bits of rock and vegetation, even a few snapped-off trees. But the rock at the wind's shimmering foot was worn bare.

The violence, the energy, were startling; it was like a waterfall, a rocket launch. A deep part of her mind couldn't accept that it was *controlled* by anything: the animal in her, conditioned by a million years of experience, knew that this lethal expression of nature's power was unpredictable, beyond propitiation.

Nevertheless she walked forward. After a few paces, she felt the first breath of wind, and a speckle of dust on her cheek.

When she got to within maybe a hundred paces of that dense wall of dust the air grew turbulent. She staggered but kept on, leaning into the wind to keep to a rough straight line, and the dust bit harder, stinging her mouth and eyes.

She shielded her eyes. Only maybe fifty paces to the dust. Forty-nine, forty-eight ... The air was a powerful physical presence, battering at her torso and face, whipping her hair, snatching the breath from her lungs.

And now she was inside the dust, suddenly, as if walking into a sandstorm. The dust was a thick glowing cloud around her, obscuring the sky, the rock, even the twister itself; and when she looked downwind she saw how she cast a kind of shadow in the streaming particles.

A fresh surge hit her, unexpectedly violent. She fell sideways, rolled a couple of times, and hit her head on a rock.

She lay there for a moment. Then she got to all fours on the worn-bare rock and tried crawling.

She fell again, rolled back, tried again. Her hands and the skin of her cheeks were streaked with tiny cuts, where sharp bits of rock had bitten into her. Still she kept trying.

Lacking a plan B, she tried again the next day.

And the next.

She tried wrapping herself in her parachute silk, to keep out the dust and bits of rock. She just got blown away faster. So she tied the silk tightly around herself, an outer-body garment with slits for her hands, a mask over her face. She managed to get further into that central wall of dust, maybe ten paces deep, before the sheer strength of the wind stopped her progress.

She tried crawling in, all the way. That didn't work.

The Hams watched all this, bemused.

She considered schemes with ropes and pitons and rock-hammers, where she would make a kind of ladder that she could 'climb', across the face of the barren windswept rock, all the way to the centre. But she had no rope or pitons or rock-hammers, and couldn't come up with any way of making them.

She explored the cave system, but found no way through that way.

And if she couldn't go under the twister wall, she surely couldn't go over it; it looked to her as if that tunnel of tortured air stretched all the way out of the atmosphere. (She did toy with insane schemes of retrieving Malenfant's lander and firing it up into some kind of Alan Shepard sub-orbital trajectory that would take her up and over the wall of air, and re-enter right into the eye of the storm. But – despite her various rash promises to Joshua to pilot him and the lander all the way to his mythical Grey Earth – she didn't know how to fly the lander, still less how to rig it for such a flight, still less how to land it.)

On the tenth day of trying, as she lay clinging to the rock, sucking air from dust through a sheet of muslin, somebody walked past her.

Mouth gaping, bits of 'chute silk flapping around her, she watched as a Ham man and child walked hand in hand into the teeth of the storm, blurring. Granted the Hams were stronger than she was – both of them probably, even the boy – but they weren't *that* strong. They weren't even leaning into the damn wind.

Then she noticed, just before they disappeared into grey-red dust, that their skin wraps were hanging loose around them. The churning air wasn't touching them.

She spent more days watching.

The Hams had always used the other side of the crater as part of their domain for hunting and gathering. They had trails leading that way, so ancient they were actually worn into the rock. When a Ham walked such a trail, heading for the crater's interior, she just carried on through the wall of wind and dust.

The Hams weren't the only ones.

A flock of bats flapped clumsily into the crimson mist one day, their fragile wings unaffected by the tearing air. She spotted a young deer, apparently lost, that stumbled out of the dust, gazed around with wide eyes at the world beyond, then bolted back into the wind storm. Even other hominids could make it through: notably Runners, and one Nutcracker she spotted.

But not herself – and, for some reason, not the chimp-like Elves, an association she found insulting.

She tried to interrogate the Hams. 'Julia, how come you can get through the wind and I can't?'

An intense frown creased that powerful face. 'Hams live here.' She waved her arm. '*Still* live here.'

'All right. But why am I kept out?'

A shrug.

'What is it I'm not allowed to see? Is there some kind of installation in there, a base? Are the Hams allowed to go up to it? Do you have any, umm, trade with whoever built it?'

None of this meant much to Julia. 'Funny stuff.' She waved her fingers before her face. 'Hard to see.'

Emma sighed. So the Hams might be wandering around or through some kind of fabulous *Homo superior* base without even looking at it, interested only in their perennial pursuits, perhaps not even *capable* of seeing it from out of their bony cages of conservatism.

And that, presumably, was why the Daemons let the Hams wander at will past their meteorological moat. The Hams would restrict themselves, going where they had always gone inside the crater, doing what they had always done, taking not a step beyond their self-imposed boundaries; they would not interfere with whatever projects and designs the Daemons were developing in there. Whereas noisy, curious, destructive *Homo sap* types like herself would not rest until they had barged their way into the Daemons' shining city.

Breaking this demeaning exclusion became an obsession with her.

She focused on the Hams. She kept trying their trails. She carried Ham tools and weapons as if intent on some Ham-type gathering and hunting. She tried walking in with a party of Hams, her slim form tucked into a line of their great hulking bodies. But the wind seemed to whip *through* their immense muscular forms, to grab at her and push her aside.

She pushed the deception further. She purloined some skins and wrapped herself up like a Ham. Slouching, bending her legs, she practised the Hams' powerful, clumsy gait. She let her hair grow ragged and filthy, and even smeared clay on her face, letting it dry in a hopeful imitation of a Ham's bulky facial morphology, the high cheekbones and the bony crest over the eyes.

Then, joining another foraging party, she slouched towards the wind, her gait rolling, keeping her distinctive *Homo sap* chin tucked into her chest.

The wind wasn't fooled.

Furious, she stamped back to the caves, and sought out Joshua.

'You have to help me.'

Joshua stared at her. He was ragged, filthy, sitting in a debris-strewn cave that managed to be remarkably ill-appointed, even by the Palaeolithic standards of this Red Moon.

'Wha' for?'

She sighed, forgiving him his squalor, and kneeled in the dirt before him. '*I want to know*,' she said. 'I want to know what they are doing in there – and who *they* are. If they are responsible for dragging this Moon around the realities – I mean, for changing the sky – I want to know why they are doing it. And to make them understand the damage they are causing, the suffering. Do you see?'

He frowned at her. 'Deal,' he said simply.

'Yes,' she said wearily. 'Yes, we had a deal. We still have a deal. You help me, and I'll try to help you get to the Grey Earth. Just as I promised.' God forgive me for lying, she thought.

But his eyes narrowed, almost calculating. 'Fin' a way.'

'Yes, I'll find a way. We'll go back to the lander and –'

His massive hand shot out and grabbed her wrist. The grip was painful, but she knew that he was using only a fraction of his strength, that if he chose he could probably crush her bone.

'No lies.'

He means it, she thought. He knows my kind too well. 'Okay. No lies. I'll find a way. Get me through the wind wall and I'll work on it, I'll find a way. I promise, Joshua. Please, my arm . . .'

He squeezed harder – just a little – but it was like a vice closing over her flesh. Then he released her. He sat back, baring his teeth in a wide grin. 'How?'

'How can I get through the wind wall? I've been thinking about that. Whatever controls the wind is too smart to be fooled by appearance. It's not enough that I look like a Ham. But maybe if I can learn to *think* like a Ham . . .'

Scarhead dragged a couple of haunches of meat from the back of the cave. For one brief moment the old guy looked the image of the cartoon caveman. He threw the meat down on the trampled ground, then went back into the cave to fetch tools.

Emma had once more donned her best-effort Neandertal disguise. She got to the ground gingerly, conscious of the need to keep her face rigid so as not to crack her mask of clay.

As usual, nobody showed the slightest interest in her – by now, not even the children.

The meat was, gruesomely, a couple of legs, intact from hoof to shoulder, perhaps from a horse. The limbs were already skinned, fresh, bloody, steaming slightly. Flies buzzed languidly around the exposed flesh.

Scarhead returned. He threw his handfuls of tools on the ground and sat cross-legged. He grinned, and the low morning sun made his scar tissue glisten.

She inspected the tools with absent interest. There were limestone pebbles gathered from the beds of rivers, used as chopping tools, and dark basalt blocks shaped into bi-faced hand-axes and cleavers. These were working tools, each of them heavily worn and blood-splashed.

Before she left the Earth she'd known nothing of technology like this, and if she had been confronted with this collection of pebbles and rocks she would have dismissed them as nothing but random debris. Now she knew differently. Tools like this, or the still more primitive artefacts of the Runners, had kept her alive for months.

Scarhead held out a hand-axe to her.

She took the rock, feeling its rough texture. She turned it over in her hands, testing its weight, feeling how it fit perfectly into her small human hand – for, of course, Scarhead had chosen it to suit her grip.

Now Scarhead held up a fresh lump of obsidian, hammers of bone and rock. He said bluntly, 'Copy.' He grabbed one of the horse legs, and began to saw at the joint between the scapula and humerus, between shoulder and leg. His stone blade rasped as he cut through tough tendons and ligaments.

She tried. Just manhandling the heavy limb proved a challenge to her; the joints were gruesomely stiff, the meat slippery and cold in her hands.

She sighed. 'Could I see the vegetarian menu?'

Scarhead just stared at her.

No smart-ass H sap jokes, Emma; today you're a Neandertal, remember?

She kept trying. She worked the knife into the meat until she had exposed the tendons beneath the shoulder. The meat, cold and slippery against her legs, was purple-red and marbled with fat; it was coldly dead, and yet so obviously, recently attached to something alive.

Turning the stone tool in her hand, she sought to find the sharpest edge. She managed to insert her blade into the joint and sawed at the tough ligaments, scraping them until they gave, like tough bits of rope.

Scarhead grunted.

Surprised, she raised her hand. The tool's edge had cut into her flesh, causing long straight-line gashes that neatly paralleled the lifeline on her palm. She hadn't even felt the cuts happen – but then the blade on a stone knife could be sharper than a metal scalpel; it could slide right into you and you'd never know it. She saw belatedly that Scarhead's working hand was wrapped in a hunk of thick, toughened animal skin, and a kind of apron was draped over his lap.

. . . And now the pain hit, sharp and deep like a series of paper cuts, and she yowled. She went to a stream to drench her cut palm in cold water until the slow bleeding had stopped.

Scarhead waited patiently for her, no expression she could read on his broad, battered face.

You aren't doing too well here, Emma.

She tried again. She spread a skin apron over her lap, and improvised a protective binding for her hand from a bit of tough leather. Then she resumed her work at the ligaments and tendons.

Think about the work, Emma. Think about the feel of the stone, listen to the rasp of the tendons, smell the coagulated blood; feel the sun on your head, listen to the steady breathing of Scarhead . . .

She reached bone. Her axe scraped against the hard surface, almost jarring from her hand. She pulled the axe back and turned it over, exposing fresh edge, and began to dig deeper into the joint, seeking more tendon to cut.

A last tough bit of gristle gave way, and the leg disarticulated.

She stared, oddly fascinated, at the bone joints. Even Malenfant, who had never shown the slightest interest in biology, might have been interested at this bit of natural engineering, if he had gotten to take it apart in his own hands.

And she was still analysing. *Wrong.*

She glanced up at Scarhead. Not watching her, apparently immersed in the work, he had begun to fillet the meat from the shoulder joint he was holding. Emulating his actions, she did the same. She dug her blade into the gap between meat and bone, cutting the muscle that was attached to the bone surface. She soon found the easiest way was to prop the scapula on the ground between her legs, and pull at the muscle with one hand to expose the joint, which she cut with the other hand. She got into a rhythm of turning the axe in her hand, to keep exposing fresh edge.

She tried not to think about anything – not Earth, Malenfant, the wind wall, the destiny of mankind, her own fate – nothing but the feel of the sun, the meat in her hand, the scrape of stone on bone.

For brief moments, as the hypnotic rhythms of the butchery tugged at her mind, she got it.

It was as if *she* was no longer the little viewpoint camera stuck behind her eyes; it was as if her consciousness had dispersed, so that *she* was her working hands, or spread even further to her tool, the flesh and bone she worked, and the trails and bits of forest and scrub and the crater walls and the migrating herds and all the other details of this scrap of the world, a scrap inhabited by the Hams, unchanging, for generation upon generation upon generation.

. . . Her hands had finished the butchery. On one side of her, a flensed shoulder-bone; on the other, a neat stack of filleted meat.

She looked into cavernous eyes, feeling the sun's heat, feeling the pleasurable ache of her arms and hands. She forgot the name she had given him, forgot her own name, forgot herself in his deep stare.

Shadows beside her. It was Joshua, and Julia . . . No, no names; these people simply were who they were, everybody in their world knew them, without the need for labels. She took their hands and let herself be raised to her feet.

The Hams led her up the hillside, away from the caves, towards the place where the unnatural wind moaned.

It was not like a dream; it was too detailed for that. She felt the sharpness of every grain of red dust under her feet, the lick of the air on her cheeks, the salty prickle of sweat on her brow and neck, the sharp, almost pleasant ache of her cut palm. It was as if a veil had been removed from her eyes, stops from her ears and nose, so that the colours were vivid and alive – red earth, green vegetation, blue sky – and the sounds were clear, grainy, loud, their footsteps crunching into the earth, the hiss of wind over the scrubby grass that clung to these upper slopes. It was like being a child again, she thought, a child on a crisp summer's Saturday morning, when the day was too long for its end to be imagined, the world too absorbing to be analysed.

Was *this* how it was to be a Neandertal? If so, how – enviable.

They had reached the crest of the crater-rim hill. They began to walk forward, in a line, hand in hand.

That wall of air spread across the land before her, a cylinder so wide it looked flat. She felt a lick of wind, touching her cheek, disturbing her hair, the first prickle of dust on her skin. She dropped her head, concealing her *Homo sap* protruding chin, and walked steadily on. She concentrated on the sun, the texture of the ground, the bloody iron scent of the dusty air.

Anything but the wind.

They went into the dust. She walked steadily, between her Ham friends, immersed in crimson light. She was ten paces inside the dust. Then fifteen, past her previous record. Twenty, twenty-one, twenty-two . . .

Maybe it was the counting. Hams did not count.

The wind hit her like a train.

Her hands were wrenched from the Hams' grip. She was lifted up off the ground, flipped on her back, and slammed down again.

The light dimmed to a dull Venusian red. Suddenly she couldn't see Julia or Joshua, nothing but a horizontal hail of dust particles and bits of rock, looming out of infinity as if she were looking into a tunnel. If she turned her head into the wind she could barely breathe.

Another gust – she was rolled over – she scrabbled at the ground. And then she was lifted up, up into the air, limbs flailing, like a cow caught by a Midwest tornado. She was immersed in a shell of whirling dust; she couldn't see ground or sky, couldn't tell how far away the ground was, couldn't even tell which way up she was. But she could tell she was falling.

She screamed, but her cry was snatched away. '*Malenfant!* –'

She was on her back. She could feel that much. But there was no wind: no hot buffeting gusts at her face, no sting of grit on her exposed skin. Nothing but a remote howl.

She opened her eyes.

She was looking up into a dark tunnel, like gazing up from the depths of a well, towards a circle of cloud-scattered blue sky. The light was odd, greyish-red, as if shadowed. Was she back in the caves? She tried to sit up. Pain lanced through her back and stomach.

A face loomed above her, silhouetted by the patch of bright sky, backlit by diffuse grey light. 'Take it easy. We don't think any bones are broken. But you are cut and bruised and badly winded. You may be concussed.' The face was thin, capped by a splash of untidy black hair. Emma stared at an oddly jutting chin, weak cheekbones, an absurd bubble skull with loose scraps of hair. It was a woman's face.

It came into focus. A *human* woman.

The woman frowned. 'Do you understand me?'

When she tried to speak Emma found her mouth full of dust. She coughed, spat, and tried again. 'Yes.'

'You must be Emma Malenfant.'

'Stoney,' Emma corrected automatically. 'As if it makes a difference now.' She saw the woman was wearing a faded blue coverall, scuffed and much-repaired, with a NASA meatball logo on her chest. 'You're Nemoto. Malenfant's companion.'

Nemoto regarded her gravely, and with a start Emma recognized for the first time the Oriental cast of her features. A lesson, she thought wryly. Compared to the distance between humans and other hominids, the gap between our races really is so small as to be unnoticeable.

'. . . Malenfant is dead,' she said hesitantly. 'I'm sorry.'

She thought she saw hope die, just a little, in Nemoto's blank, narrowing eyes.

'I don't know how well you knew him. I –'

'We have much to discuss, Emma Stoney.'

'Yes. Yes, we do.'

Nemoto slid an arm under Emma's back and helped Emma sit up. Everything worked, more or less. But her belly and back felt like one immense bruise, and she was having trouble breathing.

She was sitting on crimson dirt. A few paces away from her, waiting patiently, she saw Joshua and Julia. She grinned at them, and Julia gave her an oddly human wave back.

Beyond them was strangeness.

A yellow floor sprawled over the ground – seamless and smooth, obviously artificial. There were buildings on this floor, rounded structures the same colour and apparently made of the same material, as if they had grown seamlessly from out of the floor, as if the whole thing was a sculpture of half-melted Cheddar cheese.

Hominids were moving among the structures. They walked on feet and knuckles, big and bulky, too remote for her to make out details. Like gorillas, she thought, like the creature she had seen leaving the Zealot stockade with the ragtag army. Could they be Daemons?

She looked over her shoulder. She saw that wall of wind, streaked with dirt and ripped-up vegetation. But now she could see how it curved inwards, *around* her – confining her here, not excluding her. And when she looked up it stretched into the sky, making a twisting, slowly writhing tunnel.

She was inside the twister.

'Ha!' she said, and she punched the air. 'Fooled 'em, by God.'

Nemoto was frowning. There was an edge about her, a tension that seemed wound tight. 'It was not like that. You did not "fool" anybody. The Daemons watched your approach. They watched as you plastered clay on your face and butchered your meat –'

'How did they watch me?'

Nemoto waved at the air. 'They can see what they like, go wherever they want to, at a gesture. They call it Mapping.'

'I don't understand.'

Nemoto leaned down, thrusting her face at Emma, anger sparking. 'Your efforts to deceive them were comical. Embarrassing. They could not have succeeded. *It was me*, Emma Stoney. I was the one who practised deceit in the end; I convinced them to admit you. I tried to spin your absurd stunt into an act of true cognition. I told them that deceit is a sign of a certain level of intelligence. But I said you were aware of the shallowness of your deceit. You *intended* to demonstrate an ability to bluff and counter-bluff, thus showing multiple levels of cognition which –'

Emma raised a hand. 'I think I get it.' Holding Nemoto's hand, she pulled herself to her feet. 'I wish I could say I was so smart. Intentionally, anyhow. Umm, I guess it's appropriate to thank you.'

She heard heavy footsteps. She turned.

One of the gorilla-things was coming towards her. It – no, *she*, she had breasts – she walked using her knuckles. But she moved fast, more than a walk: it was a knuckle-sprint, a knuckle-gallop, startlingly fast for such a huge animal.

The creature must have been eight feet tall. The ground seemed to shake.

Emma felt Nemoto's hand slide into hers. 'Show no fear. Her name is Manekato, or Mane. She will not harm you.'

The Daemon stood before Emma. She straightened up, her massive black-haired bulk towering, and her hands descended on Emma's shoulders, powerful, heavy, human-like. Emma felt overwhelmed by weight, solidity, the powerful rank stench of chest-hair. She raised her hands and pressed against that black chest, pushing with all her strength against the surging muscle. Effortlessly, it seemed, the Daemon pressed closer, bringing her shining black face close to Emma's. The mouth opened, and Emma glimpsed a pink cavern and tongue, two huge spike-like upper canines, and smelled a breath sweet as milk.

Two ears swivelled towards Emma, like little radar dishes.

Then the Daemon backed off, dropping to rest her weight on her knuckles once more. She growled and hooted.

Nemoto was smiling thinly. 'That was English. You will get used to her pronunciation. Mane asks, *What is it you want?*'

'Tell her I want –'

'Tell her yourself, Emma Stoney.'

Emma faced Manekato, gazed into deep brown gorilla eyes. 'I've come here looking for answers.' She waved a hand. 'Don't you see the damage you cause?'

Mane frowned, a distinctly puzzled expression, and she peered at Nemoto, as if seeking clarification there. Just as with the Hams, Emma had the distinct and uncomfortable feeling that she wasn't even asking the right questions.

Again Nemoto had to translate for Emma. '*You think we made this. The engine that moved the world. Child, the Old Ones are far above us – so far they are as distant from me as from you. Do you not understand that?*'

Emma shuddered. But she said belligerently, 'I just want to know what is going on.'

This time, Emma made out Mane's guttural words for herself. 'We hoped you could tell us.'

That first night, Emma stayed in the shelter the Daemons had given Nemoto – despite Nemoto's obvious reluctance to share. A second bed was 'grown' inside the little shelter's main room for Emma, fully equipped with mattress, pillow and sheets; the gorilla-thing called Mane apologized to Emma for the crowding, but promised a place of her own by the next night.

Unlike the rounded, quasi-organic feel of the other structures on the disc floor, Nemoto's residence was a boxy design with rectangular doors and windows, giving it a very human feel. But, like the other structures, it seemed to have grown from the smooth, oddly warm, bright yellow substrate. It was as if the whole place was a seamless chunk of pepper-yellow plastic that had popped out of some vast mould.

But the Daemons had provided for Nemoto well. She had a bed with a soft mattress and sheets of some smooth fabric. She was given fruit and meat to eat; she even had a box the size of a microwave oven, with pretty much the same function. There were spigots for hot and cold water, a bathroom with a toilet that flushed.

Holiday Inn it wasn't, but it was close enough, Emma thought, in the circumstances. Nemoto said the flush toilet, for instance, had taken a couple of prototypes to get right.

None of this had anything to do with the way the Daemons lived their lives. They seemed to have no desire for privacy when defecating or urinating, for instance; they just let go wherever they happened to be, making sure they didn't splash the food. The magic floor absorbed the waste, no doubt recycling it for some useful purpose, and would even dispel odours. The Daemons, though, were understanding, or at least tolerant, of Nemoto's biological and cultural hang-ups.

Anyhow it suited Emma fine.

There were sanitary towels. Emma fell on these and stole as many as she could carry away.

There was coffee (or a facsimile).

There was a shower.

She luxuriated in her first hot wash for months, using soap and shampoo that didn't smell as if it had come oozing straight out of the bark of a tree. At first the water just ran black-red at her feet, as if every pore on her body was laden with crimson dirt. By the time she had washed out her hair two, three times, it began to *feel* like her hair again. She cleaned out the black grime from beneath her fingernails. She looked around for a razor, but could find none; so she used one of her stone blades, purloined from a Neandertal community many miles away, to work at her armpits.

Towelling herself dry, Emma stood by the window of Nemoto's little chalet, peering out at the Daemons' encampment.

Feeling oddly like a primatologist in a hide, she watched little knots of the huge gorilla-like creatures knuckle-walking to and fro. *H. superior* or not, they all looked alike, for God's sake. And little cartoon robots buzzed everywhere, rolling, hopping and flying. She had to remind herself that these really were creatures capable of flying between worlds, of putting on a light show in the sky to shame the aurora borealis, of *growing* a city in the jungle.

But as she watched, one of the 'gorillas' flickered out of existence, reappearing a few minutes later on the other side of the compound.

At that moment Emma knew, deep in her gut, that there was indeed nothing primitive about these shambling, knuckle-walking, hairy slabs of muscle, despite her *Homo sap* prejudices.

And it made it still more terrifying that it was not the Daemons who were responsible for moving the Moon, but another order of creatures beyond even them. She felt that she was at the bottom of a hierarchy of power and knowledge, unimaginably tall.

She hit her first soft pillow in months. Emma spent twelve hours in deep, dreamless sleep.

When she hauled herself out of bed the next day, Nemoto made her brunch (French toast, by God). But Nemoto was largely silent, volunteering little of her experiences here.

Emma, in turn, resented this silence. After all Nemoto had spent a good deal of time with Malenfant – most of his last few months alive, in fact, when Emma had been about as far from him as she could be. But Emma wasn't about to beg for scraps of information about her own damn husband.

I am not, Emma thought, going to get along easily with this woman.

Manekato came visiting. She crouched to get her eight-feet-tall bulk inside Nemoto's shelter, then sat squat on the floor, a gorilla in a too-small cage. Her accent was thick, her voice a Barry White growl. But when she spoke slowly, Emma found she understood her.

Manekato said, 'You have talked. Nemoto has shared with you what she has learned.'

Nemoto and Emma shared a glance.

Emma said, 'Actually, no.'

Mane slapped her huge thigh, apparently in frustration. 'You are the same species! You are alone here, far from home! Why can you not cooperate?'

Nemoto said easily, 'You are showing your prejudice, Manekato. You must see us as individuals. We are the same species, but that does not determine our goals – any more than you and Renemenagota had identical motivations.'

The name meant nothing to Emma.

Mane turned to Emma, her huge head swivelling. 'Very well. Em-ma? Why have you come here?'

Emma thought about that. 'I want to go home.'

Manekato said, 'I regret that is not within my gift. *I* cannot go home.'

Emma closed her eyes for a moment, letting her last sliver of hope disappear. She should have expected this, of course. If it were possible to reach Earth, Nemoto would surely have been sent there by now.

She opened her eyes and met Mane's gaze. 'Then I want to go to the centre.'

'The centre?'

'The place where everything happens.'

Nemoto grinned. 'She wants to see the world engine.'

Mane asked, 'Why?'

Emma felt angry. *Who are you to ask? It isn't yours, any more than it is human . . .* 'Because I've come this far. Because I've kept myself alive on this damn Moon that took my husband's life, and I want to know what the hell it is all for.'

'What difference would *knowing* make?'

'It just would,' Emma snapped. 'And I resent your cross-questioning.'

Mane paused. Then she said gently, 'Em-ma, how did you come here?'

'It was an accident. I, umm, fell through a portal. A Wheel, a blue circle.'

'Yes. We know of such devices. But your mate, Mal-en-fant, came here purposefully, with Nemoto.'

'He came to rescue me.'

'How is it Mal-en-fant had the technology to travel to the Red Moon? Did he invent it from scratch?'

Emma glanced at Nemoto, who showed no reaction. Mane was asking her questions to which Nemoto must already have given answers; perhaps this was some obscure test.

'No,' Emma said. 'We had travelled to our own Moon – umm, a lifeless world – long before the Red Moon showed up. The technical base was there.'

'Why did you go to this Moon? For science, for learning?'

'For politics,' Nemoto said sourly. 'For irrational purposes. For typical *Homo sapiens* reasons.'

'It wasn't just that,' Emma said, frowning. 'You don't live with an astronaut your whole life without figuring out some of the bigger picture. Manekato, we went to the Moon because we are a species that explores. We go places even when there is no immediate purpose. *Why choose this as our goal? Why climb the highest mountain? Why . . . fly the Atlantic? We choose to go to the Moon . . . because that goal will serve to organize and measure the best of our abilities and skills . . .*'

Nemoto laughed. 'President Kennedy's 1961 speech. It is a long time since I heard those words.'

'Malenfant was fond of quoting it.'

'So,' Mane said, 'you intended to live on your Moon, to colonize it.'

'Ultimately, I guess, yeah.'

'And then?'

'And then the other planets,' Emma said vaguely. 'Mars, the asteroids, the moons of Jupiter.'

'And then?'

'And then the stars, I guess. Alpha Centauri . . . You'd have been better asking Malenfant.' She studied Manekato, trying to read the expressions that passed over that broad, blue-black face. 'Every intelligent species must have the same kind of goals. Expansion, colonization. Mustn't they? Especially every intelligent variety of hominid.'

Nemoto was shaking her head. 'Not so, it seems.'

Emma was growing irritated again; she wasn't enjoying being treated as the dope of the class. 'Why are *you* here, Manekato?'

'Like you,' Mane said evenly, 'when this Red Moon appeared in our skies – and it disrupted our world as much as it did yours – we asked the question *why.*'

Emma leaned forward. 'But *why you*, Mane, rather than somebody else?'

Mane frowned. 'I came because I had no home.'

It turned out that Mane's home, which she referred to as a *Farm*, had been wiped off the face of her Earth by Red Moon tides.

'She came here because she was forced,' Nemoto said.

'You could have rebuilt someplace else.'

'There is nowhere else,' Mane said. She pulled at an ear that was all

412

but buried in thick black fur. 'It was the end of my Lineage. A Lineage that stretched back through a hundred thousand generations.' She sighed, and began to scratch at the other ear.

Emma sat, stunned. A hundred thousand generations? If each generation was, say, twenty years at minimum – why, that added up to *two million years*.

Nemoto said, 'Emma, these people are *not like us*. They are much more like the Hams. They sit on those Farms of theirs, for ever and a day. They do not covet what their neighbours possess. There is no robbery, no territorial or economic expansion, no nation, no war.'

'And if you lose your Farm –'

'If you lose your Farm, you die. Or anyhow your Lineage does.'

'That's terrible,' Emma said to Mane. 'What do they do? Sterilize you? Take your children?'

But it seemed that once again she had asked the wrong question. Mane asked blankly, '*They?*'

'Nobody has to enforce it,' Nemoto said. 'It just happens. The families let themselves die out. It is seen as a price worth paying for ecological stability. Emma, the Daemons have *evolved* this way, shaped by their cultural imperatives. Two million years, remember.'

Emma shook her head, uncomfortable under Mane's steady gaze. She felt defiant. 'Humans wouldn't live like that. We wouldn't accept it.'

Mane kept pulling her ear. 'What would you do?'

Emma shrugged. 'The family would go on. The *Mayflower* syndrome. We'd carve a place out of the wilderness –'

'But there is no wilderness,' Mane said. 'Even without war, even if you found a space not already cultivated, you would be forced to occupy a region, delineated in space, time, and energy flow, already exploited by another portion of the ecology.'

It took some time for Emma to figure that out. 'Yes,' she said. 'There is bound to be some environmental impact. But –'

'Other species would find reduced living space. Diversity would fall. And so it would go on. Soon the world would be covered from pole to pole by humans, fighting over the diminishing resources.' Mane nodded. 'Such was the ambition of Praisegod Michael. At least you are consistent.'

'The Daemons limit their numbers,' said Nemoto. 'They don't overrun their Earth. By respecting the stability of the ecosystem that provides for them they have survived for millions of years.

They even accept their short lifespans, though it would be trivial for them to do something about that.'

'A brief life burns brightly,' said Manekato.

Emma shook her head. 'I still say humans couldn't live like that.'

Nemoto said slyly, 'The Hams do. And they are *almost* human.'

'Are you saying we should live like Neandertals, in caves, wearing skins, wrestling buffalo, watching our children die young?'

Mane said, 'Are the Hams suffering?'

No, Emma thought. Actually they are happy. But her pride was hurt; she stayed silent.

Mane leaned forward, and Emma could smell her milk-sweet breath. 'The lion takes only the last deer in the herd. She does not dream of having so many cubs that the plains would be full of nothing but lions. There are simple laws. Most species figure them out; you are the exception. An ecology of a single species is not viable. A diverse, stable world would provide for you.'

Candy-land, Emma thought.

'We have a story,' Mane said. 'A mother was dying. She called her daughter. She said, "This is the most beautiful Farm in the world." And so it was. The mother said, "When I die, you will be free to act. Do with it what you will." The daughter pondered these words.

'And when the mother died, the daughter took a torch and set fire to her Farm – every bit of it, the buildings and crops and creatures.

'When asked why she had done this – for of course, without a Farm, her Lineage would be extinguished – the daughter said, "One night of glory is better than a thousand years of toil."' The big Daemon actually shuddered as she finished her tale.

'We have a similar legend,' Emma said. 'There was a warrior, called Achilles. The gods gave him a choice: a brief life of glory, or a long, uneventful life in obscurity. Achilles chose the glory.' She looked up at Mane. 'In my culture, that story is regarded as uplifting.'

Mane turned her tremendous head. 'The tale I told you is, umm, a scary story. Intended to frighten the children into proper behaviour.'

Nemoto said grimly, 'But we will go on anyhow. To the planets, the stars. If we get the chance; if we survive the human-induced extinction event that is unfolding on our Earth. Because we don't have a choice.' She eyed Manekato bleakly. 'Sure our strategy is flawed. But it has a deadly internal logic. We're stuck on this road we have chosen. We have to keep expanding, or we'll die anyhow.'

'There is that,' Mane said gently. She stood, and with startling clumsiness rammed her head against the low roof of the chalet. 'You wish to see the engine of the world. So do I, Em-ma. We will go together.'

Nemoto nodded warily. 'How? Will you Map us?'

Manekato laid a hand on Emma's scalp. It was heavy, gentle, the pads of flesh on the palm soft. 'We have found we cannot Map there. But it would not be appropriate anyway. We are all hominids together, here on this Red Moon. Let us do what hominids do. We will walk, to our destiny.'

Four of them would be travelling together: Emma, Nemoto, Manekato – and Julia, the Ham. As Emma was preparing to leave, Julia had walked out of nowhere, with every sign of staying at Emma's side until they reached whatever there was to find, at the centre of this wind-wrapped crater.

Manekato loomed over the three of them, the massive muscles of her shoulders as big as Emma's skull. 'Now we go, we four, to discover the secret of the universe.' She threw back her mighty head and laughed, a roar that rattled off the smooth-walled structures of the compound. And, without hesitation, she walked off the yellow platform floor, heading for the interior of the crater, and the forest that lay there.

The little column turned single-file and spread out. The going was easy over the dust-strewn rock, and Emma, hardened by her weeks of living rough, found it easy to keep up with Manekato's knuckle-gallop. But when she looked back she saw that Nemoto was labouring, lagging behind Emma by a hundred yards. Julia walked at her side, stolid, slow, patient, her own awkward gait endearingly clumsy.

Emma waited until Nemoto caught up. Nemoto did not look her in the eye; she plodded on, her gait showing a trace of a limp. Emma clapped her on the shoulder. 'I guess the human species isn't going to conquer the stars if we can't even walk a couple of miles, Nemoto.'

'I am not as acclimatized as you,' Nemoto said.

'Despite all that astronaut training you must have had. Whereas *I* was just thrown here on my ass from out of the blue sky –'

'Punish me if you like. Your misfortunes are not my fault.'

'Right. You came here to rescue me. Or was it just to give me somebody even worse off than I am?'

Julia moved between them. 'No' worry, Emma. I help.'

Emma grinned. 'Just throw her over your shoulder if she gives any trouble. Nemoto – even if they can't Map there, I don't understand why the Daemons haven't been to this centre before.'

'They have been studying it. They can be remarkably patient. And –'

'Yes?'

'I think they have been waiting for us.'

Emma observed, 'Nobody's carrying anything.'

Julia shrugged. 'Fores' has food. Fores' has water.'

'You see?' Nemoto glared. 'These *others* do not think as we do. Julia *knows* that the land will provide everything she needs: food, water, even raw materials for tools. It is a different set of assumptions, Emma Stoney. Just as Manekato said. *They* see the universe as essentially bountiful, a generous mother land. We see the universe as an enemy nation, to be occupied and mastered.'

'So we're inferior in every way,' Emma grumbled, resentful.

'Not that,' Nemoto said. 'But we are different. The Daemons' intellectual capacity is obvious – the rapidity of their comprehension, the richness and precision of their thinking. But they come from a world where hunters, indeed predators of any kind, cannot prosper. Even their games are cooperative, all concerned with building things.'

'What about religion? What do they believe?'

Nemoto shrugged. 'If they have a religion it is buried well, in their minds and their culture. They need not worship sublimated mothers or seeds as we do, because they control nature – at least, below the Red Moon. And without the metaphor of the seed, of renewal, they have no urge to believe in a life beyond the grave.'

'Like the Hams.'

'Yes. The Hams, Neandertals, have much more in common with the Daemons than we do. And remember this, Emma Stoney. Mane's people regard us as less intelligent than them. Save for academic interest or sentimentality, they have no more interest in *talking* to us than you would have in chatting to a Colobus monkey. This is the framework within which we must operate, no matter how hurtful to your *Homo sapiens* ego.'

They reached a patch of forest. Manekato plunged into it, seeking fruit. The others followed more slowly.

Keeping Manekato's broad back in sight, Emma stepped cautiously over a muddy, leaf-strewn ground. Roots snaked everywhere, as if put there to trip her. In some places the trees towered high. She could see the canopy, where the thick branches of each tree spread out, making an almost horizontal roof of greenery. The trunks themselves were dense with life, with lianas that looped and sagged, and ferns and orchids sprouting like underarm hair from every crevice and fork. Though it was humid and still, the moist air felt almost cool on her cheeks, as if this was fall. There was a mild, pervading stench of decaying vegetation.

A shadow flitted between the tree trunks, a round, uncertain form dimly glimpsed among the shadowy verticals.

Emma stopped dead, heart hammering.

Manekato was a massive, reassuring form at her side. 'It is a Nutcracker. A vegetarian hominid which –'

'I know about Nutcrackers.'

Manekato peered curiously into her face. 'I sense fear.'

Emma found her breath was shallow; she tried to control it. 'Does that surprise you?'

'You are already far from home. Without prior preparation, without aid, you have survived in this place for many weeks. What more is there for you to fear now?'

'Humans aren't creatures of the forest, like the Elves or the Nutcrackers. We are creatures of the open. Like the Runners.'

'Ah.' Apologetically Manekato reached for her and, with thick, gentle, leather-skinned fingers, she probed at Emma's shoulders, elbows, hips. 'It is true. You are designed for steady walking, for running, over long distances. You sweat – unlike me – so that you can control your heat loss efficiently in the open sunlight. Yes, your link with the forest is lost deep in the past. And so you see it, not as a place of bounty and safety, but of threat.'

'We have tales. Fictions. Many of them are scary. They involve dense forests, being lost in the woods.'

Manekato showed ferocious teeth. 'And if an Elf were able, it would frighten its companions with tales of being trapped in the open, with no forest cover in sight, at sunset, as the predators begin to feed . . . But that hominid appeared to be fleeing. Little threatens the Nutcrackers, here in their forest domain; they are strong and smart. Curious.' Mane loped forward, more slowly than before, her massive form moving with barely a rustle through the crowded foliage. Emma followed in her tracks.

Then Mane slowed, peering down at something on the ground.

Emma heard the buzzing of flies. Then came the stench, the rotting-meat stench: sanitized out of the world she had come from, a smell she would not get used to no matter how long she lasted on this strange, mixed-up Moon.

The smell of death.

It looked like a chimp that had been hit by a truck. Its hairy skin was broken by wounds and lesions, and a watery fluid leaked from gaping mouth and empty eye sockets. Maggots squirmed in the lesions, giving the corpse a semblance of life. The body seemed to be deliquescing, in fact, its flesh and bones dissolving right out from within its skin and pouring into the ground.

There was an infant sitting on the ground beside the adult, presumably its mother, a round bundle of misery.

'Now we know why that Nutcracker was fleeing,' Emma said.

Nemoto, panting hard, joined Emma. 'I have seen this before. Do not touch anything.'

'What is it?'

'Something like the Ebola virus, I think. It starts with a headache, a fever. As your cells fill with the replicating virus your immune system collapses. Your skin turns to pulp; you haemorrhage; your gut fills with blood; blood leaks from your eyes, mouth, nose, ears, anus. When you die your body turns to slime. If somebody picks up the corpse, they contract it too, and die in turn. There is no vaccine or cure. I guess that is why the others of this one's troupe have abandoned it, and its child.'

'I have made this one safe,' Mane murmured. 'There is no infection here.' Emma hadn't seen her do anything.

The baby raised its head and studied Emma. The little Nutcracker, surely no more than a year old, was surrounded by scrapings of thin white infant scut.

Emma said to Mane, 'It's safe to pick it up?'

'Yes.'

Emma pulled a piece of cloth over her mouth and nose and stepped forward, towards the infant. The infant cowered back, but it was weak and hungry and scared, and let Emma tuck her hands under its armpits.

She lifted it easily, though it was heavier than she had thought, a boulder of hair and bone. 'Well, it's a girl; I can tell that much.' The infant had brown-black eyes, creamy white at the edges. Her skin beneath the hair was black, and wrinkles ran across her brow, between her eyes and over her stubby ape nose, giving her a troubled expression. Her mouth was open, and was a startlingly bright pink inside. The hair on her body was thick and coarse, but on her head, over that improbable crest of bone, the hair was sparser.

Emma held the baby against her chest. The little body was very warm. The sad, small black face tucked into a fold of Emma's coverall, and Emma bent to kiss the bony crest on the top of her head. She smelled leaves.

Then the infant hugged her tight with legs and arms, tensed, and defecated in a stream that spilled down Emma's trouser-legs.

Julia made claw hands. 'Leopards. Hyenas. Chomp baby Nu'cracker.'

'Right,' Emma said. 'Smart baby. You only take a dump when your mother is holding you.'

Nemoto was watching her. 'Emma Stoney, I hope you're not considering bringing that infant with you.'

Emma hadn't thought that far ahead. 'Why not?'

'Because you do not know how to look after it.'

'Her. I don't know how to look after *her*.'

'You know nothing of the ecology of these creatures. You are sentimental.'

'She is right,' Mane said mournfully. The big Daemon loomed over the little tableau, like an adult standing over a child with her doll. 'This infant has been abandoned by its kind. It will shortly die, of starvation, predation, disease. Death is commonplace for all hominid species, Em-ma. Among the Nutcrackers, in fact, the men compete for access to groups of women and children. And sometimes if one man displaces another, he will destroy the children of his defeated opponent.'

'All very evolutionarily sound,' Emma said coldly. 'But I'm keeping her.'

She felt a massive hand on her back: Julia's. 'Lonely,' said the Ham.

'Yes. Yes, I'm lonely, Julia. I lost my husband, my world, my life. For all your kindness, of course I'm lonely.'

'All,' Julia said softly. 'Lonely.'

Nemoto prowled about the little clearing, agitated, avoiding the corpse. 'We are the lonely hominids. On Earth it is thirty-five thousand years since we last encountered another hominid species. Maybe it was our relentless expansion that drove the last of the Neandertals to extinction; maybe it was our fault – but whatever the cause it was surely the last contact. And when we look out into the sky, we see nothing but emptiness. An empty world in an empty universe. No wonder we have been at war with our planet since before records began. Earth had betrayed us, orphaned us: what else was there to do? Yes, we are lonely, all of us. Lonely and frightened. But do you really think making a pet of an orphaned Australopithecine is going to make any difference? . . .'

Emma felt Mane's heavy, gentle hand touch the top of her head, distant, comforting.

They approached the centre.

People moved over the rocky ground. They were Daemons, little clusters of them walking to and fro, bearing incomprehensible pieces of equipment, occasionally flickering into and out of existence in that baffling, utterly disturbing way of theirs.

Beyond the Daemons, Emma thought she could see light shining up from the ground, caught by swirling dust motes. She shivered.

Nemoto was silent, tense.

They reached the centre of the clearing. Emma stepped forward gingerly.

There was a hole in the ground, a few yards wide, like a well. Light shone from it, up into the dusty air, like an inverted sunbeam.

Emma felt cold with awe.

She sat on the grass with the Nutcracker infant and reached for a flask of milk from her pack. She opened up the yellow plastic-feel flask, exposing a nipple, and tipped it towards the infant's head, making soothing noises. The infant grabbed the yellow flask with hands and feet, and she began to suck at the nipple, very hard. Milk splashed into her mouth and over her face, and over Emma.

Emma wiped milk from her lap and eyes. 'I should do this with an apron.'

'You shouldn't do it at all,' Nemoto said sourly. 'You should give her back to her kind.'

'Nutcrackers don't adopt orphans. You know that.'

Mane stood over them like a block of granite. 'We could make the infant acceptable to a troupe of its kind.'

Emma scowled. 'How?'

Nemoto said, 'Emma, if they can travel between worlds just by thinking about it, the Daemons can surely fool some half-evolved ape.'

Mane reproached her, 'Nutcrackers are fully evolved. Just differently evolved.'

The infant finished the milk, or at any rate lost patience with the bottle. She threw it over her head. Then she touched the milk that had pooled on Emma's chin, and opened her mouth to make fast, rasping cries. 'Hah hah hah!'

'She's laughing at me,' Emma said.

'I am not surprised,' Nemoto said.

'I'll find some running water and wash us both up.'

Julia, watching, grinned. 'Nutcracker don' wash!'

Nemoto grimaced. 'This is not a toy, still less a human child! Soon you will be stinking as badly as her! Emma, give up this sentimentality. Give her back to her own kind.' She seemed obsessed with the issue of the infant.

Emma looked up at Manekato, and she looked into her own heart. 'Not yet,' she said.

There was a moment of stillness. In this open space the sun was warm on her face, invigorating, its light making the dusty air shine. The infant Nutcracker gurgled and plucked at Emma's sleeve.

Manekato walked to the lip of the tunnel. She stood silently, on crimson earth, peering into the well in the Moon, its diffuse light picking out the folds in her blue-black skin. Emma wondered what she was thinking, what the tunnel was saying to her.

Mane turned. 'It is time.' She held out her hands.

Yes, Emma thought. Somehow she knew it too. She stood up, brushing dust off her coveralls. The Nutcracker child clambered up into her arms. She settled her distorted head against Emma's chest and promptly fell asleep.

Nemoto stood reluctantly. Emma could see she was trembling, utterly afraid.

Mane took Emma's hand, and Nemoto's, and Julia took Nemoto's other hand. Cradling the infant, Emma walked up to the lip of the well.

The shaft at her feet was a cylinder, walled by what looked like sparkling glass, a wall that receded downwards to infinity. Lights had been buried in the walls every few yards, so the shaft was brilliantly lit, like a passageway in a shopping mall, the multiple reflections glimmering from the glass walls. Conduits snaked along the tunnel, their purpose unclear. The shaft was vertical, perfectly symmetrical, and there was no mist or dust, nothing to obscure her view.

Momentarily dizzy, Emma stepped back, anchored herself again on the surface of the Red Moon.

Nemoto said, 'What is this?'

Mane said evenly, 'It is a tunnel in the Moon.'

'But what is it for?'

'We don't know.'

Emma said, 'How deep is it?'

'We don't know that either,' Manekato said. 'We have tried sending –' she hesitated '– *radio signals* and other emissions into the well. No echo has returned.'

'But,' said Emma, 'it can't be longer than the width of the Moon. Even if it came out the other side . . . It can't be longer than that.'

'We don't know,' Mane said. '*We did not put it here.*'

Nemoto said tightly, 'What do we have to do?'

Mane regarded her with her large eyes, pupils black, the whites flecked with yellow. 'I think you know.'

Yes, Emma knew – though she didn't understand how she knew. A prickly wave of vertigo swept over her. Malenfant, she thought desperately, you should be here to see this. You would *love* it. But *me* . . .

There was no more time, no time for thinking, for doubt. Without a word, the five of them stepped off the lip of the tunnel, into the air.

For a moment they floated there in space, bathed in the light from the heart of the world, like cartoon characters for whom the laws of physics are momentarily suspended.

And then they began to sink, gently.

There was nothing beneath her feet. The air was full of light.

Slow as a snowflake, tugged by a force that felt like gravity – and yet it could not be gravity – Emma fell towards the heart of the Moon. There was no noise save the rustle of clothing, their soft breathing, no smell save the lingering iron-and-blood stink of the crimson dust of the Red Moon.

She could tell she was falling. Lines in the wall, like depth markers, were already rising up past her, mapping her acceleration. But it was as if she were suspended here, in the glowing air; she had no sense of speed, no vertigo from the depths beneath her.

She could hear her own heart pound.

Nemoto was laughing, manic.

Emma held the black bundle of fur closer to her chest, drawing comfort from the Nutcracker's solid animal warmth. 'I don't know what the hell is so funny.'

Nemoto's face was twisted, a mask of fear and denial. 'We are not in the hands of some omnipotent, infallible god. This is no more than a gadget, Emma. More ancient than our species, more ancient than worlds perhaps, very advanced – but very old, and cranky, and probably failing as well. And we are relying on it for our lives. *That* is what strikes me as funny.'

Their speed picked up quickly.

In seconds, it seemed, they had already passed through the fine layers of the Red Moon's outer geology. Now they sailed past giant chunks of rock that crowded against the glassy, transparent tunnel walls like the corpses of buried animals.

'The megaregolith,' Nemoto murmured. 'In the later stages of its formation this little world must have been just as bombarded as our own Luna. Under the surface geology, the craters and cracks, this is what you get. Pulverization, shattered rock, mile upon mile of it. We are already far beyond the reach of any human mining, Emma. We are truly sinking deep into the carcass of this world.'

Mane regarded her, curious, judgmental. 'You are analytical. You like to find names for what you see.'

'It helps me cope,' Nemoto said tightly.

The material beyond the walls turned smooth and grey. This must be bedrock, Emma thought, buried beyond even the probing and pulverizing of the great primordial impactors. Unlike Earth, on this small world there had been no tectonic churning, no cycling of rocks from surface to interior; these rock layers had probably lain here undisturbed since the formation of the Red Moon.

Already they must be miles deep.

Despite the gathering warmth of the tunnel, despite her own acceleration, she had a sense of cold, of age and stillness.

She had no real sense of how long she had been falling – it might have been seconds, or minutes – perhaps time flowed as deceptively here as space, as gravity. But she was reluctant to glance at a watch, or even look up to the receding disc of daylight above. She was not like Nemoto, determinedly labelling everything; rather she felt superstitious, as if she might break the spell that held her in the air if she questioned these miracles too hard.

They dropped through a surprisingly sharp transition into a new realm, where the rock beyond the walls glowed of its own internal light. It was a dull grey-red, like a cooling lava on Earth.

'The mantle,' Nemoto whispered. 'Basalt. Neither solid nor liquid, a state that you don't find on the surface of a planet, rock so soft it pulls like taffy.'

Soon the rock brightened to a cherry-pink, rushing upwards past them. It was like dropping through some immense glass tube full of fluorescing gas. Gazing at that shining pink-hot rock just yards away, Emma felt heat, but that was surely an illusion.

The baby Nutcracker stirred, eyes closed, wiping her broad nose on Emma's chest.

Falling, falling. Thick conduits surrounded them now, crowding the tunnel, flipping from bracket to bracket. She wondered what their purpose was; neither Nemoto nor Mane offered an opinion.

For the first time she felt a lurch, like an elevator slowing. Looking down along the forest of conduits, she could see that they were approaching a terminus, a platform of some dull, opaque material that plugged the tunnel.

She asked, 'Where are we?'

Mane said, 'Thousands of miles deep. Some two-thirds of the way to the centre of the Moon.'

They slowed, drifting to a crawl maybe a yard above the platform. Emma landed on her feet, still clutching the infant – an easy landing, even if it had reminded her of her involuntary sky-dive.

Now she glanced at the watch Nemoto had loaned her. The fall had taken twenty minutes.

The smooth surface was neither hot nor cold, a subdued white, stretching seamlessly from one side of the shaft to the other.

Emma put down the infant Nutcracker. With a happy grunt the infant urinated, a thin stream that pooled on the gleaming floor.

In this place of shining geometric perfection, all the hominids looked misshapen, out of place: Julia with her heavy-browed skull, the Daemon with her looming gorilla body, her fast, jerky motions and her eerily swivelling ears, and Nemoto and Emma, the proud ambassadors of *Homo sapiens*, huddled close together in their dusty, much-patched coveralls. We are barely evolved, Emma thought – even Mane – unformed compared to the chill, effortless perfection of this place.

'. . . Noise,' Julia said. She turned her great head, peering around. 'Noise. Lights.'

Nemoto scowled, peering around, up into the tunnel that receded into infinity over their heads. 'I cannot hear anything.'

'There is much information here,' Mane said gently. She had closed her eyes. 'You must – let it in.'

'I don't know how,' Nemoto said miserably.

Emma glanced down at the infant Nutcracker. She was crawling on legs and knuckles and peering into the floor, as if it were the surface of a pond. Emma, stiffly, got to her knees beside the child. She stared at the floor, looked where the infant looked.

There was a flash of blue light, an instant of searing pain.

The floor had turned to glass. With the Nutcracker, she was kneeling on nothingness. She gasped, pressed her hands against the hard surface. No, not glass: there was no reflection, nothing but the warm feel of the floor under her hands and knees.

And below her, a huge chamber loomed.

She felt Nemoto's hand on her shoulder, gripping tight, as if for comfort.

Emma said, 'Can you see it?'

'Yes, I see it.'

Emma glimpsed a far wall. It was covered with lights, like stars. But these stars marked out a regular pattern of equilateral triangles. Artificial, then. She looked from side to side, trying to make out the curve of that remote wall. But it was too far away for her to make out its shape, too far beyond her puny sense of scale.

'It's a hole,' she said. 'A chamber at the heart of the Moon.'

'It is whatever it seems to be.'

'The chamber looks flattened. Like a pancake.'

'No,' Nemoto murmured. 'It is probably spherical. You have the eyes of a plains ape, Emma Stoney. Evolved for distances of a few hundred miles, no more. Even the sky looks like a flat lid to you. Humans aren't evolved to comprehend spaces like this – a cave thousands of miles across, a cave big enough to store a world.'

'Those lights are regular. Like fake stars on a movie set.'

'Perhaps they are the mouths of tunnels, like this one.'

'Leading to more holes on the surface?'

'Or leading somewhere else.' Nemoto's voice was quavering. 'I don't know, Emma. I understand none of this.'

But you understand more than me, Emma thought. Which is, perhaps, why you are more frightened.

There was motion in the heart of the chamber. Blueness. Vast wheels turning. A churning, regular, like a huge machine.

The Nutcracker child gurgled, her eyes shining. She seemed

enchanted by the turning wheels, as if the whole display, surely a thousand miles across, was no more than a nursery mobile.

'Blue rings,' Nemoto breathed.

Emma squinted, wishing her eyes would dark-adapt faster. 'Like the Wheel, the portal I fell through to come here.'

Nemoto said, 'This technology has a unifying, if unimaginative, aesthetic.'

'It is the world engine,' Mane said simply.

Emma saw the turning wheels reflected in Mane's broad, glistening eyes. 'What is a *world engine*?'

'Can you not see? Look deeper.'

'. . . Ah,' Nemoto said.

At the heart of the turning rings, there was a world.

It was like Earth, but it was not Earth. Turning slowly in the light of an off-stage sun, it was wrapped in a blanket of thick, ragged cloud. Emma glimpsed land that was riven by bright-glowing cracks and the pinpricks of volcanoes. Plumes of black smoke and dust streaked the air, and lightning cracked between fat purple clouds.

'Not a trace of ocean,' Nemoto murmured. 'Too hot and dry for that.'

'Do you think it is Earth? – or any of the Earths?'

'If it is, it is a young Earth, an Earth still pouring out the heat of its formation . . .'

'The sky,' Mane said, her voice quavering, 'is full of rock.'

Emma glanced up.

. . . And for an instant she saw what the Daemon saw: a different point of view, as if she were standing on that burnt, barren land, on bare rock so hot it glowed, close to a river of some sticky, coagulating lava. She looked up through rents in fat, scudding clouds – into a sky that was covered by a lid of rock, an inverted landscape of mountains and valleys and craters.

She gasped, and the vision faded.

Emma saw again the hot young world, and another beside it now, a Moon-like world, evidently cooler than Earth, but large, surely larger than Mars, say. The two planets sat side by side, like an orange and an apple in a still-life.

But they were approaching each other.

'I think we are watching the Big Whack,' Nemoto murmured. 'The immense collision that devastated young Earth, but created the Earth-Moon system . . .'

The planets touched, almost gently, like kissing. But where they touched a ring of fire formed, shattering the surface of both worlds, a spreading splash of destruction into which the smaller body seemed to implode, like a fruit being drained of its flesh.

'The collision took about ten minutes,' Nemoto said softly. 'The approach speed was tens of thousands of miles per hour. But a collision between such large bodies, even at such speeds, would look like slow motion.'

A vast fount of material, glowing liquid rock, gushed into space from the impact. Emma glimpsed the impacting planetesimal's grey curve, a last fragment of geometric purity, lost in the storm of fire. A great circular wave of fire spread out around the Earth from the impact point.

A ring of glowing light began to coalesce in Earth orbit. As it cooled it solidified into a swarm of miniature bodies. And then spiral arms formed in the glowing moonlet cloud. It was a remarkable, beautiful sight.

'This is how the Moon was born,' Nemoto said. 'The largest of those moonlets won out. The growing Moon swept up the remnant particles, and under the influence of tidal forces rapidly receded from Earth. Earth itself, meanwhile, was afflicted by huge rock tides, savage rains as the ocean vapour fell back from space. It took millions of years before the rocks had cooled enough for liquid water to gather once more.'

'You know a lot about this stuff, Nemoto.'

Nemoto turned, her face underlit by the glow of Earth's violent formation. 'A few months ago a new Moon appeared in Earth's sky. I wanted to know how the old one had got there. I thought it might be relevant.'

Emma glanced at Mane. The Daemon stood with her knuckles resting lightly on invisibility. Her eyes were closed, her face blank. Julia's eyes were closed too.

'What do they see?' she whispered to Nemoto. 'What do they hear?'

'Perhaps more than this show-and-tell diorama. Manekato said this place, this tunnel in the Moon, was *information-rich*. Julia is as smart as we are, but different. Manekato is smarter still. I don't know what they can apprehend, how far they can see beyond what we see.'

'. . . Hey. What happened to the Earth?'

The glowing, devastated planet had blown apart. Fragments of its image had scattered to corners of the chamber – where the fragments coalesced to new Earths, new Moons, a whole family of them. They hung around the chamber like Christmas-tree ornaments, glowing blue or red or yellow, each lit by the light of its own out-of-view sun.

Other Earths:

Emma saw a fat, solitary world, banded with yellow cloud.

Here was another cloud-striped world, but the clouds swirled around a point on its equator – no, it was a world tipped over so that its axis pointed to its sun, like Uranus (or was it Neptune?).

Here was an Earth like Venus, with a great shroud of thick clouds that glowed yellow-white, nowhere broken.

Here was a world with a fat, cloud-shrouded Moon that seemed to loom very close. This Earth was streaked by volcanic clouds. It lacked ice caps, and its unrecognizable continents were pierced by shining threads that must have been immense rivers. This world must be battered by the great tides of air, water and rock raised by that too-close companion.

Most of the Earths seemed about the size of Earth – of *the* Earth, Emma's Earth. But some were smaller – wizened worlds that reminded her of Mars, with huge continents of glowering red rock and brooding weather systems squatting over their poles. And some of the Earths were larger. These monster planets were characteristically wreathed in thick, muddy atmospheres and drowned in oceans, water that stretched from pole to pole, with a few eroded islands protruding above the surface, rooted on some deep-buried crust.

The Moons varied too. There seemed to be a spectrum of possible Moons. The smallest were bare grey rock like Luna, those somewhat larger cratered deserts of crimson rock more or less like Mars. Some were almost Earth-like, showing thick air and ice and the glint of ocean – like the Red Moon itself. There were even Earths with pairs of Moons, Emma saw, or triplets. One ice-bound Earth was surrounded, not by a Moon, but by a glowing ring system like Saturn's.

Emma looked, without success, for a blue Earth with a single, grey, modest Moon.

'The Big Whack collision shaped Earth and Moon,' Nemoto murmured. 'Everything about Earth and Moon – their axial tilt, composition, atmosphere, length of day, even Earth's orbit around the sun – was determined by the impact. But it might have turned out differently. Small, chance changes in the geometry of the collision would have made a large difference in the outcome. Lots of possible realities, budding off from that key, apocalyptic moment.'

'What are we looking at here? Computer simulations?'

'Or windows into other possible realities. It is a glimpse of the vast graph of probability and possibility, of alternates that cluster around the chaotic impact event.' Nemoto seemed coldly excited. 'This is the key, Emma Stoney. The Big Whack was the pivotal event whose subtly different outcomes produced the wide range of Earths we have encountered . . .'

Emma barely understood what she was saying.

Julia grunted. 'Grey Earth,' she said. She was pointing to the tipped-over, Uranus-like Earth.

Emma said, 'Where you came from.'

'Home,' Julia said simply.

Nemoto said, 'I recognize *that* one.' She pointed to the fat, solitary Earth, banded by Jupiter-like clouds. 'A Moonless Earth, an Earth where the great impact did not happen at all. It may be the Earth they call the Banded Earth, which seems to be the origin of these Daemons.'

Mane laid gentle, patronizing hands on their scalps. 'Analyse, analyse. Your minds are very busy. You must watch, listen.'

'Ooh.' It was the Nutcracker infant. She was crawling over the invisible floor, chortling at the light show.

Emma glanced down. The various Earths had vanished, to be replaced by a floor of swirling, curdled light.

It was a galaxy.

'Oh, my,' she muttered. 'What now?'

The galaxy was a disc of stars, flatter than she might have expected, in proportion to its width no thicker than a few sheets of paper. She thought she could see strata in that disc, layers of structure, a central sheet of swarming blue stars and dust lanes sandwiched between dimmer, older stars. The core, bulging out of the plane of the disc like an egg yolk, was a compact mass of yellowish light; but it was not spherical, rather markedly elliptical. The spiral arms were fragmented. They were a delicate blue laced with ruby-red nebulae and the blue-white blaze of individual stars – a granularity of light – and with dark lanes traced between the arms. She saw scattered flashes of light, blisters of gas. Perhaps those were supernova explosions, creating bubbles of hot plasma hundreds of light years across.

But the familiar disc – shining core, spiral arms – was actually embedded in a broader, spherical mass of dim red stars. The crimson fireflies were gathered in great clusters, each of which must contain millions of stars.

The five of them stood over this vast image – if it *was* an image – Daemon and Ham and humans and Nutcracker baby, squat, ungainly, primitive forms.

'So, a galaxy,' said Emma. '*Our* Galaxy?'

'I think so,' Nemoto said. 'It matches radio maps I have seen.' She pointed, tracing patterns. 'Look. That must be the Sagittarius Arm. The other big structure is called the Outer Arm.'

The two major arms, emerging from the elliptical core, defined the Galaxy, each of them wrapping right around the core before dispersing at the rim into a mist of shining stars and glowing nebulae and brooding black clouds. The other 'arms' were really just scraps, Emma saw – the Galaxy's spiral structure was a lot messier than she had expected – but still, she thought, the sun is in one of those scattered fragments.

The Galaxy image began to rotate, slowly.

Emma could see the stars swarming, following individual orbits around the Galaxy core, like a school of sparkling fish. And the spiral arms were evolving too, ridges of light sparking with young stars, churning their way through the disc of the Galaxy. But the arms were just waves of compression, she saw, like the bunching of traffic jams, with individual stars swimming through the regions of high density.

'A galactic day,' Nemoto breathed. 'It takes two hundred million years to complete a turn.'

Oh, Malenfant, Emma thought again, you should be here to see this. Not me – not *me*.

Nemoto said, 'But *whose* Galaxy is it?'

'That is a good question,' Mane said. 'It is our Galaxy – that is, it belongs to all of us. The Galactic background is common to the reality threads bound by the Earth-Moon impact probability sheaf –'

'Woah,' Emma said. 'Nemoto, can you translate?'

Nemoto frowned. 'Think of the Galaxy, a second before the Earth-Moon impact. All those stars have nothing whatsoever to do with the Big Whack, and will not be affected by it. The Galaxy will turn, whether the Moon exists or not, whether humans evolve or not . . .'

Mane said, '*Our* Galaxy looks the same as *yours*. And it is unmodified.'

Emma snapped, 'What does *that* mean?'

Nemoto said, 'That there is no sign of life, Emma.'

'But we're looking at a whole damn *galaxy*. From this perspective the sun is a dot of light. The place could be swarming with creatures like humans, and you wouldn't see it.'

Nemoto shook her head. 'The Fermi Paradox. In our universe, and Mane's, there has been time for a thousand empires to sweep over the face of the Galaxy. Some of the signs of their passing ought to be very visible.'

'Like what?'

'Like they might tamper with the evolution of the stars. Or they might mine the black hole at the Galaxy's core for its energy. Or they might wrap up the Galactic disc in a shell to trap all its radiant energy. Emma, there are many possibilities. It is very likely that we would see *something* even when we peer at a Galaxy from without like this.'

'But we don't.'

'But we don't. Humanity seems to be alone in our universe, Emma; Earth is the only place where mind arose.' Nemoto confronted Mane. 'And *your* universe is empty too. As was Hugh McCann's. Perhaps that is true in all the universes in this reality sheaf.'

Emma murmured, 'The Fermi Paradox.'

Nemoto seemed surprised she knew the name.

'Something is happening to the Galaxy,' Mane said.

They clustered close to watch.

The Galaxy was spinning fast now. All over the disc the stars were flaring, dying. Some of them, turning to red embers, began to drift away from the main body of the disc.

Emma picked up the Nutcracker infant and clutched her to her chest. 'It is – shrivelling,' she said.

'We are seeing vast swathes of time,' Nemoto said sombrely. 'This is the future, Emma.'

'*The future?* How is that possible?'

Suddenly the stars died. All of them went out, it seemed, all at once.

The Galaxy seemed to implode, becoming much dimmer.

At first Emma could make out only a diffuse red wash of light. Perhaps there was a slightly brighter central patch, surrounded by a blood-coloured river, studded here and there by dim yellow sparkles. That great central complex was embedded in a diffuse cloud; she thought she could see ribbons, streamers in the cloud, as if material were being dragged into that pink maw at the centre.

Further out still, the core and its orbiting cloud seemed to be set in a ragged disc, a thing of tatters and streamers of gas. Emma could make out no structure in the disc, no trace of spiral arms, no lanes of light and darkness. But there were blisters, knots of greater or lesser density, like supernova blisters, and there was that chain of brighter light points studded at regular intervals around the disc. Filaments seemed to reach in from the brighter points towards the bloated central mass.

Emma said, 'What happened to all the stars?'

'They died,' Nemoto said bluntly. 'They grew old and died, and there wasn't enough material left to make any more. And then, *this*.' Nemoto pointed. 'The wreck of the Galaxy. Some of the dying stars have evaporated out of the Galaxy. The rest are collapsing into black holes – those blisters you see in the disc. That central mass is the giant black hole at the core.'

'*When* is this?'

Nemoto hesitated, thinking, and when she spoke again, she sounded awed. 'Umm, perhaps a hundred thousand billion years into the future – compared to the universe's present age *five thousand times* older.'

The numbers seemed monstrous to Emma. 'So this is the end of life.'

'Oh, no,' Mane replied. She pointed to the clusters of brighter light around the rim of the galactic corpse. '*These* seem to be normal stars: small, uniform, but still glowing in the visible spectrum.'

'How is that possible?'

'Those stars can't be natural,' Nemoto said. She turned to Emma, her eyes shining. 'You see? Somebody must be gathering the remnant interstellar gases, forming artificial birthing clouds . . . Somebody is farming the Galaxy, even so far in the future. Isn't it wonderful?'

'*Wonderful?* The wreck of the Galaxy?'

'Not that,' Nemoto said. 'The existence of life. They still need stars and planets, and warmth and light. But their worlds must be huddled close to these small, old stars – probably gravitationally locked, keeping one face in the light, one in the dark . . . I think this is, umm, a biography,' Nemoto said. 'This whole vast show. The story of a race. *They* are trying to tell us what became of them.'

'A very human impulse,' said Mane.

Emma shrugged. 'But why should they care what we think?'

Nemoto said, 'Perhaps they were our descendants . . .'

Mane said nothing, her eyes wide as she peered at the crimson image, and Emma wondered what strange news from the future was pouring into her head.

And now the Galaxy image whirled again, evolving, changing, dimming.

Emma hugged the baby hominid and closed her eyes.

Manekatopokanemahedo:

This is how it is, how it was, how it came to be.

It began in the afterglow of the Big Bang, that brief age when stars still burned.

Humans arose on an Earth. Emma, perhaps it was your Earth. Soon they were alone, and for ever after.

Humans spread over their world. They spread in waves across the universe, sprawling and brawling and breeding and dying and evolving. There were wars, there was love, there was life and death. Minds flowed together in great rivers of consciousness, or shattered in sparkling droplets. There was immortality to be had, of a sort, a continuity of identity through copying and confluence across billions upon billions of years.

Everywhere they found life: crude replicators, of carbon or silicon or metal, churning meaninglessly in the dark.

Nowhere did they find mind – save what they brought with them or created – no *other* against which human advancement could be tested.

They were forever alone.

With time, the stars died like candles. But humans fed on bloated gravitational fat, and achieved a power undreamed of in earlier ages. It is impossible to understand what minds of that age were like, minds of time's far downstream. They did not seek to acquire, not to breed, not even to learn. They needed nothing. They had nothing in common with their ancestors of the afterglow.

Nothing but the will to survive. And even that was to be denied them by time.

The universe aged: indifferent, harsh, hostile and ultimately lethal. There was despair and loneliness.

There was an age of war, an obliteration of trillion-year memories, a bonfire of identity. There was an age of suicide, as even the finest chose self-destruction against further purposeless time and struggle.

The great rivers of mind guttered and dried.

But some persisted: just a tributary, the stubborn, still unwilling to yield to the darkness, to accept the increasing confines of a universe growing inexorably old.

And, at last, they realized that something was wrong. *It wasn't supposed to have been like this.*

Burning the last of the universe's resources, the final downstreamers – lonely, dogged, all but insane – reached to the deepest past . . .

Emma Stoney:

Nemoto was muttering, perhaps to Emma or Manekato, or perhaps to herself, as she impatiently swept lianas and thorn tangles out of her path. 'Evolution has turned out to be a lot more complicated than we ever imagined, of course. Well, everything is more complicated now, in this manifold of realities. Even though Darwin's basic intuition was surely right . . .' And so on.

Carrying the sleeping Nutcracker infant, Emma walked through the forest. Ahead she could see the broad back of Manekato.

Emma let Nemoto talk.

'. . . Even before this Red Moon showed up in our skies we had developed major elaborations to the basic Darwinian model. Darwin's "tree of life" is no simple tree, it turns out, no simple hierarchy of ancestral species. It is a tangle –'

'Like this damn jungle,' Emma said, trying to turn the monologue into a conversation. 'Lianas and vines cutting across everywhere. If it was just the trees it would be easy.'

'A criss-cross transfer of genetic information, this way and that. And now we have this Red Moon wandering between alternate Earths, the Wheels returning to different Africas over and over, scooping up species here and depositing them there, making an altogether untidy mess of the descent of mankind – and of other species; no wonder this world is full of what Malenfant called "living fossils". Surely without the Red Moon we would never have evolved,

434

we *Homo sapiens sapiens. Homo erectus* was a successful species, lasting millions of years, covering the Earth. We did not *need* to become so smart . . .'

It had been some days since their jaunt into the tunnel in the Moon. Nemoto had spent the time with Manekato and other Daemons, struggling to interpret the experience. For her part, Emma had barely been able to function once those visions of the ageing Galaxy had started to blizzard over her – even though it had been, apparently, just a fraction of the information available in that deep chamber, for those minds capable of reading it.

But she remembered the last glimpse of all.

. . . It was dark. There were no dead stars, no rogue planets. Matter itself had long evaporated, burned up by proton decay, leaving nothing but a thin smoke of neutrinos drifting out at lightspeed.

But even now there was something rather than nothing.

The creatures of this age drifted like clouds, immense, slow, coded in immense wispy atoms. Free energy was dwindling to zero, time stretching to infinity. It took these cloud-beings longer to complete a single thought than it once took species to rise and fall on Earth . . .

That ultimate, dismal vision was slow to dispel, like three-in-the-morning fears of her own death. She knew she didn't have the mental toughness to confront all this, special effects or not. Unlike Nemoto, perhaps.

Or perhaps not. To Nemoto, the whole thing seemed to have been more like a traumatic shock than an imparting of information. She had come out of the experience needing human company, in her reticent way, and needing to talk. But when she talked it was about Charles Darwin and the Red Moon, or even Malenfant and the politics of NASA, anything but the central issue of the Old Ones.

Emma concentrated on the leafy smell of the child, the crackle of dead leaves, the prickle of sunlight on her neck, even the itch of the ulcers on her legs. *This* was reality, of life and breath and senses.

Manekato had stopped, abruptly. Nemoto fell silent. They were in a small scrap of clearing, by the side of the lichen-covered corpse of a huge fallen tree. Manekato lifted herself up on her hind legs, sniffed the air and swivelled her ears, and belched with satisfaction. 'Here,' she said. 'The Nutcrackers will come.' With a massive thump she sat on the ground, and began exploring the bushes around her for berries.

Emma, gratefully, put down the infant Nutcracker and sat beside her. The leaves were slippery and damp; the morning was not long advanced. She considered giving the infant some more milk, but the child had already discovered Manekato's fruit, and was clambering up the Daemon's impassive back.

Nemoto sat beside Emma. Her posture was stiff, her arms wrapped around her chest, her right heel drumming on the ground. Emma laid one hand on Nemoto's knee. Gradually the drumming stopped.

And, suddenly, Nemoto began to talk.

'They made the manifold.'

'Who did?'

'The Old Ones. They constructed a manifold of universes – an infinite number of universes. They *made* it all.' Nemoto shook her head. 'Even framing the thought, conceiving of such ambition, is overwhelming. But they did it.'

Manekato was watching them, her large eyes thoughtful.

Emma said carefully, 'How did they do this, Nemoto?'

'The branching of universes, deep into the hyperpast,' Manekato murmured.

Emma shook her head, irritated. 'What does that mean?'

Nemoto said, 'Universes are born. They die. We know two ways a universe can be born. The most primitive cosmos can give birth to another through a Big Crunch, the mirror-image of a Big Bang suffered by a collapsing universe at the end of its history. Or else a new universe can be budded from the singularity at the heart of a black hole. Black holes are the key, Emma, you see. A universe which cannot make black holes can have only one daughter, produced by a Crunch. But a universe which is complex enough to make black holes, like ours, can have many daughters, baby universes connected to the mother by spacetime umbilicals through the singularities.'

'And so when the Old Ones tinkered with the machinery –'

'We don't know how they did it. But they changed the rules,' Nemoto said.

Emma said hesitantly, 'So they found a way to create a lot more universes.'

Manekato said, 'We believe the Old Ones created, not just a multiplicity of daughter universes, but *an infinite number*.' The bulky Daemon studied Emma's face, seeking understanding.

'Infinity is significant, you see,' Nemoto said, too rapidly. 'There is, umm, a qualitative difference between a mere large number, however large, and infinity. In the infinite manifold, in that infinite ensemble, *all* logically possible universes must exist. And therefore *all* logically possible destinies must unfold. Everything that is possible *will* happen, somewhere out there. They created a grand stage, you see, Emma: a stage for endless possibilities of life and mind.'

'Why did they do this?'

'Because they were lonely. The Old Ones were the first sentient species in their universe. They survived their crises of immaturity. And they went on, to walk on the planets, to touch the stars. But everywhere they went – though perhaps they found life – they found no sign of mind, save for themselves.'

'And then the stars went out.'

'And the stars went out. There are ways to survive the darkness, Emma. You can mine energy from the gravity wells of black holes, for instance . . . But as the universe expanded relentlessly, and the available energy dwindled, the iron logic of entropy held sway. Existence became harsh, straitened, in an energy-starved universe that was like a prison. Some of the Old Ones looked back over their lonely destiny, which had turned into nothing but a long, desolating struggle to survive, and – well, some of them rebelled.'

The infant crawled over Manekato's stolid head and down her chest, clutching great handfuls of hair. Then she curled up in the Daemon's lap, defecated efficiently, and quickly fell asleep. Emma suppressed a pang of jealousy that it was not *her* lap.

'So they rebelled. How?'

Nemoto sighed. 'It's all to do with quantum mechanics, Emma.'

'I was afraid it might be.'

Manekato said, 'Each quantum event emerges into reality as the result of a feedback loop between past and future. Handshakes across time. The story of the universe is like a tapestry, stitched together by uncountable trillions of such tiny handshakes. If you create an artificial timelike loop to some point in spacetime within the negative light cone of the present –'

'Woah. In English.'

Manekato looked puzzled.

Nemoto said, 'If you were to go back in time and try to change the past, you would damage the universe, erasing a whole series of consequential events. Yes? So the universe starts over, from the first point where the forbidden loop would have begun to exist. As the effects of your change propagate through space and time, the universe knits itself into a new form, transaction by transaction, handshake by handshake. The wounded universe heals itself with a new set of handshakes, working forward in time, until it is complete and self-consistent once more.'

Emma tried to think that through. 'What you're telling me is that changing history is possible.'

'Oh, yes,' said Nemoto. 'The Old Ones must have come to believe *they had lived through the wrong history*. So they reached back, to the deepest past, and made the change – and the manifold was born.'

Emma thought she understood. So this had been the purpose the Old Ones had found. Not a saga of meaningless survival in a dismal future of decay and shadows. The Old Ones had reached back, back in time, back to the deepest past, and put it right, by creating infinite possibilities for life, for mind.

She said carefully, 'I always wondered if life had any meaning. Now I know. The purpose of the first intelligence of all was to reshape the universe, in order to create a storm of mind.'

'Yes,' Manekato said. 'That is a partial understanding, but – yes.'

'Whew,' Emma said.

Nemoto seemed to be shivering, exhausted. 'I feel as if I have been gazing through a pinhole at the sun; I have stared so long that I have burned a hole in my retina. And yet there is still so much more to see.'

'You have done well,' Manekato said gently.

Nemoto snapped, 'Do I get another banana?'

'We must all do the best we can.' Manekato's massive hand absently stroked the Nutcracker; the child purred like a cat.

'But,' Emma said, 'the Old Ones must have wiped out their own history in the process. Didn't they? They created a time paradox. Everybody knows about time paradoxes. If you kill your grandmother, the universe repairs itself so you never existed . . .'

'Perhaps not,' Manekato murmured. 'It seems that conscious minds may, in some form, survive the transition.'

'Do not ask how,' Nemoto said dryly. 'Suffice it to say that the Old Ones seem to have been able to look on their handiwork, and see that it was good . . . mostly.'

'Mostly?'

Nemoto said, 'We think that we, unwilling passengers on this Red Moon, are, umm, exploring a corner of the manifold, of that infinite ensemble of universes the Old Ones created. Remember the Big Whack. Remember how we glimpsed many possible outcomes, many possible Earths and Moons, depending on the details of the impact.'

'It is clear,' Manekato said, 'that within the manifold there must be a sheaf of universes, closely related, all of them deriving from that primal Earth-shaping event and its different outcomes.'

Nemoto said, 'Many Earths. Many realities.'

'And in some of those realities,' Manekato said, 'what you call the Fermi Paradox was resolved a different way.'

'You mean, alien intelligences arose.'

'Yes.' Nemoto rubbed her nose and glanced uneasily at the sky. 'But in every one of those alien-inhabited realities, *humans got wiped out* – or never evolved in the first place. Every single time.'

'How come?'

Nemoto shrugged. 'Lots of possible ways. Interstellar colonists from ancient cultures overwhelmed Earth before life got beyond the single-cell stage. Humankind was destroyed by a swarm of killer robots. Whatever. The Old Ones seem to have selected a bundle of universes – all of them deriving from the Big Whack – in which there was *no* life beyond the Earth. And they sent this Moon spinning between those empty realities, from one to the other –'

'So that explains Fermi,' Emma said.

'Yes,' said Nemoto. 'We see no aliens *because we have been inserted into an empty universe*. Or universes. For our safety. To allow us to flourish.'

'But why the Red Moon, why link the realities?'

'To express humanity,' Manekato said simply. 'There are many different ways to be a hominid, Em-ma. We conjecture the Old Ones sought to explore those different ways: to promote evolutionary pulses, to preserve differing forms, to make room for different types of human consciousness.'

Emma frowned. 'You make us sound like pets. Toys.'

Manekato growled; Emma wondered if that was a laugh. 'Perhaps. Or it may be that we have yet to glimpse the true purpose of this wandering world.'

Emma said, 'But I still don't get it. Why would these super-being Old Ones care so much about humanity?'

Nemoto frowned. 'You haven't understood anything, Emma. *They were us.* They were our descendants, our future. *Homo sapiens sapiens*, Emma. And their universe-spanning story is our own lost future history. *We* built the manifold. *We* – our children – are the Old Ones.'

439

Emma was stunned. Somehow it was harder to take, to accept that these universe-making meddlers might have been – not godlike, unimaginable aliens – but the descendants of humans like herself. What hubris, she thought.

Nemoto said now, 'That was the purpose, the design of the Red Moon. But now the machinery is failing.'

'It is?'

'The sudden, frequent and irregular jumps. The instabilities, the tides, the volcanism. It shouldn't be happening that way.'

Emma turned back to Manekato. 'Let me get this straight. The Red Moon has been the driver of human evolution. But now it is breaking down. So what happens next?'

'We will be on our own,' said Nemoto. She raised her thin hands, turned them over, spread the fingers. 'Our evolutionary destiny, in hominid hands. Does that frighten you?'

'It frightens *me*,' Manekato said softly.

For a moment they sat silently. Emma was aware of the dampness of the breeze, the harsh breathing of the big Daemon. On impulse she put her hand on Manekato's arm. Her fur was thick and dense, and her skin hot – hotter than a human's, perhaps a result of her faster metabolism.

'. . . Wait,' Manekato said softly, peering into the trees.

Shadows moved there: shadows of bulky, powerful forms. They paused, listening. There were at least three adults, possibly more. Emma could make out the characteristic prow-shaped silhouettes of their skulls.

The Nutcracker infant roused from her sleep. Bleary-eyed, she peered into the trees and yowled softly.

The shadows moved closer, sliding past the trees, at last resolving into recognizable fragments: curling fingers, watchful eyes, the unmistakable morphology of hominids. One of them, perhaps a woman, extended a hand.

The infant clambered off Manekato's lap and stood facing the Nutcracker-woman, nervous, uncertain.

The Nutcracker-woman took a single step into the clearing, her eyes fixed on the infant. The child whimpered, and took a hesitant step forward.

Nemoto hissed to Emma, 'Listen to me. I have a further theory. The Old Ones did not disappear into some theoretical universe-spanning abstraction. *They are still here.* Wouldn't they want to be immersed in the world they made, to eat its fruit, to drink its water? Maybe they have become these Nutcrackers, the most content, pacific, unthreatened, *mindless* of all the hominid species. They shed everything they knew to live the way hominids are supposed to, the way we never learned, or forgot. What do you think? . . .'

The infant glanced back at Emma, knowing. Then, with a liquid motion, the Nutcracker-woman scooped up the child and melted into green shadows.

Back in the Daemons' yellow-plastic compound, Emma luxuriated in a hot shower, a towelling robe, and a breakfast of citrus fruit.

Luxuriate, yes. Because you know you aren't going to enjoy this much longer, are you, Emma? And maybe you'll never live like this again, not ever, not for the rest of your life.

You will miss the coffee, though.

She dressed and emerged from her little chalet. The sky was littered with cloud, the breeze capricious and laden with moisture. Storm coming.

She saw Nemoto arguing with Manekato. Nemoto looked, in fact, as if she still wasn't getting a great deal of sleep; black smudges made neat hyperbolae around her eyes. By contrast, Manekato was leaning easily on her knuckles, her swivelling ears facing Nemoto, her great black-haired body a calming slab of stillness. And Julia, the Ham girl, was standing close by, listening gravely.

When Emma approached, Mane turned to her, smooth and massive as a swivelling gun-turret. 'Good morning, Em-ma.'

'And to you. Nemoto, you look like shit.'

Nemoto glowered at her.

'What's the hot topic?'

'Future plans.' Nemoto's foot was characteristically tapping the plastic-feel floor like a trapped animal, about the nearest she got to expressing a true emotion.

'Grey Earth,' Julia said.

'. . . Oh. The deal we made.'

'The deal *you* made,' Nemoto said. 'Over and over again. You said you would take the Hams back to their home world, if they helped you.'

'I know what I said.'

'Well, now it is payback time.'

Emma sighed. She stepped forward and took Julia's great hands; her own fingers, even hardened by weeks of rough living, were pale white streaks compared to Julia's muscular digits. 'Julia, I meant what I said. If I could find a way I would get you people home.' She waved towards the latest Earth in the sky, a peculiarly shrunken world with a second Moon orbiting close to it. 'But you can see the situation for yourself. Your world is gone. It's lost. You see –'

Nemoto said, 'Emma, you have made enough mistakes already. It would pay you, pay us both, not to patronize this woman.'

Emma said, 'I'm sorry.' So I am, she thought. But I made a promise I couldn't keep, and I knew it when I made it, and now I just have to get out of this situation as gracefully as I can. That's life. 'The point is the Grey Earth *isn't* coming back. Not in any predictable way.' She looked up at Mane. 'Is it?'

The great Daemon rubbed her face. 'We are studying the world engine. It is ancient and faulty.' She grunted. 'Like a bad-tempered old hominid, it needs love and attention.'

Emma frowned. 'But you think you might get it to work again?'

Mane patted Emma's head. 'Nemoto frequently accuses me of underestimating you. I am guilty. But you are symmetrically guilty of overestimating me. We cannot repair the world engine. We cannot understand its workings. Perhaps in a thousand years of study . . . For now we can barely *see* it.'

Nemoto shuddered. 'We are all on very low rungs of a very tall ladder.'

But Mane said, 'There is no ladder. We are all different. Difference is to be cherished.'

'And that's what we humans must learn,' Emma said.

'You will not learn it,' Manekato said cheerfully, 'for you will not survive long enough.' She sighed, a noise like a steam train in a tunnel. 'However, to return to the point, we believe we may be able to direct the wandering of the Red Moon, to a limited extent. Prior to shutting down the world engine altogether.'

'Grey Earth come,' Julia said again, and her face relaxed from its mock-human smile into the gentle, beatific expression Emma had come to associate with happiness.

Emma held her breath. 'And Earth,' she said. '*My* Earth; our Earth. Can you reach that too? . . .'

'The Daemons can make *one* directed transition,' said Nemoto gravely. 'And they are going to use it to take us to the universe of the Grey Earth.'

'Because of me?'

'Because of you.'

Emma studied Nemoto. 'I sense you're pissed at me,' she said dryly.

Nemoto glowered. 'Emma, *these are not humans*. They don't lie, the Hams and the Daemons. It's all part of the rule-set with which they have managed to achieve such longevity as species. A bargain, once struck, is absolutely rigid.'

'But what's the big deal? Even if the Daemons manage to bring us back to the Grey Earth universe, they can just send the Hams home. As many as want to go. They can just *Map* them there.'

Nemoto shook her head. 'You aren't thinking right. The deal was with us, not the Daemons. We have to get them home. Whichever way we can.'

'The lander?'

Nemoto just glared. Then she walked away, muttering, scheming, her whole body tense, her gait rigid, like a machine.

5

MANIFOLD

Emma Stoney:

Hello, Malenfant. I want to tell you I'm all right.

I know that's not what you'd want to hear. The notion that I'm alive, I'm prospering without *you*, is anathema. Right?

But then you probably aren't listening at all.

You never did listen to me. If you had you wouldn't have screwed up our entire relationship, from beginning to end. You really are an asshole, Malenfant. You were so busy saving the world, saving *me*, you never thought about yourself. Or me.

But I miss you even so.

I guess you know I'm alone here. Even Nemoto has gone, off to a different fate, in some corner of the manifold or other . . .

Mary:

There were more yesterdays than tomorrows. Her future lay in the black cold ground, where so many had gone before her: Ruth, Joshua, even one of her own children.

And there came a day when they put old Saul in the ground, and Mary found herself the last to remember the old place, the Red Moon where she had been born.

It didn't matter. There was only today.

Nemoto was not so content, of course.

Even in the deepest times of the Long Night, Nemoto would bustle about the cave, agitated, endlessly making her incomprehensible objects. Few watched her come and go. To the younger folk, Nemoto had been here all their lives, not really a person, and so of no significance.

But Mary remembered the Red Moon, and how its lands had run

447

with Skinnies like Nemoto. Mary understood. Nemoto had brought them here, home to the Grey Earth. Now it was Nemoto who was stranded far from her home.

And so Mary made space for Nemoto. She would protect Nemoto when she fell ill, or injured herself. She would even give her meat to eat, softening the deep-frozen meat with her own strong jaws, chewing it as she would to feed a child.

But one day, Nemoto spat out her mouthful of meat on the floor of the cave. She raged and shouted in her jabbering Skinny tongue, and pulled on her furs and gathered her tools, and stamped out of the cave.

She returned staggering and laughing, and she carried a bundle under her arms. It was a bat, dormant, still plump with its winter fat, its leathery wings folded over. Nemoto jabbered about how she would eat well of fresh meat.

Nemoto consumed her bat, giving warm titbits to the children. But when she offered them the bloated, pink-grey internal organs of the bat, mothers pulled the children away.

After that, Nemoto would never be healthy again.

There was a time of twilights, blue-purple shading to pink. And then, at last, the edge of the sun was visible over the horizon: just a splinter of it, but it was the first time it had shown at all for sixty-eight days. There was already a little meltwater to be had. And the first hibernating animals – birds and a few large rats – were beginning to stir, sluggish and vulnerable to hunting in their torpor.

The people capered and threw off their furs.

Nemoto was growing more ill. She suffered severe bouts of diarrhoea and vomiting. She lost weight. And her skin grew flaky and sore.

Mary tried to treat the diarrhoea. She brought salt water, brine from the ocean diluted by meltwater. But she did not know how to treat the poisoning which was working its way through Nemoto's system.

The days lengthened rapidly. The ice on the lakes and rivers melted, causing splintering crashes all over the landscape, like a long, drawn-out explosion. In this brief temperate interval between deadly cold and unbearable heat, life swarmed. The people gathered the fruit and shoots that seemed to burst out of the ground. They hunted the small animals and birds that emerged from their hibernations.

And soon a distant thunder boomed across the land. It was the sound of hoofed feet, the first of the migrant herds. The men and women gathered their weapons, and headed towards the sea.

It turned out to be a herd of giant antelopes: long-legged, the bucks sporting huge unwieldy antlers. The animals were slim and streamlined, and the muscles of their legs and haunches were huge and taut. And they ran like the wind. Since most of this tipped-up world was, at any given moment, either freezing or baking through its long seasons, migrant animals were forced to travel across thousands of miles, spanning continents in their search for food, water and temperate climes.

But predators came too, streamlined hyenas and cats, stalking the vast herds. Those predators included the people, who inhabited a neck of land between two continents, a funnel down which the migrant herds were forced to swarm.

The antelope herd was huge. But it passed so rapidly that it was gone in a couple of days, a great river of flesh that had run its course.

The people ate their meat and sucked rich marrow, and waited for their next provision to come to them, delivered up by the tides of the world.

The air grew hotter yet. Soon the fast-growing grass and herbs were dying back, and the migrant animals and birds had fled, seeking the temperate climes.

The season's last rain fell. Mary closed her eyes and raised her open mouth to the sky, for she knew it would be a long time before she felt rain on her face again.

The ground became a plain of baked and cracked mud.

The people retreated to their cave. Just as its thick rock walls had sheltered them from the most ferocious cold of the winter, so now the walls gave them coolness.

Nemoto's relentless illness drove her to her pallet, where she lay with a strip of skin tied across her eyes.

At length there came a day when the sun failed even to brush the horizon at its lowest point. For sixty-eight days it would not rise or set, but would simply complete endless, meaningless circles in the sky, circles that would gradually grow smaller and more elevated.

The Long Day had begun.

Nemoto said she would not go into the ground until she saw a night again. But Nemoto's skin continued to flake away, as the bat she had woken took its gruesome revenge.

There came a day when the sun rolled along the horizon, its light shimmering through the trees which flourished there.

Mary carried Nemoto to the mouth of the cave – she was light, like a thing of twigs and dried leaves.

Nemoto screwed up her face. 'I do not like the light,' she said, her voice a husk. 'I can bear the dark. But not the light. I long for tomorrow. For tomorrow I will understand a little more. Do you follow me? I have always wanted to *understand*. Why I am here. Why there is something, rather than nothing. Why the sky is silent.'

'Lon' for tomorrow,' Mary echoed, seeking to comfort her.

'Yes. But *you* care nothing for tomorrow, or yesterday. Here especially, with your Long Day and your Long Night, as if a whole year is made of a single great day.'

Overhead, a single bright star appeared, the first star since the spring.

Nemoto gasped. She was trying to raise her arm, perhaps to point, but could not. 'You have a different pole star here. It is somewhere in Leo, near the sky's equator. Your world is tipped over, you see, like Uranus, like a top lying on its side; that is how the impact shaped it. And so for six months, when your pole points at the sun, you have endless light; and for six months endless dark . . . Do you follow me? No, I am sure you do not.'

She coughed, and seemed to sink deeper into the skins. 'All my life I have sought to understand. I believe I would have pursued the same course, whichever of our splintered worlds I had been born into. And yet, and yet –' She arched her back. 'And yet I die alone.'

Mary took her hand. It was as delicate as a bundle of dried twigs. 'Not alone.'

Nemoto tried to squeeze Mary's hand; it was the gentlest of touches.

And the sun, as if apologetically, slid beneath the horizon. A crimson sunset towered into the sky.

Mary placed her in the ground, the ground of this Grey Earth.

The memory of Nemoto faded, as memories did. But sometimes, sparked by a scent, or the salty breeze that blew off the sea, Mary would think of Nemoto, who had not died alone.

Emma Stoney:

Alone.

Yes, Malenfant, I'm alone. I know I have company – various specimens of *Homo superior*, who you never got to meet, and the Hams, including your Julia, who didn't get to ride back to the Grey Earth. But I'm alone even so. I'm a pet of the Daemons. They are – kindly. So are the Hams. I feel like I'm drowning in chocolate.

I've decided to leave. I'm going up-river, into the heart of the continent. I'm intending to hook up with another band of Runners. I did that before; I can do it again. They range far into the continent's interior, the desert. They know how to find water, how to eat, how to survive out there. If anybody knows a way across the red centre it will be the Runners.

I want to see the Bullseye up close, that big volcanic blister. Although maybe it won't be so spectacular. Like you used to say about Olympus Mons on Mars: too big for the human eye to take in, right? Well, those mile-deep rift canyons around its base look like they'd be worth a snapshot.

But I want to go on beyond that.

Maybe I can get past the Bullseye, all the way to the other side of the continent. There is another Beltway over there, Malenfant, another strip of greenery on the western edge of the continent. Nemoto told me you didn't see any dwellings or structures, from Earth or when you orbited the Moon. But maybe there are people there even so, in the western Beltway.

Maybe they are like me. Maybe they are like the Hams, or the Daemons, or maybe another form we haven't dreamed of before. Nobody seems to know. Not the Daemons, not even the Hams.

I can hear your voice. I know what you're saying. I know it's dangerous. Doubly so for a person alone. But I'm going anyhow. I'm tougher than I used to be, Malenfant.

I'll tell you what I'd like to find, in the other Beltway, or someplace else. The place the humans evolved.

We know the Hams were shaped by conditions on the Grey Earth. We think the Daemons are descended from a bunch of Australopithecines that wandered over to the Banded Earth millions of years ago. And so on.

Well, presumably humans came from a group of Runners, similarly isolated. Maybe there were several of Nemoto's 'speciations': one to produce some archaic form, a common ancestor of humans and Neandertals – Hams – and then others to produce the Hams, and us. And maybe others. Other cousins.

I think I'd like to find that place. To meet the others.

Nobody knows everything there is to know about this Red Moon. It's a big place. It's full of people.

Full of stories.

Manekatopokanemahedo:

Babo shrugged massively, as Manekato groomed him. 'It may yet be possible to use the world engine, if only in a limited way . . .'

'To do what?'

'We can explore the manifold. We can Map to other realities. Other possibilities. You don't have to send a whole Moon to do that.'

Mane pondered. 'But what is there to look for?'

'In fact there is a valid goal,' Babo said carefully.

The Astrologers, he told Manekato, believed that the universe – any given universe – was a fundamentally comprehensible system. If a system was comprehensible, then an entity must exist that could comprehend it. Therefore an entity must exist that could comprehend the entire universe, arbitrarily well – or rather *She* must exist, as Babo put it.

'The God of the Manifold,' Manekato said dryly.

The catch was that there was a manifold of possible universes, of which this was only one. So She may not exist in this universe.

Anyhow, it – She – was to be the ultimate goal of the Daemons' quest.

'Of course,' Babo said, 'She may actually be an expression of the manifold itself – or perhaps the manifold itself, the greater structure of reality strands, *is itself* self-referential, in some sense conscious. Or perhaps the manifold is itself merely one thread in a greater tapestry –'

'A manifold of manifolds.'

'And perhaps there is a further recursion of structure, no end to the hierarchies of life and mind, which –'

Mane held up her hands. 'If we find Her: what will we ask Her?'

Babo picked his nose thoughtfully. 'I asked Em-ma that. She said, *Ask Her if She knows what the hell is going on.*'

Mane touched her brother's head. 'Then that is what we will ask. Come, brother; we have much to do.'

Hand in hand, the two of them loped towards the forest, seeking shade and food.

Shadow:

Shadow found a scrap of meat.

It was on the ground, under a fig leaf, where she had been looking for fruit. It was just a scrap, half-chewed, not much more than a bit of gristle. Shadow scrabbled it up off the floor. Her fingers were stiff now, her vision poor, and she had trouble making her hands do what she wanted them to do.

She sat on the ground and chewed the gristle, sucking away the dust and the tang of somebody else's saliva. The meat was well-chewed. There was barely any flavour, any blood; she couldn't even tell what animal it had come from. But it was tough, and the way it scraped between her teeth made her ache with hunger. She swallowed it only when she had reduced it to a shred of fibre, too ragged to hold or gnaw.

She had not eaten meat for a long, long time: not yesterday, not the days she remembered in vivid, non-chronological, blood-soaked glimpses, not as far back as she could remember.

. . . She became aware of their scent first. The scent of fur, musk, blood. Then their shadows.

All around her.

They had come on her silently. But they had been coming for her, one way or another, since the day when she had failed to kill the Nutcracker infant, in that blinding flash of light. She tried to run, willing all her strength into legs that had once been so strong. But her life had been very hard, and she was slow.

Young hands grabbed her legs. She fell face-first into the dirt.

She twisted, trying to get on her back. But those strong hands kept a grip of her ankle. Her grimace of hatred and defiance turned to a yell of pain, as bones snapped.

They fell on her. Both her legs were held. Somebody sat on her head, and dark stinking fur pushed into her mouth and nose and eyes. She flailed and got one blow on hard flesh. But then her arms were pinned down. She couldn't see who they were.

The blows began to fall. Kicks, stamps, jumps, punches. Bodies hurling themselves onto her. She glimpsed others running around the main group of assailants, landing kicks and blows when the chance came. It was a bedlam, of screams, pain, motion. Still she couldn't make out their faces.

Thumbs pressing into her eyes. Strong hands working at one of her arms, twisting. Bright red pain in her shoulder and elbow, the crunch of ligament and bone.

Termite! . . . But her mother was long dead, of course.

The pain lessened. With relief, she fell into darkness.

Emma Stoney:

You know, I think I always knew we couldn't manage to live together. But I think I always dreamed we would get to die together.

But it's been quite a ride. I wouldn't have missed it for the world, Malenfant. For *all* the worlds.

Of course there is another possibility. Maybe I should go with the Daemons, off into the manifold. If this really is a manifold of infinite universes, anything is possible. No, strike that – anything that *can* happen *will* happen, someplace.

And so there must be one reality where you're waiting for me. There *must* be. A whole universe, just for us. Kind of romantic, don't you think? . . .

I'm still blown away by what I've learned of the Old Ones.

The Old Ones created infinite possibility – infinite opportunities for life, for mind. What higher mission could there be? And what really overwhelms me is that they may have been *us*. Or at least humans from some variant of our future history. *Us*: we did this. Think of that.

You'd have loved it, Malenfant. But of course, maybe you already know about it all.

To redesign an infinite ensemble of universes: what terrible responsibility, what arrogance . . . Maybe they really were us. It sounds just the kind of thing your average *Homo sap* would do for a dare.

An *H. sap* like Reid Malenfant.

Is it all your fault? Malenfant, *what did you do*, out there in the forest of realities?

Time to go. Goodbye, Malenfant, goodbye.

Maxie:

The people walk across the grass. Maxie's legs are walking. He is following Fire.

The sky is blue. The grass is sparse, yellow. The ground is red under the grass. The people are slim black forms scattered on red-green.

The people call to each other.

'Berry? Sky! Berry!'

'Sky, Sky, here!'

The sun is high. There are only people on the grass. The cats sleep when the sun is high. The hyenas sleep. The Nutcracker-men and the Elf-men sleep in their trees. Everybody sleeps except the Running-folk. Maxie knows this without thinking.

There is a blue light, low in the sky.

Maxie looks at the blue light. The blue light is new. The blue light is still. It watches him. It is a bat. Or an eye.

Maxie grins. He cares nothing for the blue light.

He walks on, across the hot crimson dust.